WOLF'S CALLING

WOLVES OF CRIMSON HOLLOW BOOK TWO

M. H. SOARS

MICHELLE HERCULES

For my daughter Lily whose imagination never ceases to amaze me.

WOLF'S CALLING

WOLVES OF CRIMSON HOLLOW BOOK TWO

Website:
www.mhsoars.com
www.michellehercules.com

Editor: Cynthia Shepp

Cover Design: Rebecca Frank

CHAPTER 1

RED

After Valerius, the alpha of the Shadow Creek pack, called me the Mother of Wolves, he simply left without answering any of my questions, the most important one being what he plans to do with me. The bindings around my wrists don't bode well. I struggle against them, ignoring the sharp bite of leather on my skin until my wrists go numb. The feeling of impotence only serves to spike up my heart rate, and all I can hear is the pounding of my pulse in my ears.

Focus, Red, focus. Panicking won't help one bit.

I let my gaze skitter around the room, scrutinizing every single detail of my confinement. There isn't much to see. Only depressing gray walls, no windows. The metal door has a little glass opening enforced by metal bars. This is a prison, like I ever had any doubt I was in one. The fact I'm not shackled to the wall by an iron chain, but trapped to a bed instead, makes no difference.

Maybe if I shift, the binds will snap. I close my eyes, trying to tap into the wolf's essence that now swirls in my chest. But there's nothing there, not even a shred of the animal's wild energy. The raw power in my core is gone, as if it never was. *What has Valerius done to me?*

Without a window, I can't tell what time of the day it is or guess at how long I've been out cold. It could have been hours or days. If Sam, Dante, and Tristan have noticed my absence, will they know I didn't leave voluntarily? My past speaks against me. I did try to escape a few times since I was turned into a wolf, but things are different now. We're bonded.

I jerk in my bed, forgetting for a second I'm stuck. *The mating bond.* I was able to feel them even when we were apart. Maybe I can communicate with them now, tell my mates I'm Valerius's captive and, most importantly, that Seth and Lyria betrayed them.

Closing my eyes, I focus on their faces, trying to find their auras somehow, though I'm not even sure if *aura* is the correct term. I still don't know how the connection works. Before, there was a sense of awareness, almost like an invisible blanket draped over my shoulders, if they were nearby. Now, there's nothing but a big, cold void that brings an ache to the back of my throat. Why can't I feel them? Did something happen? It feels like a stone dropped in my stomach.

I hear the door unlock before it's pushed open. My entire body freezes, not knowing who will come through. A petite teenager walks in, carrying a tray of food in her hands. Her head is down, and her unbound dark hair has fallen forward, framing her face and hiding most of it.

"Who are you?" I ask.

She doesn't even glance in my direction. Instead, she approaches the bed, then presses the button that lifts the hospital bed to an upright position. The smell of scrambled eggs and bacon reaches my nose, making my stomach grumble. At least they don't plan to starve me to death. But how do they expect me to eat with my hands bound?

"What is it? Cat caught your tongue?" I press again.

The girl peers at me from under her lashes, her moss green eyes almost too large for her face. She's as pale as Valerius, with sharp, striking features. But while the enemy alpha emanated strength and health, this girl appears as if she would bend and break if hit by the softest breeze. Her high cheekbones seem more evident due to her gauntness. She's so thin I'm afraid she hasn't eaten in days. Shit, maybe she hasn't. I have no idea what kind of alpha Valerius is.

There's no malice in her eyes, but also no spark. It's like her soul has been crushed. A sharp pang in my chest makes me suck in a breath. For a split second, I feel my wolf stir inside, albeit quite subdued. My power hasn't deserted me, thank God. Maybe I'm still under the tranquilizer's effect. Once that wears off, I can attempt a shift. I'm sure the bindings won't be a match for my wolf. But first, I need to get as much information from this girl as possible.

Quiet as mouse, she grabs a spoon, the only utensil on the tray, and scoops up a bit of food. So, this is how it's going down. She plans to feed me like a baby. Even the bacon has been chopped to small pieces. I suppose a fork and knife would be too much of a risk since they could easily be turned into weapons—if I were free of my constraints.

"I'd much rather eat by myself. Why don't you just untie me?"

As expected, she simply shakes her head, bringing the spoon to my mouth. I'm tempted to clamp it shut, but I need to regain my strength, so eating is a must. My compliance seems to ease some of the tension in her shoulders. She's afraid of something.

After I swallow the lump of food, I try once more to get her to speak. "What's your name?"

She freezes as if my question were offensive or worse, dangerous. Her gaze connects with mine for a brief second before she reaches for the simple silver chain around her neck, pulling the pendant from underneath her loose T-shirt. Her name is spelled out on it—Nadine. But that's not all I notice. My attention is drawn to the scar marring her neck—three lines of puckered skin. It's as if someone clawed her throat out. A chill runs down my spine. Most likely, that's what happened.

Catching me staring, Nadine quickly drops her chin, pulling her hair over to hide her scar. A nagging suspicion takes root.

3

"You can't talk, can you?"

She shakes her head, still avoiding my gaze.

"Shit. Now I feel like an ass. Please, forgive me."

It's not an act. I do feel badly.

The teen lifts her chin. Maybe I'm wrong, but I read surprise in her eyes. The reaction doesn't last. Soon, she's staring at the plate again, scooping up more food. I take another bite, barely savoring the taste, when the loud bang of the door hitting the wall has the girl scrambling to her feet. In her haste, she drops the spoon, but she's too rattled to pick it up.

Valerius enters. Nadine takes a step back, her shoulders hunching and head dropping as she attempts to make herself even smaller. He scrutinizes the tray of food, notices I barely made a dent, and makes a tsking sound.

He swivels to me. "I take it you're still being difficult."

"Not really. You interrupted my meal, but I would have eaten faster without these." I turn my hands into fists as I stare at my bound wrists, locked to the rails of the bed. Come to think of it, why does Valerius have a hospital bed in this cell?

"Your freedom is completely up to you." He shoves his hands into the pockets of his jeans in a casual gesture, as if discussing something stupid like the weather.

Narrowing my eyes, I try my best to keep my voice neutral. "Let me guess, you're going to make me promise not to run."

Valerius's lips curl into an arrogant smirk. "Something like that, but you'll have to make me believe your words first."

I scoff. "And how am I supposed to do that?"

"Very simply, Amelia. By answering all my questions about the Crimson Hollow pack."

My heart stops beating for a moment before lurching inside, drumming fast while my tongue goes dry. Valerius wants me to betray the pack—the ones who saved my life. Does he know I've bonded with all three Wolfe brothers? He called me the Mother of Wolves before, but he couldn't possibly have gained that information from Seth or Lyria.

"What makes you think I have any worthwhile information?"

"You're the Mother of Wolves; you have information I need even if you don't know it yet."

Dread drips down my spine. There he goes again, calling me by that moniker. What does he know about the legend?"

"I'm not going to betray my pack."

Valerius frees his hands from his pockets, gripping the end of the bed railing until his knuckles turn white. His face twists into something feral, almost demonic. There's a flash of red in his pupils—not ember like most wolves—which causes my heart to beat in a staccato rhythm.

"I'm only going to say this once. You're not a Crimson Hollow wolf. You belong to me, and I don't tolerate disloyalty among my subjects."

"*Subjects?* Are you a king then? I belong to no one," I say through clenched teeth, letting my temper take control. "This is not my home, wherever the hell this is."

Valerius growls, peeling back his lips to show elongated canines. In the corner, the sound of china rattling against the metal tray diverts my attention from the deranged alpha. Nadine is shaking like a leaf in the wind, biting her lower lip.

"It seems those idiots down South didn't explain how things work among wolves," Valerius says, his voice guttural now. "A Shadow Creek wolf turned you, which means you carry the Shadow Creek wolf strain. Ergo, it makes you mine. Get used to it, *darling*."

I pull against my bindings once more, barely feeling the bite of the rough leather against my skin. "What do you want with me?"

Valerius keeps staring at me cruelly, his lips curling into that odious smirk that seems to be his trademark.

"I already told you. I want information. Later, well, we'll see how it goes."

His statement is ominous. Whatever it is, it won't be anything pleasant. I need to get out of here.

"You can't keep me here forever. They'll come for me."

Valerius chuckles. "They? You mean the dead alpha's sons?

Let them come. I've been provoking those Crimson Hollow idiots for months, trying to make them take a stand. But their alpha was too cautious for my liking. He never did anything that would justify a war. Now he's dead, and my sources tell me his sons have taken a keen interest in you. So you, my dear Amelia, just gave me the excuse I need."

A shard of fear spears my heart. A war between the two packs would have devastating results on both sides. I can't let that happen. "Are you going to attack the Crimson Hollow pack because they rescued me?"

Valerius lets go of the bed, straightening up to his full height. "It's obvious you'd do anything to avoid that."

I don't answer the man, hating he can so easily figure me out. Instead, I ask, "Since when have you been in cahoots with Seth?"

Just thinking about the enforcer's betrayal brings my blood to the boiling point. Lyria's backstabbing wasn't so unexpected. The bitch had been gunning for me since I arrived in the pack. But Seth was Tristan's closest friend. I still can't believe he betrayed us.

"Cahoots?" Valerius laughs. "I don't think I've heard that word in a very long time. It must be your grandmother rubbing off on you."

My body begins to shake. Estrangement or not, I have to protect Grandma from Valerius.

"Leave her out of this," I hiss.

He narrows his eyes, leaning forward. "I have no intention of meddling with an old witch. At least, not right now. But I can easily change my mind. Don't forget that, Amelia."

My nostrils flare, but I bite my tongue. It won't do me any good to throw demands around while I'm Valerius's captive and he's threatening open war against my family and my pack. For once in my new wolf life, controlling my temper will be my only hope of getting out of this mess.

"If I give the information you want and remain loyal to the Shadow Creek pack, can I have your word you won't attack the Crimson Hollow pack?"

The alpha doesn't answer right away, but keeps staring at me with his devilish eyes. I try to not squirm under his scrutinizing gaze. Finally, he flashes me a satisfied grin.

"Now we're getting somewhere. I knew you were a smart girl. Losing Felix was worth it after all."

"Felix?"

Valerius nods, his eyes shining with amusement. "My best soldier."

Suspicion makes my brain spin. First, my grandmother creates a ruse to send me into the woods, and now Valerius's comments... No, it can't be.

"What are you saying? Did you send that wolf to attack me?"

Valerius's smirk blossoms into a bared-teeth smile. "Oh, you poor thing. Did you think you were turned into a Shadow Creek wolf by chance?"

CHAPTER 2
TRISTAN

Goddamn it. I should have never gone in to town this morning. Maybe if I had been around, Red wouldn't have disappeared. And it was all for nothing. I made the trip to have another chat with Zeke, show him the device Mom found implanted in the back of Dad's head, and see if the imp could also sense a demonic presence in it. But he wasn't in his bakery. Since the lowly demon has an aversion to cell phones, I wouldn't be able to find him until he wanted to be found. However, he did have something for me. Somehow, he knew I would be back. It was a note with random names of people and dates next to them. Until I could figure out what they meant, it was useless to me.

I should follow Mom outside, help her get the enforcers, but I'm glued to the floor, unable to move. The hollowness in the center of my chest seems to be expanding, and drawing air in is painful. Is this how Mom is feeling right now? If so, how can she function?

"Are you all right?" Dante stops in front of me, his green eyes filled with concern.

"No. Why does it hurt so badly? Do you think it means Red is…" I can't bring myself to say the words. When had I turned into such a wimp? When had I started allowing my emotions to take control?

"She's not dead." Dante's tone is hard and certain.

"How can you be so sure? And if she's not dead, then why can't we sense her presence? If she was taken, she can't be that far."

Running a hand through his messy hair, Dante glances away. "There could be a million reasons why we can't sense Red right now."

"And none of them are good."

Dante whips his face to mine, his eyebrows scrunched into a frown. "Where did you go?"

The sudden change of subject is clearly on purpose; Dante doesn't want to dwell on what could have befallen Red. I feel the darkness creeping in, crippling and oppressive, but I can't succumb to it. I won't allow my bond to Red to turn me into a useless ball of feelings.

"I went to see Zeke, ask him about the device we found on Dad. The girl working in his shop told me he went out of town last night, but he left me this." I hand Dante the note. Maybe he can make some sense out of it.

He scans it quickly before raising his gaze to mine. "What's this? I don't recognize any of those names."

"I have no fucking clue. Maybe it's nothing. I wouldn't put it past Zeke to have left it behind as a practical joke to mess with our minds."

Dante reads the paper again, his forehead furrowed in concentration. "No, I don't think this is a joke. These names and dates mean something. Only one woman is on it, and all the others are…shit." Dante jerks his head up. "I think I know what this is."

"Know what? Did you find Red?" Sam joins us in the foyer, dressed in sensible clothes that can be stripped at a moment's notice. He's ready to go on a hunt.

"I went to talk to Zeke. Couldn't find the imp, but he left a note with names and dates," I reply.

Dante passes it to Sam, who quickly reads it. He seems puzzled. "What does it have to do with Red's disappearance?"

"I'm not sure it has anything to do with it," I say.

"Maybe it's not related to her disappearance per se, but it's definitely related to Red, or more precisely, to what she is."

Crossing my arms, I say, "I don't follow."

"Look at the dates. Those people lived around the same time this town was founded. I believe those are the dates of their deaths, and they're not too far apart from one another."

Dante stares at Sam and me expectantly, but when neither of us say anything, he continues. "What if those are the names of the original Mother of Wolves and the members of her pack?"

I let out a groan. "Dante, please. Let's not start with that nonsense now."

"No, Tristan. It's high time you start accepting what's right in front of you. The Mother of Wolves legend is real, and I'm almost one-hundred-percent sure Red is her reincarnation."

"Even if that's true, how does knowing her name in a previous life help us now?" I fire back.

"I don't know yet."

"Sorry to interrupt your useless argument, but aren't you forgetting one concerning detail?"

I glare at Sam. "What?"

"If this list is what Dante thinks it is, then Zeke is aware Red could be the Mother of Wolves, which means—"

"Other scumbags from the underworld might know as well," Dante finishes, then curses.

I rub my face, frustration, anger, and fear swirling in a dangerous mix. "Let's go find Red."

With purposeful steps, I march out of the house, but my stride is cut short by my mother's approach. Lyria and Billy are right behind her, carrying a beat-up Seth between them.

"What happened?" I ask.

"We know where Red is," Mom replies, the hard set of her jaw telling me it's not good news.

"Where is she?" Sam takes a step forward, wincing a little as he does. He hasn't recovered completely, but he seems determined to ignore the pain.

Seth lifts his bruised face, one eye completely shut and purple, his lips split and bleeding.

"Valerius sent his cronies. She's in Shadow Creek."

CHAPTER 3
DANTE

I don't take my eyes off Seth as he tells us the story of how three Shadow Creek enforcers ambushed Red and took her away with them. Seth had been around the area, heard her cry for help, but had been overwhelmed in the end.

"You said those shifters were in human form. Why didn't you shift when you heard Red's cry?" I ask, watching the enforcer closely.

Seth's jaw sets into a hard line. Grinding his teeth together, he finally bites out, "I did shift, but one of them hit me in the eye with the butt of his tranquilizer gun. Hence this." Seth touches his swollen-shut eye. "Then two of them shifted as well, and kept me busy while the other escaped with Red."

"I found Seth in the forest near the path leading to your studio, Dante," Lyria chimes in. "Those Shadow Creek wolves meant business. They would have finished Seth off if I hadn't showed up."

Lies. The word comes to my mind unbidden, as a warning. There are no visible telltale signs in Lyria's demeanor that she's being untruthful. It must be my gift manifesting, then. I watch Seth and Lyria closely now. Both had plenty of reasons to get rid of Red. They're cunning enough to realize she stood in their way of power.

Billy fidgets where he stands, drawing my attention. Our

stares connect for a brief second before he lowers his eyes to the ground. *Interesting.* Does he know something? *I need to speak to him in private.*

"I swear to God, if those fuckers touch one strand of Red's hair, I'm going to tear them apart limb by limb," Sam replies, his voice almost coming out as a growl.

You're not the only one, brother. I keep the thought to myself instead of broadcasting to him. Sam doesn't need me riling him up.

Tristan takes a step away from us, but stops when Mom calls to him, "Where do you think you're going, Tristan?"

My oldest brother can't hide the glint of surprise shining in his eyes when he looks over his shoulder. "I'm heading for my Jeep. I'm going after Red."

"No, you're not."

"You can't be serious," Sam complains.

The urge to speak out against Mom's command is paramount for me, too, but I swallow back the retort. I know very well what she's going to say next. Technically, Red doesn't belong here with us, mating bond or not. She's a Shadow Creek wolf. But Seth and Lyria don't know that yet, at least not officially. It's possible Seth got that piece of information by snooping around, though.

"I'm dead serious, Samuel. If the you three show up at the Shadow Creek pack's territory with claws and teeth bared, Valerius will have all the ammunition he needs to declare war against us."

"So what? Those fuckers have been messing with us for years. They're probably behind those mind-controlled rogue wolves, too," Sam continues.

"What mind-controlled wolves?" Lyria asks, and I immediately curse in my head. Damn Sam and his big mouth.

The ire shining in our mother's eyes tells me she also wants to throttle Sam for letting that information slip.

"I know a war should be avoided at all costs, but if we don't do anything, it will only embolden Valerius more. We need to make a stand," Tristan continues, ignoring Lyria's question.

"And we will…but with a cool head and a strategy behind it." Mom raises her chin, exerting her alpha power, daring anyone to contradict her.

Tristan balls his hands into fists by his side, clenching his jaw so hard I'm afraid he might crack a couple of teeth.

"I don't understand why Valerius would kidnap Red," Lyria says. "What's so special about her?"

Keeping the growl that bubbles up my throat contained is a great effort. Those are exactly the words I would expect from the former beta, especially considering her infatuation with Tristan and how he lost the little interest he had in her when Red came along. However, underlying Lyria's contemptuous tone, I catch a hint of deceit. She knows exactly why Valerius took Red.

"Take Seth to the infirmary. I'll be right there to have a look at his injuries," Mom says.

No sooner had Mom spoken those words than a black SUV comes up the driveway leading to the front of the alpha's manor. I freeze on the spot, sensing more than seeing Tristan and Sam tense up as well. We all recognize Mayor Montgomery's car approaching. *Fucking fantastic.*

"What is *she* doing here?" Tristan asks in a low, dangerous tone.

Pinching the bridge of her nose, Mom sighs. "I called Mayor Montgomery to let her know about your father. Likely, she came to pay her respects in person."

Mom turns to Lyria. "Go on. I don't want the mayor to see Seth like that."

Without a word, Lyria and Billy drag Seth inside the house, using the main entrance instead of the clinic's door on the side of the building. A few seconds later, the mayor's car stops in front of us. The driver steps out, then opens the back door. A slender woman wearing a sharp suit emerges from the vehicle. Her light blonde hair is pulled back in a severe bun, emphasizing her resting bitch face even more.

Her cold gaze sweeps past my brothers and me before she focuses on Mom, who stands stiffly next to Sam. Without any greeting, she approaches her, kissing her on both cheeks when she's near. I've never seen the mayor greet anyone like that, not even her husband, but I'll go out on a limb and say Mom didn't appreciate the gesture.

"I'm so sorry for your loss, Mervina. Anthony was a great shifter and leader. He'll be missed."

"Thank you, *Georgina*. Anthony was indeed a great leader."

It's strange to hear Mom greet the mayor by her first name, but due to the nature of the woman's visit, I suppose a more informal approach is warranted. They were both part of the same coven before Mom chose to be turned into a shifter. But that's as far as my knowledge goes about their previous relationship. I don't even know if they were close friends before.

"If there's anything I can do, let me know."

Mom opens her mouth, but Tristan cuts in.

"How about you grant Wolfe Corp the permits so we can resume construction?"

The mayor furrows her eyebrows. "Tristan, you're aware Valerius is claiming ownership of those lands. It's my job to make sure you're not building on property that doesn't belong to you."

"Cut the bullshit. You know very well we bought those lands legally. Our documentation is solid. Valerius has no claim over them."

The mayor's gaze turns icy cold as she narrows her eyes to slits. "I'll let that lack of respect slide taking into consideration you're grieving. Besides, I didn't come here to discuss business."

"And we know that, Georgina. Thanks for coming. But as you can imagine, there's much to be done."

The mayor runs her hands over the front of her jacket, smoothing invisible lines. "Of course. I should head back to the town hall anyway. My job as the mayor never ends."

Sam snorts a little too loudly, catching the woman's attention. She glares before returning her attention to Mom once more. "When can we expect an official announcement from you?"

"An official announcement? About what?"

"I don't want to sound insensitive, but with the tense situation between you and the Shadow Creek pack, the sooner we know who your new alpha is, the better."

The blood rushes to Mom's cheeks as her expression turns murderous. "I *am* the alpha. Is that official enough for you?"

The mayor's eyebrows shoot to the heavens as her mouth turns into an "O". "I didn't realize you planned to rule the pack alone. Is that...*wise*?"

"Are you questioning my ability to lead?"

"Oh, no, far from it. It's just this pack never had a female alpha lead alone before, and with the tensions high between you and Valerius... I just don't want to see a shifter war break out. I don't have the resources to come to your rescue, and I might not be allowed to help if Valerius has cause to demand reparations."

Fuck. The mayor is in league with that fork-tongued snake. She's already laying down her excuses not to assist us if Valerius decides to attack.

"What cause could Valerius possibly have to declare war against us? A land dispute?" Mom asks, her tone now ten degrees colder.

"Oh, no. Not a land dispute, but if he found out you broke a common shifter law, like harboring a newly made wolf who doesn't belong to your pack for instance, he will be within his right to strike you if he wishes."

Damn it. How can the mayor know about Red? Who leaked that information?

Mom's expression becomes as hard as stone, impenetrable. What she's thinking isn't obvious; she's the epitome of neutrality. "Message duly noted, Georgina. Thanks for coming."

With a brief nod of her head, the mayor turns on her heels and slips into the waiting car. It's only when the SUV disappears down the driveway that Mom speaks again.

"While I tend to Seth, I want you three to decide who is going to pay Valerius a visit and claim Red as your mate."

CHAPTER 4

RED

I blink in rapid succession while my brain grapples with Valerius's words. My stunned silence lasts a couple of beats before I can find my voice.

"You planned this? Did Seth and Lyria help you as well?"

Valerius flicks a strand of his hair back, an arrogant gesture that has me wishing I was loose so I could punch the smugness from his face.

"Oh, dear. Wouldn't you like to know?"

"You're odious." I struggle against my bindings once more. In my anger, I feel my wolf rise again from the place it had been numbed down. Maybe the key to awakening it completely is to allow the anger to spread. It had worked in my first days as a wolf when I couldn't take animal form unless I was aggravated enough.

"Odious," he snorts. "You couldn't be more boring, could you? I'd love to stay here and listen to you throw half-baked insults at me, but I have a feast to prepare."

"You're throwing a party? What for?"

"To celebrate Anthony Wolfe's death, naturally. That bastard lasted long enough. It's quite fitting he died at the hands of his own sons."

My stomach clenches painfully as I remember that terrible fight. Only a monster would rejoice in the pain of someone's death.

"Did Seth give you that information?"

"That little vermin didn't need to tell me anything. I have eyes everywhere."

Shit, he has more spies in our midst? Who? He's not going to tell me if I just ask. I need to find another way to get that information, and then get out of here so I can warn my mates and Dr. Mervina.

"If that's so, then you don't need me for intel."

"That's where you're wrong, Amelia. Your knowledge will be most helpful. You'll see."

I make a sound in the back of my throat that almost sounds like a growl.

"Now, don't be ungrateful." Valerius continues. "This is also your welcome party. The pack is dying to meet you." The man's devious smile tells me his wolves are anything but excited to greet me.

"I thought you would keep me chained up until I agreed to betray my—the Crimson Hollow pack."

Valerius waves his hand in a dismissive motion. "Nah, the bindings and this prison cell have served their purpose already."

"What purpose is that?" I hiss.

He ignores my question, switching his attention to my bound wrists. It's easy to guess the reason, though. He did it to scare the shit out of me. Bastard.

"So am I free to go?"

"Hmm, that would be too easy. Rather, I'll leave this door open. When you manage to get free of your bindings, you can walk straight out."

Yeah, right. This sounds way too easy. There must be a catch.

"You're not afraid I'm going to run away?"

"Oh, Amelia. You could try to escape, but you'll find that no one enters or leaves my domains without my permission." Valerius smiles smugly before his attention turns to Nadine.

His expression immediately becomes one of disdain.

"What are you still doing here, mutt? You have a pile of onions with your name on it to peel."

Nadine turns her gaze to the ground before scampering out of the room. I wonder if she's an omega like I was. She sure acts submissively enough.

"You shouldn't treat your wolves like that. It's despicable."

"That's how I rule my pack, and you'd better learn to fall in line quickly. Mother of Wolves or not, I won't tolerate insubordination. I'm not a softy like the members of the Wolfe family."

"You know nothing about them," I say through clenched teeth.

Valerius narrows his eyes, and his lips curl upward, revealing the hint of teeth. "If that's the case, you'll remedy it soon enough."

I open my mouth to rebuff his remark, but he swings around, leaving the room before I can say anything. But good to his word, he left the door wide open. I don't trust this. It must be a trap, but I can't simply stay here and do nothing.

Struggling against the bindings, I try to break free once more. Valerius might think it's impossible to escape his territory, but impossible to me just means someone didn't try hard enough.

As much as I struggle, I'm no closer to breaking free, though. My wrists are scratched raw, the skin close to the leather bindings red. It's no use—only my wolf will be able to break free of these.

With a deep breath, I focus on the tiny energy dancing inside of my core. It's nothing but a fragment of what my power used to be, but it gives me hope.

I don't know how long I keep my eyes closed, imagining my wolf breaking free from its prison. Hours must have passed, but I felt my wolf getting stronger with each minute. It motivates me to keep trying without stopping.

I only attempt a shift when I sense the wolf's energy

spreading through my limbs. Its essence is not as strong as it used to be, but I have wasted enough time already. At first, nothing happens. I don't feel the usual trembling sensation rip through my body. But finally, a ripple finally runs down my spine, and my fingers begin to tingle. The only problem is I sense the wolf slipping away. I'm losing it. To push it through, I bite my lower lip and think about Seth and Lyria, the two snakes who betrayed my pack. I imagine myself punching Lyria in the face, breaking all her teeth. A low growl erupts from my throat, and the picture I painted in my head changes to something way more vicious. It's my wolf's thoughts. In it, it's tearing that woman to pieces limb by limb. Such savagery should terrify me, but I'm past the point of caring. I let the beast take control. Like a tsunami, it rushes through my cells, almost erasing my human thoughts completely.

When my joints snap and my muscles begin to move and change shape, I rejoice in the sharp pain. It's working. I'm shifting. Then there's the sound of the bindings tearing off. I'm free.

I leap out of the bed, landing on four paws. The urge to howl is immense, but I can't draw attention to myself right now. I need to escape. What I do is sniff the air, then the ground, trying to pick up on any scent that might be important. There's nothing out of the ordinary besides a faint scent of ammonia, which I assume was used to clean the place.

Sticking my head out of the door, I look left and right. A long and dark corridor stretches in both directions. Besides the absence of an immediate threat, a shiver runs down my spine. This place is spooky as hell. My body is tense, and I'm on defense mode as I pick a direction. I can't tell if it will lead to the exit or not.

The place seems deserted, but the strangest detail is my door is the only one in the entire corridor. The hallway stretches several yards, and there's nothing but smooth concrete walls on both sides. However, the farther I go, the faster my heart beats as a great sense of doom hangs above me. It's a bad feeling that I can't shake off. Whether it's my sixth sense, or something else entirely warning me, I don't know. What I do know is I'm definitely not going in the right direction.

I turn around, now running toward where I came from, but finding no doors on this side as well. Damn it. Where is the fucking exit? I come to a screeching halt when I hear a low moan in the distance. It's so low I almost believe I'm imagining things. Then I hear it again, clearer this time, and I recognize the voice. It's Rochelle's, begging to be set free.

Pivoting on the spot, I turn my nose up and sniff the air, trying to catch her scent. No sign of it. It's possible she's not in this building, but nearby, and now that I'm in wolf form, I can hear her just like I sensed when the unknown black wolf was in danger. Ignoring caution, I howl just in case she can hear me. There's no reply, no soft whisper in the air. Nor is there any sign of the great wolf apparition that called me the Mother of Wolves. What I do hear is the distinct sound of gears put into motion, right before sunlight streams through the sudden opening at the end of the tunnel. This is my chance at freedom, but I hesitate, scanning the opposite direction. What if Rochelle is here somewhere?

You can't help her alone. A voice sounds in my head, and I don't know if it's my inner thoughts or someone else speaking to me. It's definitely not the wolf apparition. The great beast has a distinct voice, impossible to forget. No, it sounds like the foreign thoughts that plagued me before I became a wolf. This will be something I'll have to figure out later. I take heed of the warning, sprinting toward the exit before the door slides shut.

Despite my guilt about Rochelle, my heart rejoices at being out in the open after hours of being kept captive. But it doesn't last long when my eyes register the pack of wolves waiting for me. Among them is the scarred wolf who attacked Rochelle and Billy.

Fuck. I knew this was a trap.

CHAPTER 5
DANTE

There's a moment of stunned silence before Sam speaks, "What?"

Mom turns to us. "Valerius can't know that all three of you imprinted on her. That's dangerous information, and I don't want anyone to know yet. But the only way to get Red back and avoid Valerius from rightfully declaring war against us is if one of you is openly mated to her."

"I don't see how that's going to help." Tristan crosses his arms, glowering.

"There are shifter laws older than the ones we have now. A true mating bond would justify us not leaving Red to die in the woods, even if we knew she had been infected by a Shadow Creek wolf."

"So you want one of us to claim we imprinted on her on that same evening?" I ask.

"Yes. It doesn't guarantee Valerius will let Red go free, but if he decides to declare war against us, we can count on support from our allies."

Tristan scoffs. "Montgomery won't help. It's clear she's on Valerius side."

"No, she won't. Her hatred toward our pack runs deep. Now that Anthony is gone, she sees it as the perfect opportunity to get rid of me for good."

"What happened between you two? You never talk about your time before you became a shifter," I say.

There's a moment of silence while Mom's thoughts seem to turn inward to the past. She finally lets out a heavy sigh, hunching her shoulders as she crosses her arms and stares at the ground.

"Georgina and I never saw eye to eye. Since our initiation in the Midnight Lily Coven, she viewed me as competition. Things didn't improve when your father and I got together. You see, Georgina and Anthony dated briefly before I came along, and then she became obsessed with him to the point of threatening the relationship between the witches and the wolves. I had to leave the coven to avoid a full-blown interspecies war."

No one speaks for a moment. No one seems surprised either about Mayor Montgomery's actions, but hearing Mom talk about Dad a day after his passing rips open my chest. The image of the Grim Reaper sucking Dad's soul from his body is all I can see. Nausea rolls in as my stomach twists viciously. We've been so focused on Red's disappearance that ignoring the ache of our father's death was easier.

Mom lifts her face, her eyes now brighter than before. "It doesn't matter if Georgina doesn't help. In fact, failing to assist will only work against her in the long run. Day by day, the supernatural community is losing faith in her leadership."

"But she still has control of the witches and also the sheriff's department." Tristan points out.

"True, but the Midnight Lily Coven isn't the only one in town," Mom replies.

Frowning, I glance at my brothers. Both seem as confused as I feel. Focusing on Mom once more, I ask, "What do you mean? Mayor Montgomery would never allow an independent coven to form in Crimson Hollow. She craves power too much."

A spark of mischief shines in Mom's eyes. "Who says she's aware?"

"Forget the witches. Who will step forward as Red's mate?" Sam cuts in, sounding annoyed.

I open my mouth to reply, but Tristan beats me to it. "I will."

Sam makes a disgruntled sound in the back of his throat. "Why you?"

The hard set of Tristan's jaw tells me he won't be dissuaded of the idea, and I know why. As the oldest, he feels it's his job to risk going to the Shadow Creek territory alone. He has always been like that, putting himself in the line of fire to protect Sam and me.

"Because I'm the one everyone expects to take on the alpha role one day. They think I'm the strongest."

Scowling, Sam opens his mouth, most likely to tell Tristan off, but he raises his hand and continues. "I know it's not the case, but false perceptions will help us now. I don't expect my announcement to go well. Let them believe I'm the biggest threat."

"I don't like that idea at all," I say. "But I can't fight your logic."

"What the hell, Dante?" Sam throws his hands up in the air.

"Tristan is right, Sam," Mom chimes in, her solemn face telling me she dislikes the idea of her oldest son risking his neck as much as we do. "While Tristan is busy distracting Valerius, we'll gather our allies and wait for him to deny Tristan's right."

"You know he will," Sam replies, sounding a little defeated.

Mom nods. "Yes, and that's precisely why we need the numbers. If our pack goes alone, the losses will be too great."

"But if Valerius sees several supernaturals are against him, he won't risk engaging in battle," I add, then grind my teeth, thinking Tristan's risk will be for nothing if Seth is indeed a traitor. I need to find that out before he can feed Valerius more information.

At that precise moment, I catch Billy striding away in the distance. He must have taken the clinic's side exit. This is my chance to corner the kid without anyone around.

"I'm fine with Tristan going to Shadow Creek," I say, then begin to move toward the omega.

"Where are you going?" Sam asks.

"I'm going to do a little investigation of my own."

My vague response earns a string of curses from Sam, but he doesn't follow me. I don't want to spook Billy or make him feel like he's in trouble. Omega or not, Billy is Seth's brother, and even though he will be compelled to answer my questions truthfully, there's nothing keeping him from tipping Seth off.

Billy veers toward the cluster of small bungalow-styled apartments where some of the wolves in our pack have taken up residency. There's no one around the courtyard, which is sheer luck. At this hour, there's usually always someone roaming about. I pick up my pace, not wanting to be caught paying Billy a visit. The kid enters his apartment, but before he can shut the door, I brace my hand on it, keeping it open.

"What the he—oh, Dante. It's you." Billy takes a step back, allowing me to enter his place. "How can I help you?"

Shutting the door, I spend the next few seconds taking in the omega's measure, reading his body language and facial expression. He doesn't maintain eye contact. Instead, he keeps his gaze glued to a random spot on my right shoulder. That's due to the fact I'm exerting my wolf dominance, letting the essence ebb freely from me.

"What do you know about your brother's attack?"

Billy whips his face to mine, his eyes a little rounder, as if my question took him by surprise.

"What do you mean?"

"You were acting a little tense when Lyria was explaining how she found Seth."

"Of course I was. My brother was ambushed."

There's a rise to Billy's voice, and a little tremble at the end. He's lying. Narrowing my eyes to slits, I take a step forward.

"Billy, have you forgotten who you're talking to? You can't hide shit from me."

The kid's Adam's apple bobbles as he swallows hard. It

seems to me his face has gone a little paler, too. Everyone knows I have the sight, but only my family is aware I can't call my gift at will. What the wolves do know is I can read minds, even when I'm not in wolf form. Sam let that bit of information slip on purpose when we were younger—to terrorize the other young wolves.

Running a hand through his hair, Billy looks away. "I heard my brother during the attack. I ran as a wolf to his location as fast as I could. When I got to him, he had already shifted back and was in bad shape. Lyria was helping him."

Billy pauses to rub his face. He seems torn about what he's going to say next.

"There's more, isn't there?"

The kid glances my way, his expression twisted in anguish. "Seth said three Shadow Creek wolves attacked him and ran away with Red, but there was no scent of any other wolf— or of Red for that matter. Also, I didn't find him on the path leading to your studio, but in a secluded area deeper in the woods."

My nostrils flare as I take in the meaning of Billy's confession. I want to march out of here and throttle Seth with my bare hands until he confesses he's colluding with the enemy. But I can't do that without solid proof he's a traitor. The mood within the pack is too volatile right now; there's no stability. It won't take much for the pack to turn against us.

When I don't say a word, Billy continues. "You don't think Seth is behind Red's kidnapping, do you?"

I shake my head. "I don't know, Billy. Do you think your brother would be capable of such betrayal?"

Billy lets out a heavy sigh, staring at a point over my shoulder. "I'd like to think no, but Seth has been different since Red showed up. And I've caught him sneaking out of the compound to meet with Lyria. At first, I thought they were hooking up, but now, I don't know."

"I hate to put you in this spot, Billy, but we need to discover what your brother is up to. If he sold us out to Valerius, he needs to be dealt with."

His eyes turn as round as saucers. "Would you kill him?"

"That's not for me to decide. Only the alpha can make that call. The question is, where does your loyalty lay? With the pack or with your brother?"

CHAPTER 6
SAMUEL

Stupid Dante and his secrets. I almost followed him just to piss him off, but I have other urgent matters to attend to since everyone in my family decided to ignore my opinions. While Mom went to patch Seth up, Tristan headed into town to speak with the sheriff. I still have my doubts the woman will be able to do anything since the mayor pays her salary. For that reason, it's high time I pay Hell's Hole a visit.

A notorious dive bar, Hell's Hole is the favorite spot of the most unsavory citizens of Crimson Hollow, humans and supernaturals alike. It's also the place to gain intel that's impossible to obtain through legal means.

I'm still sore everywhere and I can't walk a step without wincing in pain, but arriving at Hell's Hole driving a damn car won't do. So I suck up the discomfort, hopping onto my Ducati. It was a gift from my father when I turned eighteen. I remember the day as vividly as if it happened yesterday. My brothers and I were suffering from a major hangover after we spent the night celebrating our birthdays. We never made it back to the house, choosing to sleep in the forest to avoid our parents. Dad found us nonetheless, but he didn't give us grief. Instead, he took us to the compound's parking lot where our gifts waited for us. Dante and Tristan got the cars they wanted, and I got the Ducati, even though Mom had been against me owning a motorcycle. She didn't think I was responsible enough. Like being a wolf shifter was less dangerous than going over a hundred miles an hour on the bike. For a regular wolf, maybe, but not for me.

The memory does something to my chest, and I need a moment to recover from the overwhelming sorrow that takes a hold of me. A rogue tear escapes the corner of my eye, which I promptly dry with the sleeve of my jacket. I can't have that; there's no time for it.

I turn on the engine, revving it up before I peel out of the garage. My stomach dips a little as my heartbeat accelerates. Riding my bike is the closest state of freedom I can find when I'm not in my wolf form. The wind on my face, the speed, the sensation that I'm flying, it's almost the same feeling I get when I'm running on four legs. Today, with my heart as heavy as it is, I don't get as much joy. Sadness and fear are overriding my ability to enjoy the ride, but at least I'm doing something to keep my mind occupied.

Going as fast as I can, I make it to town in less than ten minutes. It takes me another five to arrive at my destination. Hell's Hole is in a depressing area of Crimson Hollow where most of the houses and buildings have seen better days. Graffiti everywhere, smashed windows, and most places in those constructions could use more than just a fresh coat of paint. Hell's Hole is not any different. What once was an off-white façade is now dark grey in spots where street art—and I say that loosely—is not covering the surface. The neon sign is not on during the day, but at night it spells "ell's ole" since both Hs have gone out and no one cared to replace them. It's not like the clientele care about the ambience of the place.

The moment I enter the dark space, the stench of cigarettes and cheap beer reaches my nose. There are other smells in the mix as well that I prefer not to think about. I hate coming here for that reason alone. It's not like I can put a damper on my enhanced senses, and there's no getting used to the smell.

Baldwin, the beefy bartender, is in his usual spot, doing

his usual thing, which is to polish the wooden surface of the bar. It's the only thing that gleams in this place. Without stopping his routine, he raises his head, acknowledging me with a nod. To humans, Baldwin just appears to be a man who loves his body-building exercises. Completely bald, he kind of resembles Mr. Clean. But that's his disguise. Baldwin is in fact half troll, half human. In his true form, his skin is silvery gray and decorated with the most intricate tattoos. He's only shown his true face once in my presence, and that was when a group of intoxicated lowlifes were hitting on Gretchen, Baldwin's lover. Suffice to say, those punks hadn't showed up here again. Since they were humans, their memories had probably been erased by either witches or druids, too.

Knowing why I'm here, Baldwin's dips his chin to his left. I follow the movement. Sitting in the darkest corner is the person I came here for. I don't acknowledge the other patrons as I head in that direction.

Without bothering to look up, Nina Ogata, the slyest fox shifter that ever was, speaks when I reach the edge of her table. "I heard you had to kill your dad."

She had to go right for the jugular. I wince as if she physically slapped me, but I couldn't expect less from Nina. She's savage, and that's why she's the best at what she does. A supernatural spy for hire, she sells information to the highest bidder, not caring in the slightest who is paying. She was born missing a moral compass.

The fox lifts her face, not an ounce of emotion showing in her expression. "That sucks."

"You have such a way with words, Nina. It's touching, really."

She shrugs, then brings the glass she's holding to her lips, finishing up whatever fuel was in it.

"Leo is pissed at you."

I raise both eyebrows in surprise. *Anger* and *Leo* are two words that don't usually come together in the same sentence. He's the most laid-back shifter I know, and that's why he's the glue that holds The Howlers together. He's also a kickass drummer.

"Whatever for?"

"Don't know. He's been bitching and moaning for four days. I honestly can't stand his whining anymore."

"Then why the fuck don't you move out?" I pull up a chair because me standing is drawing too much attention.

Nina glowers, and I crack a sardonic smile. She can kiss my ass.

"Because… Well, I don't like to live on my own, okay? And the only person I can tolerate is Leo. We shared a womb for crying out loud."

"Right, it has nothing to do with Leo's excellent housekeeping skills."

Nina's glare intensifies as her back hits the padded booth. "You didn't come all the way here to talk about my brother. What do you want?"

"I need you to do some recon work for me."

Nina's expression changes from annoyance to sudden interest. Leaning forward, she rests her elbows on the table. "Are you thinking about robbing a bank, Sammy?"

Ignoring the childish nickname she likes to call me, I continue. "How familiar are you with the Shadow Creek territory?"

She narrows her eyes. "What do you want with them? Their new alpha is dangerous."

"I know. He took something from me, from the pack. We want it back."

"Something or *someone*?" She purses her lips.

Fuck. I forgot for a second who I'm talking to. "Someone. Her name is Amelia—"

"I know who she is. Wendy's granddaughter." Nina pauses for a second, peering over my shoulder. Then she leans closer as if she's about to share a secret. Whispering, she continues. "I've heard rumors Valerius is planning to take over your territory."

A spike of adrenaline rushes through my veins. "Where did you hear that?"

"I won't disclose my sources, but you guys have to watch your backs."

"Tell me something I don't know. The question is are you going to help me or not?"

"Getting into that deranged alpha's territory will be dangerous. I'm a dead fox if I'm caught. What are you willing to pay?"

"Name me your price."

"It depends on what the job is. Is it an information only type of mission or am I rescuing the girl?"

I'm so tempted to tell Nina if she has the chance to free Red, to take it. But that won't do us any good. Valerius can get her back at any time by claiming she's a Shadow Creek wolf.

"I want to know everything about Valerius's territory, how many wolves he has in his pack, who his allies are, and, most importantly, how to get in and out of his domain without him finding out."

"Why do you want that information if you don't plan on rescuing your girlfriend?"

"Who says Red is my—never mind. Can you do it or not?"

"Yes, it will be tricky, but I can. It's going to cost you big time, though."

"Money is not a problem."

"I don't want any money. I want that sweet Ducati of yours. It was a gift from your dad, wasn't it?"

Curling my hands into fists, I bite my tongue so hard the coppery taste of blood fills my mouth. "Why do you want that? I can pay you twice as much what that bike costs."

She curls her lips into a wicked grin. "I know, but it wouldn't be as much fun as taking that beloved gift from you. There are just some things money can't buy, and I crave priceless treasures."

CHAPTER 7

RED

The scarred wolf takes a step forward, growling as he shows his impressive canines. I'm paralyzed for a few seconds as adrenaline mixes with fear, enough to give the other wolf a sense of superiority. He thinks I'm easy prey because I wasn't able to best him the last time we faced off.

It's with great effort I manage to snap out of it, bracing for the imminent attack. Lowering my body closer to the ground, I step forward, growling as the hairs on my back stand on end. This is the wolf who almost killed my friends. I won't let him get the upper hand again.

His other companions are all watching me with aggressive stances, but they stay back. If I hadn't met the Shadow Creek's alpha already, I would have pegged this wolf to be the one.

He attacks in the next second, and I manage to leap out of his path just in time. But he's too fast for me, not giving me the chance to retaliate before he attacks again. This time, his paw connects with my side, sending me careening to the ground. I see stars for a moment, a dizzy feeling washing over me. The other wolves begin to howl, as if they're cheering their companion on. Fuckers.

I get back on my paws before Scar—that's what I'm calling the enemy wolf now—pins me to the ground and ends this fight. He's stronger and more vicious than I am, but he's not smarter. I can win this. I *have* to win this. Sam, Dante, and Tristan can't help me this time. I also don't want to summon the great wolf apparition in front of the enemy. Instinct is telling me it's not information I want them to have.

Baring my teeth, I launch at Scar, making the mistake of not protecting my face. I feel a sting when his teeth graze the skin, but it's not enough to deter me. I'm consumed with bloodlust. I find my mark, clamping my jaw shut on my opponent's shoulder. Sinking my teeth deep, I try to not gag when his blood fills my mouth. He begins to thrash and buckle, attempting to displace my hold on him. As much as I would like to hang on until I inflict enough damage, I can't risk falling and leaving myself exposed for an attack. So I leap off while I have the upper hand.

His entire side is drenched in dark red, but Scar doesn't seem affected by his wound. He simply shakes his head, preparing to attack once more. Jumping on me, he uses his larger body to push me to the ground. *Damn it. So much for my advantage.* My hind legs fold despite all the effort I put into staying upright.

My body freezes as a bolt of blinding pain rushes through my limbs. I let out a whine without meaning to do so. But the strangest thing is that Scar is not the reason for it. He's no longer on top of me, but on the ground a little farther way, shaking as if he, too, is in excruciating pain.

What the hell?

Grinding my jaw, I push my thoughts toward him, trying to connect with him. I remember my first lesson about the telepathic ability of wolves, how communication only happens when we drop our mental shields. I have no idea if this will work. His mind is blocked, but it's a weak barrier that disintegrates with a mere push from me. I didn't intend to invade his head like that, not expecting his mental shield to simply give away. Once inside his mind, all I hear is static, similar to the first time I encountered him, and, for whatever reason, he let me hear his thoughts. The only difference today is there isn't a repetitive command to maim and not kill.

Lifting my snout, I stare over Scar's crumpled form when I notice the silence that has taken over the group of wolves surrounding us. Their aggressive stance has changed into one of submission as they part to create a path for a dark grey wolf to come through.

Valerius.

I wait for my wolf to acknowledge his power as my alpha, for the compulsion to yield to him to hit, but it doesn't come. If I weren't crippled by pain, I'd howl to the wind in celebration. I'm not a Shadow Creek wolf despite Valerius's words. I may have their wolf strain, but I belong to the Crimson Hollow pack.

Valerius glances in Scar's direction before switching his attention to me. Just as swiftly as the pain had come, it disappears. With shaking legs, I get onto my paws, growling at the enemy alpha.

I feel an invasive nudge against my barriers, something akin to claws scratching at a blackboard. Not letting him in right away, I instead watch the increased annoyance grow in Valerius's eyes. He peels his lips back with a snarl.

My wolf makes a sound that resembles a chuckle—if wolves were capable of that—then I open the communication channel, using the technique Dante taught me. I'll only allow Valerius to see what I want.

"You dare block me from your mind? How did you do that?" he demands.

"Wouldn't you like to know?" I spit back the same reply he gave me earlier, which earns me another growl from him.

"I should kill you right now for your insubordination."

"But you won't because you need me."

I'm aware I'm playing a dangerous game here, considering the fact that whatever Valerius did to Scar also affected me somehow. But my ability to block Valerius out of my mind rattled the alpha, and I can't miss this opportunity to see how far I can push him.

Valerius seems to grow larger as he stands up straighter. I realize he's emanating all his alpha power. He wants me to lose my defiant stance. If I hold my ground, he'll know I'm not under his influence. Worse, he'll be humiliated in front of his pack. He might follow through with his threat and kill me. But if I pretend to submit to his influence, it might benefit me in the long run. I don't know how long I'll be here after all. If I'm stuck, I might as well earn the alpha's trust to try to unveil the plans he has for my true pack.

So I lower my nose, letting out a whine for good measure.

"That's more like it," he says to me, but to the pack, he howls.

The other wolves imitate him, but I don't join the fray. I have no idea what's that all about. Scar remains on the ground, unmoving except for the slight tremor of his body. Our gazes connect, and I risk speaking to him one more time.

The static is still there, but I also catch a thread of actual thought. Not knowing if he can hear me, I ask. *"Are you okay?"*

Scar closes his eyes before shaking his head slightly. Maybe he had heard me. I want to keep probing, but Valerius turns to me again.

"Congratulations, Amelia. You passed your test. You're now officially a Shadow Creek wolf."

CHAPTER 8
TRISTAN

Valerius will try to kill me. I have no doubt about that. That's one more reason why I should be the one heading to his territory to claim Red as my mate. I don't know who will be more enraged—him or her. I bet she'll be furious to be claimed as if she were livestock. She's a firecracker, and it's no wonder we butted heads in the beginning. I don't need Dante's gift to know we'll continue to do so many times over in the future. Despite that, I miss her so damn much. The emotions are so strong it's impossible to grasp she just came into my life. Now, I can't imagine living without her. My greatest fear is that the Shadow Creek motherfucker has hurt her.

A growl emanates from my throat, savage and wild. If Valerius or any of his wolves touched an inch of her hair, there will be hell to pay. I want to head to Shadow Creek right away, but I can't be a hot head now. I need back up, or I'm dead meat. Going to enemy territory on my own is suicide.

The first order of business is to pay Sheriff Arantes a visit. She's not a supernatural, but she has ties to the community. It was one of the reasons she was elected for the job. The only drawback is that she has to follow directives from Mayor Montgomery due to her position. However, not even the mayor will be able to prevent the sheriff from intervening this time. According to Mom, anyway. I hope she's right.

I'm about to slide into my SUV when Lyria finds me. My spine goes taut as I brace for another argument with the former beta. Her stern expression tells me she means business. Once upon a time, I used to appreciate that determined, unwavering trait of Lyria's personality. Now it only grates on my nerves. I can't believe I entertained the idea—however briefly—of engaging in a relationship with the enforcer.

"Tristan, may I have a word with you?"

I let out a loud sigh. "Lyria, I don't have time for whatever complaint you have now."

"Where are you going in such a hurry? You don't even want to speak to Seth, your *best* friend?"

I don't miss the emphasis she puts in her final remark. Checking on Seth should be a priority—to find out everything about his ambush—but I don't think he'll be able to tell me more than he already did.

"I'll talk to him later. I have an urgent matter to attend to." I make a motion to enter my car, but Lyria holds the door.

"Come on, Tristan. I know I'm no longer the beta, but I'm one of your best enforcers. I deserve to know what's going on. What do you plan to do about the Shadow Creek pack?"

I watch Lyria closely while I debate telling her at least something. She was the former beta. Keeping her at arm's length might only fuel the distrust already running among some members. My faith in her has diminished profoundly thanks to her actions, but since it has been decided I must claim Red as my mate, I might as well tell Lyria that.

"You wanted to know earlier why Valerius would send his enforcers to take Red. He did because the rogue who attacked Red belonged to the Shadow Creek pack."

Lyria's eyes turn rounder as she processes the news. Then her eyebrows furrow, her gaze flashing annoyance. "You lied to us. Worse, you broke the rules."

"I know, but I had no choice." And here goes nothing. "I imprinted on Red the moment I laid eyes on her. There was no way I could leave her in the forest to die or send her to Shadow Creek."

The enforcer takes a step back, clutching her chest as if my confession physically hurt her. "Red is your mate?"

"Yes."

Blinking fast, Lyria lets out a humorless laugh. "That explains a lot."

"Valerius doesn't know, so it's a matter of time before he attacks us thinking he's in the right."

Staring into the distance, Lyria doesn't speak for several beats. "What about Rochelle and the hunters? We still don't know what happened to her."

My hand grips the door handle tighter. "I know. I'm headed to speak with Sheriff Arantes to let her know about everything that happened in the last few weeks."

"Then I'll come with you." Lyria takes a step toward the car.

"No. I'm going alone."

"Tristan, that's not fair. Sure, I had my differences with Red, but Rochelle was one of my closest friends. Don't keep me out of it."

"I'm not trying to keep you out of anything, Lyria. But I need you here. Gather the wolves. You have my permission to tell them what I told you."

Lyria's eyebrows rise until they almost meet her hairline. "You want me to tell them Red is your mate?"

I get her surprise. Such news should be delivered by me. But I don't have the time. Despite her dislike of Red, I trust her to deliver the news tactfully. Lyria knows what's at stake. She won't betray me or undermine the safety of the pack.

"Yes. I can imagine there's much unrest among the wolves. I need you to reassure everyone. We can't have instability within the pack when Valerius is getting ready to decimate us."

Her sharp gaze becomes hard as she squares her shoulders. "Don't worry, Tristan. You can count on me."

The conversation with Lyria went better than I expected. I was surprised she didn't throw a temper tantrum when she learned Red was my mate, even though she knows there's nothing to be done when a wolf imprints. We can't fight it, and it can't be undone. I do feel bad about my deception, but wolves don't deal well with change, and there's never been a case where three wolves imprinted on the same female. If the pack were to find out now, so soon after the death of my father, who knows what would happen.

I'm so consumed with my thoughts I barely notice the drive into town. As I park in front of the sheriff's office, I'm relieved to see her car there. What I don't expect is to find the pandemonium inside. There are several distraught people—mostly humans—yelling and demanding a solution from whoever is taking their statement. The bench in front of the reception is occupied, while the folks standing are pacing or having loud conversations with one another. The theme seems to be the same, loss of livestock due to gruesome attacks, sightings of strange things at night. One person even claimed to see a wolf running across the town square a few days ago.

The place is so packed I have to elbow my way through to the front of the counter. A gruff, bearded man turns my way, glowering. "Hey, wait your turn, pal."

I don't even attempt to temper down the wolf, leveling the human with an animalist glare. It works, and the man mumbles something incoherent under his breath, moving away from me. The officer manning the reception is Santiago Kane, a powerful druid who is more than a thousand years old, but who still appears as if he just graduated high school.

"What's going on here?" I ask.

Unbothered by the chaos, the druid glances in my direction. "It seems Crimson Hollow is experiencing one of those days where everything spooky decides to happen all at once."

"I need to speak with Sheriff Arantes."

"She's busy right now. Xander Rodriguez has been locked in her office for over an hour."

I peer over the druid's shoulder toward the sheriff's office. The blinds have been shut, so there's no way to tell what's going on inside. If the alpha of the Thunderborn sleuth is here, it means something terrible must have happened. They rarely like to come down the mountain. No wonder we didn't hear back from him about the hunters.

The door to the office bursts open, and out comes a furious bear shifter. People in his way clear out quickly, picking up on his wild nature that he's not trying to hide. A big guy with wild curly hair that reaches his shoulders, he'd be terrifying even if he were taming the beast.

Xander locks his eyes on mine. When he's near enough, he says under his breath, "Tristan, I'd like a word with you."

Shifting, I see the office where Sheriff Arantes is now standing in front of her door with hands on her hips. The usually collected woman looks troubled.

"I need to speak with the sheriff," I say.

"Forget her. Look at this place. It's a zoo. She won't be able to help you. Just like she said she can't help me."

"Fuck."

"Go with Xander," Santiago says. "Officially, the sheriff's office can't do anything. Mayor Montgomery issued an order that we're only supposed to work on human-related cases."

Surprised at his blasé use of "human," I quickly take in the three people standing next to us. They must have heard Santiago, but none of them even blinked. Noticing my stare, Santiago continues. "They can't hear what I'm saying. Druid trick."

"Why am I not surprised?" Xander says with unveiled contempt, which Santiago ignores.

"Unofficially, a few of us are meeting at my son's place in an hour."

The druid turns to the man in front of him. Just like that, I know whatever spell he cast is gone.

"Let's get the hell out of here before I bite someone's head off." Xander moves toward the exit, not caring who he's pushing out of his way.

Once outside, I follow him across the street and away from the busy entrance to the sheriff's precinct. It seems half the town is experiencing some type emergency. Because this is Crimson Hollow, they don't call. People like to vent their issues face to face.

"What brought you down here? You hate people," I say.

"I do, but I didn't know what else to do. Three members of my sleuth have been slaughtered."

For the first time since I got to know the bear shifter, I see fear shining in his brown eyes.

"How?"

My immediate thought puts the blame on the hunters who attacked Red and kidnapped Rochelle.

"I don't know." Xander stares sightlessly at a point far into the distance. "Some kind of beast tore through them, ate their intestines while they were still alive."

"How do you know they were still alive when it happened?"

Xander whips his face to mine while blasting me with his pissed-off bear energy. Shit, he's really on edge.

"Because I found one still clinging to his life."

I swallow hard as I picture that type of horror. "Were they…"

"They were in bear form, which makes it that much worse. What kind of creature would be able to take down three of my best shifters in one fell swoop like that?"

"A demon?"

Xander rubs his face before turning to me. "Yes, I considered that possibility, which is why I came down here. My pack is strong, but when it comes to those filthy beings, we're no match."

Damn it. None of the shifters can go against a demon

without assistance from the witches or druids. Angels, the most natural guardians against evil, can't be counted on.

"You must be here about the hunters who were in your territory, right? I'm sorry I didn't reply to your mother's message, but now you know why."

Shaking my head, I reply. "Yes, I came here to warn the sheriff about the hunters, but also because the Shadow Creek pack is about to declare war against us. They also kidnapped my mate."

Xander stares at me without blinking. "It seems hell is about to descend on Crimson Hollow again."

The bear doesn't need to say more for me to get his meaning. Are we about to have a reprise of the Thirteen Days of Chaos? Fuck, the town barely survived then, and we had the magical supes all working together. But with Mayor Montgomery in charge of the witches, we definitely can't count on them.

CHAPTER 9

RED

After the announcement that I have officially been inducted into a pack I have no intention of belonging to, Valerius shifts back and leaves the area. His wolves don't move until he's gone. Even then, only a handful shift back to their human forms.

The state they are in shocks me. In their wolf form, I couldn't see how badly injured some of them were. There isn't one without some kind of wound on their bodies. If I had any doubt Valerius is a despicable alpha, here is the proof.

Scar hasn't moved from his spot since he collapsed. I don't know if he's still in pain or if he simply got rendered incapable. When he cornered Rochelle and Billy in the woods, he was being controlled by Martin, one of the hunters with the raven tattoos on their necks. Is it possible the controlling device implanted in his brain is also capable of inflicting pain? But why was I affected as well?

Shit, do I have an implant in *me*? I was out for a few hours, and I did wake up tied to a hospital bed. The urge to shift back and check the back of my head for an incision scar is overpowering, but at the same time, I don't trust changing back into my vulnerable human form while in front of those strange wolves.

A tawny brown wolf approaches Scar. For a split second, I think he's going to check on his companion, but I'm taken by surprise when the wolf bites Scar's hind. The fallen wolf whines loudly in pain, but he doesn't fight back. He doesn't resemble the vicious animal set on killing me in the forest not too long ago. When other wolves close in on him, I sense they're about to gang up against Scar as well.

What's wrong with them? Where's the sense of fucking comradery?

Without thinking, I push the brown wolf off Scar, snapping my jaw at him in warning. My action makes the others pause. Not knowing if I can communicate with them, I push my question telepathically anyway.

"Why are you going after him? He's hurt."

I don't hear a reply for several beats, until one voice finally sounds in my head.

"They can't hear you. Valerius tampered with their telepathic channels so only he can speak mind to mind to his wolves."

When I turn to my right, Nadine is there in her human form. It was her voice I heard. *"How are you able to hear me then? You're not even shifted."*

"I'm not like them."

No shit, Sherlock. I figured that out already. I don't tell her Scar was able to hear me. Well, at least I think he did. *"Why are they going after him? I thought he was the beta or something."*

"This pack has no beta."

While I'm focused on the telepathic convo with Nadine, the brown wolf tries to sneak up behind me, but I sense his approach, pivoting out of the way to snap viciously near his face, grazing his ear in the process.

With a whine, he retreats, lowering his nose in a submissive gesture. I take one step in his direction, snarling a warning. A woman with stringy salt-and-pepper hair gets between us, her hand outstretched in supplication.

"Please don't hurt him. He's young and trying to prove himself to the others."

I wish I could tell her that I don't want to hurt anyone, but I won't tolerate bullying in front of me. Since I can't communicate with her in my current state, I bark instead, hoping everyone will take it as a sign to leave.

From the corner of my eye, I catch Nadine signaling fast with her hands. The woman who spoke nods once before motioning for the others to follow her. I have no idea where they're going, not seeing any other buildings in the area besides the one I escaped from.

Nadine comes closer, but maintains a certain distance from me. She doesn't appear as fearful as before, but her eyes still carry a haunted shadow.

"What now?" I ask.

"Valerius sent me to take you to your new quarters."

"What about him?" I glance at Scar.

"You can't help him, and you shouldn't try. Victor will only be free of his paralysis when Valerius wants."

His name is Victor? Scar suits him better. *"Why is Valerius punishing him?"*

Nadine's eyes connect with mine. *"Because he can."*

"That's not a good enough answer."

My rebuff seems to make the girl smaller. It wasn't my intention to scare her. She's already living in a nightmare from the looks of it.

"Victor is Valerius's older brother, and was the former alpha's beta. When Valerius killed the alpha, he gave Victor that scar."

Oh my God. The more I learn about Valerius, the worse the picture gets. *"He's punishing his own brother? What kind of monster is he?"*

Nadine surveys Victor. The wolf, despite his precarious condition, seems to move slightly to see the teen as well. After a moment, Nadine turns toward a path that disappears into the woods.

"We should go. Valerius will be displeased if I don't return to my duties in the kitchen soon."

Without waiting for my reply, the girl moves away. I'm torn between assisting Victor and following her. The wolf seems to guess my dilemma. He howls, as if he's telling me to leave.

"I'll find a way to help you. I promise." I send the thought out, not knowing if it was received on the other end.

When I catch up with Nadine, I notice she seems closed off again. I can't miss this opportunity to ask her about the Shadow Creek pack. I don't know when I'll see her alone and while I'm in wolf form again.

"When did Valerius become the new alpha?"

"Six months ago."

"Was the former alpha as ruthless to his members as Valerius is?"

I somehow doubt it, although my mates had nothing nice to say about the Shadow Creek pack. It seemed to me their animosity ran for way longer than six months.

Nadine shakes her head. *"No, he wasn't that bad. The pack was loyal to him. Valerius's leadership isn't natural."*

"How can he be the alpha then?"

"No one will dare challenge him, not after what he did to the former alpha's inner circle."

I'm so caught up in my questions it takes me a minute to notice we've arrived at a small square. In its center stands the charred remains of a gazebo, a black skeleton of what had perhaps been a beautiful construction.

"What happened here?"

"That's where Valerius killed the alpha. Instead of slashing his throat and killing him mercifully when the alpha yielded, he dragged him there, tied him to the structure, and set fire to it." Nadine shudders, squeezing her eyes shut. *"I can still hear his screams as he was burned alive."*

Bile rises up my throat when I remember I was crazy enough to taunt the alpha earlier. This is the shifter who is set on destroying my pack. I need to warn my mates about Valerius somehow. They don't know who they're dealing with.

"Your new place is over there." Nadine points at a dilapidated shack that has seen much better days. It should be condemned. Without waiting for my comment, she heads that way.

"Is this place even livable?"

"You're lucky to have a roof over your head. I sleep in the forest."

Breathing deeply, I try to control the sudden anger that spreads through my veins. I may not know much about the supernatural community, but I don't understand how Valerius has been allowed to get away with so many atrocities and for so long?

"If you wanted to run away, could you?"

It's a dangerous question to ask. Nadine is under Valerius's thumb; she fears him. Who's to say she won't feed all this information to him?

Ignoring my question, she pushes the rotten wooden door open. The stench of mold reaches my nose almost immediately. Moving into the darkened house, she begins to open the windows. When the light illuminates the decayed room, it doesn't make things better. Now I can see the horror that is my new home. The scarce furniture is on the verge of collapsing, seeming more like it should be in a trash heap. A thick layer of dust covers every single surface. Horrified, I realize I'll be sharing the space with several spider families. If I were in human form, I might cry.

"This place has been shut since Valerius rose to power. I can help you clean up once I'm done with my daily duties."

Even though I like the idea of Nadine's companionship, I don't want her to work more than she needs to. *"If you can get me some cleaning supplies, I'll manage."*

"I can bring them later. I'm not sure if the stove works, but I know for sure the fridge is busted."

"Great."

"You won't have access to food supplies anyway. We all

must eat together in the barn per Valerius's rules."

Feeling more defeated with each minute I spend in this place, I survey my surroundings. The kitchen opens to the small living room. There are only two doors down the hallway. If I had to guess, I'd say they lead to a bedroom and bathroom. God, I'm afraid to know what disgusting condition the bathroom must be in.

Nadine catches me staring. *"I would relieve myself in the forest as a wolf if I were you. There's a creek nearby most of us use to get clean."*

"I don't have any clothes."

The realization just hit me. I completely ruined the ones I had on when I shifted.

"I put some in your room. They're new."

The fact she pointed that out makes me suspect not everyone here has access to new clothes—or even basic livable conditions for that matter. Valerius is terrorizing the pack into submission by debasing them to the lowest levels.

"I have to go. Dinner will be served in two hours. Sometimes Valerius will ask one of us to bang the gong to signal the start of the meals. Sometimes he won't. Wolves who fail to attend or arrive late are severely punished."

"Where is the barn exactly?"

"On the other side of the gazebo. It's impossible to miss."

Shit, I don't have a watch and I'm terrible at telling the time using the sun's descent on the horizon.

Guessing where my thoughts are, Nadine continues. *"Don't worry. I'll come get you."*

"Thank you."

She heads toward the door, but stops, glancing over her shoulder. *"In answer to your earlier question, I could run away, but I choose not to."*

"Why not? This place is hell on Earth."

"True. But someone has to bring Valerius down."

Before I can ask her how she plans on doing that, she slips away.

So either Nadine is another trap set up by Valerius to test me or she's speaking the truth. I don't know which alternative is more dangerous.

CHAPTER 10

SAMUEL

As much as I hate to admit I just made a terrible deal, I couldn't say no to Nina's price. The fox is the best at what she does. Even if she's one of the sneakiest supernaturals in Crimson Hollow, I'd rather pay her than any other shady creature. I've known her my entire life. Sure, she plays tough, but I know she won't betray me.

When I left Hell's Hole, I didn't go back to the compound right away. Instead, I went to my place in town. I haven't been there in a while. Actually, I haven't been there since Red came into my life. It's hard for me to wait and do nothing, so I must keep myself busy.

Unlike Tristan, who keeps a studio apartment above Wolfe Corp's office, I own a townhome in one of the nicest areas in Crimson Hollow. It's absolutely suburbia, and my friends thought I was crazy for picking a house in such a family oriented neighborhood. This is the place where Stepford wives are made. It's in a gated community and shit. The main reason I bought it was to piss off the proper and trim humans and also Mayor Montgomery, who owns the biggest house in the entire neighborhood.

At first, my new neighbors all complained about having a bad boy rocker move into their pristine haven. The husbands were the most worried ones. To be fair, I flirted with all their wives, but I never slept with any of them. While the husbands were busy looking in my direction, their wives were entertaining other company.

The two cars parked in front of my house tells me my bandmates are here. I soundproofed the basement so we can practice there. They must think I'm the worst for bailing on them a week ago without even bothering to let them know I was still alive.

I'm sure they know about my father by now, so no one is going to grill me. However, their pity would be just as bad. What I need from them is help. Sure, I hired Nina to find me a way into the enemy's territory, but we'll need muscle to face Valerius. Besides Leo, who is a fox shifter, there's Jared, a druid who knows everyone and has a wicked arsenal of spells, and Armand, a hybrid half vampire, half who-the-fuck-knows.

Pushing the front door open, I find my bandmates sprawled on the couches in the living room, eating all my food and making a fucking mess.

Armand, who had his feet over the coffee table, pulls his legs back as he sits up straighter on the couch. "Sam, I didn't expect to see you here."

"Clearly." I make my way to the kitchen, in dire need of a beer.

Leo joins me. In his true form, he doesn't say a word, just shoves his hands in his pockets and watches me closely.

"What?" I snap.

"I didn't expect to see you. Isn't today your fa—"

"Yes, but I don't want to talk about it."

"Okay. We're here for whatever you need, man."

Twisting the cap off the beer bottle, I maintain eye contact with Leo. "Good to know because I have a problem. The pack has a problem."

Jared jumps from the couch, all wired up and ready for action. "Is this related to your father's death?"

Narrowing my eyes, I curl my fingers tighter around the

cold bottle. "In part. What have you heard?"

"What everyone in the supe community has. That you and your brothers challenged your father to protect the new girl."

Throwing my head back, I take a large sip of my beer. I should have expected as much. Such tragedy wouldn't be contained to the compound for too long. Some of our wolves are worse than churchgoing ladies when it comes to gossip.

"Something was done to my father at the alpha meeting in Vancouver. He wasn't the same when he came back. He attacked Red for no reason. We had no choice but to stop him."

"What do you mean something was done to him?" Jared leans forward, intent. "A hex?"

I take a couple of more sips of the beer to buy time. My bandmates are my most trusted friends, yet I'm hesitant to reveal my father had a controlling chip in his brain. Considering the first device we found had a demonic energy embedded in it, a hex is not too far from the truth.

"Something like that."

"The new Shadow Creek alpha was in the meeting, wasn't he?" Leo crosses his arms.

"Yes, and he's our prime suspect."

"His antecessor was an asshole, but there's been rumors he was tame compared to Valerius. Something really nasty is going on in that pack." Jared's stare is hard and full of anger.

His comment makes my stomach clench painfully. Red has been in Shadow Creek for too long already. Every hour that passes gives that deranged male more time to harm her. My wolf is bouncing inside of me, begging to be set free to go after his mate.

"Valerius took Red, and I need your help getting her back."

My statement is met with surprise by all my friends.

"Why would Valerius kidnap Wendy's granddaughter?" Armand asks.

"Because she was infected by a Shadow Creek wolf."

"Ah fuck, man," Jared places his hands on his hips, giving

me a stern regard. "He's totally in the right as much as I hate to say it."

"That would be true if Red wasn't my mate."

There, I said it. The plan was to have only Tristan admit he was bonded to Red, but fuck it, I won't lie to my friends.

"Fuuuuck…" Armand says, his French accent becoming even more pronounced.

Jared swings around, his green eyes as round as saucers. "You imprinted on a Shadow Creek wolf? That's brutal, man."

My nostrils flare as I throw the druid a glower. He's just stating a fact, but his comment rubs me the wrong way.

"What's brutal is that piece of garbage took my mate, and he thinks he has every right to do it. We're about to go to war with Shadow Creek and I'll need your help."

"You can count on me, mon amie. It's been a while since I fought, but it's like riding a bicycle, no?" Armand rolls his shoulders back as if warming up already for combat.

"Shit. Of course I'll help you," Jared says. "Even if you had zero fucking rights to pick a fight with Valerius, I'd be game. That dude is bad news, and no one in the supe community will be sad to see him go."

I glance at Leo, who hasn't spoken a word since I announced Red is my mate. His arms are crossed in front of his chest, his chin dipped low.

"Leo?" I ask.

When he lifts his face, I'm shocked to see so much turmoil and emotion on it. What the hell is going on with him?

"Yeah, of course I'll help," he says, his voice a little choked up. I've never seen him act so strange. His sister's words come back to haunt me. She did say Leo had been brooding for days. I can't imagine why.

"Good. Things are about to get nasty, and I don't know if we can count on the mayor or Sheriff Arantes."

"My grandfather said it's mayhem at the sheriff's station. Lots of weird shit has been going on around town. The sheriff is under strict orders from the mayor to only assist in cases dealing with humans. The supe community is on their own."

I curse under my breath. There goes our hope the sheriff would be able to send some support. Tristan can't go to Shadow Creek alone. He'll be killed for sure.

"Tell me again why Georgina Montgomery is still the mayor of this town?" Armand asks.

"It's complicated," Jared says. "Anyway, there's a supe meeting at my dad's place in a little over an hour. If the mayor won't help us, we'll have to take matters into our own hands."

"So, what's the plan?" Leo asks. "Are you going to storm Valerius's territory? Demand he give up Red?"

I can't tell them Tristan is already doing that. My mother will have a cow if I reveal to my friends that my brothers and I imprinted on Red, even if it will soon be common knowledge in the supe community. But for now, she doesn't want the pack finding out, so the fewer people who know, the better.

"As much as I'd love to make a big show of it, I'm thinking more in the lines of a covert operation. I hired Nina to get me intel on Valerius's territory."

"You sent my sister into that viper's domain alone? Are you insane?" Leo takes a step in my direction, his eyes flashing with anger, a rare thing for him.

I lift both my hands. "Your sister is a supernatural spy for hire. Getting into dangerous situations is her job."

Leo rubs his face with a jerky movement, body tense.

"Relax, dude." Jared taps him on the shoulder. "Nina can handle herself."

Armand gets busy with my freezer, pulling several frozen blood bags from inside. Since he spends most of his time here, I always have his favorite meal stocked, which is AB negative, the rarest. It would be a fucking pain to get it without raising suspicion there's a half-vamp in town. Thankfully, Zaya, the head nurse at Crimson Hollow's hospital and also a supernatural, hooks me up without asking any questions.

"What are you doing?" I ask.

"If we're going behind enemy lines, I have to build my

strength up to the max."

I count the bags on the counter. There must be at least twenty there.

"That's at least a week's supply. Are you planning to drink all that in one go?" Jared asks.

Armand's lips crack into a crooked smile, revealing the pair of fangs he usually keeps hidden. "I'd require less blood if it was fresh."

Jared takes a step back, covering his exposed neck. "*No way, Jose.* Keep your fangs away from me."

Armand reaches for one of the bags, but I grab his wrist, stopping him. "You realize if you go full vamp, everyone will know about you."

My friend's usual laid-back attitude changes into something dangerous. A predator. I don't know if it's his vampire side showing or the other half he never speaks about. "I'm done with hiding."

I don't know what to say. Armand never told us his reasons for keeping his true identity a secret, nor how he wound up in Crimson Hollow. He made us swear a blood oath we would never tell anyone. For that reason, not even my brothers know The Howlers bass player is a half vamp.

"If we want to make it to the meeting at my dad's, we'd better get going," Jared moves toward the front door.

My stare returns to the blood bags. "What exactly will happen if you drink all that blood at once?"

Armand shrugs. "I don't know. It's been a while since I indulged in such a large quantity. I guess we shall soon find out."

CHAPTER 11
DANTE

There's not even a moment of hesitation on Billy's face before he replies, "My loyalty is with the pack."

His tone is firm, resolute. Billy had always been an atypical omega. A little too outspoken, which got him in a lot of trouble. But it seems the events of the last few days have helped him shed the submissive omega cape. Now I see a wolf with so much more potential than being the pack's punching bag.

"Good. I'm counting on you to keep an eye on your brother. Report his every move to me."

Billy nods, then his gaze seems to go inward. "If my brother turns out to be a traitor, the revelation will destabilize the pack even more. Not everyone is happy Dr. Mervina has taken on the alpha's role."

My nostrils flare. We can't let that kind of sentiment take root. "Who has been more vocal about it?"

"Harold and Deacon. I heard them talking smack in Hell's Hole. They were drunk. Didn't even care they were discussing pack business loud enough for anyone to hear."

I let out a curse under my breath. I'm not surprised those two morons are behind it. They have the muscles but not the brains. There's something else in Billy's answer that caught my attention, though.

"What were you doing in Hell's Hole? That bar is a dive,

and no place for a kid like you."

Billy puffs his chest out while lifting his chin in a stubborn manner. "I'm not a kid. I'm nineteen."

Clearing my throat, I pin him with a cut-the-bullshit look. Redness rushes through Billy's cheeks before he lowers his face to rub the back of his neck.

"Uh, it was a dare."

"A *dare?*" I raise an eyebrow.

"Well, some of the guys were talking about girls they would…er—"

"Have sex with?"

"Yeah, and Greg said he'd bang Nina Ogata. I laughed. Told him not even in his dreams."

I have to agree with Billy's assessment. She'd probably eat the teen alive and spit out his bones.

"What was the dare, Billy?" I insist. Knowing how the younger wolves in the pack taunt him, I can imagine it was anything but easy.

"I had to find Nina and kiss her."

Oh dear Lord. If my life weren't in shambles at the moment, I would laugh. Quickly perusing Billy's body, I check for injuries.

"You seem to have all your pieces intact. I assume this happened last night?"

"Yes. I didn't mean to disrespect the mourning, but I figured I could distract the unrulier wolves by going along with the dare. I'm sorry."

The dull pain in my chest becomes more acute. I've been trying my hardest not to think about Dad and what had been done to him. Knowing he's in a good place doesn't help with the ache or ease the hollowness in my heart.

"There's no need to apologize. Just please tell me that your little stunt didn't put your name on Nina's target list."

Billy's brown eyes turn a little rounder. "She didn't punch me. I think that's a good sign?"

"You're lucky you left with your balls intact."

Not having anything else to add to the conversation, I remind Billy to come to me as soon as he gets new information about his brother's plans before I take my leave.

Despite Billy's pledge of alliance to the pack, it must be extremely difficult for him to betray his brother. I'm not sure if I can trust him completely yet. Only time will tell. What I learned from him only served to make me more certain that Seth and Lyria connived with Valerius. I don't have solid proof, but not revealing my suspicions to Mom would be foolish and dangerous.

I seek her out. She's no longer in the infirmary taking care of Seth. Neither is the traitorous enforcer. Luckily for him. I don't think I could keep my hands to myself if I were alone with that snake.

On a hunch, or maybe it's my gift manifesting, I head to the place in the forest where Mom goes when she needs alone time. There's a natural pond hidden from view by a cluster of trees, and I remember watching Mom sit by the bank and dip her toes in the chilly water when I was a kid. She'd always known when I spied on her. Sometimes, she would ask me to join her.

Today, I find her in the same spot, legs halfway into the water. She turns when I step closer, her tear-streaked face shocking me.

"Mom…"

Wiping her cheeks with the sleeve of her jacket, she avoids my stare. "You always knew where to find me."

I move closer and sit next to her, crossing my legs instead of dipping them into the water. "I don't think I've ever seen you cry."

She laughs without humor. "Oh, I've cried—many, many times. But only when I'm alone. I never wanted you or your brothers to see me like this. I wanted you to believe I was strong even if I wasn't born a wolf. It's kind of silly when I look back. Crying is not a sign of weakness."

"I'm sorry you felt you had to hide your emotions from us."

"And now I have to do it all over again for the sake of the pack. But it's so damn hard, Dante. I still can't believe your father is gone. He was my entire world."

My eyes start to prickle, and I bite the inside of my cheek to avoid losing my shit.

"He's in a good place, Mom. He's in peace."

"Do you really believe so?"

I don't know if I should tell her I saw the Grim Reaper and the angel who took Dad away. It all seems like a hallucination now. In the end, I decide to tell Mom. Maybe it will help her get through the hardest part of her pain.

"An angel came for Dad's soul. I saw him."

Mom's eyes turn wider as her mouth drops open. "You did? You saw an angel?"

"Yeah."

Mom reaches for my hand, then squeezes my fingers tight. "Thank you for telling me this. Some of the witches I grew up with used to say shifters didn't have souls. I'm glad they were wrong."

I smile—albeit it's a tight and sad one—before moving my attention to the serene pond.

"I came looking for you because I have something to share," I say in a low voice.

"Why are you whispering?"

"Because I don't want to be overheard." I give her a meaningful glance.

In turn, Mom's lips tighten. "You have a suspect for who leaked information to Georgina?"

I nod. "Not only that, I'm almost one-hundred-percent sure the same person assisted in Red's kidnapping."

"Seth."

"Yes, and possibly Lyria as well."

Mom takes a deep breath before exhaling the air in a loud sigh. "I feared as much. Seth was evasive when I asked him for more details about the ambush. Lyria also kept trying to distract me by changing the subject."

"I just came from a talk I had with Billy. He said his brother has been acting suspiciously since Red's arrival, and he's been sneaking out to meet with Lyria."

"We can't accuse them without evidence. I know some members of the pack aren't happy I'm the sole alpha. We'll need undeniable proof Seth and Lyria helped Valerius."

Throwing a small pebble in the pond, I watch the ripples form in the quiet water. "Tristan and Sam need to know, especially Tristan."

"Yes, tell them after the secret meeting."

"What secret meeting?"

"I received a message from Wendy. Some leaders are meeting at Kane's place in a couple of hours. It seems we're not the only ones dealing with serious issues."

"Things are about to get really bad before they get better, aren't they?"

"I can't tell. My sight has not returned. Let's hope not."

Standing up, I offer Mom a hand. She shakes her head. "I'm not coming with you. I must prepare for your father's funeral. I'll give him a proper farewell even if I'm the only one attending."

Guilt sneaks into my heart, squeezing it in a tight hold. "I'll be there, Mom. I promise."

Mom gives me a pitiful smile. "Don't make promises you can't keep, Dante."

CHAPTER 12

RED

Alone in my new home, I shift back into human form only because I want to check if I have a scar on the back of my head. Searching with the tips of my fingers, I feel nothing out of the ordinary, no bumps, no tenderness. Knowing eliminates one of my worries, but my heart is still squeezed tight in my chest. I hug myself, rubbing my arms up and down to get rid of the sudden goose bumps. It's not coldness that made them appear, but the great sense of foreboding hanging over my head. And this decayed house is not helping one bit.

Watching where I step, I make my way toward the door I'm guessing leads to the bedroom. Taking Nadine's words, I'll avoid the bathroom for now. I push the door open, and the sound of old hinges creaking reminds me of a horror movie soundtrack. Swallowing the huge lump in my throat, I remain frozen as my eyes adjust to the gloom—all the windows here are still shut.

I scan the small space. There's one iron-framed bed with a stained mattress. From where I stand, I can see all the lumps. I guess I'll be sleeping on the floor then. A wooden armoire is on the opposite side of the bed, the only piece of furniture that seems to be in halfway decent shape. I force myself to enter the room, even though every fiber of my being is demanding I turn on my heels and the get the hell out of here. Maybe I can sleep in the forest as well, just like Nadine does. However, I know that would piss Valerius off.

On top of the mattress, I find a small pile of folded clothes—a pair of jeans, a colorful top, and some underwear. They're indeed brand new with the labels still attached to them. What's more surprising is they're from my favorite store. I know without trying them on they will fit like a glove. Valerius did say I wasn't attacked by a rogue Shadow Creek wolf by chance. How long had he been spying on me? And did Grandma know I'd be turned by the enemy when she set me up?

The first order of business after I get dressed is to air out the moldy and dusty smell from here. Sunlight shines through when I open the windows. I remain under it for a minute, soaking up its warmth. Turning away from the light, I cringe at the filthiness that covers every single surface. There are spider webs in every corner. I shudder. I hate spiders.

My thoughts immediately veer toward Dante, Sam, and Tristan. Sadness overwhelms me. Out of nowhere, I choke on a sob. *No, I can't give in to despair.* I need to remain strong. But the feeling I'm missing something vital remains, almost making me sick. It must be the mating bond at work. I remember when I tried to resist Tristan, how ill I got.

What are they doing right now? How are they coping with everything? I want to reach out to them so badly to tell them that, despite everything, I'm okay. I need to let them know I didn't run away. But as much as I focus, as much as I push my thoughts out as if I'm casting a net in the netherworld, I can't find them.

A lonely tear rolls down my cheek, and I hastily wipe it off. If I can't communicate with them via the bond, then I have to find another way to let them know where I am and what Valerius is planning to do. Well, first, I have to learn what that deranged wolf wants.

Fuck. I need to get answers fast or I'll go mad.

$\mathcal{T}$he time has finally come for me to meet the rest of the pack. There wasn't a gong announcing dinner tonight, but Nadine came to fetch me as she promised. Even so, after I put my new clothes on, I sat by the window and kept close watch of the goings-on outside. Not only did I not want to miss dinner in case Nadine wasn't able to come, but I was also hoping I could learn more about the members of the pack.

Unfortunately, I didn't gain any intel since the square with its burned-down gazebo was deserted most of the time. Around six, groups of bedraggled people began to appear, most showing signs of clear abuse and malnutrition. Their pace was slow and defeated. There were a few exceptions, shifters who look a little better than the others. Perhaps they were Valerius's favorites.

I was about to head out by myself when I caught sight of Nadine hurrying toward the house. She looked a little flustered, but I couldn't tell if it was because she was running late or something else had spooked her.

The girl was right; the barn is impossible to miss. Once we circle the charred remains of the gazebo, it's the biggest building in the square. I'm glad to see it isn't in a condemned condition. On the contrary, it seems it has been recently renovated and painted like the ones in storybooks, red and white. I don't know much about construction, but even the roof looks like high-quality shingle.

With Nadine, I join the fray of folks trudging in silence into the building. Just like the group of wolves who were waiting outside my prison, these shifters all seem to be underweight and their clothes have seen better days. The new ones Valerius gave me makes me stick out, and now I realize he did it on purpose. I have the impression that all eyes are on me, and some are positively ill-wishing glares. It's like déjà vu. I also didn't feel welcomed by the Crimson Hollow pack, but that seems like it happened ages ago.

The layout inside the barn is similar to the one in the mess hall at the Wolfe compound. Picnic tables and benches are spread throughout. On the far side, a few people are serving food. The line moves fast, and the reason becomes obvious to me right away. There's only one type of food being served from a huge metal pan. Is this what Valerius calls a feast?

I take a step in the line's direction, but Nadine touches my arm, shaking her head.

Frowning, I whisper. "Why can't I get any food?"

In answer, she points at the fancy table on a dais located on the opposite side of the room. It's set up in a way that whoever is sitting there can see the entire eating hall. There are only two padded chairs in front of the table covered in a white linen cloth. One for Valerius and the second for a lucky guest. *Shit. I guess that's me.*

"You want me to sit there?" I ask.

Nadine nods in affirmation, making me stiffen. First, I get new clothes, and now I'm sitting at the table with Valerius. He definitely wants me to stand out. I'm sure receiving preferential treatment from the ruthless alpha is not going to endear me to the rest of the pack. Valerius doesn't want them to warm up to me. That has become crystal clear. Why else would he order Victor to attack me only to punish him later? Even the disgusting house he assigned to me is a luxury here.

I'm drawing attention by not moving, but it's going to be even worse if I take the seat Nadine pointed at. I'm tempted to just ignore the girl and get in line for whatever grub they're serving. In that prison cell, I barely ate anything and my stomach is hollow.

I don't get to act upon my decision as I'm shoved forward by someone. It's a miracle I don't fall flat on my face. Pissed off beyond measure, I spin around, ready to defend myself.

"Get out of my way, bitch." A preteen sporting a shiner on his left eye sneers at me.

He's just as skinny as Nadine, but a little taller. The T-shirt he's wearing is too big, faded, and has several holes. I can't bring myself to fight with a kid who has seen his fair share of abuse.

"Didn't your mother ever teach you manners?" I ask instead.

"Fuck off," he says before he heads for the food line.

Suddenly, the conversation around us ceases. A prickly sensation tingles on my neck. I turn just in time to see Valerius pull out the chair from his table and take a seat. He didn't come in through the same entrance as everyone else, that much is obvious.

He has changed since the last time I saw him. Before, he was dressed casually in jeans and a long-sleeved T-shirt. Now, he's in a dark suit jacket with a white button-down shirt. His long hair gleams under the light. His entire ensemble is a stark contrast to what everyone else is wearing. He dressed like that to demonstrate the sheer difference between him and his *subjects*. He does think he's a king.

Does he not know that half the kings throughout history died terrible deaths? The morbid thought gives me pleasure.

When his cold gaze finds mine, I sense a malefic energy reach out for me. Just like the nightmare from the night before. My mouth becomes dry. His evil stare switches from me to Nadine, immediately putting me on high alert. From the corner of my eye, I catch the girl become smaller. Damn it. I didn't even pause to think that my refusal to sit at Valerius's table would get Nadine into trouble.

Ignoring the hatred aimed my way, I stride toward the dais, keeping my gaze glued to the son-of-a-bitch's face. I don't want him to know he's intimidating the hell out of me right now. I have to remember he's a dangerous and completely unhinged wolf. Any wrong move on my part could be deadly.

"I thought for a second you would refuse to dine with me. That would displease me immensely," he says when I sit next to him.

"I wouldn't dream of it."

"Sarcasm doesn't suit you, Amelia." He reaches for the

glass of red wine in front of him.

I bite my tongue, stopping myself from digging my grave deeper.

"We don't eat?" I ask instead, since there are no plates in front of us.

He snorts. "Not that grub."

No sooner does Valerius utter those words than Nadine and two other young girls approach with trays and serve us a feast worthy of kings. Different cuts of meats, steamed vegetables, scalloped potatoes, and salad. The smell reaching my nose is absolutely divine, but my appetite is nowhere to be found, not when all around us wolves are eating scraps no better than dog food.

From the corner of my eye, I catch some hungry glances thrown in my direction, more precisely at my plate of food. I turn to the table nearest to us, and my heart breaks when I see it's a family with young children ogling my meal.

"You're not hungry, my dear?" The words are casual, but Valerius's tone is dangerous.

Turning away from the starving family, I begin to cut my meat, but guilt makes it almost impossible to swallow the food. It's a miracle I don't choke on it. My nose begins to burn as my vision turns blurry. I'm on the verge of crying, heartbroken that I'm witnessing such undiluted cruelty. Nadine was right; Valerius needs to be stopped.

He needs to die.

It's the voice that doesn't belong to me, nor to the wolf apparition. Who is in my head?

Look deeper within yourself and you'll know the answer.

I freeze mid-chew while I fight to get air into my lungs. What the actual fuck? Am I being possessed or something?

"The food is not to your liking?" Valerius asks, that hint of warning in his tone again.

I swallow the lump of food in my mouth, which goes down like a rock. Reaching out for the glass of water in front of me, I take my time drinking it, trying to recover from the strange convo going on in my head.

"No, not all," I reply.

A commotion at the entrance demands Valerius's attention. Two young men are being dragged by the collars of their shirts as if they were garbage. I don't recognize the shifters holding them, but they look as evil as Valerius.

"My, my, what do we have here?" the odious alpha asks.

"They were late, and tried to sneak in without being seen," replies the wolf who looks more like a crow due to his dark hair and hawk-like nose.

"Is that so? Excellent." Wiping his mouth with the napkin, Valerius turns to me.

I don't like the glee in his eyes one bit.

"I love when that happens," he continues.

"Why?"

"Because it means entertainment." He turns to the assembly. "Clear out the tables."

My heart sinks. Most of the people haven't had a chance to finish their meals yet. In fact, I see people rushing to shove their mouths with food while others scramble to push the tables against the walls.

As soon as enough room is made in front of Valerius and me, his enforcers shove the two youngsters roughly on the ground. Both have lacerations on their faces and a bit of swelling around their eyes. Those poor kids. I curl my fingers tighter around my knife and fork, while my body shakes with anger. Or maybe it's my wolf trying to leap through and take charge.

"I don't know how many times I must go through the rules with you lot. Tardiness is not tolerated in this pack. You know what to do." Valerius leans back, delight written all over his face.

I want to claw that expression off.

When the youngsters don't move right away, the enforcers start to kick them.

"Get going, you disrespectful sods."

I make a motion to stand—no, to leap—over the table and stop this torture, but a clawed hand sinks into my forearm, piercing the skin.

"Don't even think about it. If you interfere, those boys die."

"You're a monster," I say under my breath.

"Aren't we all?" He smiles, revealing his sharp canines. Then he releases my arm. I don't need to look down to know he left marks on my skin.

The enforcers have stopped their aggression. Now, the two teens are slowly removing their clothes. They're going to shift, but why?

"What are you going to make them do?"

"Isn't it obvious, my dear Amelia? They will fight each other… to the death."

"What? Your punishment for being late is death?"

"Well, it isn't their first strike." Valerius picks at his nails, as if the matter is of no consequence.

"You can't do that. It's insane."

Valerius throws his head back and laughs. When he's done, he says. "Oh, if I knew how funny you would be, Amelia, I would have gotten you here sooner."

"If you keep going at this rate, pretty soon you won't have a pack left to rule over."

My words seem to give Valerius pause. In slow motion, eyes narrowed, he cocks his head. "You're worried about me? I'm touched."

I might be going crazy, but I don't think Valerius is being sarcastic right now. He does believe I'm worried about him. Maybe that's how I'll get him to trust me, through his ego.

"Why wouldn't I be? Isn't this my pack now, too?"

Valerius keeps staring at me as if he's trying to read my mind. I think he's smelling my bullshit. Maybe I went too far. He finally turns to the two boys on the ground, who are now naked and waiting for their alpha's command.

"Commence."

They shift, the process taking longer than any Crimson

Hollow wolf's shifting I'd seen. Could it be that lack of food and strength are the reason? A minute later, two wolves are circling each other, snarling as they go. Then one attacks, and the gratuitous violence begins. Not wanting to appear weak, I watch it all, not averting my gaze. The battle turns bloody fast with one wolf coming out as the clearly superior animal. Pushing his opponent to the ground, he goes for the jugular. This is it—he's going for the kill. I'm sick and furious that I'm impotent. Valerius will kill them both if I try to stop it.

A loud piercing noise echoes in the room, making me wince as I try to protect my ears with my hands. Damn enhanced wolf's senses. Valerius is the one responsible for the shrill noise. He has an airhorn in his hand.

The victorious wolf leaps off his opponent, turning to Valerius.

"That was pathetic. Shift back, the both of you."

The teens do as they're told. The moment they're back into their human forms, Valerius's henchmen cover their faces with a black sack and tie their hands behind their backs. What's worse, no one seems surprised, not even the unresisting teens who don't bother to struggle.

"What are you doing with them?"

I get my answer in the next second. Martin Black, the hunter who took Rochelle, walks into the barn followed by three companions. If the mood wasn't already somber enough, it becomes ten times more sinister. Without being conscious of doing so, I peel my lips back, feeling my gums start to ache. Martin's dark gaze finds mine when he stops next to the bound wolves. He smirks, then veers his attention to Valerius.

"Got me some fresh blood?"

CHAPTER 13
DANTE

Brian Kane's house—Jared's dad—is on the opposite side of the range of mountains that houses our compound, but flatter lands don't mean less nature. In fact, his house is so secluded that if it weren't for the sign pointing toward the dirt trek that leads to his property, one could miss it entirely. The dark stones and wood used in the construction also helps it blend with its surroundings. The roof has an organic form, and the windows that jut out of it have a round shape, creating a continuum effect.

Ancient trees surround the property, and the deep moss hanging from some of them adds the feeling that we have left civilization behind and ventured into the jungle. Besides the remote location of his house, the entire perimeter is also protected by druid magic. I feel the energy barrier as I cross the invisible line, a slight vibration over my skin. I wonder what would happen if someone not welcome tried to trespass.

I find several cars already parked in front of the place, but not enough to make me think we've got reps from the entire supernatural community here. I'm curious to see who has come. Definitely not any witch from the Midnight Lily coven.

I park my car next to Tristan's SUV, noticing Sam's Ducati is also here. So all my brothers received the memo about this meeting. As much as it is convenient that our allies are congregated under one roof, I'm not sure how much help we'll receive if other members of the community are also experiencing problems of their own.

I don't have to wait long to find out about the mood inside. From where I stand on the front porch, I can hear the angry voice of Xander, the alpha of the Thunderborn sleuth. All eyes turn to me when I enter the room, and Xander—who stands in the middle of the living room—stops midsentence to look at me as well. His angry expression morphs into a solemn one before he lowers his gaze. He's giving me his condolences for Dad's passing.

One by one, the others present do the same. Some of the faces here aren't unexpected. They're usually always at the town meetings. There's Brian Kane's entire family, of course, who alone could fill an entire room. Brian and his wife have so many children I've lost count. And let's not forget the cousins.

Zaya is also here, which is good and bad. Good because she has access to important information before anyone since she works at the hospital. Bad because she must have information for this meeting, and it's probably not good. The one person I thought would be here for sure was Wendy Redford, and her absence makes me worry. She knows Red was kidnapped by Valerius. I don't think for a second that she doesn't care. So why isn't she here?

"Mom is not coming?" Sam asks, distracting me from my troublesome thoughts.

I see he brought his bandmates, Armand, Jared, and Leo.

All I do is shake my head and cross my arms, not even trying to communicate with him telepathically. I don't need to; he knows the reason.

"Send Mervina our deepest condolences." Brian Kane takes a step forward, his light brown hair showing no visible signs of his age, which is not surprising considering his father is immortal.

"Thank you, Brian. I will." I turn to Tristan before Xander

has the chance to resume his angry speech. "Did you tell them about the hunters and Red's kidnapping?"

"Yes."

"And I was just telling Tristan that as much as I would like to help get the girl back, I have my sleuth to worry about. I need to deal with the demon who killed my bears."

"You don't know if it was a demon," Tristan replies.

"If it wasn't a demon, then what the hell was it?"

"Your members weren't the only casualties," Zaya chimes in. "Two nights ago, we admitted a goat farmer. He was badly injured; something tore through his leg when he went to investigate the ruckus his animals were making. It wasn't a clean cut made by a blade. It was messy, definitely done by a beast."

Xander throws Tristan a victorious glance. "What did I tell you?"

"So you're saying you're not going to help us in case Valerius attacks?"

The bear shifter scrubs his hands through his hair, cursing under his breath. "I didn't say that at all. I'm just saying I can lend you only a couple of my bears when you go demand your mate back."

Ah, so Tristan already told the bear alpha he's Red's mate. Good, at least that part is already over with. I'm glad that I missed it. It's bad enough that only he can say he's bonded to Red.

"Wait, what?" Leo speaks loudly, earning everyone's attention. The fox is known to be quiet, so his outburst sounds a little peculiar.

I notice The Howler's drummer is not the only one staring at Sam with equally stupefied glances. Armand and Jared are both frowning in my brother's direction.

"Red is *Tristan's* mate?" Jared cocks his head, staring intently at my brother.

"Eh…" Sam's panicked gaze finds me. For fuck's sake. Did my brother open his big mouth?

Opening up my channel, I send a question to him telepathically. *"What have you done?"*

"I told my friends the truth. I couldn't lie to them."

Flaring my nostrils, I fight hard to keep my irritation contained. Why can't Sam follow simple instructions? I want to throttle him.

"Is there something going on that we should know?" Brian asks, staring directly at Tristan, who seems like he's about to explode. Actually, a vein on his forehead is throbbing already.

Now that Sam's friends know, keeping up the lie will be futile and only serve to lose our allies' trust.

"Yes, as matter of fact, there is. But this is information that cannot leave this house."

"I see. I have wards in place. No one outside this room can hear anything."

"I'm afraid that won't be enough," I say.

Brian's eyebrows furrow together as his lips become a thin line. "Are you asking me to cast a silencing spell on everyone present?"

Because of my special ability, I've always had a curiosity for anything related to the occult. Since there's such a big druid community in Crimson Hollow, I learned as much as I could about their ways and powers. So I know exactly what they're capable of.

"Yes," I answer with certainty.

"What the hell is a silencing spell?" Xander asks, darting his attention from me to Brian.

"It's a precaution spell, a small compulsion that prevents people from discussing certain things," Carol, Brian's wife, answers.

"Hold up." Armand raises his hands. "I didn't sign up for having my mind messed with."

"Why are you even here? You don't have any supernatural powers anyway," one of Brian's younger sons says. I can't remember his name now.

"He's here because he's my friend," Sam replies before

turning to Armand to whisper something in his ear. The lanky guy furrows his brows, face going rigid.

With a sigh, he finally says, "Fine. You can do your druid mojo on me."

I don't know what Sam said to his friend to make him change his mind so fast, but I'm glad he was able to convince him since we're in this tight spot thanks to his big fucking mouth.

Brian glances at Xander, who shrugs and replies, "I'm fine with it."

When no one else opposes, Brian and Carol close their eyes and begin to chant some incantation in a foreign language. My guess is it's Gaelic. I feel a light vibration in the air surrounding me, but it vanishes after a few seconds.

The druid opens his eyes again, then declares the spell has been cast.

"Now, can you tell us what the hell is going on? This meeting is taking too long already." Xander cuts right to the chase.

"Tristan is Red's mate. But that's not all. Red is also mine and Sam's mate." When no one utters a word, faces confused, I continue. "All three of us are mated to Red."

After another long silence, Brian finally speaks. "That's, um, *interesting*."

"I don't see how that changes anything. So you guys have some crazy imprinting going on in your pack. I have a demon to deal with. Priorities."

"This is a waste of time." Tristan motions for the door. I was planning on stopping him from storming out when the familiar prickling sensation on the base of my spine manifests.

I'm about to have a vision.

CHAPTER 14
TRISTAN

I'm ready to head out. I'm too angry to stay. Fuck. I've always known Xander was a stubborn shifter, but his refusal to offer support when we most need it is a blow I didn't expect. All this was indeed a waste of time. I could have already gone to Shadow Creek and forced Valerius to show his hand. But most importantly, I could have already made sure Red is okay.

Dante's sudden groan is what makes me stop in my tracks. He's clutching his middle, his face covered in sweat. His gaze is darting everywhere in a manic frenzy. I've seen him act like that enough times to know he's about to have a vision. He's searching for something to paint the images that are most likely already beginning to flood his mind.

"What's wrong with him?" Brian's younger son asks, his blue eyes going wide.

"Get him a piece of paper and pen," I say. When nobody moves, I snap, "Now!"

Carol hurries out of the living room, returning a moment later with a few sheets of paper and markers in her hands. Lost to his strange gift, Dante grabs the supplies with a jerky movement before dropping onto his knees to maniacally begin drawing.

No one besides my family has ever seen Dante in one of his episodes, and I'm thankful he insisted Brian cast a silencing spell on this group. I'd hate if anyone blabbered about this. Having the sight is not a gift to be taken lightly, and many people don't understand how it works. It's an erroneous assumption to think it can be called at will.

As if in a trance, Dante draws sketches that look like nothing but a mess of angry lines from where I stand. He stays busy at it for at least ten minutes before he finally stops, sitting on the balls on his feet. His breathing is erratic, and his hands are stained black and red from the markers. His eyes remain glazed; maybe he's still lost to the vision.

"Can anyone explain what just happened here?" Xander asks.

Sam approaches Dante, crouching in front of him and his mad sketches. Dante doesn't blink when Sam begins to lay out the pieces of paper side by side, moving them until a picture begins to form.

"Holy cow. Is that a battlefield?" Brian's son, Gideon, asks, taking a step closer.

"That's me in bear form, and some of my enforcers," Xander says in awe.

"Plus the Crimson Hollow wolves," Armand starts, "and—"

"Every other supe who is not bound to Mayor Montgomery," Zaya completes.

"Fighting a demon," Carol pipes in. "Maybe your demon, Xander." She glances meaningfully at the alpha.

"But most importantly, look who is leading the charge." Sam points at the woman who has become our entire world. Red.

Xander studies the image closely, squinting, before standing up straighter. "That's Amelia Redford, isn't it?"

"Yes. That's our mate, and she's fighting that demon. Are you sure you don't want to help us now?" I say, daring the alpha to say no.

"So Dante has the sight; is that it?" Xander switches his attention to my brother, who hasn't moved at all since he finished his artwork.

"Yes," Sam and I answer together.

"How often do his visions actually happen?" Zaya asks, her eyes narrowed and glued to the drawing on the floor.

I glance at Sam, who in turn shrugs before saying, "Always."

We don't know that for certain. It's possible there may have been visions Dante never told us about, which never actually happened. Mom's sight is also not one-hundred-percent accurate. But I won't contradict my brother.

"Well, I guess that settles it then." Brian rubs his hands together. "When are we going to Shadow Creek?"

"Nobody is coming with me," I say, hoping my hard tone will be enough to convince the others.

Sam opens his mouth to argue, but I cut him off. "We're sticking to the original plan. Only the people in this room know Red is mated to the three of us, and it will remain that way. There's no reason Valerius should be made aware."

"That's suicide, Tristan. Valerius will kill you," Sam replies, his electric-blue eyes crackling with determination.

"He won't be going alone," a newcomer announces from the front door.

I turn to find Mrs. Redford there, flanked by two other women I don't recognize. One is tall with red hair brushing the middle of her back, possibly in her late twenties. The second is a brunette, maybe ten years younger than Red's grandmother herself, dressed as if she just came from a Renaissance fair.

"Wendy, how in the hell did you get past my wards without triggering the alarm?" Brian asks.

"Please, Brian. Have you forgotten who you're dealing with?"

Carol laughs, and her husband grumbles something unintelligible.

Ignoring the convo between the druid and his wife, I focus my attention on Mrs. Redford. "I am going alone. That's the plan."

"To Valerius, it will appear you're alone, but that doesn't mean it's the truth. With my help and hopefully Brian's, we'll be able to conceal the presence of your brothers and anyone else who decides to come. If things get dicey for you, we'll be there to help."

"Is that possible? Can it work?" Sam turns to Brian.

"There's only one way to find out, isn't there?"

"So is it settled then? When do we go?" Xander asks.

I glance at him, then out the window, noticing the sun is about to set, which means we missed Dad's funeral. A grand sense of guilt washes over me, but at the same time, there's no time to waste with such futile emotions. My father was betrayed, and everything points to Valerius as the guilty party. The best way to honor my father is to kill the bastard responsible for his death.

Crossing my arms, I ask Xander, "How long until you can gather your bears?"

His eyes become dangerous, feral. "Give me an hour."

CHAPTER 15

RED

"They're not the best, but see what you can do with them," Valerius replies to Martin's question. As much as I want to keep quiet and learn by observation, I can't.

"Where is he taking them?"

Valerius places a cold hand over mine, a gesture that makes my skin crawl. "You were concerned earlier I might not have much of a pack left to rule. Martin is the person ensuring that's not the case."

He must be behind the chip controlling the wolves, but what else is he doing to them to make them super strong?

"How?" I ask.

"That's not your concern." Valerius snaps his fingers.

It's a sign for his lackeys to take away the young wolves. The men accompanying Martin reach for them, grabbing their arms roughly before dragging them out. Martin remains behind.

"Say hello to your friend Kenya when you see her, will you, Red? I think we really hit it off." The chilling message makes my blood grow cold, and my heart squeezes tightly.

"Stay away from my friend." My voice comes out rough, almost a growl.

"I didn't realize you knew each other," Valerius says, and I catch a hint of annoyance in his tone.

Interesting. It seems he and Martin aren't completely in sync. I add that tidbit of information to my list. Any scrap of intel I can get to undermine Valerius's ruling, I'll take.

"We met a few days ago in town by chance. The mayor's daughter introduced us."

"I see. You can leave now. You have a job to do."

"Certainly." Martin lowers his head, but before he turns around, his gaze connects with mine. His face is a perfect mask, not a visible shred of emotion showing on it. His eyes, however, are an entirely different story. Mischief is all I can read in them.

Why would he provoke Valerius in that manner?

The spectacle is over. So is the meal, it seems. No one puts the tables back where they were before. Instead, Valerius's wolves remain frozen to their spots, waiting for their alpha's command.

I angle my body so I can get a better view of the shifter, and that's when I notice the tremors on his hands and the dark veins that appear on them, spreading up his arms and under the sleeves of his jacket. I whip my face to his, noting the hard set of his jaw and the perspiration that has pooled on his forehead.

"Valerius?"

He doesn't answer. Instead, he stands up abruptly and jumps off the dais, striding toward the back door through which he came in earlier.

What the hell was that?

It doesn't seem he's coming back, but no one is willing to resume dinner or stick around. Like ants marching to work, the Shadow Creek wolves head for the door, hurrying as fast as they can. Not knowing what to do, I get up and make a motion for the exit as well. Somebody touches my elbow, and I find Nadine next to me.

Damn it, I really wish I could communicate with her while in human form. But since I can't, I'll have to wait until we're back in my new accommodations to shift so I can ask her all the questions I have.

Nadine makes a detour. Instead of heading straight to my shack, she takes me to the back of the barn where the kitchen is. Several heads turn our way when we enter, but no one speaks a word to me. Nadine ignores the curiosity as well, grabbing a broom and bucket filled with cleaning supplies.

I don't want her to help me clean up now. It's late. But if I say anything in front of these shifters, it might cause suspicion. However, I really need to be alone with Nadine again. When we hit the square, it's deserted. There are other houses besides the one I'm occupying, but I don't see any light coming from inside them. All the shutters are closed. It looks like a ghost town.

With everything that happened, it didn't occur to me to check if I had electricity in my newest lodgings. Mercifully, there is. Nadine turns on the light switch as she enters the house. The single white bulb dangling from the ceiling flickers to light, but it's weak and barely illuminates the room. I shut the door behind me, but it does little to make me feel safe. When Nadine begins to sweep the floor, I stop her.

"No, you don't need to clean right now. I want to talk to you."

The girl stops, putting the broom aside. She keeps staring at me, and it takes me a moment to understand she's waiting for me to shift. Not wanting to destroy the new clothes I got, I take them off, then I shift fast.

"You want to know what Martin does with the wolves he gets." Nadine's voice echoes in my head as soon as I lower my shields.

"Yes. That's one of the many questions I have. But first, what happened to Valerius just now? He was shaking, and his hands... what were those dark veins?"

Nadine goes paler than she already is. *"That's the price Valerius paid for his rise to power."*

"I don't understand."

Shuddering, the girl closes her eyes. *"I... I can't tell you anything about that."*

Not wanting to push Nadine about this topic and risk her leaving, I focus my attention back on Martin.

"Okay. What about Martin? Where did he take those wolves and what does he do to them?"

"I don't know what he does to them. All I know is that some never come back, and the few who do come back are changed."

"Changed how?"

"Stronger. Meaner."

Ruthless, just like Victor was when I first encountered him. That's why Valerius doesn't care that the wolves under his thumb despise him. He's turning them into mindless killing machines without free will.

"Did Valerius always work with Martin from the beginning?"

Nadine shakes her head. *"No, the Ravens only showed up here a few months ago."*

"Ravens? Is that what they call themselves?"

"That's what I call them, you know, because of their tattoos." Nadine touches her neck in demonstration.

"Martin took an enforcer from the Crimson Hollow pack. Rochelle. She has red hair and is a little bit taller than me. Have you seen her?"

"No, I'm sorry. But it doesn't surprise me that Valerius is taking wolves from other packs. He wants to build an army."

It makes total sense. If he's using a chip to control his wolves, what's keeping him from doing the same with wolves from other packs? A thought occurs to me. Valerius must be keeping those wolves nearby. He did say no one enters or leaves his domain without his permission.

"What else is in that building where Valerius kept me prisoner?"

"I don't know. The first time I set foot there was to bring you food."

I begin to pace, restlessness taking a hold of me. *"It's a huge building, but I couldn't find any other rooms besides my cell. Is it possible that's where Martin is taking the wolves?"*

Nadine doesn't answer my question for several beats. Instead, her gaze loses focus. *"Once when I was sleeping nearby, I heard whines of pain in the distance. At first, I thought it was coming from somewhere in the forest, but there was a strange echo to it, as if the sound was coming from inside somewhere."*

That's it. I bet there's where Martin is taking Valerius's wolves. Maybe Rochelle was in that building after all.

"We have to go back there."

Nadine shakes her head. *"No. You shouldn't leave the house at night, especially tonight."*

"Why especially tonight?"

Hunching her shoulders forward, the teen hugs her middle as if she's trying to create a shield around herself. *"Trust me on this. Tonight, no one is safe."*

I want to keep on probing. Why is tonight worse than the other nights? Does it have anything to do with what happened to Valerius during dinner?

Sudden loud voices outside keep me from continuing my interrogation. With a snap of some unknown string inside of me, I feel the bond as strong as ever. Tristan, Sam, and Dante are here. They've come for me. The only problem is I'm not sure I'm ready to be rescued yet.

CHAPTER 16

RED

I don't think I can trust my wolf not to run away with my mates, so I shift back to human form before I head out. The shouts I heard came from the Shadow Creek wolves, who decided to re-emerge only to taunt and throw insults at their visitors. It seems whatever it was that made them hide away after dinner is no longer an issue.

Even in human form, I can't control the impulse to run. I pass the gazebo, slowing down only when I reach the circle of shifters who have gathered in front of the barn. Two lampposts in front of the building provide light to an otherwise dark square.

"So have you come for your punishment?" Valerius asks from the middle of the circle.

I can't see who he's talking to, but I don't need a visual to know my mates are there. Ignoring caution, I elbow my way through the crowd until I gain a front and center location. Despite having felt Sam and Dante's presence, only Tristan is standing opposite Valerius, his body tense and ready for a fight. He doesn't break eye contact with the enemy alpha, but I'm certain he can feel my presence.

"No, Valerius. I came here because you took something from me."

Valerius throws his head back and laughs. "Oh, sweet Lord.

I didn't peg you to have any sense of humor, Tristan. Isn't it the other way around? You took something that didn't belong to you. But I'm afraid your stupidity for showing up here alone won't stop me from taking revenge against your entire pack."

Alone? What is Valerius talking about? Tristan is not alone. Sam and Dante are somewhere here. They must be hiding.

"You can try, but you won't succeed. Unlike you, I have allies. If you attack the Crimson Hollow pack, you'll feel the full wrath of our community."

Narrowing his eyes, Valerius snarls. "Lies. You broke the rules. Those law-abiding freaks won't dare come to your rescue."

Tristan curls his lips into an arrogant smirk, the same one I hated when I first met him. "I did no such thing."

The odious alpha smiles, a chilling expression taking over his features. "Shall I remind you that you rescued a human who was attacked by one of my wolves? Amelia doesn't belong to you."

I belong to no one, you jerk. That's what I want to say, but I bite my tongue, recognizing now is not the time to antagonize Valerius.

"She's my mate. You can't keep her here."

My jaw goes slack. I did not expect Tristan to confess to that. Valerius turns to me, his glare so intense it shakes me to the core. There goes my plan to try to gain his trust.

"It makes no difference to me. Amelia is not going anywhere."

My nostrils flare at the same time my entire body starts to shake. My wolf is begging to be set free.

"Then I'll challenge you." Tristan speaks loud and certain, and my wolf simmers down a little. He's going to fight for my freedom? I should be the one fighting for myself. I'm not a damsel in distress.

Valerius opens his arms, indicating the crowd. "Did you hear that, folks? He's challenging me. This lowly beta who needed the help of his two brothers to kill his father thinks he can beat me."

My heart gets stuck in my throat. After what Valerius did to his former alpha, I know Tristan won't be able to win this challenge. He's going to die. I can't let him do that.

"Tristan, please don't do this." I take a step forward.

He turns to me, his face as hard as stone. My heart rejoices and breaks at the sight. He won't back down. He's made his decision. All along, he planned on challenging Valerius. But why is he claiming to be my mate alone? Where are Sam and Dante? I can still feel their presence nearby, but it seems I'm the only one around who can.

"You're my mate. You belong with me."

Such a caveman thing to say, but my heart clenches painfully in yearning. It feels like I haven't seen him in months. The worst thing is it may be the last time I will ever see him alive. He's going to hate me for what I'm about to do, but I can't let him throw away his life for me.

"I don't belong with you. I renounce the mating bond."

My chest aches as I take in the hurt in Tristan's eyes, the sting of betrayal. I wish I could tell him telepathically why I'm doing this, but I don't think he would understand.

"You're not serious," he says in a whisper, more to himself than anyone else.

Valerius lets out a long whistle, then laughs. "My, my, that was unexpected."

"I am serious. Go home, Tristan."

"Oh, no, no. Bond or not, Tristan trespassed into my territory and challenged me. A fight to the death we shall have."

I whip my face toward Valerius so fast I might have pulled a muscle in my neck.

"No," I say feebly. I was an idiot for believing he would simply let Tristan go unharmed.

Ignoring me, Valerius angles his head from side to side, cracking his shoulders. Then he shifts, ripping his fancy clothes. Tristan almost doesn't have the time to shift before

Valerius is on him. Unfortunately, he isn't fast enough to avoid the grey wolf's bite. Dark blood stains Tristan's white pelt, but he doesn't seem to notice as he peels his lips back, revealing sharp teeth. I don't think I've ever seen him so enraged and savage. He's not holding back. But it's clear Valerius has the upper hand. He's stronger and faster, and he seems to guess every move Tristan is about to make.

Nadine told me Valerius's leadership isn't natural. What if his strength is the result of a scientific experiment? I remember Anthony Wolfe was almost unbeatable, and it took his three sons to defeat him. And Valerius doesn't seem to care his wolves are weak and malnourished. He must have another way to make them strong.

I taste blood in my mouth, and that's when I realize I'm beginning to shift. I'm going to join the fight, and there's nothing anyone can say to stop me. All my ideas to discover Valerius's plans are unimportant. All I care about is my mate who is losing this damn fight. Right before I surrender to my wolf, I feel a familiar nudge against my mental barriers and I freeze, stopping the transformation.

"Dante?"

"Red, are you all right?" His voice is not clear. It's sort of garbled, as if he's speaking from inside a bubble.

"Where are you?"

"Near."

"You need to help Tristan. He's losing."

A loud yelp brings me back to the fight. Tristan is on the ground, trying to get up. His white fur is almost entirely covered in blood. Valerius snarls as he circles him, and I know he's about to deliver the final blow.

"No!" I yell.

Valerius snaps his head to see over his shoulder, his eyes glowing red like he's a demon. Then he turns to Tristan, who has managed to get onto his paws, but I can tell it's costing him. Everything seems to happen in slow motion next. Valerius prepares to jump at the same time I break into a sprint, not knowing if I can shift in time to tackle him before he attacks Tristan. A blinding flash zaps between Valerius and Tristan, and when it fades, Grandma is there, accompanied by Brian Kane—a quiet man who owns an herbal tea store in Crimson Hollow—and a tall and strong guy with long hair. He oozes raw power. On instinct, I realize he's a shifter; I just don't know what kind. No sign of Dante and Sam, though.

None of Valerius's wolves do anything. They seem kind of frozen by a spell.

"This ends now," Grandma speaks, her voice clear and hard. Gone is the fragile state I got used to in the last two years I lived with her.

Valerius shifts back, but not completely. His hands are still clawed paws and his face is a deformed atrocity, half human, half wolf. It's a sight that shows exactly what he is. A heartless monster.

"How dare you come here, witch? Do you know who you're dealing with?"

"We came to make sure you wouldn't break the laws that all supernaturals must abide by. My granddaughter renounced the bond to the Crimson Hollow beta. You have no cause to kill him."

"He trespassed on my territory."

"So did your wolf," the shifter replies.

Valerius doesn't speak for several beats, but his body is shaking. I don't know if the tremors are caused by anger or something else. It seems small dark veins are spreading through his back, just like it happened to his hands earlier.

"I don't know how you managed to hide yourselves from my sentries, but it's of no issue. I don't need to kill that pathetic excuse for a wolf. I have what I want, and she's made her choice." Valerius glances in my direction, smiling victoriously.

If I could punch that smugness off his face I would—with relish. *Your time will come, Valerius. Mark my words.*

Grandma turns to me with worry in her gaze. The sting of

her betrayal is still in my heart, and her presence here is not helping with the pain. On the contrary, it only serves to raise more questions, making me doubt her motives even more. I don't know who she is.

Before she can ask the question obviously on her mind, I say, "I'm staying. I'm where I should be." *For the time being.*

A low murmur spreads throughout the crowd. I can only imagine what kind of conclusions this pack is making. First, I get special treatment at dinner and now this. God, what if they think I'm going to become Valerius's mate? The thought alone makes me want to puke. And worse, what if that's what Valerius wants? I'll kill him if he tries anything.

"Not if I kill him first." Dante's voice sounds in my head. *"Red, what are you doing?"*

"I can't go back to Crimson Hollow yet. Valerius is up to something. Staying is the only way to discover what it is."

"It's dangerous."

"I can take care of myself. I found out—"

"Get out of here before I decide to show you what my wolves are capable of," Valerius spits out with all the venom he can muster, disrupting my train of thought.

Tristan's stare lingers in my direction, almost as if he's pleading with me to reconsider my decision. I shake my head in answer and I see it then, the fire extinguishing from his wolf gaze.

Grandma lifts her chin in a defiant way before turning away from Valerius. She doesn't need to say anything to deliver the message that this isn't over. And she's right; this isn't over by a long shot. The circle of wolves breaks apart, creating a path for Grandma and her two companions to walk out. The tall shifter waits for Tristan to go first while he brings up the rear. It's with great effort that I keep my feet planted to the ground. The compulsion to follow Tristan is almost overwhelming.

"We have to go. The cloaking spell is weakening," Dante says, his voice in my head almost a whisper.

"Valerius is working with the hunters," I say, but I don't

hear a reply. Shit. *"Dante? Are you still there?"*

I'm so focused in my communication with Dante I don't notice Valerius until he's standing right in front of me. I have to suppress a gasp for he's still in his mid-shift state, watching me with those devilishly red eyes.

"You surprised me tonight, Amelia." He reaches for my face with his clawed hand, but seems to notice and stops before he actually touches me. He lowers his arm. With a grimace, his face returns to full human.

"Excuse me, I have to attend to unavoidable business." His voice is wound tight, as if he's in great pain now.

I don't move from my spot as I watch Valerius stride away from the square and vanish into the night. One by one, his shifters disperse, crawling back to where they had retired for the night. In my short life as a supernatural, what happened here tonight was one of the most surreal things I've witnessed so far.

Nadine touches my arm to catch my attention, then points in the direction of my shack. When I don't move right away, she pulls my arm and starts to drag me.

Planting my feet firmly on the ground, I say, "I'm not going back there. I'm going to find Rochelle."

CHAPTER 17
RED

As soon as I'm out of the square and sure there's no one around, I take off my clothes and shift. It will be easier to search for clues about the missing wolves if I can tap into my wolf's enhanced skills. Also, I need to be able to communicate with Nadine. Something has the girl terrified more than usual. Tense, she keeps peeking over her shoulder every five seconds.

"Why don't you shift?" I ask.

She doesn't answer my question, only says, *"We shouldn't be out tonight. This is a bad idea."*

Even through the telepathic connection, I sense the fear in her words, the trepidation in her reply. I feel bad for putting her in a risky situation, but I can't simply go back to my shack and do nothing. Now that I'd renounced my bond to Tristan, the stakes are much higher. Valerius will attack the Crimson Hollow pack as soon as he gathers his army of mindless wolves. But if I can find the location where he's taking the wolves he conscripts, then maybe I can end his reign of terror.

I wish Nadine would shift; we would make progress much faster through the forest. But for whatever reason, she prefers to remain in her human form and runs after me. It doesn't take long to find the path that leads to the eyesore building I spent the night in. It's nestled at the base of a cliff, a fact I missed entirely when I escaped. From our side, the descent down the mountain is not that steep. I find the path I took earlier, making my way down as fast as I can. Nadine is swift on two legs as well, but I believe all shifters have better dexterity than humans.

I don't pick up the scent of any wolf nearby, which means there are no sentries in place. If this is where Valerius keeps the wolves he kidnaps, I find it odd there is no one guarding it. Or maybe the reason there are no sentries is the same as why Nadine doesn't want to be out tonight.

Stopping in front of the building, I stare at it intently. I came out from this side, I'm sure of it, but there's nothing but smooth concrete wall where there should be a door. I move closer to inspect it better, but I find nothing that indicates there's an exit there. An invisible door would indicate high technology, just like the chip controlling the wolves. How did Valerius manage to get hold of it? Maybe it's Martin Black and his hunters who possess the technology. Damn it. There are still so many questions without answers.

If I can't find a way in, maybe I can pick up Rochelle's wolf signature through the doors, just like I heard her before. Closing my eyes, I concentrate, expanding my awareness outward. I have no idea what I'm doing, I'm totally going on instinct here. A minute goes by, and all I hear is the sound of my breathing. Shit. This trip is turning out to be an epic fail, but I refuse to give up.

"We need to leave. There's no way in," Nadine says.

"Not yet. I'm going to circle back, maybe I can find another entrance."

With my nose glued to the ground, I trot around the perimeter of the building, keeping close to the wall. I catch nothing out of the ordinary besides the smell of overgrown grass and earth, until I sense a shift around me. I can't really explain it. My nose picks up on something, but it's not a smell. Following the strange pull, I stop by an ordinary spot and begin to dig. There's something down there. I only stop when my paw scratches something hard, a small rock.

Nadine crouches next to me, fishing my finding out after I uncover it. It's a smooth river pebble with a strange design etched on it.

"What is it?" I ask.

"I think it's a rune." The girl wipes the excess dirt off the top to better inspect it. Suddenly, something even more peculiar happens. The wall in front of us shimmers briefly, revealing a rusty metal door where before there was nothing.

"Holy crap." I can't keep from sending that outburst via the connection.

"So that's how he's doing it. Valerius must have used magic to conceal all the entrances to this place."

"If he's using magic, then he has more allies," I reply as my chest tightens. First the hunters, and now magic. How is my pack going to fight Valerius?

"It would appear so."

The more I dig, the grimmer the situation becomes. I'm new to the supernatural world, but I know an evil person like Valerius having access to magic is definitely not a good thing.

Nadine turns the door handle, but the door won't budge. "This is heavy, but I don't think it's locked."

"I'll shift back to help you."

Somehow, I'm not surprised Valerius wouldn't bother to lock the entrances. If he has all of them concealed there's no point. His cockiness will be his downfall. Bastard.

My arms break into goose bumps when the late-night breeze kisses my skin. I really wish there was a way for me to store my clothes somewhere. I don't think I'll ever get used to parading naked in front of others.

Nadine switches places with me so I can try the handle. I put all my muscle strength into it without success. Why couldn't I get a bolt of strength when I became a shifter?

"What now?" I ask out loud.

An icy blast of wind comes out of nowhere, and I shiver. Hugging myself and rubbing my arms up and down, I attempt to keep warm, but it's no use. I have to shift back into a wolf if I don't want to freeze to death.

"Jesus, where's that wind coming from?"

Nadine seems frozen as well, but for entirely different reasons. She's staring into the forest as if there's a huge threat lurking behind those trees. I open my mouth to ask if she's sensing a sentry or something, when she grabs my arm and drags me in the direction we came from. My surprise doesn't slow me down. My preservation instincts have kicked in. Whatever is behind us, it's bad, and it can find us. A great sense of doom takes hold of me, as if all the good and joy in the world has suddenly vanished and only darkness remains. The malign presence is getting stronger, nearer. We'll never make it back to the square before it catches up with us. We need to find a place to hide now.

Nadine is still dragging me, but I don't think she actually has a plan. I spot a huge tree trunk that is wide enough to conceal us both if we stand behind it. It's not perfect, but it's the best option we have. I take the lead, pulling the girl with me. She struggles as I push her back against the tree. Wrapping my arms around her shoulders, I try to keep her in place.

"We can't outrun whatever is coming. We need to hide," I whisper.

Tears are streaming freely down Nadine's face as she begins to shake. I hug her tighter, wishing I had listened to her and not dragged her out here. If something happens to her tonight, it will be solely my fault.

The forest becomes shrouded by fog, an unnatural occurrence for sure. I close my eyes, calling upon the great wolf apparition because I don't know what else to do. At first, nothing happens, and my heart squeezes tighter. The evil presence is upon us, a few more seconds and we'll be discovered. Then, my core becomes a little warmer as a soft caress brushes my mind.

"We are here," the strange voice sounds in my head.

I open my eyes when I feel the tree behind us tremble

slightly. The branches are moving, covering our bodies as if they're embracing us.

What the hell. The tree is alive? Are Ents fucking real?

The branches keep moving until they form a cocoon around us. It's claustrophobic, and I begin to worry how I'm going to get us out, when I sense it, stronger than ever, the malign presence floating right in front of us. Squinting, I try to catch a glimpse from the cracks between the branches, but all I can make out is a great shadow and the smell of sulfur.

Nadine is trembling so much I have to hold her tighter to keep her bones from rattling against the bark. Neither of us breathe until the dark being has gone. Even so, we wait frozen for another minute, not daring to move.

Slowly, the branches move again, releasing us from their wooden embrace. I'm still shaking, not exactly sure what the hell we just escaped from, when Nadine throws her arms around my neck, holding me for dear life, and begins to cry in earnest.

CHAPTER 18

SAMUEL

I'm so fucking angry I could kick something. What the hell happened back in Shadow Creek? We let Tristan take a beating from that freak and did nothing to stop it. *Nothing*. I wanted to leap from my hiding spot and sink my teeth into that fucker's throat so badly I actually tasted blood on my tongue. But Dante stopped me; he actually physically tackled me to the ground and kept me from joining the fray while our companions just stood back and watched. Even Armand managed to keep his cool after all that blood he drank earlier at my place. Then, Wendy and Brian combined their powers to zip themselves into the square to stop a tragedy.

I only quit struggling when Dante told me he had managed to speak to Red mind to mind. She was on the verge of fighting Valerius, but Dante was trying to convince her not to. That's why I promised to stay put. I didn't want Dante to lose his connection to Red because he was busy restraining me. Worse than watching my older brother almost get killed by a lowlife wolf would be to witness Red fight the bastard.

I can't help feeling defeated as we head back to the compound. I insisted on riding my Ducati despite the consensus it would be better if we split into groups and went by car. Fuck that. I have too much pent-up energy, and being confined inside a vehicle for an hour with other supes would drive me crazy.

Plus, I'm trying to avoid my bandmates, especially now that they know I withheld information from them.

Shit, what a mess.

When I see the junction on the road ahead, I slow down. I'm not ready to go to the compound yet. On top of dealing with the frustration of our epic fail, there's also the guilt. We've missed our dad's funeral, and being in the alpha's manor right now will only make everything worse.

Revving up the engine, I veer left toward town. I haven't given Nina much time to come with up the intel I need, but maybe seeing my face again so soon will motivate her even more to get rid of me.

It's past ten, which means Hell's Hole is slowly filling up with its usual clientele. I park my Ducati on the street parallel to it, not wanting to advertise I'm in the establishment in case Nina is not there yet. She might avoid the place if she's not ready for me.

Heads turn when I walk in, making me feel like I'm in a western movie entering a saloon. My presence here is not unusual, but tonight, it seems the animosity toward me is turned up several notches. Releasing the wolf energy I usually keep contained when I venture into town, I let those motherfuckers know they'd better not start anything with me or there will be hell to pay. I have a lot of suppressed aggression I'd be more than happy to unleash.

With a purposeful stride, I make a beeline to the bar, and the conversation that had ceased for a moment when I came in resumes. Parking my ass in one of the high chairs, I make eye contact with Baldwin, the bartender.

"Twice on the same day." He wipes a glass, then raises it toward the light to make sure he didn't miss a single spot. "Things getting rough?"

Rubbing my jaw, I lean forward. "You have no idea."

"I'm not sure about that." He turns to the counter behind him, letting me stew on that not-so-subtle comment.

"What have you heard?" No sense beating around the bush.

Flipping the dish towel over his shoulder, he turns to me. "What everyone who wasn't deaf heard last night from the mouths of two of your people."

"I need to know whose ass I'll be kicking later and what they said."

"Harold and Deacon. I had to give them a dose of *Goodnight, Cinderella* to get them to shut up."

"Right, you gave them a potent sleeping concoction to help protect my pack. I don't buy it."

The half-troll smiles with his full teeth, his eyes gleaming with danger. "They were getting rowdy. I didn't want a fight to break out here, not when the sheriff's department is too busy to send an officer."

"Since when do you need law enforcement assistance to deal with your customers?"

The smile vanishes from Baldwin's face. For a brief second, his troll markings appear on his arms. Oops, sore subject.

"Since I received a warning from our illustrious mayor that if I use magic to deal with humans again, she'll shut down Hell's Hole."

He must be referring to the two assholes who were harassing Gretchen. Damn, the mayor is not winning any points with the supe community. What the hell is her end game? Why is she antagonizing the very people who put her in power and siding with the enemy? I would bet my right arm that whatever scheme Valerius is concocting, the mayor is involved.

Son of a bitch.

And now we have a possible demon on the loose that can only be dealt with by magic or celestial powers. Since the angels have pretty much deserted us, we can only count on garden-variety spells from druids and witches—witches she controls.

"What did Tweedledee and Tweedledum say?" I veer back to the problem at hand.

"They think your mother's leadership is weak, and that someone ought to challenge her for the alpha's position."

My hands curl into fists, my nails becoming claws that dig into my skin. So it has started already. My father has not been dead for two days yet, and those vultures are already vying for power. Mom would never allow us to stay put to offer her protection, though. She also knows that now that we're mated to Red, our primal instinct is to protect her, not our own mother. It's the way of the wolves, but it doesn't make me feel less guilty we can't be there in case she's challenged.

"Did they say who they think should be the new alpha?" My voice is low and dangerous. I'm not doing anything to hide that I'll kill those disloyal bastards when I get my hands on them.

Baldwin crosses one leg over the other, leaning against the counter behind him. His gaze narrows while he studies me. He either doesn't want to tell me or he doesn't know.

"No names were mentioned, but they were clear that neither you or your brothers were good contenders. They said you were weak. That it's high time the Crimson Hollow pack has a different type of leader."

"What type of leader?" I growl.

Baldwin shrugs. "Someone who respects the hierarchy of wolves."

Ah. So the fact we helped Red and welcomed her into the pack is coming back to haunt us. I wonder where those poisonous thoughts are coming from; Harold and Deacon are incapable of an original idea.

"Anything else?"

Baldwin shakes his head, then looks over my shoulder. "No. That's when I gave them the *Goodnight, Cinderella* and dumped their sorry asses on a bench in the square. I hope they got arrested for loitering."

We both know that's highly unlikely considering Sheriff Arantes's officers are spread thin, according to the report Tristan gave us. I wouldn't be surprised if that was also a fucking lie. As much as I would like to believe the sheriff has our backs, she has always been the mayor's right hand.

Maybe she's also dirty.

If that were true, it would be a huge blow to all of us.

Baldwin's attention gets diverted to the entrance. "The person you're looking for just came in."

I turn halfway, trying to be inconspicuous but failing miserably at it. Nina indeed had come in, appearing a little rattled from what I can see. The moment she spots me, her spine goes rigid and she strides in my direction.

"Did you get my text?" It's the first thing out of her mouth.

Pulling my cell phone out of my jacket, I check the screen. Sure enough, there's one text from her. I must have missed the ping while I was busy having murderous thoughts about Harold and Deacon.

"Never mind," she says, pulling up a chair. "You need to get your girl out of Valerius's territory."

My heart immediately goes on overdrive. I'm already off my seat, ready to get the hell out of this bar and fly back to Shadow Creek. "Why? What happened? What did you see?"

Nina grabs my arm, pulling me none too gently onto the chair. "Settle down. You're making a spectacle out of yourself. And I haven't given you any information yet, you idiot."

"Spill it out already then."

"When I was out in the Shadow Creek woods, I encountered something vile and..." Nina closes her eyes, body visibly shuddering. "I have never been so scared in my entire life."

"What did you find?"

For Nina to confess she was terrified of something, it must have been truly terrible.

"A demon was roaming freely through Valerius's woods. I've never felt a more malevolent presence, and that's saying a lot in my line of business."

"How did you get in there without being seeing?"

Turning to the bar, Nina taps the counter once to catch Baldwin's attention. He returns a moment later with two shots of tequila, which Nina polishes off in two seconds flat. Both of them.

"I took advantage of the cloaking spell Wendy and Brian cast."

"So you're basically saying you have not found a way into Shadow Creek that won't alert Valerius's sentries. Is that it?"

"There's a way to get into his territory, which is not well patrolled. Between Shadow Creek and Xander's territory, you'll find a forgotten hunting cabin. Not too far from there, across a creek, the wired fence surrounding Valerius's lands is falling apart. That's how I slipped in. I would have gotten more intel if that demon hadn't showed up. But fuck it, I'm not going back there."

"Fine. I don't need you." I stand up.

Nina's gaze changes, as if she's worried about me.

"That's suicide. The sentries alone would be a hard challenge, but with a demon around, you can't hope to escape alive if he catches you. You need magic to fight that kind of power—a lot of magic."

An idea sprouts in my head, and I realize what I need to do first. "Then I guess I'll have to ask Mrs. Redford to give me some kind of amulet to help conceal my presence."

Wouldn't a cloak of invisibility be handy now? Why do all the cool magical gadgets only exist in movies and books?

"Wait, don't go yet." I watch Nina pull off a ring from her middle finger. It has a blue stone in the middle, with intricate swirls around it and on the band. "Here." She hands it to me.

"What is it? A marriage proposal?"

"You can't be serious for one second?"

She glares at me, but then her criticism sobers me up. She's right. I shouldn't be making jokes, but it's how I react in times of extreme stress. I'll either joke or make very bad decisions.

"It's a special ring. It's has the ability to store a spell for a few minutes or hours, depending on the type and how you use it. That's how I was able to slip under Wendy's cloaking spell even when I was nowhere near you guys."

I bring the ring to eye level, inspecting it. It doesn't look like anything special or expensive. "Where did you get this?"

"Where I got it is not important. If Wendy agrees to help you, then you can store the spell in that ring and use it when you arrive in Valerius's territory."

"Ingenious."

Not understanding why she's suddenly been so helpful, I ask, "Why are you giving me this, though?"

"Like I said, that demon is bad news. I don't know why it's roaming the Shadow Creek lands. Whatever it is, it's not safe for your mate."

Narrowing my eyes, I stare hard at the fox. "How did you know Red is my mate?"

"Leo didn't blabber if that's what you're worried about. But I also can't tell you how I know."

Under other circumstances, I would have insisted she tell me the truth. Brian cast a silencing spell on everyone present, after all. But I need to find Wendy and convince her to give me some kind of spell for tonight's mission. I'm getting Red back whether she wants to come with me or not.

CHAPTER 19
TRISTAN

I don't say a word during the trip to the compound. Xander, who is driving, doesn't attempt to engage in conversation, either. His people, two burly bears who have the don't-mess-with-me vibe are mute as well. That's why I chose to ride back with them, instead of with Brian, Mrs. Redford, and Dante.

The bruises on my body and the scratches on my face sting, despite the fact they're already healing, but the pain in my chest is another story. I lost to Valerius, badly. I failed my pack. Most importantly, I failed Red. I'm not surprised she renounced the bond even if my head tells me there's a reason why she did it. My heart is dead, as if by denying the bond and refusing to come back with us Red tore it to pieces.

I don't notice we have arrived at the compound until Xander parks the car and slides to face me. "We're here."

Blinking out of my stupor, I stare at the alpha's manor, which is shrouded in darkness. Not a single room is lit inside. Mom must not be in the house, which is not surprising. I wouldn't want to be in that mausoleum either—not where every nook has my father's memory etched in it. Maybe I should have gone to my apartment in the city, but that place is now filled with bittersweet memories.

With a deep breath, I open the door, but before I close it again, the door behind me, Xander speaks.

"It will be okay, Tristan."

That coming from the guy who didn't want to help to begin with is rich. He's only being supportive now thanks to Dante's vision. I can't even summon the strength to resent him. He's the alpha of his sleuth; he needs to put his members first and foremost.

Without a word, I shut the door, not moving from where I stand until Xander drives off. Then, I turn away from the house and head in the direction of the forest. I don't know where my feet are leading me; I just want the solitude only nature can provide. In another time, I might have shifted into my wolf form, but I don't have the will to do so.

I don't realize where I'm going until I recognize the spot where Red was attacked. I'm in Irving Forest, which means I've been walking for at least thirty minutes without noticing. The pressure in my chest intensifies, almost caving it in. With a closed fist, I massage the spot, as if by doing so it will make the pain go away.

Damn it, Red. Why didn't you come back with us? Why are you risking your life like that?

With heavy steps, I amble toward a mossy boulder, the same one Dante threw the rogue wolf against, killing him instantaneously. Leaning against the rocky surface, I slide down until my ass hits the ground. Bringing my knees up, I rest my forearms on them, letting my head fall between my shoulders. Being away from her is agony, and the constricting in my throat soon becomes a burning in my eyes.

My ears prickle at the sound of leaves being crunched. I raise my head, now in high alert as I search my surroundings. Then her scent hits me, and I manage to relax a fraction. Lyria breaks through the trees in the next moment, her steps sure as she makes her way to me. In her hand, I notice she carries a bottle.

"You're a hard wolf to track." She plops next to me.

I snort. "I find that hard to believe."

"True that. You weren't at your father's funeral."

Fuck. Why does she have to remind me of that? "I want to be alone, Lyria."

"Fine. Don't tell me why you missed such an important event. Here, I brought this for you. I figured you would need it."

She hands me the bottle of whiskey, my favorite brand. I curl my hands around it, not making eye contact with her.

"How was it?" I ask finally.

"Sad. Your father was a respected alpha."

I nod. He truly was, until he fell prey to Valerius and that controlling chip.

"I know you're hurting, Tristan, but you need to get your head straight. The pack needs you."

"The pack has my mother. She's the alpha."

Lyria laughs without humor. "You don't truly believe she'll be able to hold that position for long, do you?"

I whip my face toward the enforcer. "What do you mean?"

"Half the pack hasn't accepted her as a true alpha. You need to intervene, Tristan. You need to take what's rightfully yours."

"You want me to challenge my own mother? You don't think killing my father was enough?" My voice comes out as a growl that echoes in the silence of the forest.

"I'm not saying you should engage her in a fight. But you should talk to her. If she steps down in your favor, the pack will back you up as the new alpha."

A bitter laugh bubbles up my throat. That's until they learn Valerius kicked my ass.

"I'm serious, Tristan. If you don't do it, someone else will challenge your mother."

"Warning duly noted, Lyria. You can leave now."

She stands, brushing her pants as she goes. "Fine. Be stubborn like that. No one can say I didn't try."

She's halfway out of the clearing when I say, "Thanks for the gift."

Lyria doesn't stop or turn around. Soon, she disappears into the forest. I wait until I can no longer hear her footsteps to break the seal of the bottle and drink full swallows from it. It was wishful thinking to believe the wolves would just accept Mom as their alpha. But there's nothing my brothers and I can do to stop her from being challenged. The alpha role has to be earned. If we intervene, she wouldn't be a natural alpha, much like Valerius isn't one. I could sense his wolves don't respect him. They fear him, which is not the same thing.

My throat burns as the liquid goes down, and the warmth that spreads through my limbs is a welcome balm. Soon, the ache in my chest become less noticeable and the thoughts in my head turn fuzzy. After a few more sips, I can't even remember anymore why I was so worried. My last coherent thought is that I've never reacted this way from drinking whiskey before. But then, welcome darkness takes over me.

CHAPTER 20

SAMUEL

It's a little before midnight when Mrs. Redford finally returns home. I headed to her chalet in the woods as soon as I was finished with Nina. Needless to say, I was going out of my mind waiting. Sitting on her front porch step, I jump to my feet when her car's headlights reach me. She parks by the side of her house, and I wait for her to walk around. She doesn't seem surprised to find me there. Without a word, she walks by me, unlocks the front door, and then leaves it wide open for me.

"Would you like some tea? I'm going to brew some." She heads for the kitchen, and I follow.

"I'll pass on the tea. I came here to ask you a favor."

She fills the kettle with water from the sink, then turns on the stove before she replies, "I thought as much."

"I need you to cast a cloaking spell again."

She chuckles as if my request is a joke. "Pray, dear boy. What for?"

"I'm going back to Shadow Creek. I'm getting Red back."

My answer finally extracts a reaction from the elderly woman. She turns to me with round eyes and mouth agape. "She doesn't want to leave. She made that very clear."

"Things have changed. I've learned there's a powerful demon roaming freely in Valerius's territory. Red can't go against a demon; you know that."

"You're underestimating my granddaughter." The lady frowns.

"Are you going to help me or not?"

"You know if Red doesn't want to leave, there's nothing you can do to change her mind."

I open my mouth to say I'll bring her back even if by force, but Mrs. Redford continues. "If you kidnap her, she'll never forgive you. Remember how poorly you handled her transition into the pack."

Fighting for control, I plant my hands on the kitchen table, leaning on it. She's right. We pretty much forced Red to stay with us, then threw her at the wolves without training. We did her wrong.

"I'll give you a cloaking spell, but you can't go back there tonight."

I raise my head, a glim of hope dangling before my eyes. "Why not tonight?"

"Because I said so. Trust me."

"With all due respect, Mrs. Redford, I can't trust you completely. You lied to your granddaughter her entire life."

She winces at my words, almost making me feel guilty, but I stand by what I said. Red and I have not spoken about her grandmother's betrayal, but it obviously hurt her deeply. And I can't be sympathetic to anyone who hurts her.

"She wasn't ready to hear the truth. I know it sounds like a half-baked excuse, but it's a fact."

"Do her parents know you're a witch?"

"My son does, but he doesn't have the gift. Quite frankly, he never cared to learn more about his heritage. He couldn't wait to get out of Crimson Hollow. As you can imagine, he was against the idea of Red moving back here to take care of me."

Since it seems I'm not going anywhere for the time being, and the lady won't give me what I came for, I might as well get some answers. "Were you ever truly sick or was that a ploy to get Red to move to Crimson Hollow?"

Mrs. Redford's gaze becomes hard, her lips turning into nothing but a slash. "Watch your tone, Samuel Wolfe. I won't tolerate disrespect in my house."

"It sounds to me like you're evading the question. It's a simple yes or no."

"It's not so simple as you put it. Yes, I was diagnosed with cancer, but when Red moved here, I went into remission."

"Let me guess—you never told her about that. You let her believe you were still sick."

Guilt shines in her eyes before she nods. Anger bubbles up my throat, making my hands turn into fists. I want to break something. "You let Red worry about you all these years. How could you?"

"I did what had to be done. Red had a strong attachment in Chicago. I take it she never mentioned Alex to you."

"Who the hell is Alex?" Jealousy spikes my heart, twisting into it viciously.

"Alex Flint, her high school sweetheart. The end of their relationship left Red brokenhearted. Right after I received the news I was cancer free, Alex reached out. If I had told Red the truth, she would have returned to Chicago."

"To be with Alex," I complete, the words bitter on my tongue.

Mrs. Redford nods. "I couldn't let that happen. I knew Red had a destiny to fulfil here in Crimson Hollow. So I lied, and now you're mated to my granddaughter. So in a sense, you have me to thank for that."

I can't fault her logic even though her methods were shady as fuck. She could have told Red the truth or at least part of it.

"Now sit down and have tea with me. I need to recover my strength before I attempt another cloaking spell. Although, I don't know if it will work. I usually have to be nearby."

"Don't worry. I have something with me that will do the trick."

"Oh? What is it?"

Tired of playing games, I pull the ring Nina gave me out

and show it to Mrs. Redford. She takes it from my hand, inspecting it closely.

"My, my, where did you get this?"

"Doesn't matter." I offer my palm up, wanting the ring back. She drops it on my hand with the disapproving clicking sound of her tongue. A shrill whistle coming from the stove announces the water is ready.

I'm not a tea drinker, but tonight, I'll indulge the old lady. While she pours steaming water into my cup, my mind returns to what she revealed, about Red and her ex. Is she still in love with him? She's bonded to us, but does she love us? It's hard to tell when the strength of the mating bond takes over everything. Despite that, I'm certain I'm falling in love with her. It's almost a feeling apart from the magic that connects me to her. And knowing she loved another before us makes me crazy with jealousy.

"What is it, Samuel. Cat caught your tongue?"

"How involved was Red with this Alex?"

"Ah, you're still thinking about that, huh?"

I shrug, trying to downplay my interest. "Red and I haven't had much time to get to know one another."

"That's true. Unfortunately, I can't answer that question. You'll have to ask Red."

I grumble, like I'm going to ever remind Red of her ex. Mrs. Redford drops a satchel of herbal tea in my mug, and the aroma fills my lungs. I can't tell what flavor it is.

"What is it?"

"Just green tea." She drops a satchel in her own mug before sipping tentatively.

"How long until you can cast the spell?"

"What's the hurry? I already told you that you can't go tonight."

The muscles around my jaw lock tight. I'm at the lady's whim, and I don't like it one bit. I have half a mind to just take off and deal with the sentries in Valerius's territory. I have to see Red tonight.

"It's almost like you don't care about your granddaughter's well-being."

She cuts me a glare so powerful I almost cower in my seat. "I am thinking about Red's safety. That's why I don't want you to invade Valerius's territory looking for her tonight. Have you stopped to consider the repercussions if you're caught together?"

Damn the old lady. She knows exactly what to say to make me feel horrible. To hide the consternation on my face, I bring the cup of tea to my lips, taking a huge gulp that burns my tongue. The tea has a sharp tang to it, almost bitter, but despite that, it doesn't taste like green tea.

"Ugh, what the hell is this?" I stare at the contents as if it has done me great injury. In a sense, it did.

"A special brew to calm the nerves."

I raise my gaze to the old lady, finding her staring at me almost expectantly. Then it hits me, the numbing sensation. My eyelids become heavy as tiredness takes hold of me.

"What is in this tea, witch?"

"Mint, ginger, and a pinch of *Goodnight, Cinderella.*"

Ah fuck, Red's grandmother drugged me. Son of a bitch.

CHAPTER 21
DANTE

Talking to Red, even if mind to mind, helped relieve a little of the pain in my chest, but the unease still lingers there. She wants to play spy, find out what Valerius is planning, and it does make me proud, but at the same time, I hate she's risking her life, that we aren't there to protect her.

Valerius is an unhinged motherfucker. The way he keeps his wolves submissive is unnatural. A quick glimpse at the assembly and I could tell the wolves present hate their alpha with an unwavering passion. So why don't they revolt?

I'm betting the reason is what Red wanted to tell me but couldn't. I need to find a way to return. It's against my nature to simply wait for her to discover something worthwhile while I sit on my ass.

When I returned to the compound, I searched for my brothers. There's still the matter about Seth they need to be made aware of. I couldn't find either. Even casting out my senses, I couldn't locate their essence, which told me they weren't on the property.

I search for Mom instead, even though her words come back to haunt me. I'd promised we would be back to attend Dad's funeral, but we broke that promise, just like she said we would. I head for the clinic at first, but an odd pull in the opposite direction makes me stop in my tracks. Curious, I follow the invisible thread that leads me to a smaller building next to the gymnasium where our wolves train. The door is unlocked. At this hour, it tells me someone is still in the building. When I push the door open and enter the grand hallway, I see illumination at the end of it, coming from the library.

Realization comes to me now that I'm in close proximity with her. The odd pull I felt was my link to Mom. She's the one burning the midnight oil in the small community library. I find her with gaze down on one thick book, reading and completely absorbed in her task. She doesn't even glance my way when the door shuts behind me.

"Mom, what are you doing here?" I head her way.

"Looking for answers."

I pull up a chair opposite hers. "Answers to what exactly?"

She finally glances up, her eyes bloodshot and unbelievably sad. My chest becomes tight, and the thickness in my throat renders me silent for a moment.

"I'm so sorry about tonight, Mom," I say telepathically instead.

This is a loaded apology. I'm sorry for missing Dad's funeral, for not being able to see before it was too late that he was under the influence of a controlling chip, and also for fucking it up tonight at the showdown with Valerius. I didn't try to talk to my brothers before we parted our separate ways. Didn't tell Tristan about my suspicions of Seth and Lyria. My brief telepathic convo with Red left me reeling, feeling hollow and impotent.

Mom seems to read that in my eyes. Her gaze is understanding and forgiving when she reaches over and covers my hand with hers.

"I know how much you loved your father, Dante. But the mating bond is the strongest link between wolves. You had to go after your mate."

"How was it?" I finally find my voice.

"Sad, but also enlightening. I was able to tell exactly who I can count on, and who wants me gone."

"Let me guess. Seth and Lyria were among the disloyal scumbags?"

Mom lets out a humorless laugh. "Seth tried to hide his true feelings, but Lyria didn't even make that effort."

"Who else?" I spit out, anger turning my nails into claws.

"A few other enforcers." She shakes her head. "Nobody I can't handle or best in a fight if push comes to shove. You don't need to worry about me."

"I have to worry, Mom. Seth and Lyria delivered Red to Valerius. I know it in my bones. We're not dealing with honorable wolves here."

Mom turns her gaze to slits. "You don't need to tell me that. I wasn't born yesterday, son. I survived being a member of one the most ruthless witches' covens for years before I turned into a shifter. I can handle a few backstabbers."

I open my mouth to protest, but Mom cuts me off. "Enough about pack politics. I found something that could be useful to you."

Mom slides an old leather tome with faded golden letters printed on the cover across the table. I can't discern what it says.

"What is it?"

"The chronicles of Crimson Hollow's founding members. Maybe you can find some of the names from the list Zeke Rogers left for us in it."

I take the book, opening to a random page. "I'll have a look."

Mom tries to suppress a yawn, then closes the book she was reading when I came in. "I need to try to get some rest. You should, too, Dante."

We both rise at the same time, me with the chronicles tucked under my arm, and Mom with a handful of books in hers.

"What are those books about?"

"Witchcraft. It's been a while since I dabbled with the gift."

Her admission gives me pause. I only ever saw Mom as a

shifter who had a peculiar gift like mine. I kind of brushed aside the fact she was a witch before she made the change.

"Do you think you'll need to use your witch powers?"

Her gaze turns more somber, if that's even possible. "I don't know, Dante. It doesn't hurt to be prepared."

I walk with Mom back to the manor, then ask her if she wants me to stay, an offer she refuses. So I head to my studio, brooding about everything that has happened and everything that has yet to come. My last vision comes to the forefront of my mind. The original artwork remained at Brian's place, but I have it memorized. Red is once again at the center of the picture. This time, leading the charge against a foul creature that can only be a demon of grand order. She'd appeared fierce in that image, a true warrior. It made me love her even more.

That vision should have given me solace that Red will not perish at Valerius's hands, but it doesn't mean she won't get hurt. I try not to think about what that brute is doing to her, where he's keeping her. Before I know it, I'm pacing in my studio, pulling my hair in a maniac motion. I hate not being able to do anything.

Out of sheer frustration, I kick the nearby table, sending everything on top flying to the floor, including the chronicles I brought home with me. I had set it there as soon as I entered my place. It drops at my feet, face down and opened in the middle.

Since I have nothing to do and I'm going out my mind, I might as well do some research. I grab the book and the list of names before heading to the couch, eyeing the liquor cabinet as I go. I shake my head. No, I can't get drunk tonight, I might miss something. Plopping my ass down on the sofa, I peruse the table of contents first before diving in. Nothing jumps out at me, so I'll start from the beginning. It's going to be a long night. Maybe I should make some coffee.

It's not until way past two in the morning that I reach the middle of the chronicle and a name jumps out at me. *Robert E. Saint.* It's the second name on Zeke's list. He was Crimson

Hollow's mayor from November 1876 until April 1878, when he died from a mysterious illness not mentioned in the book. He was the youngest man to ever be elected mayor, only thirty-one.

There's still one member of the Saint family living in Crimson Hollow, a man rumors say came from the past during the Thirteen Days of Chaos. Could he be related to Robert? More importantly, if the rumors are true, could he have lived during that same time?

Maybe that's why Zeke gave me this list, so I could trace back to Albert Saint. I read everything about the illustrious mayor, noting the date on the list is exactly what I suspected it was—the date of his death. Invigorated by my discovery, I ignore the fatigue and keep on reading. A couple of hours later, I reach the end of the book, not finding any of the other names in it. But if they were shifters, then they wouldn't be recorded in the chronicles of the founders. It's highly likely that, back then, supernaturals weren't integrated with human society.

Suppressing a yawn, I put the book aside, then let my head hit the pillows on the couch. Exhaustion has finally taken over, but it has not erased the worry. *Red, please be safe.*

A loud knock on my door has me reeling. With a groan, I peel my eyes open, noting it's still early in the morning by the way the light is hitting my living space.

"Who is it?" I throw my legs to the side of the couch, wincing as a blinding headache flares on my forehead.

"It's Billy."

Springing to my feet despite my muscles' protests, I shake out my body, knowing I shouldn't have slept on that couch. With long strides, I reach the front door, opening it with a brusque movement. Bad idea. The morning light hits me square in the eyes. I have to use my arm to block it.

"It's damn early, kid. You'd better have a good reason to be here."

"Yes, I have information for you."

"Oh?" That piques my interest. I hope Billy has found proof his brother is a rat.

I move out of the way, opening the door further. Billy enters, still wearing yesterday's clothes.

"What do you know?" I ask.

He turns to me, his face solemn and hard. "There's a demon roaming Valerius's lands. Red is not safe there. We need to rescue her."

It takes a moment for my foggy brain to catch up with the omega's words. I raise my hand, closing my eyes for a brief second. "Whoa, back up. I thought you had information about your brother."

"No, I haven't seen Seth since he left the infirmary."

That I don't like to hear. "What's this nonsense about a demon in Shadow Creek?"

Guilt flickers in the kid's eyes before he lowers his gaze. "I went to Shadow Creek on my own last night. I didn't know you'd be there."

"Why in the world would you do that? That was reckless and stupid. You could have been caught or worse—killed. What the hell, Billy?"

Billy winces at my outburst, his shoulders sagging forward as he becomes smaller. "I just wanted to help. And nothing happened to me. I even saved Nina's life."

I raise my hand once more. "Slow down. What now?"

"Nina Ogata was there. Sam hired her to gather intel on the Shadow Creek's territory, find a way in without alerting the sentries."

Eyes on the ceiling, I curse. It was such a Sam thing to do, involving that freaking spy to help, a fox who can't be trusted by anybody. She was shunned by her parents for crying out loud. I hope Sam hasn't told her anything that she can turn around and sell to the highest bidder.

"So, what are we going to do?" Billy asks.

I arch an eyebrow. "*We?* We aren't doing anything. I gave you a task, which is to find out what your brother is up to. My brothers and I will handle Valerius."

Billy tenses up, but he refrains from speaking back. Smart kid.

"I'll go look for Seth, but...you're going to get Red out of Shadow Creek, right?"

Placing my hands on my hips, I glare at him. He's shedding his omega shell and turning into something more, maybe even a beta if he puts his mind to it.

"Yes. We're getting Red out of there."

I don't know why I felt the need to answer him. I don't owe the kid any explanation, but I can read the signs of rebellion. He already went rogue once and broke into Valerius's territory. There's nothing keeping him from doing it again, even with the promise of severe punishment. Maybe he knows I wouldn't punish him for something that needs to be done.

He takes his leave, and I turn around to change and grab last night's literature from where I'd dropped it on the floor. It's time I pay Albert Saint a visit.

CHAPTER 22

RED

I couldn't let Nadine go to sleep in the forest, not with that thing from nightmares roaming about. As soon as I managed to soothe her, we made a break back to my shack. Even behind closed doors, the poor teen couldn't stop shaking. I told her to take the bed. Even if the mattress is a piece of shit, it's better than sleeping on the floor. She didn't want me to leave the room, so in the end, I laid down next to her and held tight. It took a while for her fragile body to stop trembling. In the end, I believe exhaustion took over and she finally relaxed in my arms.

I don't remember falling asleep myself when the sound of the front door banging loudly against the wall jars me awake. I jump out of bed, my heart stuck in throat and my body poised in a defensive stance. A few seconds later, two burly shifters wearing muscle shirts, jeans, and combat boots fill the doorframe. I angle my body in an attempt to hide Nadine, but they can see her.

"What's this? Doesn't this pack know the meaning of privacy?" I say through my teeth.

One of the shifters, the tallest of the duo, sneers. "Privacy is a word you should erase from your vocabulary, sweetheart. You belong to Valerius now."

There are so many things I'd like to tell this asshole, but

the insults die in my throat. I'm in no position to get into an argument with these guys. And I thought my first days with the Crimson Hollow pack were tough. They were a trip to Disneyland compared to this.

"What do you want?"

"The alpha has requested your presence," the second minion answers before his gaze travels over my shoulder. "And he'll be pissed to learn that useless mute spent the night here."

Narrowing my eyes, I take a step forward. "Leave her out of this."

Before I can stop her, Nadine walks around the bed toward the door. Her gaze is down when she stops next to me.

"You don't give us orders, bitch," the first asshole replies. "You may have dined with our alpha last night, but that doesn't mean shit around here." He turns around and stalks away, followed by his buddy.

I don't move right away, so Nadine grabs my arm and makes me follow them. Valerius's minions are waiting by the front door. The moment their gazes zero in on Nadine's hand on my arm, she drops it.

Their pace is brisk, and both Nadine and I have to sprint to keep up. Like déjà vu, there's a circle around the red barn, but this time, the crowd parts for Valerius's brutes, and consequently for Nadine and me.

Valerius is standing proudly in the middle of the circle. Gone are the dark markings on his skin. He looks refreshed, but also seems more evil than ever when he glances my way. His eyes flash red when he sees Nadine. With a snap of his fingers, he commands the girl to stand by his side. She keeps her gaze down as she walks toward him, and I want more than anything to protect her, but I know if I try, I'll only make matters worse for her.

My attention diverts to the two hooded figures kneeling opposite Valerius. Behind them are two hunters.

"Good morning, my dear Amelia. I hope you're well rested."

"Who are those men?" I point at the captives in question.

"Men?" Valerius chuckles. "Those aren't men. They're maggots."

On cue, the hunters remove the hoods from their captives, revealing two wolves I recognize. I don't remember their names, but I know their faces. They're from Crimson Hollow.

Bound and gagged, they grunt and struggle against their bindings as if trying to tell me something.

I whip my face back to Valerius. "You kidnapped them? Why?"

"To punish them for being such loudmouthed vermin. They were talking trash about you, my dear, for everyone in Hell's Hole to hear. I don't tolerate that kind of disrespect. You are one of my wolves, after all."

"I don't care they were speaking ill about me. You need to release them."

"You'd better watch your mouth," he growls, then straightens his button-down shirt. "Now, I'm bored with this talk." He glances over the two Crimson Hollow wolves as if he's inspecting live cattle in a market. "Release that one over there with the ugly goatee."

The hunter behind the guy in question does as ordered. The moment the shifter is ungagged, he lets his tongue loose.

"You filthy bastard. You don't know what's coming to you. My pack is going to decimate you and this poor excuse for a pack."

The nearest hunter pulls his leg back and kicks the wolf in the ribs, sending him to the ground. "Shut your mouth, vermin," he says.

"Make him shift already. I don't have all day." Valerius waves his hand.

What? Make him shift? How?

I have my answer in the next second. The hunter pulls a syringe from his vest pocket, then jabs it into the fallen wolf's neck. There's a grunt from him, and his body starts to tremble. The shift begins slower than usual, and I have a hunch it is because it's happening against the wolf's will.

A brown wolf finally appears, and it snarls viciously in Valerius's direction. The second hunter pulls his captive's head back by the hair, then presses a sharp hunting knife against his throat.

"I'd think twice before doing anything," Valerius warns the wolf. "One wrong move on your part and your companion dies."

The wolf glances at his friend and loses the bravado.

"What are you waiting for?" Valerius glowers at me. "Shift already so we can get this over with."

"What?"

"Are you fucking deaf? I didn't go through the trouble of bringing those two losers here just for you to stare at them. Avenge your name."

"You want me to fight him?" My heart is thundering inside my chest while my mouth goes dry.

I know the answer before Valerius replies. Of course he does. I realize I'm asking stupid questions to buy time because I really don't know how I'm going to get out of this situation and save my peers.

"No. I want you to invite him for tea. Shift already. I'm losing my patience, Amelia."

I hesitate for one second, and that's enough stalling for Valerius. He grabs Nadine by the hair, pulling it so hard she can't hide the pain in her face.

"If you don't do as I say, you'll force me to take out my frustration on sweet Nadine here."

Seething, I ground my teeth. There's no winning Valerius over, no gaining his trust. He's deranged and evil. I don't bother taking off my clothes before I shift. I'm too angry and frustrated for that. The emotion only doubles in wolf form, making it almost impossible to aim my aggression toward the Crimson Hollow wolf. I want to rip Valerius's throat instead. He knows that, which is why he's using poor Nadine as a shield.

Turning toward the other wolf, I try to communicate with

him telepathically. I find his mental shield, but he doesn't open it for me. Damn it. If he was talking badly about me, then he won't trust me. I'm proven correct when he attacks, teeth bared, ready to take a chunk out of my face. I leap out of his reach, but don't go on the offensive. Instead, I attempt one more time to get him to talk to me. Finally, he allows it.

"Nothing you can say is going to change how I feel about you. I knew you were up to no good, you filthy Shadow Creek spy."

"I'm not a spy. I was taken, just like you were."

"You're one of them, and I'm going to kill you before I end your alpha."

He comes at me again, more furious than before. I have no choice but to go on the offensive. I don't know his rank in my pack, but he's not the strongest opponent I've faced since I was bitten. Without much effort, I scratch the side of his face. Before he can recover, I jump on his back, biting his shoulder. I could inflict more damage, sink my teeth deeper, but I don't want to hurt him too badly. I just want to keep Valerius from killing him and his friend.

The reluctance to hurt is only on my side, though. This wolf never liked me before, and now it seems his animosity has evolved to full-on hatred.

Trying to use his larger body mass against me, he jumps in my direction, not realizing I'm much faster than he is. I manage to slide away before he can pin me to the ground, but I'm running out of time. Valerius will get bored and punish all of us. I have to end this. Keeping my body lower to the ground, I wait for the wolf to try to jump on me again. When he does, I leap out of the way at the last second, twisting mid-jump to clamp my jaw around the side of his neck. This time, I do bite, hard enough to take the steam out of him.

He folds on his front legs with a whine, and I let go.

"I don't want to hurt you more. Yield and let this be over with."

The wolf tries to get up, but he collapses again. He must

have had other injuries I didn't see before the fight started. He was already running on fumes. Surprisingly, he shifts back, painfully slow. I don't know if the drug has worn off or if he's doing it on his own.

I step back, turning to Valerius. He knows I want to kill him, there's no point pretending otherwise, so I bare my teeth, emitting a low growl from deep in my throat.

"What are you waiting for? Kill him," he commands.

His venom hits me like a cannonball. I sense the malevolence, Valerius's will bearing down on me. He's using his alpha influence at full strength, but he doesn't know it doesn't affect me. I'm not bound to him.

Unwilling to shift back and defy Valerius as human, I shake my head, the only way I can communicate I'm not doing it.

"You have to do it," Nadine says in my head. *"Don't challenge Valerius."*

"I can't kill that wolf, Nadine. That would make me a monster."

She goes silent, then her gaze shifts to the crowd behind me. The hairs on my back stand on end as I feel the arrival of more wolves, the *other* wolves—Valerius-controlled freaks. Adrenaline kicks in as I swing around in time to see Victor lead the group into the middle of the circle. The other shifters who are still in human form give the former beta a wide berth.

"End it." Valerius's chilling words reach my ear. A second later, following Victor's lead, his wolves descend on the Crimson Hollow shifter.

No!

I make a motion to keep the wolves away, but a sharp prickle on my side followed by a burning sensation that spreads through my body like wildfire renders me useless. My legs give out from under me, and I lose the ability to control my muscles. I've been shot by a tranquilizer gun again.

In horror, I watch Valerius's killing machines tear the poor shifter apart in a frenzy. His desperate screams seem to go on forever until the soil surrounding him turns crimson. His friend can't help him, either. He's down on the ground. Held there by the boot of one hunter pressing down on his neck.

Finally, Victor and his companions spread out, revealing nothing but a pulp of torn flesh and blood in their wake. The only part intact is the shifter's head. I let out a whimper, hating myself for not being able to stop the carnage. What made me think I could bring Valerius down on my own? I'm no match for him.

Unable to move now, I only see Valerius approach when his boots appear in my line of vision. He crouches in front of me, his face twisted into something so vile it's almost demonic.

"It's a pity that it has to come down to this, Amelia. I really had high hopes for you. It seems the information I received was false after all. There's nothing special about you. You're just like the others, insubordinate and weak."

He unfurls from his crouch, turning to someone in the crowd.

"Take her to the lab."

CHAPTER 23
TRISTAN

I feel the hard throbbing on my temple first, as if my skull is splitting in two, then comes the ache all over my body. Finally, I blink my eyes open. At first, I'm disoriented, not knowing where I am until the foul taste of ashes in my mouth jars my memories. I'm in Irving Forest. I came here last night looking for solitude. Then Lyria found me, holding a bottle of my favorite whiskey in her hand—a bottle I must have drunk all of.

Movement on my periphery catches my attention.

"Billy? What are you doing here?" I ask, and the kid jumps on the spot, as if startled. "I decided to go for a run. Found you passed out here."

I groan as I try to sit up straighter. "What time is?"

"A little over seven. Did you...sleep here?"

"It would appear so."

When I manage to stand up, the entire world begins to spin. I have to focus on a point out in the distance to try to find my balance. "I need to get back to the compound."

"Tristan, I need to tell you some—"

"Damn, Tristan. Did you spend the night here?" Lyria asks from behind, her loud voice making me wince. Why does she keep popping up when I least want to see her?

Massaging my temples, I ask, "Why are you surprised?

You're the one who gave me the booze."

"I didn't think you would drink the whole bottle."

Lyria's attention switches to Billy, and I hope she won't start picking on the kid now. I can't deal with bickering this early when I'm suffering from a massive hangover.

"I'm going back to the compound. I have a raging headache," I say.

"That's why I came looking for you. Seth and I need to have a serious conversation with you."

Fuck, that sounds as much fun as sticking my head into a beehive.

"Oh, yeah? About what?" Billy asks, and I know that will earn him a tongue lashing from the enforcer.

In true form, Lyria glares at Billy. "Nothing that would concern an omega. Don't you have chores to do?"

"Leave him alone, Lyria. Come on. Let's go." I begin to walk toward the forest, hoping she will follow me. Anything to avoid Lyria getting all confrontational with the pack's omega. I can't deal with that bullshit right now.

She does follow me. As soon as we're out of earshot, I ask, "What's this meeting all about?"

"I think it's best if we discuss that when we're not out in the open."

I have a bad feeling about this covert meeting. I bet Seth wants to discuss the future of the pack, more precisely, my role in it. He'd better not come with some bullshit talk that Mom can't be the alpha and I should challenge her for the role. She's more than capable of ruling. Quite frankly, after what happened last night, I'm the last wolf who should be the alpha of anything. I'm a disgrace.

The feeling of failure doesn't leave through the entire trek back to the compound. Lyria leads me to Seth's apartment, which is in a complex building reserved for the enforcers. Of all the things I could expect from Seth, an ambush wasn't it. And that's exactly what it feels like when I enter his place and find all our enforcers there, waiting for me.

"What's this?"

"Tristan, before you jump to conclusions, let me just start by saying we have the utmost respect for Dr. Mervina and for what she's done for the pack," Seth starts, confirming my suspicions.

"But that won't stop you from stabbing her in the back," I say through my teeth, barely keeping in check the anger that is now running through my veins.

"She was a great alpha's consort, but she's not a true leader. The pack needs a strong hand at the helm, especially now that Valerius is threatening war against us," Seth insists, and everyone shows their agreement with a nod of their heads.

So it seems the news of my defeat hasn't reached down here yet. I wonder how long it will take for Valerius's cronies to spread the news. I'm sure Seth and the others will be singing a different tune when they find out.

"Trust me on this. Our best bet at survival is if my mother remains the alpha."

"You can't be serious, Tristan." Lyria takes a step forward with disbelieving eyes.

I don't buy for a minute her charade. Something is not right here. I can almost smell the deceit.

A sharp bolt of headache has me blinded for a second. I wince, closing my eyes and trying to breathe through the pain. I never felt anything like it. It's almost like a flash migraine of sorts.

"Tristan, are you okay?" Seth asks.

"Yes, I'm okay. I need painkillers."

I sense the unrest that spreads in the room and the judgmental glances of the enforcers on me. Am I making a mistake by not siding with them? If I say no to replacing my mother as the alpha, who are they going to pick as the next contender? Shit, I can't think straight. My mind is boggled up in a giant mess. Lyria should have known better than to bring me to this meeting after I drank all night. Booze that she provided. Maybe that was her plan, get me so drunk I couldn't think straight the next day.

A loud screech outside has all the enforcers on their feet in the blink of an eye. Fuck, is Valerius attacking already? I'm the first out of Seth's apartment, and the first thing I see is Jeanine Smith sobbing nonstop as she clutches a box.

"What's going on?" I take three steps at a time until I'm down in the courtyard.

Vincent, a young wolf who hopes to join the enforcers this season, answers. "The Shadow Creek pack delivered a package this morning and a note."

He hands me the small piece of paper and there, written in neat block letters, the message.

This is the just the beginning.

"What's inside that box?" Seth asks before I can.

Jeanine opens it, her hands shaking visibly, before she pulls out what's inside. Deacon's head.

Disgruntled sounds echo all around me. A kid bends over and pukes. But soon those sounds become muffled as a ringing in my ears gets louder and louder.

"Where did you find that package?" I manage to ask.

"In front of the north gate," Vincent replies.

"Get me the footage of the security camera. I want to see who came within our borders."

My vision turns double. If I don't lay down somewhere, I'm just going to pass out. I've drank myself to a stupor before, but never in my life have I felt as shitty as this the next day.

"I'll get the footage," Seth says.

I feel a hand on my lower back, then Lyria's face appears in my line of vision. "Tristan, you look like you're about to hurl. You should rest."

"I can't rest. There are things to be done." I step out of her touch.

"Has anyone seen Harold?" someone in the crowd asks. I can't tell who.

"He went out with Deacon last night," Vincent answers.

"Do you think he's dead, too?" Jeanine turns to me, her eyes bright and frightened.

"I don't know, but we should expect the worst."

Immediately, I know my bluntness is not well received. Maybe I should have given them a less pessimistic answer. That's what my mother would have done. One more reason why she's the rightful alpha, not me.

"That's unacceptable. Are we just going to sit around and wait for Valerius to pick us off one by one? We need to attack those motherfuckers." Charles, one of our most experienced enforcers, says.

I understand his anger and frustration, but all his words did was add more fuel to the fire. Pinching the bridge of my nose, I say, "We can't simply storm Valerius's territory without a plan."

"So what's the plan, then?" Lyria asks, which makes me distrust her even more. She knows I don't have a plan, but she sure wants to out me in front of the entire enforcer squad. Fucking fantastic.

"Let's wait to see the video footage first, then I'll get in touch with our allies. We'll need all the backup we can get."

"Since when do we need help from other supes to handle our problems? Your father would have already dealt with Valerius." Charles crosses his arms, glaring at me openly.

Even though my brothers and I were responsible for my father's death, his demise was triggered by someone else, maybe even Valerius. But I don't voice that out loud.

"I said we'll wait for the video footage," I say with a growl. "I'm still the beta of this pack. Everyone here ought to remember that."

Swinging around, I head back to the manor. I can't stay here and listen to all this nonsense. These wolves don't know what we're up against. My headache is worse than before now, but even so, I think I hear someone whisper, "Not for much longer."

Any other day, I would have turned around and dealt with the discerning voice, but something keeps my feet moving forward as if I no longer have free will.

CHAPTER 24
DANTE

Albert Saint and his wife Madison live in a quaint farmhouse near Wilmington's orchard. The two-story wood-paneled construction has all the charm of a small-town home, but none of the creepiness that seems to attach to every single building in Crimson Hollow. It's like the town's curse. Even the alpha's manor has some otherness to it, as if silently shouting that supernaturals live there.

As far as I know, Albert and Madison are one-hundred-percent human. Per the official agreement put in place after the events of the Thirteen Days of Chaos, every non-supe inhabitant who came into contact with us had their memories altered. The supe community tried their best to keep the truth contained. However, if Albert is indeed a time traveler, my assumption is that he knows the truth. If not, then fuck. I'll be breaking the accords by telling him about the supernatural world. It's a risk I must take. I need to know what the connection is between his relative and Red. Zeke wouldn't have left that list for nothing.

Madison owns The Little Witch Cafe, a popular spot that serves not only the best coffee in town, but also excellent sandwiches and cakes. Albert is a history teacher at Crimson Hollow's high school. Since school is out for the summer, I'm hoping to catch him home.

Standing on his front porch, I ring the doorbell, but I can't seem to remain still as I wait. I'm fidgety. For the past hour, I've been feeling a great sense of unease, a constant pain in my chest. I don't know if it was Billy's story about his close encounter with a demon or if something happened to Red, but I won't rest until she's back with us. The time to tread carefully has passed. Whether Red wants it or not, we're getting her out of there.

I hear footsteps approach. A moment later, the front door swings open. Albert is in his mid-forties, but he looks ten years younger. His brown hair is combed back and styled impeccably. The same can be said about his attire, which is slacks and a button-down shirt. I have a hunch those are his leisure clothes.

"Dante Wolfe?" He opens the screen door, his eyes narrowing a little.

"Hello, Albert. I'm sorry to bother you. I was hoping you would help me with a history question I have about the town's founders."

"Oh?" The man arches his eyebrows.

"May I come in?"

"But of course. Where are my manners? Forgive me." He opens the door wider to let me through.

I take a quick glance at the space. Dark wood flooring offers a nice contrast to the pale gray walls. To my right, a cozy living room seems to have been decorated by someone from the HGTV channel. I even spot one of my paintings hanging above the fireplace.

Albert follows my line of vision. "Madison and I love that piece. It really spoke to us."

It's one of my most abstract and colorful works, and one of the few not inspired by my visions. Those paintings I'd never sell.

"I'm glad it found a great home."

"May I offer you something to drink? Coffee, tea, or water perhaps?"

His British accent is noticeable, which makes me even more suspicious that he's indeed not from our time. It was common for wealthy families to send their sons to study in England back in the nineteenth century. I couldn't find any trace that Robert E. Saint had a relative named Albert, but it means nothing. At least, I'm hoping it means nothing.

"I'm fine. Thank you," I reply.

Albert points at the couch. "Please take a seat."

I follow his instructions and Albert sits across from me, crossing one leg over the knee. "How can I help you?"

"I'd like to know more about one of you ancestors. Robert E. Saint to be precise."

I can see the change in the man's expression. It becomes guarded, his entire body tenser. "What would you like to know about him?"

"I'll cut straight to the chase. Rumor has it that you're not from this time. Is that true?"

Albert's gaze narrows as he stares without saying a word. His jaw is locked tight, and I'm afraid my bluntness will make him clamp up.

"Where did you hear that?" he finally asks.

"Do you know what I am?" I lean forward, resting my elbows on my knees.

"Yes," he answers simply.

"Did you come from the same time as when Robert was the mayor of this town?" God, I feel like I'm a cop in an interrogation room. But there's no time to waste beating around the bush.

"Yes, sort of." Albert looks away, rubbing his face. "I haven't spoken about this with anyone besides Madison. Not even our kids know."

"I won't breathe a word of this conversation. You have my word."

Albert nods, his gaze going a little out of focus. "Robert was older than me, twenty-seven and already a man of his own when I boarded the ship to England. He helped build this town, literally brick by brick."

Finally, some good news. "Did he have any friends?"

"I suppose he did."

"Does the name Natalia Petroviski sound familiar to you?"

There's a flash of shock in Albert's eyes as they become wider. "Yes, as a matter of fact. She's the lass Robert fell desperately in love with. This is one of the most vivid memories I have of my cousin. Right before I was to leave Crimson Hollow, Robert took me out for drinks, only something happened in the course of the night that distressed him profoundly. He was usually a responsible man, but that evening he got drunk to the point he couldn't walk home. He told me about Natalia, the love of his life according to him, and how he could never marry her."

"Why couldn't he marry her?" I ask, already on the edge of my seat.

"Because she wasn't one of us. At the time, I didn't understand what he meant. I thought that perhaps she was from a lower class. But now, knowing what I know, I think she might have been a supernatural."

"A wolf shifter," I say more to myself than to Albert.

"It's possible. How did you come across that name? I've read every book and chronicle I could get my hands on about that time, and she wasn't mentioned in any of them."

"It was a list someone gave to me. Here." I give Albert the folded piece of paper. "Do you recognize any of the other names in it?"

"No. I'm afraid not. I'm sorry." He returns the list.

"Did he say anything else on that evening about Natalia? Where she was from, where she lived?"

"No, but he did tell me they used to meet by Silver Falls."

"That's near the Ravenwood border, isn't it?"

"Yes, indeed."

My mind is whirling, which makes me silent for a moment. So Robert and Natalia were involved. I'd bet all my money that Natalia was the original Mother of Wolves—what I'm not sure about is whether Robert was human by the time of his death. He married another, that much I know. But he could have been made a shifter and been part of Natalia's pack in the end.

"I'm sorry I can't give you more information. As I said before, I left Crimson Hollow and didn't return until a few years later, and then, well, I didn't stick around that time for much longer."

"No worries. The information you gave me was helpful." I stand up, and Albert does the same. "I'd better get going. Thanks for your time. I really appreciate it."

"Natalia Petroviski might not be in any official record or book, but Madison's former roommate, Cher Suzuki, found a chest filled with old witches' diaries around the time I came here. Sadly, the chest has disappeared."

"Cher Suzuki? Who is she?"

"A witch. She left Crimson Hollow soon after things calmed down around here. Not even Madison knows where she is or if she's still alive."

Fuck, another dead end.

"Do you think she took the diaries with her?"

"That I'm not sure, but if the diaries remain in Crimson Hollow, I can only think of one person who might have them."

A name immediately pops in my head, and Albert promptly confirms my hunch.

"Wendy Redford."

CHAPTER 25

SAMUEL

I don't know what wakes me from the most peaceful sleep I've had in weeks, but when I finally manage to open my eyelids, it feels like I'm underwater. My muscles are languid; I have no strength in my body. It takes me a moment to remember why I feel so strange. Mrs. Redford drugged me with *Goodnight, Cinderella*, a potent sedative capable of knocking out a bear for hours.

Somehow, she managed to drag my sorry, sleepy ass to her couch in the living room. There's no way she could have done that without the help of magic. I'm pissed she drugged me but in the end, it was my fault for not being more careful. Mrs. Redford's sweetly innocent face is just a façade. She's a powerful, cunning witch, and I keep forgetting that.

I sit up, and the room begins to spin. Throwing my legs off the couch, I rest my head in my hands and close my eyes. My temples throb, a sure sign that a brutal headache is coming.

"Ah, you're awake." Mrs. Redford enters the room. "Good. I made fresh coffee, and there's bacon with eggs if you wish to eat."

"You drugged me, witch."

"For your own good. Now, you should eat. *Goodnight, Cinderella* has nasty side effects. You'll feel better on a full belly."

I glare at the old lady. The first thing I notice is her clothes. She ditched her usual granny dress, going for sensible khaki pants, a button-down plaid shirt, and hiking boots.

"Where are you going?"

"We're going on a little trip. I'm just waiting for—"

A knock on the door interrupts what she was about to say. "Ah, it must be him."

"Who?"

Ignoring my question, she opens the door...and color me surprised, Dante is standing there.

"Good morning, Mrs. Redford. I—"

"Yes, yes. I know why you're here. Come in. I bet you also haven't had anything to eat."

Dante crosses the threshold, and I wish I had my phone with me to capture his expression of utter shock when he sees me there. My brother is not taken by surprise easily. He doesn't need to have a vision to guess stuff, thanks to his gift.

"Did you spend the night?" he asks.

"I had a date with Cinderella last night."

Scrunching his eyebrows together, Dante turns to Mrs. Redford. "I just came from an interesting visit with Albert Saint."

Fine. Ignore the fact the shady grandma poisoned me last night, brother dearest.

"Oh, and what prompted you to visit him? A question about Crimson Hollow's history, perhaps?"

"As a matter of fact, yes. Zeke Rogers left town in a hurry, but before he did so, he left a list with names for us. Robert E. Saint was on that list, and also the name of only one woman, Natalia Petroviski."

"And what did Albert have to say about his cousin?"

"Whoa, hold up." I raise my hand. "I'm feeling a little lost here. Would any of you care to explain what the hell you're talking about?"

Dante looks over his shoulder and blows out a heavy breath. "Albert Saint traveled through time twenty-five years ago when the portals to different dimensions opened. He's from the nineteenth century. Robert E. Saint, one of the names on the list, was his cousin. It seems Robert fell in love with Natalia Petroviski, but due to her otherness nature, they couldn't be together. Albert didn't know much about her, but he hinted something about some old diaries."

Dante turns to Mrs. Redford again. "You have those diaries, don't you?"

"What diaries?" I ask. "And why do they matter?"

Ignoring my question, Mrs. Redford nods to Dante. "Yes. Cher Suzuki asked me to guard them during her absence."

My body is achy, I have a shitty headache, and being left out of the loop is grating on my nerves. Irritated, I stand, hands on my hips and all. "Who the hell is Cher?"

"She's not important, Sam," Dante snaps. "Stop asking stupid questions."

"Fuck you, Dante."

Mrs. Redford turns her glare to me. "You'd better watch your tongue, boy. You're in my house, and I won't tolerate that kind of language."

Ah, shit. That's exactly what I need. To be scolded like a little child. I bite back an angry retort. Antagonizing the witch more won't do me any favors, not when I need her to give me the cloaking spell.

"I'm sorry," I mumble, looking at my feet.

"I'd like to see those diaries. I'm not sure why Zeke left that list of names for me, but I assume it's important. Maybe if we learn more about Natalia and her relationship with Robert, we can figure out how she ties in with Red and the rest of us."

Mrs. Redford seems to get lost in her head, and she doesn't speak for a minute. Then, she locks gazes with Dante first, then me.

"I never dared to look into those diaries. They were the personal accounts of witches from the past, and it felt like an invasion of their privacy to read them. But I feel in my bones that dark times are coming once more, so I'll take you to them."

"I don't have time to go in search for some stupid diaries. I'm going after Red."

Dante turns to me, his face twisted into a grimace. "Let me get this straight. You want to go into Valerius's territory in broad daylight without knowing where they're keeping Red? Are you out of your goddamned mind?"

"Language, Dante." I raise an eyebrow, and all Mrs. Redford does is shake her head. So I get a tongue lashing and Dante gets nothing? I see how things are. Clearly, Red's grandmother has a favorite.

"You're not going there. It's a foolish, suicidal mission."

I lose all my attempted levity in a split second, taking a step toward my brother. "Did you know Valerius is in cahoots with a demon, Dante? Did you? We can't let Red stay with that deranged alpha for another second. Can't you feel the heaviness in your chest? Something has happened to her. I know it deep in my bones."

A flash of pain shines in Dante's eyes. He's been too relaxed about Red's kidnapping, and I would like to believe he knows something we don't. But if that was the case, he would have said something.

"Yes. I've sensed something is off. But we have to wait until nighttime at least, and Tristan should come with us. We need the numbers, Sam."

A growl bubbles up my throat. Inaction is not how I roll.

"I guess none of you are hungry, so we should get going."

"Where are we going?" I watch the old witch through slits.

"Do you think I'd keep the diaries here? In my home? I'm not foolish."

Crossing his arms, Dante asks. "So where are they?"

"In the place people would least expect. Come on, let's go. It's a little bit of a drive and then a ten-minute hike."

Mrs. Redford walks out, but Dante and I don't follow her right away.

"So, Red's grandmother drugged you, huh? I bet you didn't

expect that from her."

"Nope. Lesson learned. She ain't fooling me anymore with that sweet grandmother face. That lady is ruthless." I pause for a second before asking, "How is... Mom?"

"She's hanging in there. Found her at the library studying witchcraft."

"That's unexpected. I didn't think she still practiced."

"She didn't, but I think she needs it now, you know? To connect with a part of her that wasn't linked to Dad."

I nod, unable to imagine what it must be like for Mom right now. I can't dwell too much in the sentiment or it will take over me, so I change the subject. "Albert Saint is from the past, huh? No wonder he loathed the textbooks he had to teach from. The inaccuracies must have driven the man insane."

"That's right. The rumors were true. I forgot he was your teacher in junior year. He didn't have much to say besides the fact Robert E. Saint was romantically involved with Natalia. I think she was a wolf shifter, Sam. I think she was the Mother of Wolves."

"Do you think there will be information about her in one of those old diaries?"

"It's a long shot. But it's all I have to go on right now. Maybe if we learn about Natalia, we can begin to understand Red's strange powers."

A strand of suspicion sneaks into my mind, making my heart clench painfully. "Dante, do you think Valerius knows about Red's special abilities?"

Dante opens his mouth to reply, but Mrs. Redford sticks her head in and interrupts. "I thought you wanted those diaries, boy. My granddaughter can't save your asses without some kind of help."

I wait until she heads out once more to turn to Dante. "When did Mrs. Redford become so impertinent?"

"At least now we know who Red got her feisty personality from."

CHAPTER 26
TRISTAN

Headache or not, I go look for Mom. There's no time for mourning, not when we're on the brink of war. I find her in Dad's old office, her ear glued to the phone while she paces back and forth in front of the massive mahogany desk. She glances briefly in my direction when I enter the room, but that's the only acknowledgement I get from her.

"When do you think you can get here?" she asks.

A moment later, she replies, "Thanks, Simon. I appreciate it."

Ending the call, she turns to me. "You look like hell."

"I feel like hell. Was that Simon Riddle on the phone?"

Simon is the alpha of the London pack, the oldest in the history of wolf shifters. There are other packs in England, but Dad didn't have a strong relationship with any of them. Simon was one of Dad's closest friends, and also present at the dinner that resulted in my father getting a chip implanted in his head.

"Yes. I've spent the morning calling all the alphas who belong to the World Council of Wolves to let them know about your father and also to give them an update on Valerius's movements."

"And what did they have to say about Valerius?"

I haven't forgotten that someone in my father's inner circle betrayed him.

"It's hard to tell over the phone. They all expressed their condolences and said wonderful things about Anthony, but are their sentiments sincere?"

"Simon was with Dad during that dinner in Vancouver." I don't need to say more to convey my meaning.

Mom crosses her arms, letting her chin hang low and sighing loudly. "I know. He was the most distressed to hear about your father and Valerius. Either he's a terrific actor or he didn't betray your father. We shall find out soon enough."

"What do you mean?"

Mom lifts her face, her gaze turning cold and hard. "I've requested assistance from Simon and also from the other alphas present during your father's dinner. If we're dealing with a traitor, I want them exposed sooner rather than later."

I don't disagree with the plan, but they might arrive here too late. I keep my worries to myself, though.

"We have a problem. A bigger problem. Valerius just declared war on us. He sent Deacon's head inside a box as warning of what's to come."

The blood drains from Mom's face. For a brief moment, I catch a hint of fear in her eyes. But then, she squares her shoulders, lifting her chin up as determination takes over her countenance.

"Where are the enforcers? I want a task force ready and sentries spread out throughout our territory."

That's exactly the order I should have given the enforcers before I came here. *Fuck.* Why the hell didn't I? I can't put all the blame on my damn hangover. Did losing to Valerius affect my confidence that much?

"I asked Seth to retrieve the security tape from the North gate. That's where the package was delivered."

"That's useless. We already know Valerius did this. I don't care who he sent to deliver the package."

I wince as if Mom's words physically slapped me. I'm already feeling like an utter failure, having her criticize my decision is the cherry on top of the cake.

She motions for the door, ready to play the alpha role, but I have to warn her. "Mom, wait. There's something you need to know."

"What is it, Tristan?"

"Before Valerius's package arrived, I was at an impromptu meeting organized by Seth. The most experienced enforcers were there, and they were questioning your leadership. They wanted me to take the place of the new alpha."

Mom's expression doesn't reveal anything. She has the perfect poker face on, but it must be killing her to hear her wolves don't trust her.

"I see. And do you feel you can be a better alpha, Tristan?"

I become rigid in an instant. That's not a question I want to answer. "You are the alpha."

"I might not be the alpha of this pack for much longer. But is there only *one* wolf who can take the job?"

"Are you referring to Dante and Sam?"

From the moment I began to understand how pack politics worked, I knew that if any of us became the new alpha, the other two would be forced to leave or die. We're just too equally matched in strength, and the wolves would force the alpha to fight the other two. An alpha is not a true alpha if he can't make his entire pack yield to his dominance. Because I'm the oldest, it was always assumed I'd be the one to take my father's place. But now, I'm the last wolf qualified for the job.

"You and your brothers possess different qualities, but you all have the alpha strand, the fire and power to lead. This has never happened before, but you're also mated to the same wolf. A shifter who possesses extraordinary gifts."

"I don't follow where you're going with this, Mom."

"Think about it, Tristan. Three equally matched alphas mated to the same woman. This pack is not meant to have one new alpha. It's meant to have three. You and your brothers are the legitimate alphas of this pack."

I stare at Mom for several beats without blinking. What she just said is insane and impossible.

"The pack will never accept that. You know it, Mom."

"It will be hard, and you'll have to prove that's how it's supposed to be. Why do you think I decided to remain the sole alpha? There's been too much instability already, and the pack needs to be prepared for the change. I wish we didn't have to deal with a shifter war while we're at it, but that's how things are. Now, the question is, are you ready to step up to the challenge?"

I open and close my mouth, but no sound comes forth. The old Tristan would have said yes without an ounce of doubt. Why am I feeling hesitant, unsure of everything?

"You don't need to give me your answer right now. Where are your brothers?"

"I haven't seen them yet."

The pinch of Mom's lips tells me she's very displeased to learn that. She tries to reach them by phone, but she's unsuccessful in both attempts.

"They'd better be doing something productive and not getting into trouble."

I wish I could jump to their defense, but knowing Dante and especially Sam, they're probably up to no good. God, what if they decided to go back to Shadow Creek and rescue Red?

"Let's go." Mom heads for the door. "We have a war to prepare for."

CHAPTER 27

RED

The first sense that returns to me is my hearing. There are two people talking nearby, a man and a woman. They're in the same room as me, and they don't seem to care if I overhear their conversation. They must believe I'm still sedated. So I try my best to not move a muscle.

"How long until the sedative wears off?" the man asks, and it takes me a second to recognize his voice. It's Martin, which means I must be inside the mysterious building protected by the rune spell.

"Another hour or so. The operation was successful. The chip is in place," the woman replies.

Chip? Fuck, no. They've put a controlling chip in my brain. What am I going to do?

"Good. Valerius will be pleased. You used the regular chip, right?"

"Yes, like you specifically told me to. I don't get why Valerius didn't want to use the special chip on that one. She looks like she could use a bolt of extra strength."

"You're not here to question my orders."

"Chill out, Martin. I'm not questioning anything. Anyway, we're almost out of both kinds. Actually, the one I installed in that girl was the last of the regular type."

"How many do we have left of the other one?"

"Ten, but with the way your boss keeps recruiting new subjects, we should be out of those in a week."

Martin curses. "Why the hell didn't you tell me this before, Felicia?"

"It's *Dr.* Felicia," the woman seethes. "And I didn't tell you because we still had a few of the first prototypes, but you destroyed them."

"Those have proven to be unreliable. I don't need a fucking rogue wolf turning on my team."

"So, what are you going to do?"

"What do you think I'm going to do, moron? I'm going contact our supplier and ask if they can send more this week."

My heart is thundering in my chest, and I'm afraid it will give away that I'm awake with the way it's beating so loudly. Valerius is creating an army. His strife is not only with the Crimson Hollow pack. That's obvious.

"When will she be ready for testing?" Martin asks, shoving the knife of fear deeper in my chest.

"As soon as she wakes up."

"Good. Let me know when that happens. I want to personally oversee that."

"As you wish, *boss*."

I detect the sound of a door gliding open, and then Martin's and the woman's voices begin to fade away. They're gone. I count to sixty in my head before I open my eyes to slits at first. I don't see anyone else around, so I open them fully now. I'm in a hospital room, white and sterile, similar to the one Valerius put me in on my first day of captivity. Once again, my hands are bound to the bed's side railing.

The first thing I search for is a security camera. I'm certain Valerius has them installed everywhere. Sure enough, I find one in the upper corner of the room. Damn it. How long until Martin returns to make sure I've turned into a mindless wolf? And what was all that talking about a special kind of chip and extra strength?

No time to think about that now. I need to get out of here.

Inspecting the bindings around my wrist, I notice they're the same kind as the ones Valerius used before. Unyielding and unbreakable while I'm in human form.

The bed is completely flat, which limits my view range. One thing I can see is that this room has big glass windows to the hallway, which leaves me completely exposed. Raising my head as far as I can, I try to see beyond the room. No one is around, but it doesn't mean I'm alone. Martin is still somewhere nearby. Who knows, maybe he's watching me struggle through the camera feed and laughing his ass off.

I'm running out of time, so if I want to get out of here, I have to shift before Martin turns on the chip in my head. Focusing on the energy inside my core, I call forth the wolf. It's there, restless, begging to be set free, but something is keeping it bound, contained. For fuck's sake. What did Martin do to me? My hands turn clammy as I curl them into fists, sweat pooling on my forehead. Grunting, I struggle to free my wolf until I finally feel my gums ache. *Yes!*

My celebratory sentiment dies as fast as it came when the gliding door opens again, and Martin fills the entrance.

"Give up, Amelia. Your days of shifting at will are over."

"We'll see about that."

A woman with bright red hair comes in carrying a medical chart in her hand. She must be the fucking doctor who put the chip in my head. Deep lines form on her forehead as she peers intently at me.

"Hmm, the sedatives wore off sooner than I predicted." She approaches the bed, bringing forth a small flashlight to check my eyes.

"Get away from me." I turn my face away from her, not letting the bitch do her routine checkup. If they think I'm just going to lay here and let them to do whatever they please, they're sorely mistaken.

None too gently, she grabs me by the chin and turns my face in her direction. I keep my eyes shut.

"Martin, a little help here?" she says, frustration lacing her words.

He chuckles. "Oh, no. I want to see how this will pan out."

"Open your fucking eyes, bitch. I don't have all day." The slap to my face comes swift and hard. I almost laugh. All the sharp pain did was to snap some of the invisible bindings keeping my wolf in place. My canines descend. Before the stupid doctor realizes what's happening, I sink my teeth into her hand.

She yells and tries to pull away, but the more she struggles, the harder I bite.

"Martin! Get this bitch off me."

I'm too lost in my bloodlust to notice the hunter walk around the bed with a syringe in his hand before it's too late. I feel the prickle on my neck, and a second later, my entire body begins to numb. The sellout doctor finally manages to break free when my jaw slackens.

"Why did you sedate her again?" she asks, clutching her bloody hand against her chest.

"Did you want to lose an appendage?"

"You could have activated the chip, idiot."

Martin is on the doctor in a split second, lifting the woman off the ground by her neck. "Who are you calling an idiot, butcher?"

"Let go of me." She tries to pry his fingers open to no avail as she kicks her legs.

My eyelids are getting heavy, but I fight the numbness with every fiber of my being. I don't want to go under again.

"Not until you apologize."

"I'm sorry. Put me down." She's getting purple by the second. Perversely, I want Martin to keep squeezing her neck.

"Aren't you forgetting the magic word?"

I have no doubt he'll choke her to death if she doesn't comply.

"Please, put me down," she manages to say with effort.

He drops her as if she were a sack of garbage. Gasping for air, she leans forward, bracing her hands on her legs. "You're fucking crazy," she says after taking a few deep breaths.

"Yes. And you seem to have lost your brain. Do you think I'd be stupid enough to test the chip before you finish examining the girl? Nothing can go wrong with her."

"What's so special about that bitch?"

Valerius thinks I'm the Mother of Wolves, that's what's so special about me. But he doesn't know that I can bring forth a powerful beast capable of shredding my enemies to pieces. Too bad my connection with the great wolf apparition seems to be on the fritz since I was brought to Shadow Creek. I only sensed its presence once when Nadine and I were running away from the demon.

"That's not your concern," the hunter says dismissively, leaving no room for further questions.

The sedative is finally winning the battle. I close my eyes, unable to prevent succumbing to the void.

My head is throbbing and there's a foul taste in my mouth. I'm not sure how long I stayed under. I'm still in the same room, but not alone. Martin is sitting in a chair in the corner, his eyes like a hawk on me. Déjà fucking vu. Only this time, it's not Valerius waiting for me to wake up. I can't say Martin is a better visitor.

"Welcome back."

I bite back an angry reply. Since I don't know the next time I'll be alone with the hunter, I decide to pester him with questions even though my brain feels sluggish.

"Why are you helping Valerius? What's in it for you?"

Narrowing his eyes, he leans forward. "I'm not going to waste my breath explaining my reasoning to you. It doesn't matter, anyway. You're his to do with as he pleases. You're never getting out of here to pass on the information to your friends in Crimson Hollow."

"We'll see about that."

"You keep saying that. Yet, there you are, still bound to the bed at my mercy."

"I'll take great pleasure ripping your throat out."

"I'm sure you mean it, but that ship has sailed, Amelia."

He stands up, then approaches the bed. I can't see what he's doing, but suddenly, the bindings securing my wrists slacken. I immediately want to jump at the opportunity to claw the smug smile off Martin's face. But just as my muscles tense for the action, the will to hurt the man vanishes. It's then that I notice the little remote control in his hand.

"Good, girl. Now I want you to calmly get out of bed and shift."

I fight the compulsion to obey with all the strength I have, but in the end, I succumb. Glaring at Martin, I swing my legs to the side of the bed, but when I try to stand up, dizziness makes my head spin. I have to hold on to the wall to keep upright.

"I don't know if I can shift," I say in almost a whisper. I'm totally exaggerating. I want Martin to believe I'm weaker than I am.

"You can. Now do it."

The compulsion to obey comes again, stronger than before. It's the strangest thing, because in order to shift, I have to connect with my wolf's essence, but now, I can barely feel it inside of me. And yet, my muscles begin to change shape as if they have a will of their own. Grinding my teeth, I throw Martin another glower. The motherfucker will pay even if it's the last thing I'll do in my life.

To add insult to injury, the transformation is twice as painful. Maybe because it's not a natural shift. By the time it's complete, I'm panting, still riding the ache. Instead of the wolf's energy and wild instinct in my head, all I can hear is static. The chip must run interference between the connection with my human conscience and the wolf's. I want to growl, bare my teeth at Martin, but of course, nothing happens.

"Very good. We'll start with a few simple tricks first. Sit."

Before I know it, my rear is on the ground. My wolf's body did it without me being conscience of the action.

"Good girl. Now roll."

This is humiliating. Martin has me doing dog tricks, and there's nothing I can do to stop it.

You're wrong, Amelia.

The voice again. The one that always spoke to me when I let my thoughts wander. This time, instead of ignoring it, I decide to talk back.

I don't know what to do. The chip is controlling everything my wolf does. It has cut off my connection to it.

The chip does nothing but create dissonance. They're waves of energy. They can be breached.

Who are you?

You haven't figured it out already? I'm you.

"Ah, Penelope, perfect timing." Martin addresses someone, interrupting my crazy conversation with the voice in my head. What did she mean she's me? Have I been hearing my own conscience this whole time?

A blonde, short woman with hair pulled back into a severe bun is staring at Martin as though she hates his guts. She would gain points in my book if she weren't wearing a white lab coat and carrying a chart in her hand. She must be another butcher doctor, so she can burn in hell as far as I'm concerned. An image of a towering fire comes to my mind, and that's exactly what I want to see. I want to raze this building, burn it to the ground until there's nothing left but charred soil where it once stood.

The voice—be it my conscience or not—goes silent, but her last words to me are all I can think about. That is, until a command blasts through my brain, almost an electric-shock. White-hot pain makes me whine out loud, and, for a moment, my sight deserts me. When my vision returns, Martin is standing in front of me with a perverse smile on his lips.

What the fuck was that?

The static noise becomes louder in my ears, then it morphs into a command in a robotic voice. *Attack the woman. Maim, do not kill.*

My wolf growls even if part of me knows this is crazy. Martin's companion widens her eyes as she sees my aggressive stance.

"What did you tell the wolf to do?"

The robotic voice keeps repeating the same command, which only makes my aggression increase every time it sounds in my head. This is the exact same command I heard coming from Victor in our first battle. It's maddening, enough to drive anyone insane.

I take a step forward, the hairs on my neck standing on one end. Even though I don't want to, I will attack this woman. Sure, I hate her guts on principal for what she is involved in, but I'm not a murderer.

"Martin, cut it out. This is not funny." The woman takes a step backward, ready to flee. I pick up her scent of fear, which only serves to fuel the savageness of the beast more.

No. I don't want to do this. I can't turn into Victor.

They're just waves of energy, Amelia. They can be breached.

My conscience, she's still here, albeit not as strong as before. She's right—the command, it's resonance—it doesn't have any real substance. To get out of its prison, I have to find a different frequency. The chip's command is pretty high, which means to break free from it, I need to go low. The question is—how do I do that?

I feel my leg muscles tense; my wolf is ready to attack the woman. I have maybe a few seconds. The repetitive command is as high as music in a club. And what did I use to do to be overheard over the loud music? The common instinct is to try to speak louder than the noise, but what really works is to speak at a lower frequency. I think I know what to do. Let's hope it will work.

I push my will barreling toward the robotic noise, tuning it out by concentrating on a low humming in my head. I still find resistance, but it's much less. With a mental grunt, I manage to get to the other side where my wolf's energy is spinning out of control. I shoot my human conscience straight into the eye of the storm, realizing a second too late that this could have been a terrible mistake. If I can't control my wolf's essence, I'll be lost to the bloodlust.

It's a struggle, a battle of wills, until, in the last second, I, Amelia Redford, become one with the wolf. Our thoughts are in synch. Most importantly, we're in control. The bindings controlling my wolf's body snap. I could attack Martin instead, but if I do so, the woman will sound the alarm. No, the best course of action is to make Martin believe he has complete control over me.

Doing as the command said, I attack the idiotic woman who is too slow trying to escape. She barely turns when I jump on her back, sending her to the floor.

"Get her off me!" She flails under me.

I know Martin is watching every movement I make, and the command was to maim, not kill. I bite her shoulder, letting my sharp teeth sink into her flesh. She yells in pain. For a split second, I feel bad. But then I remember she's part of Valerius's nefarious operation and the sentiment evaporates. She's lucky I'm in control. I could have done some real damage to her otherwise.

"Martin!" she begs.

I receive another command to let go of her, which I promptly obey, like the good dog that I am.

The woman gets onto her knees, trembling nonstop, and throws a murderous glare in Martin's direction. "You'll pay for this, asshole."

"Oh, come on. It wasn't that bad. You're not even bleeding that much."

She manages to get onto her shaking legs and then scrambles out of the room.

"Shift back, Amelia. Let's get you settled in your new quarters."

I do as he says, making sure I prolong the process for as long as I can. One thing I noticed is that controlled wolves take longer to shift, so I must keep up with the charade. I failed to convince Valerius I was a loyal Shadow Creek wolf, but now that I have a chip in place, I can't let them know I'm able to override it. This is my last chance to bring Valerius down from the inside. If they find out I'm not controlled by them, they will kill me.

Once back in my human form, I hug my knees, trying to appear smaller and afraid. "Where am I going now?"

"Don't worry. It's definitely better than that hovel Valerius put you in. Unlike him, I take care of what's mine."

"I thought Valerius owned all the wolves."

The corners of Martin's lips twist up, mischief shining in his eyes. "That's what he thinks."

CHAPTER 28
DANTE

I've lived my entire life in Crimson Hollow, and I've never been to this particular part of Misty Forest. On higher ground, it spans three mountain ranges, making it the largest forest in the area. Eighty-percent of the time, it's shrouded by mist, hence its name. I never knew if the occurrence was natural or put in place by a supe with something to hide.

Soaking my surroundings in and registering peculiar details is the only way I can distract my mind from worrying about Red. I don't need to read Sam's mind to know he doesn't think I care enough. Fuck, he couldn't be more wrong. But I see the chaos brewing in his eyes, the mad will to seek revenge. And Tristan, shit, I don't know what's going on with him. So I have to remain sane, be the one who's thinking clearly for once. In a way, I swapped places with Tristan, and it sucks to be in his shoes.

The ride becomes rough when we veer into a dirt path up the mountain. The strangest thing is that I've been on this mountain before several times, and this particular trek I've always missed.

"Where did this road come from? I don't remember ever seeing it," Sam asks from the backseat.

"It's concealed by magic. Only a few are able to see it."

"Why?" I ask, keeping my eye on the road ahead. The path

is narrow, and wild vegetation on both sides seems to want to swallow the vehicle.

"Because of what lays ahead. It's not safe."

"Where exactly did you hide the diaries? Satan's lair?" Sam grumbles.

"Not quite, but equally dangerous."

Great. Now Mrs. Redford is going to speak in riddles. What's wrong with giving straight answers? *Look who's talking*, my conscience says. I grind my teeth and ignore the thought. I, too, withhold information. We all did, especially to Red. If we hadn't been so wrapped up in pack politics and procedures and had taken the time to explain things to her, maybe she wouldn't be in Valerius's hands right now. I wish I had the power to go back in time.

After listening to Mrs. Redford give directions for about half an hour, we finally come to the end of the path. A great ancient tree trunk blocks the road.

"What now?" Sam asks.

"Now we walk the rest of the way." Mrs. Redford gets out of the car, and we have no choice but to follow her.

Here the forest is so dense, the tall trees block most of the sunlight. Only a few rays manage to break through their canopy. Mrs. Redford climbs atop the fallen tree, nimble as a cat, then jumps to the other side. Next to me, Sam curses under his breath.

"What's the matter?" I send the question to his mind.

"Look at her, Dante. As healthy as she can be. I can't believe she lied to Red all these years about her illness. It makes me sick."

I don't say anything for a couple of beats. I'd hate to pass judgment on Red's grandmother. She must have had her reasons for doing so. I hope that, with time, Red can forgive the old lady.

"Maybe she didn't think she had any other choice."

"Whatever. I don't trust her. She fucking drugged me last night, Dante, although I don't think you care."

"Were you about to do something foolish?"

"Yeah, maybe."

"Then I'm glad she did. We can't be hotheads now, Sam. Any wrong move on our part could put Red at even higher risk."

"Oh, like the stupid stunt Mom had us do, letting Tristan go up to Valerius to claim Red as his mate?"

That backfired, royally. I have to give that to Sam. Returning to Crimson Hollow without Red was one of the hardest things I've had to do. I couldn't let Sam see that at the time, though. If he had read the despair in my eyes, there would be no dissuading him from leaving without her.

"Are you two done gossiping?" Mrs. Redford asks from a little ahead. "It's rude to talk telepathically when you're among people who are not part of the conversation."

"Like drugging people isn't?" Sam retorts, earning a glare from me.

"Will you let it drop?" I say under my breath.

Mrs. Redford chuckles, and it's obvious her reaction only irritated my brother further.

"How much longer until we get to where we need to be?" I ask before Sam decides to antagonize the witch more.

"Not so much longer now."

"Where exactly are we going? Did you bury the diaries deep in the forest? That can't be good for paper," Sam grumbles.

Shit, I don't think he'll ever forgive Mrs. Redford for sedating him.

"No. I've hidden the diaries in a place no one will dare cross."

From the corner of my eye, I catch Sam open his big mouth again. To keep him from spewing another barb, I elbow his arm. *"Enough already. I thought you wanted Mrs. Redford to cast another cloaking spell."*

"Fine. I just want this to be over with. I really don't see how a bunch of old diaries can help us rescue Red."

It would be pointless to try to explain to Sam how acquiring knowledge can be beneficial. Never mind that he hired Nina Ogata to get intel. Sometimes, I can't understand my brother's thought process.

When I think the vegetation can't get any thicker, it suddenly gives way to reveal a clearing. Straight ahead, a cave surfaces, almost hidden from view by the moss and vines that curl around the rock. In fact, the green entrance curtain is so thick I can only see a sliver of darkness between the branches.

A gust of wind coming from inside the cave disturbs the vines, and a shiver runs down my back. Deep in my bones, I know that's no ordinary breeze. It curls around my spine, an invisible touch, cold and malevolent.

"What's this place?" Sam whispers, as if not wanting to disturb the strange vibes he's probably picking up as well.

"This used to be a torture chamber in the nineteenth century, where witches were persecuted and killed."

"What?" Sam almost shouts. "Why would you hide the diaries there?"

"Because the ghosts of the witches who died in there still haunt the place. No one gets in without their permission."

Sam takes a step back, shaking his head. "I'm not going in there."

I roll my eyes. I had forgotten about Sam's irrational fear of ghosts.

"Fine. You can stay here, but be warned—the ghosts are not bound to the cave. They can roam freely in the area nearby as well," Mrs. Redford replies with a smirk on her lips.

Seeming spooked, Sam moves closer to me. "Fine. I'll stick with you guys. But this better not be another trap."

With a disapproving click of her tongue, Mrs. Redford takes a couple of steps forward, stopping suddenly when the wind picks up, creating a mini tornado of dried leaves around her. A disembodied voice echoes in the clearing, sounding like several people speaking in unison.

"Who dares trespass upon our resting ground?"

Sam steps closer, clutching my arm. "What the fuck was

that?"

Mrs. Redford raises her arms, closing her eyes as she does so. "It is I, Wendy Redford, one of you, sisters."

"Who have you brought with you?"

"Allies."

The wind changes direction, coming straight to us. I feel phantom hands all over my body, prying thoughts that try to breach through my mind. Next to me, Sam remains quiet, but he's shaking nonstop. The invasion seems to last forever. When the spirits finally take what they were looking for, I feel drained. I might not fear ghosts like Sam does, but shit, that was unpleasant. They're fucking leeches. To remain tethered to this plane, they must feed off the energy of the living.

"What have you come here for?" the ghosts ask.

"I came for the treasure I hid here twenty-five years ago."

"Those tomes do not belong to you. You cannot take them."

Mrs. Redford drops her arms. In the next moment, a red glow appears between her hands.

"Do not test me. I've allowed you to remain here, but I can just as easily banish you to the Land of Lost Souls."

Sam and I trade glances, then he asks in my mind, *"Land of Lost Souls? What the hell is she talking about now?"*

"Beats me. It's the first time I've heard of such a place."

"And since when can Mrs. Redford create balls of energy?"

"Are you regretting antagonizing the woman knowing now she could have fried your ass at any time?" I can't help but tease Sam, despite the situation. He asked for it.

"Bite me."

"How dare you threaten us after what we've been through?" the ghosts shriek, but I can almost sense them retreating back to the cave.

"You've had your revenge, now quit being difficult and let us enter." Mrs. Redford takes a step forward.

They don't answer, but the vines blocking the entrance whoosh inward, indicating something just passed through. The ball of energy between Mrs. Redford's hands vanishes right before she peers over her shoulder.

"Let's go before they change their minds. Those ghosts are finicky as hell."

"They felt evil. Why don't you just get rid of them?" I ask.

With a sigh, Mrs. Redford sags her shoulders forward. "Banishing poltergeists is not a walk in the park. It's just easier to let them stay here. They aren't harming anyone, and we've put several wards in place to keep people away from this cave."

"But you just threatened to send them to the Land of Lost Souls, wherever the hell that place may be," Sam pipes in.

"Well, I have a good poker face."

"Wait. Do you mean you were bluffing?" Sam's voice rises, making me elbow him in return.

"Louder so the evil ghosts can hear you."

Sam emits a growl from deep in his throat while giving me the stink eye. Mrs. Redford ignores us both as she plunges into the cave's darkness.

"She lied to Red all these years. Why are you surprised she tricked those ghosts?" I ask.

"You're right. I shouldn't be. But damn it, Red's grandmother is shady as fuck."

I don't comment because I'm beginning to agree with Sam's opinion. In silence, we follow the witch inside the cave, noting it's no longer completely dark. Mrs. Redford whips out a flashlight, which gives us a faint glow to follow. Our steps echo in the narrow tunnel, making everything more sinister. No surprise, Sam is glued to my side again.

"Stop being such a ninny. You're a wolf for crying out loud."

"I don't think being a wolf gives us any advantage when dealing with evil spirits."

"You were ready to storm Valerius's territory even with a demon roaming freely, but you're terrified of ghosts?"

"I'd rather face a demon."

I shake my head. *"You're nuts."*

Mrs. Redford's flashlight goes out, and I'm about to ask if she's okay when brighter illumination reaches us. We come to the end of the tunnel, stepping into a round-shaped chamber. Mrs. Redford is busy going around the space, lighting up torches mounted on the walls. As the entire room becomes visible, several wicked apparatuses are revealed. The torture devices.

"What the hell? This is not disturbing at all," Sam points out.

"Why are those machines still here?" I reach the one closest to me, a donkey-like apparatus, which is actually a vertical wooden board with a sharp V-wedge on top of it.

"What the hell is that?" Sam comes closer, frowning as he inspects the object.

"That's a Spanish Donkey," Mrs. Redford replies from the center of the chamber. "One of the most gruesome torture devices broadly used during the Spanish Inquisition."

"Do I want to know how it worked?"

A shiver runs down my spine when the idea of how this worked comes to my mind. "No, definitely not."

Crossing his arms in front of his chest, Sam turns to Mrs. Redford. "Okay, witch. Let's grab the diaries and get the hell out of here."

Mrs. Redford closes her eyes, ignoring Sam's comment. She begins to chant words I don't recognize, but I soon feel the power of her invocation deep in my bones. A whoosh of energy emerges from the ground, and if I squint my eyes, I can almost see flecks of multicolored light dots floating in the air. The empty space in front of her begins to tremble, just as if there were a ripple in the air, and then slowly, a wooden chest materializes. Once it becomes solid, Mrs. Redford bends in front of it, then lifts the top.

Sam and I approach her, finding several leather-bound diaries inside the chest, some newer than others. One in particular catches my attention. When I reach over to retrieve it, I'm shoved to the ground by an invisible force.

"You're not worthy of that knowledge," the ghosts say while trying to get into my mind.

My skull feels like it's going to split in two, and I let out a cry while clutching my head with both hands.

"Dante!" Sam yells. "Fuck! Do something, witch."

My gums ache as my canines elongate. The pressure against my mental barrier is too much, and the spirits manage to breach it. I begin to shift without having wanted to do so. My wolf sensed the danger, and it's taking control.

"You're not like the others, are you?" A distinct woman's voice sounds in my head. *"You're worried about one of our own, someone who has been hunted through several lifetimes."*

I can't answer her. My thoughts are frozen. Then the cave vanishes, and I'm looking at a lab of sorts from a vantage point. Men and women wearing white lab coats are running about, and then dark-clad hunters storm the place. Soaring above them, I reach the end of a corridor. It's then I see her, Red, trying to escape. Rochelle is with her.

The vision vanishes at the same time the ghosts depart my head. I take in deep breaths as if I have gone without air for several minutes. Sam's face is above mine, staring down on me with panicked eyes. I manage to halt the shift, returning to my full human form.

"For fuck's sake, Dante. Are you all right?"

"What happened?"

"You stopped moving and breathing for almost two minutes while stuck in mid-shift. I thought those ghosts were choking you with their invisible hands."

"Red!" I sit up suddenly. "I saw her, Sam. She's in danger. We need to get her now."

"I got the diary we need," Mrs. Redford says. "Let's go."

CHAPTER 29
TRISTAN

Outside the alpha's manor, we find a flurry of activity already. From the youngest of our members to the oldest, wolves are coming and going with a sense of urgency in their step. Teenagers who are too young to fight were tasked with carrying boxes and materials to be used to barricade doors and windows. It seems someone has taken the reins. For a moment, I think perhaps Dante or Sam have returned, but I soon discover that's not the case.

Folks slow down when they see Mom next to me, and some even drop their gazes to the ground as if they have something to hide. Damn it. I hope the topic of my conversation with the enforcers hasn't spread throughout the compound. Slowing down my pace, I let Mom take the lead. There can't be any doubt in their minds that she is the alpha. She strides across the quad fast, heading toward the mess hall.

Seth is in front of the building surrounded by three enforcers, busy giving out orders. Raising his head, he stops talking when he senses his alpha's approach. Mom is projecting her power to the max. The other enforcers stare in our direction as well, bracing for what Mom is going to say. They seem cagey, and it's no surprise. Not even an hour ago, those shifters had been plotting to replace Mom.

"Seth, what's the current status of the situation?" Mom cuts straight to the point. She doesn't ask why her wolves are busy doing things she didn't order.

"I've doubled the number of sentries to cover the compound's perimeter and also the area surrounding it. Our security cameras have not picked up any activity yet, but it's a matter of time before Valerius attacks."

"Is that a guess or are you basing your opinions on facts?"

"Valerius killed Deacon and sent his severed head as a warning. His attack is imminent," Charles replies, his tone a little disrespectful.

"So, it's based on nothing but fear," Mom replies, earning a glower from Charles, and the other two enforcers, Trent and Gareth. She chooses to ignore the angry expressions, turning to me instead.

"Tristan, I want a task force organized. Select our stealthiest enforcers and—"

"Actually, Dr. Mervina," Seth interrupts. "I already took the liberty of putting a team together."

Mom's eyes widen a fraction, the only reaction that shows her surprise. I, on the other hand, feel several conflicting emotions. I'm pissed Seth went over Mom and me to put together the team, but also glad he took the initiative. But I'm mostly angry at myself for not being more proactive. Instead of running to find Mom, I should have given out orders first.

"Good. Who is on the team?"

"Charles, Trent, Gareth, and Lyria."

It's a good team, but Mom's face goes cold, staring hard in Seth's direction. She's not pleased with his choices.

"I want Lyria to stay in the compound. Tristan will join the team."

"She's one of our fastest enforcers," Trent says.

"We can't send our best wolves out and leave the compound unprotected. Lyria and Seth will stay."

"What about your other sons? I haven't seen their faces in almost a day." Charles crosses his arms, lifting his chin in a defiant manner.

That's enough. Fighting the lethargy that is keeping me subdued somehow, I take a step toward the enforcer.

With a barely contained growl, I say, "You'd better watch your tongue, Charles. You're speaking with your alpha."

"Dante and Samuel are not your concern." Mom's tone is hard, leaving no room for argument. "They have their own assignments."

Charles grinds his teeth, but refrains from speaking again. Good. I'd hate to put him in his place by force. We can't fight among ourselves.

"I'll let Lyria know she's staying behind," Seth chimes in. "But what's the plan?"

"The task force will head to Shadow Creek and get any intel they can find. Valerius already caught us unprepared once. I want to know exactly when he begins to move his wolves into our territory."

"That's risky. What if the team gets caught?" Trent is the one posing the question, not out of defiance from what I can gather from his tone and body posture, but out of understandable concern.

"It's a risk we must take. We can't go head to head against Valerius blind."

"When do we leave?" I ask before someone else decides to contest Mom's orders.

"As soon as possible."

No sooner does Mom give the command than a sentry comes running toward us, breathless and naked. He obviously just shifted back into human form, and didn't have the chance to put clothes on.

"What's the matter?" Mom and Seth ask at the same time. She stares at him through slits for a split second before turning her attention back to the sentry.

"Well?" she asks again.

"I spotted a group of fifteen Shadow Creek wolves coming our way from the northeast side of Irving Forest."

"Did they see you?" I ask. "And how far were they from the

compound?"

"I don't think they saw me. They were ten minutes out when I caught sight of them. They should be here any minute now. I'm sorry. I ran as fast as I could."

"I guess you're too late, *Alpha*. Valerius is already upon us." Charles makes the snide comment.

Faster than anyone can blink, I grab Charles by the collar of his shirt, lifting him off the ground. "You say one more disrespectful word to your alpha, and I'll make sure it will be your last day in this pack."

My wolf is churning inside, begging to be set free. A vein throbs in my forehead, followed by the terrible headache that has plagued me since I woke up this morning. But I push through the pain, not wanting to show weakness in front of the enforcers.

"Look who's finally found his balls," Charles sneers.

Before I know it, I'm throwing the guy to the ground.

I'm ready to shift and end this when Mom puts a hand on my shoulder. "Enough, son. Save your energy for the enemies that are coming."

I taste blood in my mouth, realizing a second later I must have bitten my tongue. My body is shaking, and that's due to trying to stop the shift from happening. I glance at Seth, who's watching me with rapt attention. Our gazes collide. For the first time since I can remember, he can't hold my stare. True, lower-ranked wolves usually can't maintain eye contact with alphas and betas, but I've rarely exerted my power on Seth and I'm most definitely not doing it now. So why is he acting like he has something to hide?

Charles gets up, shoving away the helping hand from Trent.

The sentry who came with the news hops from foot to foot in a fidgety motion. "Er, what should I do?"

"You go warn those not fighting to stay behind closed doors, then join your usual sentry post."

"Yes, Alpha." The guy takes off, mercifully not questioning Mom's orders. At least some wolves still have sense left in their brains.

He has barely disappeared from view before Mom is in her wolf form. We all follow suit, then dash after her in the direction the sentry spotted the enemy. Soon, we're joined by Lyria and two other enforcers, but we're still outnumbered.

"Stay sharp and don't make foolish mistakes. They have more wolves, so we need to be very careful." Mom's voice echoes in my head, and I'm sure in the others as well.

"We should call for backup," Seth says.

"There's no time," I say. *"We need to stop those wolves from reaching the compound."*

"It's protected. The electric fence is on," Lyria replies.

"That won't stop them," Mom's voice says.

I hear what Mom doesn't want to say. There's a traitor in our midst. That wolf can simply turn off our defense mechanism, making it easy for a breach.

Not a minute after we reach the forest, the enemy's stench reaches my nose before I get a visual. At the same time, my headache flares up, affecting my vision in the process. White, hazy spots appear, as if I'm peering through a window specked with water drops. Closing my eyes for a split second, I shake my head, trying to get my sight to return to normal. It only makes the pain that's splitting my skull in two intensify, but at least the spots disappeared. Just in time because there's a Shadow Creek wolf barreling in my direction.

He leaps on a fallen tree trunk, taking advantage of the higher ground to gain leverage and land on top of me. I saw exactly what the wolf was planning to do. I would have had enough time to jump out of the way, but my legs freeze in the last second as if the command my brain sent them wasn't registered. In consequence, I'm pushed to the ground with the enemy on top of me, his jaws and sharp teeth too dangerously close to my neck. The impact of the fall snaps me out of my paralysis, and I manage to avoid getting a piece of my face chewed off. I still can't dislodge the wolf; I'm pinned underneath him. It's only a matter of time before he manages to sink his teeth into my jugular.

Then a sharp pain in my chest comes out of nowhere, robbing me of breath. It's intense and soul crushing, the same sensation I felt when Red disappeared. Something happened to her. The knowledge she's in grave danger gives me a bout of strength. Adrenaline kicks in, giving me enough muscle power to push the wolf off me. He doesn't fall far, and he's already on his paws by the time I stand up, getting ready to come at me again. I don't give him the chance.

Baring my teeth, I body slam against his side, pushing him down on the ground again. Angry snarls and growls reverberate all around me, the sound of wolves fighting, but it's dulled, as if I'm cut off from the noise by an invisible barrier. I think about Red, about the last time we saw each other, how she sacrificed herself to save me, and I see crimson. My teeth find the enemy's neck, and I'm slashing his throat open in the next second. The taste of the enemy's blood on my tongue only fuels my need for revenge more. These motherfuckers took my mate from me. I'm already searching for my next target before the fallen wolf has died. I'm thirsty for blood.

I see nothing but a red haze. I want to kill all these wolves until there's nothing left but their putrid carcasses. Then I spot a Shadow Creek mutt breaking away from the group, dashing from the battleground. *No!* I can't let a single one of those bastards escape. Forcing my legs to run faster than ever before, I give chase. The fleeing coward is much smaller than me. It's probably a very young wolf, but I don't care. I jump on his back, clamping my jaw around his shoulder hard, until, with a whine, his front legs give out from under him. The sudden fall sends me flying against a boulder nearby. The side of my head collides with the hard surface, rendering me useless for a couple of beats. Just enough time for my prey to run away. I get up, ready to go after him, when Mom's voice echoes in my head.

"Tristan. Where are you?"

"One of them is trying to escape. I'm going after him."

"No, I need you back here. We've lost Trent and Gareth. We're surrounded."

Mom's words should have propelled me to action immediately—*they're in danger*—but it takes a few seconds for my body to respond to what my brain is telling it to do. Finally, I force my legs to move, running back to where I left the others. The sounds of vicious fighting get amplified when moments before they had been dulled somehow. It's as if I removed a plug from my ears.

I reach the spot where Mom and our remaining enforcers are, right in time to see two of our wolves killed by the enemy. Now there's only Mom, Seth, Lyria, and Charles against nine wolves, which are circling them like prey. Without thinking, I attack the closest to me, biting one of his hind legs to swing him away like a rag doll. Two wolves break away from the circle to come at me, but I'm ready. I'm still riding on the bloodlust from before. I don't even know how I kill the next wolf, but suddenly, I find myself circling only one of them, my body low, closer to the ground. I'm ready to pounce on him and end this fight quickly when a whine of pain distracts me. I break eye contact with my opponent for a split second, finding Mom down with a wolf on top of her. I should help her, but I do nothing. I just stare like an idiot.

White-hot pain on my hind diverts my attention from the scene, making me howl. This moment of distraction cost me, and I'm now down as well. I try to get up, but my muscles seize as if my body is being electrocuted. The pain is unbearable. I can't move; I can't do anything. I have no sense of what's happening until the assaults stops.

"Tristan, open your eyes. Are you okay?" I think it's Seth's voice in my head. I can't be sure, because everything is muffled.

"Mom?"

"She's hurt, but I think she'll be okay."

"What happened?"

"You caved, that's what happened," Charles answers now.

"If it weren't for Seth, you would be dead."

Charles's reply is loaded with meaning. Mom couldn't fend off the enemy, and I couldn't step up to the plate and help her. This will not bode well for either of us, but somehow, I don't have the strength to care.

CHAPTER 30
RED

Martin wasn't kidding when he said my new quarters would be an improvement from the condemned shack Valerius assigned to me. Clutching the lapels of the white lab jacket he tossed my way before we left the hospital room, I follow him through a thick metal door that leads to a different area in the building. Even without the separation, I'd be able to tell we're not in the lab area anymore. The colors on the walls are gray instead of bright white, and even the floor changed to concrete instead of linoleum.

The facility reminds me of the college dorm room I visited in Chicago before I made the decision to move to Crimson Hollow. I was set to attend Northwestern University, one of the best schools in the country, with my ex Alex. We couldn't entertain the idea of going separate ways after high school graduation. But instead, he broke up with me after our senior year trip to Scotland, shattering my heart. With time, the pain went away, making me question if I had ever been in love with him for real. I definitely didn't feel the constant pain I do now. My heart aches for three impossible wolves, and the idea I might never be with them again, that this chip in my head will obliterate who am I, has the ability of ripping my soul apart if I let it take root in my mind. I have to find a way to remove the implant.

Martin comes to halt in front of a simple white door. There's nothing on it to differentiate it from the other doors lining the hallway.

"Here we are, home sweet home." He pushes it open, revealing a minuscule room that can barely fit one person inside.

One single bed is pushed against the wall, leaving just enough room for me to get to the other side. No windows, no desk. The only other piece of furniture is a nightstand with a couple of drawers.

"Where's the bathroom?" I glance over my shoulder, finding Martin's gaze fixated on me. His dark eyes are unnerving; they almost don't feel natural. I wonder if he's something other than human. He definitely gives out creepy vibes.

"It's communal, down the corridor."

I let my eyes wander freely around the space, taking in everything—not that there's much to see. At least the mattress doesn't look like it could be housing a colony of bedbugs and the sheets are clean.

"So this is it? Am I supposed to stay here and wait for orders?"

Martin shrugs, a casual gesture that's at odds with what he represents. "You're lucky you're one of Valerius's special wolves. Not everyone in his army is so fortunate."

"What do you mean?"

"I mean, not everyone has a clean bed and a roof over their heads."

A nagging suspicion sprouts in my head. "Where does Victor stay?"

The mood changes immediately, and I sense my question awakened Martin's predatory nature. He narrows his eyes, his dark pupils glinting with malice. "I guess that rat Nadine managed to tell you a little bit about the history of this pack."

Crossing my arms, I glare at Martin. I won't let him intimidate me. "She told me Victor was the former beta, and also Valerius's older brother."

"Did she also tell you that she's Valerius's little sister?"

"What?" I can't help my tone of surprise. Sure, they have the same pale skin tone and dark hair, but my brain never considered they could be related.

Martin chuckles. "I guess not. It doesn't matter. To answer your question, Victor stays in a far less comfortable place than this. I swear to God that wolf is alive only due to sheer willpower. He has seen hell."

Cocking my head to the side, I stare at Martin more closely, wishing I could hear his thoughts. His last comment is not something I'd expect from him. Who is this guy?

"It almost sounds like you pity him. I didn't think you had it in you."

A spark of anger turns his gaze murderous right before he takes a menacing step in my direction. "Watch your tongue, Amelia. Just because Valerius thinks you're something special doesn't mean you can't be punished. Inside this building, I'm the king."

I suck in a breath when Martin's eyes flash red for a split second. *What the hell?* I saw the same thing happen to Valerius, but he's a wolf. Our eyes can glow different colors when we're angry, mostly amber from I what I could tell. I just figured because Valerius is evil incarnate, his eyes were different. Maybe Martin isn't human after all. My eyes drop to the tattoo on his neck. The raven seems to be moving as if it were alive. I peel my gaze away before he can notice I'm staring at it.

"You're free to roam in this part of the building. As you can see, the door has no lock."

"So you trust me now?"

"Oh, trust isn't involved. But you see? When I can control you with a snap of my fingers, I don't need locks. Also, it's so much fun to watch new occupants try to escape."

I can only imagine the kind of nasty traps Martin has in place.

"What's the food situation here? I'm hungry."

Not in the slightest, but if the wolves staying here are free to walk about, I want to get to know them as soon as possible. Acquiring intel quickly will be my best bet to find a way out. I'm breaking out of this prison at the first chance I get.

"Let's go. I'll show you. Wouldn't want you to wander and get lost."

Following Martin without attacking the guy is an exercise in self-control. I feel my nails turn into claws, so I curl my hands into fists to hide the partial shift, puncturing my own skin in the process. The pain helps me focus on the end goal, which is escape, not killing Martin—at least not yet. When we reach the end of the corridor, he veers right, then left before we arrive at a common area where a few tables and chairs are spread around. The room is painfully bare, like everything else here.

"Valerius likes to keep his wolves hungry to the point of starvation. It's his way to show he's in control. When I get the ones for the implant, I waste weeks nursing them back to their top shape. I wish Valerius would treat his subjects better. We would have conquered Crimson Hollow already if he wasn't so savage and stupid."

My spine goes taut at the mention of my home. "Is that what Valerius is planning to do? Conquer the entire city?"

Ignoring my question, Martin opens a cupboard door and grabs a few bags of chips from inside. "This should hold you over until dinner. You're still expected to come to the barn. Valerius must be dying to see you." The sarcasm is duly noted. He hates Valerius's guts, which is an interesting fact to know.

Martin drops the bags of chips on the counter, then walks away without another word. Fuck. I'm not done with my questions yet.

"Where is everyone?" I ask before he disappears around the corner.

He stops, glancing over his shoulder. There's a strange glint in his eyes—not quite malicious, but definitely mischievous.

"I almost forgot to ask," he says with an upward twitch of

his lips "What's Kenya's favorite restaurant?"

I'm rendered speechless for a few seconds, my brain having a hard time processing Martin's question. Throughout my ordeal, I hadn't stopped to think about my non-supernatural friends.

"Don't you dare go near Kenya."

Martin pretends to be crestfallen, as if I have no reason to issue such a statement. "What? Why? I like her. She's funny and cute, and I gotta say, I think she's into me, too."

Fear for my friend overrides caution, and I find myself taking a couple of steps in Martin's direction, a low growl stuck in my throat. "You stay away from her."

Instead of lashing out, which I totally expect him to do, he simply laughs. "Oh, Amelia. You crack me up. So I guess that means you aren't going to help me. I'll just have to figure it out by myself then."

He turns the corner and I want to go after him, stop the guy from leaving, but someone calls my name, distracting me. I spin around, coming face to face with Rochelle.

CHAPTER 31
SAMUEL

I'm about to hurl when we finally arrive at the abandoned hunting cabin between Xander's and Valerius's territory that Nina told me about. Dante drove like a maniac up the mountain, and all the twists and turns put a knot in my stomach. Or maybe I'm just too fucking worried about Red and the fact we couldn't reach Mom or Tristan when we called them.

I'm the first out of the car, taking deep breaths of fresh mountain air to recover from the ride from hell.

"Do you think that ring will work?" Dante walks around the car to stand next to me.

I reach under my T-shirt, pulling out the ring that I attached to a thick metal chain. I don't want to lose it in case I have to shift. A faint blue glow emanates from the stone on it. Mrs. Redford cast the cloaking spell as soon as we were a safe distance away from the cave of evil witches. We didn't think it would be wise for her to tag along, so we dropped her off on the side of the road, as close as we could to town. She would call somebody to pick her up.

"There's only one way to find out," I say.

I turn up my nose, sniffing the air with purpose. The scent of a creek nearby reaches me, confirming we're in the right spot.

"That way." I point.

I hate that we're going in blind. Nina really didn't tell me anything. We have no fucking clue where Red is being held. The moment we got on the road, I started trying to sense her through the bond, getting nothing. I still can't get anything as we cross the creek, which only serves to increase my anxiety. Why can't I feel her?

We find a hole in the wired fence big enough for us to pass through. The moment my feet land on Valerius's territory, I sense a shift in the air, a feeling of wrongness. I bring my fisted hand to my chest, trying to massage the sudden ache there to no avail.

"Do you feel that?" I whisper.

"Yes," Dante hisses. "There's bad energy all around. I can't exactly pinpoint where it's coming from."

"What about Red? Can you sense her?"

My brother shudders as he closes his eyes, scrunching his eyebrows together. "No."

I curse under my breath. I'd hoped Dante could pick up something with his special gift. He did manage to speak to Red the last time we were here. A great feeling of defeat takes hold of me, darkening my mood.

"Wait," he says suddenly. "I think I got something. The connection is weak, as if it's been blocked by an unnatural barrier."

"Is it enough to locate her?"

Dante doesn't speak for several beats before he finally answers, "Yes. Let's go."

We head deeper into Valerius's lands. While Dante is busy focusing on the bond to Red, I expand my senses to pick up any scent of sentries nearby. Sure, we have Mrs. Redford's spell, but I'd rather not put it to the test if I can help it.

Within a minute of going down the mountain, I pick up the stench of Shadow Creek mutts. Holding Dante's arm, I point to my forehead. Dante is the only one who can initiate a telepathic convo while in human form.

"I smell them, too," he says.

"We should circle around them."

He shakes his head. *"We can't. My bond to Red is getting stronger. We're going in the right direction. I'm afraid if we deviate course, I'll lose it."*

"Then let's hope the witch's spell works."

"You should be more concerned about the gadget Nina gave you."

"I trust Nina. I can't say the same thing about that old hag."

Rolling his eyes, Dante turns his face away, continuing his fast-paced trek toward Red. I don't care about what he thinks. Mrs. Redford is on my shit list.

We come across two sentries in the next minute. They move almost silently through the forest like ghosts, their paws making no sound on the ground. The spell is supposed to conceal everything, including smell and sound, yet, on edge, I continue to walk in the opposite direction when those sentries cross not even a yard from us. They don't glance in our direction, which means the spell worked.

"How far are we from Red?" I ask after another minute, walking blindly in the woods. I hate not knowing the lay of the land, and even though I trust my brother with my life, it doesn't mean there isn't a trap waiting for us wherever Red is.

"I can't say for sure, but we're very cl—"

The sound of laughter interrupts Dante's train of thought. We both stop and listen.

"What's the matter, Nadine? Cat got your tongue?" one man says, followed by the laughter of a second companion.

I take a good whiff of the air, picking up the scent of two humans and a shifter. I'm not sure if she's a wolf from Shadow Creek or from another pack. Her scent is strange. But one thing I do notice is the smell of fear coming from her.

There are noises of struggle before the second guy says, "Squirm all you want, little wolf. No one will hear you, and you can't scream for help."

Dante and I stare at each other. In sync, we move toward the commotion. Untamed bloodlust tinges my vision crimson when we see what those two fuckers were trying to do. One of them has a wisp of a girl pinned against a tree, grinding against her. She's putting up a struggle, trying to break free, but they only laugh at her attempts.

"I'll take the one with the girl," I say before I make a run toward the man.

Dante leaps onto the second guy, catching them both by surprise. The man assaulting the girl swings around.

"What the fu—"

His words die in this throat when I slash his neck open with a partially shifted claw. He falls on the ground with a muffled thud. A gurgling sound erupts from his mouth as he slowly suffocates on his own blood. Shifting my attention to the left, I see that Dante dispatched the second guy with speedy efficiency as well.

Movement on my peripheral catches my attention, and I turn around to find the barrel of a tranquilizer gun pointed at me. The teenager's grip on the gun is pathetic, and with the way she's shaking, chances are she'll miss me by a mile.

Raising my hands up slowly, I say, "We're not here to harm you."

She switches her aim to my right, where Dante now is. "Please put the gun down," he says in a soft tone.

Slowly, the girl drops her arms, but she's still eyeing us with wariness. The fear has not left her scent.

"What's your name?" Dante continues.

She shakes her head, before rubbing her neck.

"I don't think she can talk," I say. *"Are you able to reach her mind?"*

"I've tried. She's keeping herself closed off."

Then something occurs to me. *"She can see us. The spell doesn't work on her."*

With the end of the gun, she begins to draw on the ground. Moving closer, I see she spelled Red's name followed by a question mark.

"Yes, we're here for her. Do you know where she is?" I ask,

forgetting to keep my voice down.

She nods, then motions for us to follow her.

"Do you think we can trust her?" I ask.

"She's leading us toward the bond, but I can't tell yet if she's friend or foe."

"Those men harassing her were hunters."

"Yes, but just because she was their victim doesn't mean much if she's a Shadow Creek wolf."

"I guess we'll find out soon enough."

CHAPTER 32
RED

Relief washes over me. Rochelle is alive and seems okay despite the visible weight loss and dark circles under her eyes. In the next second, she's hugging me, an act that catches me completely by surprise. My stiffness only lasts a split second before I'm hugging her back.

"Are you okay?" we both ask at the same time, easing off the embrace.

"Yes," I reply. "And you?"

"I don't know. The last couple of days have been a blur. Why are you here?" Her face falls as the implications of my presence finally dawn on her. "You were captured."

"Yes. I've been here for a few days. But we're getting out soon. I promise."

Rochelle's eyes widen in fear as she shakes her head slightly. "I'm forsaken. Something was done to me. I have no control over what I do anymore."

I grab Rochelle's hands, keeping them together between mine as I lean closer to whisper, "There's a chip in your head, controlling everything you do."

"Yes, I gathered as much. That dark-haired man, Martin, is running the show here. He came in to see me when I woke up in a lab of sorts. He made me do things I didn't want to. He forced me to shift."

"Where are the other wolves?"

Rochelle's eyebrows furrow together. "What do you mean? I'm the only one here. I haven't seen any other wolf."

"But I thought…" I close my eyes for a brief second. "Martin gave me the impression there were others here, Valerius's favorites."

My mentioning of the Shadow Creek alpha does something to Rochelle. Her face twists into an expression of fear as she hugs her middle, her body now trembling. "He…visited me a couple of days ago." She drops her chin, staring at the floor instead as if she can't sustain my gaze.

"What happened?" I ask softly, instinctively knowing this is a delicate matter.

She shakes her head. "I don't want to talk about it."

Seething, I dig my nails into my palms, trying to control the sudden fury that begins to pump in my veins. "Did Valerius do anything to you, Rochelle?"

The enforcer lifts her chin, her green eyes now filled with unshed tears. "He made me do things, and I was powerless to stop him. He forced me to shift and…and he took me."

Fat tears roll down Rochelle's cheeks, but this time, she doesn't hide from me. Breaching the distance between us, I hug the woman again. Her sobs are steady, silent, and don't last very long. Before we break apart, I whisper in her ear, "I'm getting us out of here today. And I'll make Valerius pay for what he did to you. I swear."

"I'd like to say that Valerius is mine, but I don't think I can go against him, Red. Even speaking his name renders me impotent." She takes in a shaky breath, peering over my shoulder. "I feel so ashamed, not for what he did to me, but to not have the drive to rip his throat out."

I touch her shoulder, not knowing exactly what to say to make her feel differently. No words can soothe the raw pain she's feeling. "Hey, there's nothing to be ashamed of. What he did to you was despicable and evil. I can't presume to understand what you're going through, but believe me, you will heal; you will persevere."

"How can you be so sure? We're stuck here at his mercy. There's nothing keeping him from coming back to torment me again. I think that's what I'm most terrified of, that the nightmare has only started."

"I'll kill him before I'll let him touch another strand of your hair." I feel a surge of power coming from within as I speak these words. The voice doesn't even sound like mine; it sounds like the voice I hear in my head.

Rochelle's sharp intake of breath clues me in she noticed the difference, too. "Oh my God. You are really her, aren't you?"

"Who?" I take a step back, rubbing my hands together. I know exactly what Rochelle's answer is going to be.

"The Mother of Wolves."

Taking a deep breath, I run a hand through my hair. "I'm not sure what I am. My grandmother is a witch—that could account for my strangeness." I'm not sure why I'm so reluctant to accept I'm the reincarnation of some badass wolf. Stubbornness or fear of failure?

"All I know is we need to get out of here now," I continue.

"I've looked everywhere. I can't find the door out of this section. It's been driving me crazy because I remember vividly the way I came in, but there's nothing there anymore, just a smooth wall."

"Valerius is using spells to keep exits concealed. There are rune wards surrounding this building. I'm sure he has runes inside, too."

Rochelle wipes off her wet cheeks, shuddering in the process. "How are we going to find the exit if it's concealed? Wolves don't deal with magic well."

"What do you mean?"

"We're supernaturals, but we're at the mercy of spells and hexes, just like humans are. The shifter community was almost annihilated completely during the Thirteen Days of Chaos."

"Everyone keeps mentioning that, but I still don't know

exactly what happened here twenty-five years ago. I think it's something I should know."

Rochelle nods. "It's part of our history. Lots of good people died, supe and humans alike."

The pressure in my chest increases as a lump lodges in my throat. If I don't put a stop to Valerius's plans, more deaths will occur for sure. I glance up, searching for a security camera. I don't see any, which makes no sense. There's no way Valerius would leave this part of the building unmonitored.

"Come on, let's go." I grab Rochelle's hand, pulling her toward the hallway I came from.

"Wait, even if we manage to escape, Martin can activate the chip at any time. We're prisoners even out of here."

Pivoting on the spot, I grab the woman by the shoulders. "You can fight the chip's command, Rochelle. I was able to, so can you."

My words of encouragement have the opposite effect on the enforcer. She's downcast instead of motivated. It takes me a moment to understand why. Damn it, she must be feeling worse now, knowing she could have fought Valerius's control.

"How? I tried so hard, especially when…he showed up."

"The chip emits a sequence that blocks your human's conscience from the wolf's essence. But it's possible to breach that barrier if you concentrate."

She steps away from me, turning her face to a wall. Her jaw is clenched tight, and she doesn't speak for a few seconds, before finally, she gives me an angry retort.

"Don't you think I tried everything?"

"I'm sorry. I didn't say you didn't."

The angry scowl marring her face softens a little as she sighs loudly. "I'm sorry, too. I didn't mean to snap at you. There's a darkness here." She taps her forehead. "Tainting my thoughts, telling me I'm not good enough. I got what I deserved."

"I'm not sure what you're referring to. I didn't sense anything like that."

Rochelle's gaze seems to go inward. "Or maybe it will

come with time. I don't know. I didn't feel it at first either. Only when Va—that monster came."

Biting my lower lip, I ponder this new information. What if Rochelle got the other chip Martin mentioned? I realize suddenly I can't simply run away without trying at least to grab the stash of remaining chips. Without them, Martin can't strip other innocent wolves of their free will.

"Besides Valerius, has anyone else been here? Martin said I'm expected to attend meals in the barn."

"Yes, Martin came a few times to bring me food. I haven't been out since I was brought in."

A somber thought occurs to me. Maybe I did hear Rochelle when I escaped my first prison cell. If Valerius is keeping doors concealed with spells, who is to say he didn't do the same thing in that empty hallway? Rochelle had been crying for help. Oh my God, what if it was the time Valerius went to see her and I simply ran away? Guilt begins to gnaw at my insides, but I can't let Rochelle suspect my inner turmoil.

Turning around, I take us to the corridor I used to get here with Martin. As Rochelle mentioned, there's no sign of a door leading out. The corridor is actually a loop that brings us back to the common area.

"I told you there's no way out. And if there are magical runes in place, how are we going to find them?"

"I was able to locate the rune outside, but I was in my wolf form."

Rochelle runs a nervous hand over her hair. "I haven't been able to shift since Valerius's visit."

Her subdued tone hints to me that trauma is keeping her from turning into a wolf. But it could also be the chip interfering with her ability. Does that mean I won't be able to shift either? There's only one way to find out.

"I'll try."

Closing my eyes, I focus on my core, on the swirling energy there. Immediately, white noise fills my head, blocking my connection to my wolf. That's so odd; I didn't feel the interference before when my nails turned into claws or when my canines elongated. Both times I had Martin's death in my mind. Could it be that's the only way to override the controlling chip is through anger? Why must everything wolf-related have to be so volatile?

Instead of thinking about how I'm going take revenge on Martin, I focus on Valerius instead, the bigger monster in the picture as far as I'm concerned. Thinking about what he did to Rochelle is enough to give me bloodlust. The white noise fades away to almost nothing, liberating the wolf's wild energy. It spreads through my body like a summer storm, bending and stretching my muscles until I'm on my knees and the world around me changes.

"I can't believe it. You did it," Rochelle says.

There's awe and resentment blended in her voice. Sometimes I forget I'm a brand-new wolf. It must not be easy for those born a shifter to see a newbie able to do things they can't. And they don't know even half of what I'm capable of.

Trying not to worry about that now, I bring my nose down and expand my wolf senses, searching for the hidden runes I believe are here somewhere. It takes me a moment before I detect a hint of something different, a disturbance to the air, straight ahead. I make a beeline for it with Rochelle close behind. We don't have much time. If the runes are hiding the exit, they must also be hiding the security cameras. How long until Martin storms here to stop us?

I skid to a halt when I locate the source of magic. Peering closely, I notice two very thin lines in the skirting board as if a portion of it had been cut and glued back together. It's probably four inches in length. This is it.

I turn to Rochelle, hoping she can guess what I've found without me having to shift back into human form. In my haste to find the runes, I forgot to take off the stupid lab jacket Martin gave me, and it's now torn in half. I'd prefer not to parade naked as we try to escape.

Crouching next to me, she examines it. "Oh my God. You

found it."

She grabs the small section, but due to the depth of the board, she can only hold on to it with the tips of her fingers. "Ugh, it's stuck. It must have been glued together."

I push her out of the way to try to dislodge the section with my paw, but it's too big. What we need is something sharp, like a knife.

"I wish I could partial shift and turn my nails into claws." Rochelle sits on the backs on her feet, sounding rejected.

That's it. I can't believe I didn't think about it sooner. The ability to give myself fingers and opposable thumbs while keeping the nails long and sharp is one of a shifter's talents. I've never attempted a partial shift deliberately before. Every time it happened, it had been spontaneous. I follow the same process I do when shifting between forms completely. This time, I picture exactly how I want my body to be. It doesn't take long for the partial shift to occur—either the urgency of the situation or I'm getting really good at the whole shifter thing. It doesn't matter. I focus on the task at hand until the little piece of wood comes off and with it, the hidden rune pops out.

Copying what Nadine did before, I rub the design on the small rock off, and ta-dah, a door with a window appears on the wall next to us, but also the security cameras mounted above it. Whoever is monitoring the feed must be either taking a nap or distracted with something else.

Rochelle springs to her feet, and then peeks through the window.

"It's the lab, but I don't see anyone. I think the coast is clear."

I don't trust this at all. It smells like a trap. It's just too easy. I want to stay in my wolf form, not only because I ruined my only clothes, but because I feel better knowing I can defend myself with my claws and teeth. But I forgot to tell Rochelle I need to look for the chips first before we look for the exit. Since I don't possess Dante's gift to speak mind to mind when the other shifter is on two legs, I have no choice but to return to my more fragile form.

"What are you doing?" Rochelle asks.

"I have to tell you something. We need to find out where they're keeping the chips used for mind control."

"No, we need to get the hell out of this place. Maybe the remote control doesn't work across great distance. Maybe I can escape before they activate it."

"We can't leave those chips behind. Martin is kidnapping wolves from other packs to turn them into mindless assassins. If he doesn't have the chips, he can't increase his numbers."

"You don't know where he's getting those chips. Even if we steal all the supplies he has here, he might be able to get more within a few hours. We would be risking our necks for nothing."

"No. I've heard Martin talking to the doctor who operated on me. They only have ten chips left, and another shipment won't arrive for a week."

Rochelle furrows her brow, on the verge of arguing with me further, so I press on. "A week might not seem like a lot of time, but it could give us a break. We need any advantage we can get."

Not breaking eye contact with the enforcer, I can almost see her conflicted emotions jarring against one another.

"Okay. Let's look for those chips, but if we don't find them in a minute or two, we're going."

"Fair enough."

I take the lead, wanting to protect Rochelle from any nasty surprise waiting for us on the other side. Pushing the door open slowly, I stick my head out first, glancing left and right before I venture to the other side. Rochelle was right; there's no one around. All desks and rooms are empty. A clock mounted on the wall across from us tells me it's almost six. Where did the time go? Oh shit, soon someone will come here to take me to the barn.

"If you were a chip, where would you be?" I ask myself.

Rochelle points at the door not too far from us. "The plaque says Dr. Felicia Smith."

"Bingo. That's the butcher who put the chip in me. Let's start there."

I turn on the knob, discovering the door is locked. "Damn it."

"Move to the side. I got this."

I make room for Rochelle, who bends her legs before bringing her right foot up to deliver a powerful kick to the door, breaking it off its hinges. It falls forward, landing on the floor with a loud thud, making me wince. So much for stealth. I hope no one is in the building.

We both don't waste any time going through the doctor's drawers and cupboards. I don't find anything in the first places I check until I come across a small safe on the bookshelf, semi-hidden behind some heavy binders. Shit, I bet the chips are in there.

The sound of loud voices fills the silence. The lab personnel must have heard the ruckus. Shit. Shit. Shit.

Rochelle turns to me, eyes startled. "We need to go. Now!"

I glance one more time at the safe, then, just for kicks, I try to open it, not for a moment believing I'll succeed. My jaw slackens when the damn door swings open, revealing a clear box with tiny chips inside.

"I got them."

I don't pause to think about my sheer luck, just clutch the box to my chest and head for the door, revealing myself to the group of lab workers who are now at the end of the corridor.

"Hey, stop! Sound the alarm." The voice is panicked and high-pitched.

Rochelle and I run in the opposite direction, not knowing where the damn passage will lead. At the end, we veer right. An annoying sound blasts through the entire facility. The damn alarm. We're so doomed. We just need one more strike of good luck to find the exit because, right now, we're running blind. I skid to halt when I come across an intersection. The corridor to my right looks exactly like the one where I had been held. Dark and without any doors on either side.

"This way." I don't wait for Rochelle to follow before I bolt in the different direction.

"Are you sure? This doesn't look like it leads anywhere."

When I run by the only door in the hallway, I'm relieved to see it's my first room in this hellhole. We're in the right place.

"The exit is straight ahead."

"There's nothing but a smooth wall."

"Trust me. It's there. There must be a rune somewhere. I just need to fi—"

A disgruntled sound cuts me off. I look over my shoulder, finding Rochelle down on her knees and clutching her head.

"Rochelle!" I make a move to get her, but she lifts her hand.

"No. Don't come any closer. They've activated my chip. Oh, God. It's happening."

Fuck. She's shifting. Her body is already getting deformed while grunts escape her lips. When she meets my eyes, her irises have a different color, ember with a hint of red.

"Rochelle. You can fight it, please try."

"I can't. Run, Red, please run."

"I'll come back for you. I promise."

She closes her eyes with a whimper. "I need a favor. If I can't overcome the controlling chip, kill me fast. I don't want to live like this."

"Rochelle…"

She drops to the ground, twisting in agony as her bones snap and her muscles change shape. It wasn't enough to strip the wolves of their free will. No. Valerius had to make them suffer while they shift. I wish I could kill him a thousand times over. And Martin, too.

The sounds of pursuit become louder, prompting me to swing around and turn toward the hidden door. Halfway there, intense pain flashes in my head, almost making me falter in my steps. I brace against the wall, unable to draw air in. The command comes, the compulsion to shift making my entire body tremble. My chip has been activated. Gasping in controlled pants, I concentrate on overriding the order. I'm able to see the waves of disturbance the chip is causing in my brain this time, which makes it much easier to pierce through it. Once I'm out of that vortex, the pain subsides, becoming a faint throb instead. But the moment it took me to regain control costs me. Rochelle has shifted, and hunters have just rounded the corner, barring my way.

I take off, not knowing how I'm going to get the door open. I hit the wall with all my strength, pounding with my fists against it. As far as I know, the runes only conceal the door; it doesn't make it disappear altogether. I quit hitting the hard surface when I accomplish nothing. Instead, I begin searching for a button, conscious I might only have a few seconds left before the hunters are on me. I can't help peering over my shoulder. The hunters have now reached Rochelle, but she has not moved from her spot. She's trying to fight the chip's order. Maybe she can. I'm about to yell an encouragement to her when she jumps forward, teeth bared and with soulless eyes. I won't have enough time to shift before she's upon me, so I lean against the wall and prepare to fend her off with my bare hands.

A swooshing sound catches me by surprise before the wall at my back disappears, making me lose my balance. Strong arms catch me, and I'm suddenly staring at Sam's beautiful face.

"Hello, Red. Miss me?"

CHAPTER 33
RED

I can't believe my eyes. Sam is here. He's holding me. I don't know if I should laugh or cry. But then the sound of pursuit breaks me from my stupor. Sam rights me before dragging me with him up the hill. I sense Dante before he comes into view. Nadine is next to him holding a tranquilizer gun in her hand as they emerge from behind the trees ahead.

"Wha—"

"No time for questions. We need to move now." Dante's gaze lands on my face for a fleeting moment, before his attention diverts to the commotion behind us.

I dare to turn around, counting at least five hunters carrying guns, plus Rochelle. I can't believe they haven't reached us yet. And then they do something completely unexpected. They run in the opposite direction of where we are, not even glancing our way for a second. We're in plain view.

"I don't understand. Where are they going?"

"They can't see us," Sam replies with a cheeky smile on his lips. Oh my God. How I missed that smile. Despite the danger of this situation, my heart is full, or almost full.

"Where's Tristan?"

Sam and Dante share a glance, before Dante replies, "There was no time to get Tristan. I got a vision you were in trouble while we were at the—while we were with your grandmother.

We had to come straight here."

Nadine frantically motions with her hands, signaling us to follow her. Sam, who is still holding my hand, makes me follow her next, with Dante bringing up the rear.

"How did you manage to get here, and how did you find Nadine?" I whisper to Sam, not knowing if there are sentries nearby.

"We drove here. Well, Dante flew here. I didn't think we'd arrive in one piece. He's a maniac."

Dante grumbles behind us, the sound a balm to my sore heart. I'm giddy beyond comprehension that they're here.

"And Nadine?"

"We found her. The cloaking spell didn't work on her. Thank God she's not with the enemy." Sam squeezes my hand, sending chills up my arm.

A howl sounds in the distance, answered by a few more. The hunting party has been assembled.

"What's the plan? Valerius has several controlled wolves at his disposal, plus the other members of the pack."

"I wouldn't worry about those emaciated wolves. Their spirits are broken; they wouldn't put up much of a fight," Sam replies.

"Don't count them out just yet. You would be surprised what desperate wolves will do to survive," Dante chimes in, earning a curious stare from Nadine.

"To answer your question, we don't have a plan," Sam continues.

"How are we getting out of here then?"

"The same way we came in. There's an old hunting cabin ten minutes away from Valerius's border. We parked there. Then we're scot-free."

"What about the whole pack politics that I belong to Valerius? Won't he try to get me back?"

"He will try, but we'll be waiting for him."

Sam sounds confident, but they haven't seen what I have. They don't know what Valerius is capable of.

"What's that you're clutching so hard? Couldn't find any clothes, but you got the first item in your way?" Sam asks in his usual casual manner.

"No. These are the last chips Martin had in the lab. He's planning to create an army of controlled wolves and..." Shit, I need to tell them I have a chip implant, too. I have no idea how they're going to react. Their father had one, and they had to kill him in the end.

"And?" Sam stops suddenly, turning me to face him "What is it, Red?" There's no sign of levity in his expression anymore.

The howling of the wolves pursuing us gets closer, which makes the situation ten thousand times worse. I don't want to tell them what has been done to me now.

"It will take at least a week for him to get more. Would that give us enough time to stop him?"

Sam opens his mouth to reply when Nadine grabs his jacket sleeve, urging him to keep moving. She's frantic now, and I understand the reasoning in the next second. A cold breeze comes out of nowhere and with it, the stench of sulfur.

"We need to go," I say.

I'm the one pulling Sam with me now. Dante is no longer behind us, but next to me, running as if he knows what's in the forest as well. A demon. The sense of foreboding hangs all around us, turning my blood ice cold.

Nadine stops suddenly, and we almost collide with her.

"What—" I start, but then clamp my mouth shut. Farther ahead, where the vegetation is so thick that it resembles an impenetrable dark wall, two pairs of red glowing orbs stare at us. My heart lurches inside my chest when a low growl follows. Two of Valerius's devilish minions are blocking our way...and turning back around isn't an option.

"I thought they couldn't see us," I whisper.

Sam glances at a ring hanging from a chain around his neck, a piece of jewelry I don't remember him wearing before. It glows with a faint blue light, so it must be a magical object.

"There's still juice left in my ring. The cloaking should be working still."

Dante moves closer. "Something must have broken the spell. It doesn't matter. We need to shift now."

Both brothers drop to their knees, shifting faster than I had ever seen before. Clutching the prize I stole from the butcher doctor, I try to do the same, but I can't find my wolf's essence anywhere. What the hell? I can hear the chip's disturbing waves in the background, but it's weak, so it can't be the reason why I can't connect to my wolf. As I struggle inside, Sam and Dante engage with the enemy wolves. Shit, one of them is Victor.

Nadine is frozen to the spot, trembling, before she finally raises the tranquilizer gun, taking aim. But with the way she's shaking, she might shoot Sam or Dante by accident. I step toward her, taking the gun from her hands.

"It's too risky."

Cold tendrils of air reach my naked back, just like in the dream I had after my kidnapping. The demonic presence is approaching, and I feel deep in my bones that we can't be caught by it. Nadine glances toward where I feel it coming, her eyes turning rounder with fear. Tears roll down her cheeks, but I'm not even sure if she's aware she's crying.

Sam and Dante are too busy fighting off Valerius's wolves, and I don't see it ending any time soon. By then, it will be too late. We need help. I close my eyes and think about the great wolf apparition. They called themselves guardians, and they said they would always protect me.

Please, if you're there, I need your help.

Nothing happens for several seconds, making me lose hope. When I hear a sob, I don't know if it came from me or Nadine. Then, the cold wrapped around my body is replaced by warmth. Energy shoots from the ground, curling up my legs, grounding me. Cracking my eyes open, I could almost cry in relief when I see the great wolf, mighty and powerful, emerge from the forest. Made out of sticks and stones just like the last time, it stares at me with its blue light eyes.

"You came. I thought you had abandoned me."

"We were blocked out. There's terrible magic in this place."

The wolf glances toward the part of the forest where the nefarious presence is coming from. *"You can't stay here. You're not ready to face what's coming. Go. Now."*

I turn my attention to Dante and Sam. I can't leave them behind.

As if reading my mind, the great wolf lets out a roar that no real wolf could ever make, putting a stop to the vicious fight for a brief moment. Then he barrels toward the closest enemy wolf, the one fighting Dante, who manages to leap out of the guardian's path in the last second, landing awkwardly on his side.

Victor remains paralyzed as he watches the great wolf tear at his companion. Sam takes the opportunity to jump on him, getting him on his shoulder.

"No, Sam! We need to run."

Stopping, he glances in my direction. Dante howls before he runs to my side. Victor is down, and Sam seems torn between fleeing or ending his opponent. Nadine, who had been crying silently next to me, takes a step forward, then pulls her arm back to throw a rock close to Victor, as if she's trying to get his attention. Then she motions with her hands, signaling him to flee. Of course she wants to protect him. He's her older brother.

Victor shakes his head as he gets back on his feet. His eyes still have a faint red glow, which means he's still under the chip's control. If he doesn't flee, the great wolf will kill him. But the whole point of summoning the guardians was for giving us the chance to run away. As much as my heart breaks for Nadine, I can't let her delay our escape any longer. Grabbing her arm, I force her to come with us. She shakes her head, trying to pull free from my grasp, but I won't leave her behind.

"You're coming with me. You can't help Victor now."

A disembodied sinister laugh echoes in the forest, giving

me the worst case of chills. My skin breaks into goose bumps as the temperature suddenly seems to drop ten degrees.

Fear grips my heart mercilessly, and I don't even see Dante shift back to human before he lifts Nadine over his shoulder. "Let's go."

We break into a run, letting Dante take the lead. Sam remains in his wolf form, staying close behind us. We're flying through the forest blindly, as if the devil were after us. Not if, the devil is probably coming for us. I hope we're faster.

As we put distance between ourselves and the great wolf, I feel my connection to it fading away. But when the temperature returns to normal and the sense of darkness lessens, I allow myself a sigh of relief.

We come across a creek, which Dante crosses without stopping. The water is cold and the rocks are slippery, but thanks to my enhanced coordination skills, I blaze through them without losing my balance. The old me would have tumbled down for sure.

"The fence is straight ahead," Dante says under his breath.

Nadine is no longer struggling, but it doesn't mean she won't return to Victor if given the chance, so I appreciate that he didn't put her down.

"If we return to the compound, we'll lead Valerius's wolves straight to them."

"I don't think he cares anymore. He's already declared war on us."

The wired fence comes into view. It's not well kept. There are several spots where the wires have been torn either by hands or the passage of time, allowing us to go through without scratching our backs. Dante has to put Nadine down to avoid bumping her against a sharp edge. Holding her by her shoulders, he asks, "You're not going to run away, are you?"

She shakes her head before ducking to pass through the fence. Dante follows next, then it's my turn. He makes a motion to continue down a beaten-down trek, when Sam lets out a low growl. His brother turns, and I can tell they're speaking mind to mind.

"What is it?" I whisper.

"Sam picked up the scent of other wolves. The hideout has been compromised."

"How are we going to get out of here?"

A twig cracks nearby, followed by the sound of foliage rustling. Damn it, something is coming. I move closer to Dante and Nadine, putting my body in front of the girl on purpose. A brown bear emerges from behind the thick shrubbery. Of course, the first thought that pops in my head is now we're really screwed.

Taking a step back, I prepare for Dante's command to flee, but the words that come out his mouth are anything but that.

"Jesus, how did you find us?"

The bear's body starts to vibrate, its form changing. A tall man with broad shoulders and wild hair is standing before us, his glorious body naked. I'm not even ashamed to have noticed. I'd have to be blind not to. It's the same shifter who came with my grandmother when Tristan challenged Valerius. Are any of the wildlife in Crimson Hollow really ordinary animals?

"I wasn't looking for you. Another member of my sleuth was murdered earlier. Then I caught the stench of Valerius's flea bags, and I came to investigate." The shifter's gaze turns to me. "So you've decided to rescue your mate after all."

"Who are you?" I ask.

"This is Xander, the alpha of the Thunderborn sleuth," Dante replies, then turns to the bear shifter. "We need your help getting back to the compound."

"I can't leave my territory tonight. Something is hunting down my bears, and I need to discover what is."

"Can't you lend us a car?" I ask.

"I didn't drive here, and it would be too risky taking you down to my chalet through the mountains tonight. Valerius is not keeping his wolves within his borders. The best I can do is let you use my cave."

Thoughts of Xander hibernating in a remote cave fill my head. The question is on the tip of my tongue, but Dante speaks before I can make an ass out of myself.

"Thank you, Xander. We'll accept your offer. Please, lead the way."

Xander's nostrils flare as he takes in a deep breath. He whips his face toward Nadine, and the question that leaves his mouth comes out almost as a growl.

"Who is she?"

I put myself in front of Nadine, not liking one bit the way Xander is regarding her. "She's a friend."

"She was instrumental in getting Red out of Valerius's clutches," Dante adds because Xander is still glaring in her direction. What's his deal?

"Is she a wolf from Shadow Creek?"

"Why does it matter?" I ask through clenched teeth.

"It matters because she's hiding something. I can smell it from where I stand."

"Are you for real?" I curl my hands while letting some of my pissed-off wolf's vibe loose. I hope he's sensing that.

"Bears don't trust easily, and Xander has cause to be suspicious of strangers. His father was betrayed by a close friend," Dante speaks in my head.

"Well, he'd better quit glaring at Nadine. His Neanderthal attitude is scaring her. She's been through enough shit."

"I vouch for her, Xander," Dante says out loud. "Please, help us."

Grumbling, the guy turns around. "If she pulls a stunt, I'll hold you responsible."

"I don't like him. He's an ass," I tell Dante, knowing our telepathic connection is still on.

"Xander is an acquired taste."

"Just like Tristan," Sam's voice says in my mind, and I can't keep my jaw from dropping.

"How in the hell did you get into my head? I thought only Dante was able to do that."

"Wait? You heard me?" Sam asks in surprise.

"Yes."

"Maybe Red used my connection to you," Dante replies. *"That's amazing."*

"Dude. We hit the jackpot. Red is amazing. What can't you do, babe?"

"Ugh, don't call me that."

Sam's reply is a lighthearted chuckle that makes my body tingle. But the feeling of floating on air doesn't last long. I'm reminded of our dire situation when out in the distance, I hear Valerius barking orders. Several howls echo in the forest in response. My guess is that at least ten wolves answered that demented alpha's call. I pray they don't catch our scent, not sure if I can summon the great wolf apparition again, and without the guardian's help, we can't win.

CHAPTER 34
RED

They don't come after us, and we manage to leave Shadow Creek behind without more incidents. I'm told we're now in the Thunderborn's territory, but I can't tell one forest from another, at least not in the darkness. As we go up the mountain, the air becomes cooler, and I'm thankful it's summer. I haven't considered what it will be like shifting in the dead cold of the winter. But first things first, I need to survive until then.

At a certain point during the trek, Dante threw his arm over my shoulder, pulling me closer to his warm body. I've been trying since then not to let my mind go straight to the gutter, but I'm all too aware of every inch of my skin that's rubbing against his, of how the contact is electrifying me, arousing me. There I go again, turning into a nympho at the most inappropriate time possible.

Sam rubs his fur against my leg, before he decides I need a good lick. Fuck me. He must know I'm on the verge of combusting on the spot. My nipples are hard and begging for attention. I clutch the metal box against them tighter, not wanting the brothers to see what they're doing to me, which is pointless. They know. Hell, they can probably smell how turned on I am.

Oh, shit. If they can sense that, so can Nadine and Xander.

Mortification makes my face feel hot. Yet, I can't bring myself to step away from Dante or Sam. This is going to be a very long night.

We finally arrive in Xander's cave, which I totally expected to be simply a hole on the side of the mountain, the one bears use for hibernation. I most certainly didn't think I'd find a state-of-the-art facility protected from intruders by a garage-style door instead. Xander presses the code on a small panel hidden behind branches, and the door slides open.

The walls inside have been carved and smoothed out, and there's actually flooring on the ground. Soft yellow light turns on as we enter, revealing a room made for entertainment with comfortable couches, arcade games, a dart board, and even a pool table.

"Shit, Xander. This place is badass." Sam's voice echoes in the stony walls. I was so distracted taking everything in I didn't even notice him shift.

Xander grabs a blanket that was draped over the back of one of the couches and hands it to me.

Blushing, I step away from Dante, covering myself. "Thank you."

The bear alpha eyes Nadine for a second, as if debating getting a blanket for her as well. But she's wearing jeans and a long-sleeved T-shirt, so in the end, he doesn't. He could have offered one, though.

Pulling my attention from our sullen host, I resume my inspection of the place. Besides all the cool stuff, the room is also equipped with a modern kitchen, but the only thing I don't see immediately are places to sleep or a bathroom.

"The sleeping quarters are behind that wall." Xander points at the far end of the room where a big home theater screen hangs from the ceiling.

"Please tell me there's a restroom here."

Xander cocks his head to the side, frowning a little. "You really don't know anything about shifters, do you?"

"What's that supposed to mean?"

"Xander, ease off, man." Sam pulls me to him, kissing my neck and igniting a raging fire within my core. Why is he torturing me like that?

Unfazed by Sam's display of affection, Xander rolls his eyes, which is an odd contrast to his grumpy demeanor. The guy doesn't have a chip on his shoulder; he carries a boulder around.

Nadine has wandered off from the group to check out the pinball machine pushed against the wall. When she presses one of the buttons, the whole thing lights up with a loud noise. She jumps back, clutching at her chest.

"Jesus, what are you doing?" Xander goes after her. So do I. I won't put it past him to drag poor Nadine away from his precious toy by the hair.

She's staring at the game without blinking, more precisely at the black jaguar drawing on the scoreboard of the machine. I notice she's also clutching her necklace so hard her knuckles have turned white. Xander's gaze drops to the scar on her neck, and then his annoyed expression changes into something else. I don't think it's pity, but it definitely made him stop glowering at her.

"Nadine?" I touch her shoulder, making her jerk with a start. "It's okay. You're safe now."

"I need to go," Xander announces. "There is food and drink here. I'll come back for you in the morning."

"Any chance there's also a phone?" Dante asks.

"No. The point of this hideout is to take time off from the real world."

"Have you heard anything from our mother? We couldn't reach anyone in the compound before we arrived in Shadow Creek."

"No, the murder of another one of my bears made me a little bit preoccupied." No one misses the bite in Xander's remark. He's indeed a difficult shifter, and this is me being kind.

Sam's eyes turn to slits, but before he throws an angry retort at Xander, Dante continues, "We really appreciate all the assistance you were able to offer our pack so far."

Xander turns his attention to me, his gaze now extra sharp. "You know I only did it because of your vision of her."

That's new. Glancing at Dante, I ask, "What vision?"

"I'll tell you later. Let's get your friend settled for the night." Dante nods toward Nadine, who is still transfixed by the pinball machine. Has she never seen one?

I try to hide my disappointment as I take Nadine's hand, guiding her to where Xander told us the bedrooms were located. In fact, there are only two accommodations, and a small bathroom with a shower and toilet. At least we don't have to pee in the woods.

Both rooms have two bunk beds, which is a relief and a curse in a way. This will be the first time I'll ever spend the night with Dante and Sam together. Based on my wanton reaction to both, I'm not sure how I'm going to survive it. I'm craving both of them like I have gone years without a man's touch.

"Which room do you prefer?" I ask Nadine.

She shrugs, choosing the one in the far end of the corridor. I follow her in, not knowing what to say. She just abandoned the only family she has left, and the burden of that action must be weighing on her. I hope she doesn't resent us for freeing her from Valerius.

Nadine sits down on the edge of the bed with shoulders hunched forward and head hung low. Clasping her hands together, she stares at the soft white rug beneath her feet. I take a seat next to her, then cover her hands with mine, squeezing a little.

"You know we couldn't leave you behind, right?"

She nods, not glancing my way.

"I'm sorry about Victor. If there's a way to help him, I promise we'll find it."

Nadine snaps her face to mine, her big doe eyes shining with hope. Then she throws her arms around me, hugging me tight. Resting her head on my shoulder, she sinks into me as if I'm her lifeline. In the short period of time I remained in Shadow Creek, I've witnessed enough atrocity and cruelty to give me nightmares for ages. Nadine has been under her brother's reign of terror for months. I can't begin to imagine the state of her mind. So I don't ease out of the embrace, knowing this is probably the first act of kindness she has experienced in a long time. An intense sense of protectiveness overwhelms me. With it, the urge to make Valerius pay for every awful thing he did to her comes unbidden.

I will avenge you, Nadine—Rochelle, too—even if it's the last thing I do.

A knock on the doorframe breaks our moment. I ease off, facing the entrance. Dante is there, no longer completely naked, but still showing those delicious abs that make my mouth water.

"Is everything okay here?"

In answer, Nadine scoots up the bed, getting under the covers as she lays down.

"Yeah, as okay as it can be."

I go to him. I haven't even touched him yet, but the air is already crackling with electricity. Shame takes over me. Crazy desire is making me want to jump Dante's bones right here, with Nadine in the room. I don't care if it's the bond at work or a wolf thing. I need to have better self-control.

I slip out, unable to avoid rubbing against Dante since he didn't move out of the way. He follows me, but before I can get to the second bedroom, he grabs my arm, pivoting me on the spot. His mouth is on mine before I can draw air in, causing a sensory explosion all over my body. With a contented sigh, I surrender to the assault, urging him to take everything he wants. His hands are on my face, then Dante slides them down my body, leaving a path of scorched skin, and grabs my butt.

"I missed you so damn much," he says in my mind.

"I missed you, too."

He lifts me off the ground. My legs immediately wrap

around his waist, bringing my sex flush to his taut skin. I'm so horny I can't think straight any longer. Thoughts of animals in heat come to mind, and I wonder if I'm suffering from that as well.

The wall disappears from my back, so we're on the move. Thank God someone is thinking clearly, because I would let Dante take me in the hallway, right outside Nadine's room. What's wrong with me?

"Man, I can't believe you guys started the reunion party without me," Sam says from somewhere nearby, making me break the kiss with Dante.

He must have sensed the sudden tension in my body because he puts me down, despite the raw desire that's now shining in his wolfish ember eyes. We're now in the second room, the three of us together, and I don't know what to do.

"I... this is..." I cover my face with my hands. "Oh my God. I want you both. Is this wrong?"

Sam's strong arms circle around my middle, bringing me flush against his naked flesh and very hard erection. "You're mated to the both of us. How can this be wrong, sweet Red?"

"I've never slept with two men at once before." I drop my hands from my face, but I still can't make eye contact with Dante.

Sam begins to nibble at my neck, his teeth sharper than usual, while he brings his hands up to play with my breasts. Throwing my head back, slightly tilted to allow Sam better access to the sensitive spot below my ear, I close my eyes, enjoying my surrender moment.

"There's a first time for everything. This is a first for me as well. I never shared a woman with any of my brothers," Sam whispers in my ear.

"I can leave if it will make you more comfortable," Dante's says, his voice rough with desire.

My eyes fly open, and I finally allow myself to lock gazes with him. "No! I want you to stay."

Relief washes over his face. "Oh, thank the Lord. I think I'd die if couldn't be with you right now."

He comes closer, then drops to his knees in front of me, bringing his nose to the apex of my thighs. I can't hear anything besides the rushing in my ears. My heart is pounding with anticipation. Dante's tongue darts out as he begins to tease me, licking near my throbbing core. When I moan loudly, Sam captures my earlobe and pulls it gently. His hands continue to pay attention to my breasts, but now his fingers are making lazy circles around my nipples, sending currents of pure pleasure throughout my entire body. I don't know where to focus; my attention is split between Dante's exploration below and Sam's ministrations.

I reach back with one hand, needing to touch Sam's face to ascertain he's indeed here. At the same time, I run my fingers through Dante's hair, pulling it a little to guide him to where I so desperately need him to be.

A low growl comes from deep within his throat before his tongue darts out, finding my clit. My legs buckle, and if it wasn't for Sam holding me tight, I would have collapsed on the floor. When Dante sucks my bundle of nerves into his mouth, I lose myself completely, coming harder than I ever have before. I don't scream; I don't call their names; I can't emit any sound because the bliss is too intense. It's short circuiting all my nerves.

I want to return the favor, but I also need to be taken swiftly and hard.

"You can do both, sweetheart," Dante says.

"Did you just hear my thoughts?"

"Impossible not to. You were shouting in my head."

"Red, my naughty little wolf, were you thinking of doing *The High Five*?"

"The what?"

Dante rises from his crouch, then cups my cheek with his hand, pulling my face to his for a crushing kiss. Sam forgoes my boobs to run his fingers down my back. Desire curls around the base of my spine, making me shiver and melt at the same time.

When Dante pulls away, letting go of my lips with a pop, there's a satisfied grin on his face. He takes a step back, then Sam pushes me down gently until I'm on my knees. It dawns on me in that moment what he has in mind. I've never done anything kinky in my life. Not too long ago, I thought being in a relationship with three brothers was bold enough for me. But if I'm mated to them, then I guess I must get used to group sex. I'm not complaining; it's just a new experience.

Leaning forward, I brace my hands on the soft rug that covers the hardwood floor, then I peek up at Dante, who is gliding his hand up and down his shaft. The tip of my tongue darts out. Coquettishly, I lick my lower lip. His eyes turn into molten lava, ferocious, but before I can do anything, Sam's fingers are probing at my entrance, spreading my juices around my clit. I let out a groan when he inserts two of them, then begins another onslaught of torture.

Dante grabs me by the hair, lifting my face up to his again. He's watching me with such adoration in his gaze that any shameful feelings I had disappear. Reaching for his erection, I pull the tip into my mouth, licking the soft curve as if it were a popsicle. He throws his head back, letting out an animalistic sound that's definitely more wolf than human. At the same time, Sam replaces his fingers with his cock, entering me fast and with precision. I think he's also done with foreplay. He grips my hips, digging his fingers into my skin as he pulls back to enter me again, going deeper this time.

My attention is split. It's hard to concentrate on what my mouth and tongue are doing to Dante while trying not to come too quickly. As hungry as I am for them both, I'd like to prolong our carnal reunion for as long as possible. Pumping Dante's erection with my hand while I suck the tip of his cock, I end up letting a sliver of doubt enter my mind. What if I'm doing it all wrong?

"Sweetheart, you're doing great. Don't worry. Your tongue feels amazing on my cock."

"Probably just as good as her pussy feels wrapped around mine," Sam says.

"Wait, how are you doing this again? Is this a thing now, us having a three-way convo telepathically?"

"I think you're the conduit, Red." Dante replies. *"It doesn't surprise m—oh fuck, I can't hold it any longer."*

Dante's cock becomes bigger inside my mouth, right before his release fills it completely. Behind me, Sam's thrusts increase in pace as his grunts turn louder. He leans forward, letting go of one of my hips to reach between my legs. When his fingers brush against my clit, it's game over for me. I'm sent straight over the edge. I'm glad I can't really make a lot of noise while my mouth is busy milking the rest of Dante's release.

Sam lets go of my other hip to completely embrace me from behind, bringing his torso flush with my back. I feel the sharp pain of his bite on my shoulder the moment he orgasms. He continues to move in and out of me until he's completely emptied out. I'm so spent that my limbs can no longer hold me in the kneeling position, so I collapse on the floor. Not expecting it, Sam falls on top of me, almost crushing me.

"Shit. Red, are you all right?" He rolls off me. When I don't turn my face to his, but keep it hidden underneath my sprawled hair, he brushes it out of the way.

"I'm fine, silly. I'm just embarrassed that I fell, that's all."

His lips turn into a crooked grin. "Never be embarrassed to become boneless due to sex, my love."

I try to lean on my elbow, but even doing that is impossible. Giving up, I lay down on the rug again. "This was… I have no words to describe it."

Dante crouches in front of me, and I'm surprised to see he still has an erection. Or maybe he's recovered and is ready for round two. Just the thought makes my core throb in anticipation. Damn, I can't even get up from the floor and I'm already thinking about having sex again.

"I know the feeling. Now, come on, you can't lay here all

night. You need rest. There's much to be done tomorrow."

Dante's words about the near future puts a chink in my heart, erasing all of my post-sex bliss. I finally manage to sit up, but it takes me a few seconds to gather up the courage and tell them what happened to me.

"I have to something to tell you."

Sam and Dante both turn serious with matching frowns, but neither speaks, waiting for me to continue.

"I have a controlling chip in my head."

And by the way the blood drains from their faces, I might have just taken the pin out of a grenade.

CHAPTER 35
TRISTAN

I'm pacing back and forth in front of the clinic room where Zaya is treating Mom. According to the nurse, Mom was very lucky that the savage bite on her thigh missed a major artery. By the time it took me to carry her from the battlefield back to the compound, she would have bled to death otherwise. I managed to stop the bleeding, staying with Mom until the nurse arrived. But Zaya kicked me out of the room when my nervous pacing got under her nerves.

Besides the deep cut on her leg, Mom sustained other injuries, and the nurse has been busy for hours. Night has already fallen, but at least there hasn't been any more reports of another imminent attack. While I waited, I tried reaching my brothers once more, getting nothing. Where the hell are they? They're alive and not in danger. I'd feel it deep in my soul if something had happened to them. Similar to the bond I share with Red, my brothers and I have a deep connection, probably because we're triplets.

The door to the clinic opens with a loud bang. Billy comes sprinting in. My first thought is that our break is over and Valerius is attacking again. The kid is as white as a ghost, and his labored breathing tells me he's been running for a while.

"What's the matter?" I ask.

"I have to tell you something. It's very important."

"Is it Valerius?"

"No, it's about what Dante asked me to do."

Shit. Why would Dante ask Billy of all people for help?

"Spill it already."

"He suspected that my—"

Billy stops talking suddenly when several enforcers, Seth included, storm the hallway. I brace for more bad news.

"How is Dr. Mervina?" Seth takes the leadership, stopping in front of the others.

"Zaya is still with her. I haven't heard any update. What's going on now?"

Charles answers with a growl. Suddenly, I sense something I hadn't picked up when they entered the clinic. A challenge. He doesn't think I'm good enough to be the beta. Expanding my awareness, I pick up the same feeling from the other enforcers, but what shocks me the most is to find out Seth feels the same way.

"So it has come to this?" I ask.

"I'm sorry, Tristan. The pack feels Dr. Mervina's claim to the alpha role is not valid, and that you're not up to the task."

"So are you challenging me?" I take a step toward him, seething.

"I don't want to fight you. But let's face it, you haven't been the same since Red was taken. We need someone who will put the pack first, not some hot piece of ass."

I'm on Seth in a split second, lifting him off the ground while I pin him against the wall. "Don't you dare talk about my mate like that."

"Mate or not, the pack's safety should always come first. You know that."

As a tidal wave, the fight in me recedes. I drop Seth down, taking a step away.

"And who's going to be the new alpha? You?" Billy asks before I can, surprising everyone, including me.

Seth watches his younger brother through slits, catching the dissenting tone from the omega.

Charles takes a step forward, pulling his arm back to strike Billy across the face. My hand flies out, grabbing the enforcer's wrist before he can touch Billy.

"You won't punish him, not on my watch." I shove Charles back, taking a protective stance in front of the younger wolf.

"First the Shadow Creek bitch. Now you're protecting a lowly omega? You're a disgrace to your father's legacy. He'd never disrespect the pack's hierarchy like that," Charles spits out.

As I curl my hands into fists, the anger comes back with a vengeance. I feel the shift descend upon me, unbidden. Controlling the beast seems impossible, but I somehow manage not to turn into a wolf. If I let that happen, I won't stop until Charles is in shreds.

"Don't make things harder, Tristan. The pack has voted. It was unanimous. They want me to take the alpha's role, at least for the time being. We need unity, not a civil war." Seth's eyes are pleading and his voice sounds sincere, but I don't buy it. For the first time, I can see past his mask. Dante was right; Seth is too ambitious to be trusted. I was such a fool.

"Over my dead body. You're not alpha material. You never have been."

Seth's eyes flash red, something I've never seen before. What the fuck is going on with him? He nods subtly to the others. Suddenly, they all pull guns from behind their backs. They must have them tucked under their waistbands.

"What the hell is this? Guns? We're resorting to that now?"

Seth shrugs. "Valerius has more wolves in his army than we previously thought. And let's not forget the hunters. It's high time we embrace more advanced ways to protect ourselves."

"You're a fool. Bullets are useless against demons," Billy spits out.

"Demons? What the fuck is your brother talking about now?" Charles turns to Seth.

Seth raises his arm, pointing a gun straight at his brother. Before I can move to stop it, Billy is clutching at his chest.

"Seth... what did you do?" Billy asks before he collapses. I catch him before he reaches the floor, seeing the tranquilizer dart protruding from his chest.

I turn to Seth, not hiding an ounce of my rage. "You'll pay for this."

"Take them to the holding cell, then meet me in front of the mess hall. We have a war to prepare for."

CHAPTER 36

RED

Dante and Sam keep staring at me in silence for several beats until I can't take it any longer.

"Say something."

Sam pulls me into his arms, hugging me so tight that breathing becomes hard. "We'll find a way to remove the chip, Red. You're not going to end up like our father."

Leaning back, I manage to ease off Sam's embrace. "The thing in my head might be different than the one your father had."

"What do you mean?" Dante scoots closer, touching my knee.

"It seems there are two types of chips. A regular one, which is the one implanted in my head, and a more powerful chip that gives wolves extra strength. Those were the chips I stole from the lab."

Dante rubs his face before glancing in Sam's direction. "The chip we found on the rogue who attacked Red was embedded with a demonic presence."

"And there's definitely a demon roaming freely in Shadow Creek," Sam adds.

A shiver runs down my spine. "Do you think the chips I brought here are cursed by a demon?"

Dante's eyes turn darker. "It appears so."

I let out a heavy sigh. "Then I should be lucky that what I have is demon free. Actually, even the butcher doctor thought it strange that Martin wanted the tamer version for me."

"Wait a second, Martin is one of the hunters?" Sam's eyes widen while Dante curses under his breath.

Nodding, I continue. "Yes. He and Valerius are working together. But I don't think there's any love lost between them. As a matter of fact, Martin seems to hate Valerius."

"We suspected they might be working together when we came across hunters in his territory. What else did you find out?" Dante probes, his eyes taking on a calculating gleam.

I tell them everything I know, from the way Valerius treats his wolves, to how he killed the former alpha, and how he now tortures his own brother. When I mention Rochelle, I can't bring myself to reveal everything. It doesn't change the fact that Valerius is a monster. Besides, Rochelle must be the one to share what happened to her if she chooses to do so.

"What about the girl?" Sam asks.

"She's Valerius's sister and one of his many victims. She helped me despite the risk to herself."

"We need to reach Mom and Tristan as soon as possible. Now that you escaped, Valerius will descend on us with all his might."

I suck in a breath, realizing now I never told them the most crucial information. "Seth and Lyria are traitors. They were the ones who delivered me to Valerius."

"Son of a bitch." Sam jumps to his feet, his body now shaking with rage. "We need to get the hell out of here now."

"Calm down." Dante gets up as well. "Mom knows about Seth. She won't be caught off guard."

"That doesn't make me feel any better."

Bringing my knees up to hug them, I wrestle with the heavy weight crushing my chest. "How is Tristan?"

Both brothers turn to me, their expressions revealing nothing.

"We haven't talked to Tristan since he went to Valerius to

claim you," Dante says, his tone almost apologetic.

Dropping my chin on top of my knees, I close my eyes for a moment. My nose begins to burn. If I don't control my emotions, I'll start to cry. "I hurt him so much when I refused the bond. Do you think he'll ever forgive me?"

Dante reaches for my arms, lifting me off the floor. "Hey, don't worry too much about Tristan. Deep down, he knows you did what you thought was best."

"How can you know? You said you haven't spoken to him since that evening."

"Because I know my brother. He likes to play tough, but he's the most sensitive of the three of us."

"For sure." Sam runs his fingers up my arms in a soft caress. "Tristan is all about woe is me."

A lonely tear escapes the corner of my eye, and I hastily wipe it off. I appreciate Dante's and Sam's attempts to make me feel less guilty, but deep in my heart, I know that what I did to Tristan crushed his soul. It almost felt like I reopened an old wound.

More than ever, I wish the voice in my head would make an appearance. I don't know what she is, but I could use her motivational words.

Dante moves in front of me, capturing my face between his callused hands to stare deep into my eyes. "Stop worrying about Tristan for now. You need to rest. It's been a long day, and tomorrow promises to be even longer."

"I'm too wired up to sleep."

Sam comes from behind, wrapping his arms around my waist and kissing me on the shoulder. "Maybe we can help you relax."

Despite my worry, my body reacts to Sam's caress, and the yearning for both wolves returns as strong as before. Tired of feeling wretched, I relinquish control, allowing the bond to overcome the sadness wrapped around my heart. I won't feel complete until Tristan is with us, but for the moment, being loved by Sam and Dante has to be enough.

I don't know who leads me to one of the bunk beds, but suddenly, I'm tumbling down on the soft mattress, sandwiched between Sam and Dante. After that, everything is a blur of limbs, hot kisses, and out-of-this-world pleasure. I lose count of how many times I orgasm before I'm too exhausted to remain awake.

A loud knock on the door wakes me with a start. Then Xander's booming voice calling for Sam and Dante lifts any remains of sleepiness from my mind. I fell asleep between my mates. When they try to get out of bed without jostling me, it becomes the most uncoordinated effort I've ever seen. I'm poked in the ribs by Sam, then Dante hits his head on the bed when he miscalculates the height of the second bed on top.

"Ugh, guys, stop moving for a second."

"Sorry," they say in unison.

Sam, who is on the edge, gets out of bed first, then I do the same, followed by Dante.

Glancing down at my naked body, I'm overcome with shyness when Dante tells Xander to come in. A stupid reaction for sure since the bear shifter has already seen me sans clothes and he didn't bat an eyelash. I still have to work on my former human hang-ups. Nonetheless, I step behind Sam.

"Jesus Christ. I've been banging on the door for five minutes."

"We were exhausted," Dante replies.

"Yeah, I figured. I take it the reunion went well." Xander's tone is cold and practical. He's not trying for levity here. He still has a stick up his ass.

"Any news from our pack?" Sam asks.

"Yes, they aren't good. Valerius attacked the compound yesterday; there were losses."

"Who?" I ask, fearful that Tristan was among them. I don't

know how the bond works, but maybe my sadness could be linked to… no, I can't think like that.

"I don't know. Seth didn't really elaborate."

"Seth? Why the hell are you're getting updates from Seth?" Sam takes a step forward, not taming the raw energy one bit.

"That's the bad news. It seems there's been a coup. Dr. Mervina got hurt during the attack, and the pack voted her out of the alpha role. When I asked about the seriousness of your mother's injuries, Seth said she would recover, but that's all I got before I got disconnected."

Meaning before Seth ended the call.

"Son of a bitch!" Dante turns, punching the bunk bed's side, his fist going right through it. I expect Xander to say something, complain Dante just destroyed his property, but the bear remains silent, his face a stony wall.

Sam, on the other hand, watches his brother as if he's seeing another person. "Calm down, Dante."

He turns around, his eyes flashing anger. "I'm tired of being the calm one. I knew this would happen. I warned Tristan over and over again about that snake." He pauses, glaring at the ceiling. "Shit. Mom knew they were plotting to remove her, but she dismissed my worries, saying she could handle things."

"She probably didn't count on getting hurt," I interject, touching his arm and forcing him to look at me. The fury in his eyes dampens a little, but he isn't calm by far.

"Tristan should have taken her place." Sam glances at Xander.

"I don't know the details. When I asked to speak to Tristan, Seth said he wasn't available."

"It means that bastard made his move already. I'm going to kill him." Sam's body starts to shake, and I sense he's on the verge of shifting. Placing a hand on his shoulder, I make him look at me, too. I can't have both Sam and Dante losing their minds now.

"He will pay. But we can't be foolish now. We need a plan."

"I don't understand what's going on here. Why would Seth plot against Tristan? I thought they were best friends."

"Seth is vile. He's responsible for Red's abduction. He's working with Valerius," Dante replies.

Xander's face twists into an angry scowl as he projects a great power from his frame. I feel the blast of it, and it's enough to make me shake from head to toe. *Jesus.* These shifters are intense.

"You knew Seth was a traitor and you didn't think it was wise to warn the rest of us?"

"We had no proof," Dante argues.

"It doesn't matter. Now Valerius has access to two packs. He won't stop until he conquers the entire town."

"He's also colluding with human hunters, and I think he made a deal with a demon," I say. I don't mean to add more fuel to the fire, but if we're going to fight Valerius, Xander needs to know everything.

The alpha whips his face to mine, his eyes becoming slits. "You're telling me that piece of shit summoned a demon?"

"Yes." I lift my chin higher, even though the desire to keep my gaze to the floor is great.

"It must be the demon preying on your bears," Sam says.

"No shit, Sherlock." Xander runs a hand through his unbound hair. "We're doomed on our own. We need magical folks on our side."

"We have the druids, and Mrs. Redford's circle of rogue witches," Dante chimes in.

Hearing Grandma's name associated with rogue witches feels surreal. I'm not close to forgiving her, but I'll eventually have to find a way to have some kind of relationship with her. She's my blood.

"What about Sheriff Arantes? She can provide the manpower to at least go against the hunters. And isn't Crimson Hollow the home of other shifters?" I ask.

"The foxes won't interfere. It's in their nature to keep to themselves."

"What about coyotes, or are there any big cats around?" I glance at my mates, then at Xander, who is now watching me like I'm a fool.

"What? Do you think all zoo animals are shifters?"

Crossing my arms, I throw him a glower. "Are you saying there aren't tiger or lion shifters?"

"Yes, but not here in Crimson Hollow. There used to be a pride of jaguars, but they were all killed during the Thirteen Days of Chaos," Dante says.

"What the hell happened here twenty-five years ago? I'm sick of everyone talking about that event, but not actually saying anything useful."

All three shifters stare at me like I've sprouted a second head.

"What?"

"I'm sorry, Red. There hasn't been any time. To be honest, I don't know much about it either." Sam switches his attention to Dante, and I follow his line of vision.

"No one who lived through those days likes to talk about it, so no details are ever shared. I think they're afraid if the knowledge becomes widespread, it will happen again. I just know what everyone does. Some powerful supernatural occurrence opened portals to several dimensions, including hellish ones. The town was invaded by the foulest creatures anyone had ever seen, and only the combined forces of Crimson Hollow's supe community was able to close those portals."

I shift my attention to Xander. "How about you?"

His lips become a thin line before he replies. "I was only three when it happened, and my parents sent me away. All I know is Crimson Hollow became Grand Central Station for all kinds of supernatural beings, good and evil alike."

"If you want to know about what happened here, maybe we should pay Albert Saint a visit when this is all over. He not only lived through it, but he also came through one of the portals." Dante adds, becoming intrigued. "I wish I knew for sure who he was before, I would have tried to get the information on the Thirteen Days of Chaos a long time ago."

"Came from where?" I ask.

"From the nineteenth century."

"Wait, there's a dude here who's a time traveler?" I throw a haughty glance at Xander. "And you were all condescending when I asked about big cat shifters."

The alpha crosses his muscled arms, rolling his eyes as he does so. "Get ready. I'm bringing you back to Crimson Hollow."

"The question is where to." Dante stares at a point in the wall, and I can almost see the gears in his head working nonstop.

"If Seth wants the alpha position for himself, how long do you think he'll let Dr. Mervina and Tristan live? We need to come up with a rescue plan ASAP," I say.

"We should head back to Brian's. I'll feel better if we have druid power with us when we confront Seth. We don't know what that snake has under his sleeve." Dante crosses his arms, but Sam makes a disgruntled sound in the back of his throat.

"We got into this mess because we kept over-planning everything instead of taking action. The longer Seth stays in control of the pack, the more time he'll have to implant a controlling chip in all of them."

Xander lifts both hands. "Hold on. What the hell are you taking about now?"

"Valerius has been turning his own wolves into mindless killing machines by installing a chip in their brains. Under the influence, those wolves have no free will, no control of their actions. Plus, they also become stronger."

I turn to Sam. "You don't need to worry about that for the time being. I stole his last supply of chips, remember?"

"My vote is to return to the compound and regain control of your wolves," Xander says.

"Who says you get a vote? You didn't even want to help us in the first place." Sam throws his hands up in the air.

"I'm helping now, aren't I?"

"Stop! This bickering is useless and we're just wasting ti—"

A loud boom outside diverts my thoughts. Xander is the first out of the bedroom followed by Dante, Sam, and me last. The acrid smell of smoke fills my lungs when I enter the living room, and I see bright flames licking away at the stove.

"What the hell did you do?" Xander yells at someone. It's only when I step from behind him that I see Nadine sprawled on the floor directly opposite the flames.

"Nadine!" I run to her, but calling her name doesn't get her attention. Her gaze is fixed on the fire in the kitchen. Crouching in front of her, I search everywhere for burn wounds. "Are you okay?"

She begins to make fast gesture with her hands, but I never learned sign language, so I don't understand. "Slow down."

Closing her eyes for a brief moment, she seems to take in a deep breath before she resumes her explanation. She first draws a small square in the air, then she points at my head. "Are you talking about the chips?"

She nods, then she hits her closed fist against her palm, before pointing at the burning stove. Xander is busy trying to put the flames out.

"You wanted to destroy the chips, so you stuck them in the oven?"

When I get another nod from her, I turn to Sam and Dante. "I guess the chips are toast. I suppose it's a good thing."

"Would roasting electronic chips cause an explosion?" Sam peers at the charred mess in Xander's kitchen. He's definitely never going to invite us over again.

"I don't think so." Dante sounds unsure.

"Well, if you thought the chips were destroyed, think again." Xander pulls the clear box containing the chips from the stove, not a sign of damage on it.

I stand up, going to inspect the box myself. Xander drops the object on the counter and takes a step back, doing the sign of the cross as he goes. I know exactly what I'll find. Perfect chips.

"How is that possible?" I whisper in disbelief.

"Zeke said only Eternal Fire could destroy the demonic presence embedded in the chips."

"And where do we get that?"

Dante lifts his face from the box, staring intently at me. "We need a circle of witches."

CHAPTER 37

RED

The guys spend most of the trek down the mountain arguing about what we should do first. Get help from the druids or head straight to the compound to end Seth and Lyria's party. Wrapped up in the blanket I took from Xander's hideout, I remain quiet, refusing to weigh in on the matter until I know what I think is best. Both plans have their merits and risks.

From time to time, I check on Nadine, wishing I could shift so I could talk to her. But I'm afraid once I turn into a wolf, it will be harder to resist the compulsion from the electric device in my head. I can still feel it pulsing, albeit it's so faint now I've managed to ignore it for the most part. I'm sure my resistance to Martin's weapon must be driving him insane.

Nadine's clothes are covered in soot, and there are some patches where the fire ate away the fabric of her hoodie. Other than that, she doesn't have any visible burns, but I sense failure in destroying the chips is pressing down on her.

When we finally arrive on Xander's property, a small chalet partially concealed by tall trees with a detached workspace where logs have been piled up almost to the ceiling, the alpha mutters something about getting clothes for us inside, not inviting any of us in. I can't blame him after what we did to his hideout. Sam and Dante continue to discuss strategy while Nadine wanders off from us to sit on a fallen tree trunk nearby. Closing my eyes, I take that opportunity to turn my thoughts inward. Maybe the voice in my head can point me in the right direction.

"Hello, are you in there?"

I hold my breath, waiting to hear a reply. It doesn't escape my notice that I sound like a crazy person.

"Please, I could really use your help. I don't know what to do."

Seconds pass by and nothing happens, which makes me lose hope. Then I feel something, not in my head, but a change in the air surrounding me. My legs begin to tingle as tendrils of energy erupt from the ground, crackling around my limbs as it travels up my body. A curse nearby makes me open my eyes. Sam and Dante have taken a fighting stance as they stare out in the distance. I follow their line of vision, finding the spirit of the great wolf between the trees at the edge of the clearing. This time, the guardians didn't use natural elements to build themselves a body.

"Why are you here? Are we in danger?" I ask.

"We're here because we heard your call."

"I was trying to reach the woman's voice in my head."

"We do not sense her in you anymore."

"Who was she?"

The wolf cocks his head to the side, such an odd gesture that completely conflicts with its ethereal form.

"She's your former conscience."

"What? I don't understand."

"Why were you seeking her help?"

"I don't know what to do. Tristan is in danger, but would we be foolish to try to rescue him without assistance?"

The wolf doesn't answer right away, but I think I hear a low chuckle coming from it.

"What's so funny?"

"You misunderstand us. We're not amused. We're resigned. He truly loved you, so much so he managed to follow you here to this time."

"What are you talking about?"

"You have the answers you seek within you."

"Stop being so frustrating. If I have the answers, then how do I unlock them?"

"Get Tristan and return to the place it all began. You might find more than what you seek."

The wolf becomes more and more translucent until it disappears completely. His departure makes me feel so drained that my legs give out from under me and I collapse ungracefully to the ground.

"Red!" Sam and Dante say at the same time, both running to me.

"What happened?" Dante asks first. "Why was that beast here?"

Still staring at the spot the great wolf was standing on, I answer, "I accidently summoned it."

"You were staring at it for the longest time without saying a word. You freaked us out," Sam says.

I blink several times before I switch my attention to Dante and Sam. "It said stuff about me and Tristan. I must return to the place it all began to find answers about myself and my past. But I have no idea what it meant by that. All I know is that we need to get Tristan right now."

"That's what I've been telling Dante this whole time, but Dante can be such a mule." Sam kicks a loose pebble in a frustrated gesture while Dante keeps staring at me without blinking.

Finally, after seconds of silence, he replies, "Okay."

Sam pivots on the spot, his mouth agape. "What? I spent thirty minutes trying to convince you and you wouldn't budge, but now that Red is on my side, you agree?"

Dante rolls his eyes at the same time a smirk plays with his lips. "I trust Red's judgment."

Sam flips his brother off with both hands from behind his back, making me chuckle. He can be such a child sometimes.

"He's giving me the finger, isn't he?" Dante asks.

"Yup."

Offering me his hand, Dante says, "Come on. You're getting dirt all over you."

I twist my face into a scowl, being reminded belatedly I'm naked and I probably have mud up my butt crack. Gross.

"Zeke Rogers left us a list with names, and one of them was Robert E. Saint, the town's mayor back in the nineteenth century. I have reason to believe Robert was involved with Natalia Petroviski."

"What do those people have to do with me?"

"Red, I think Natalia was the Mother of Wolves."

I feel the blood drain from my face when a piece of hidden knowledge seems to click in my brain. "Oh my God. Do you think I'm her?"

Dante nods before saying. "I went to visit Albert, the time traveler. He was Robert's cousin, and he mentioned a spot Robert used to meet with Natalia in secret. They were lovers."

My chest becomes unbearably tight, as if I'm suffering a brutal heartache. "Do you think that's the same place the great wolf was referring to?"

"It's possible. We've also retrieved an old diary we believe belonged to Natalia. Your grandmother has it."

Xander exits the house, carrying a bundle of folded clothes in his arms. He stops halfway down the steps, glancing in Nadine's direction. The teen has her chin down, gaze glued to the ground. She seems dejected. Surprising me, Xander veers in her direction first, offering her a clean hoodie that looks to be twice her size. Nadine raises her head, frozen for a moment, before accepting Xander's offer. Then the alpha returns to us, distributing the clothes he's holding.

"I don't have any women's clothes here, so these will all be too big for you."

"Don't worry about it. They're more than fine. I'm tired of parading around naked."

"I don't mind." Sam winks at me.

"That's because you're a pig," Dante retorts, earning a snort from Sam.

"Pot, meet kettle," he says, and I squirm when I realize he's referring to last night. My cheeks become warm, which prompts me to give my back to the three of them so they can't see that my face resembles a tomato now.

Indeed, the borrowed clothes are enormous on me. The sweatshirt alone could double as a dress, and I need to roll the pants up several times. Despite the wrong size, I feel a hundred times better now that I'm covered up. I wish I had shoes on, but beggars can't be choosers.

"Have you made a decision about what you want to do?" Xander asks.

"Yes," I turn around. "We're going back to the compound. It's time to unmask that son of a bitch who betrayed us all."

And then, I'm going to find out once and for all if I'm indeed the Mother of Wolves reincarnated.

CHAPTER 38
TRISTAN

We have a small holding facility in the compound, but we rarely had to use it. The last time this prison was occupied was when Seth brought one of the hunters here. He said the guy killed himself before he could be interrogated, but now I suspect Seth was responsible for it. I can't believe I've been so stupid, so blind. Dante warned me several times that Seth shouldn't be trusted, but I ignored my brother's warnings. My misplaced trust in the enforcer might have doomed us all.

In the cell next to mine, Billy didn't move a muscle throughout the night besides the low rise and fall of his chest. I spent the entire evening wide awake, trying to formulate an escape plan and also worrying about Red, my brothers, and Mom. My solace is that Zaya is with her, and I'm confident she won't let Seth touch a strand of my mother's hair. I'm hoping one of Zaya's gifts is super hearing and she heard what Seth did to Billy and me.

Morning has come and with it, wariness that has seeped through my bones. Staying wide awake wasn't the best idea. A low murmur catches my attention. Swinging around, I see Billy slowly emerge from his sedation. He stretches his body, then rubs his eyes before blinking in rapid succession as he stares at the ceiling.

"Billy," I shout-whisper.

He turns at the sound of my voice, frowning. "What happened?"

"Seth has betrayed the alpha and taken over the pack. He shot you with a tranquilizer gun."

Wincing, Billy sits down on the bench. "I feel like I've been hit by a bulldozer. My head is throbbing like crazy."

"I hope you're rested at least. We need to find a way out of here to warn my brothers."

Billy's eyes turn as round as saucers, as if he just remembered something. "There was wolfsbane residue in the bottle of whiskey Lyria gave you."

My nostrils flare as I deal with this new betrayal. I'd known I shouldn't have trusted Lyria, not after I put a stop to her advances to be with Red. Goddamn it. Has my brain deserted me?

Rubbing my jaw, I start to move inside my small cell, not able to remain still. "Things make sense now. No wonder I couldn't think straight after I woke up. I wasn't suffering from a hangover."

Billy pats his clothes, as if searching for something. He freezes, but then lets out a relieved sigh. Pulling a coin from the inside pocket of his jacket, he smiles.

"What's that?"

"Something Nina gave me. She said if I got into trouble, this would alert her."

Narrowing my eyes, I move closer to the bars separating our cells.

"Why were you hanging out with that fox? She's a mercenary."

"It's a long story. You shouldn't be too quick to judge her. She was the one who discovered you had been poisoned by wolfsbane. Besides, Sam trusts her."

"That doesn't comfort me."

Billy frowns, standing up. "You're one to talk. You trusted my brother, and look where that landed you."

Damn. When had Billy become something more than a

lowly omega? I don't even sense the submissive nature in him anymore. He has evolved.

"Touché. How does that coin work exactly?"

"This is not a coin, but a dual-sided medallion." A blush creeps up Billy's cheeks. I don't get his reaction.

"Fine. How does the *medallion* work?"

"Like this." Billy presses his right thumb in the middle, and a faint glow bursts from the object. The light fades in the next second.

"Now what?"

The young wolf lifts his face to mine, then shrugs. "Now we wait."

I hate having to rely on the help of a mercenary like Nina, but what choice do I have? Sitting down on the metal bench in my cell, I lean my elbows on my knees. "Since we're not going anywhere for the time being, why don't you tell me how you got tangled up with Nina Ogata?"

Billy glances at his feet, rubbing the back of his neck. "I met her during a dare. Then, when I slipped into Valerius's territory on the—"

"Wait a second. What the hell were you doing in Shadow Creek?"

Glancing at the ceiling, Billy makes an exasperated sound only teenagers are able to. "Please spare me the lecture. Dante already covered that."

Forcing my jaw shut, locking it so tight it hurts my cheeks, I count to ten in my head. I'm not equipped with the patience to deal with a rebellious teenager.

"Anyway, we came across a demon and I helped Nina escape. I guess now she owes me one."

Pinching the bridge of my nose, I fight the sudden headache that is flaring up again. I have no idea how long wolfsbane will remain in my system. Or maybe the cause for my headache is the fucking bad news that keeps piling up. Now Valerius has a demon on his side. What other surprises await us? Can we even win this fight?

Loud shouts outside pull me out of my pity party, then comes the desperate yelling of women and children. We're under attack. I get off the bench, then I turn to the small barred window in my cell. It's not on my eye level, so I jump, grabbing the bars while my feet push against the wall.

"Do you see anything?"

"No. This window faces the forest, and there's no one coming from there."

I let go of the bars, landing back on the stony floor with soft feet. Billy is tense in his cell, bending his knees and curling his fists at his side. The screaming continues, but it's not as loud as before, which means our people are either running in the opposite direction of us or they were taken. Wrapping my fingers around the metal bars of my cell's door, I try to force it open. All I accomplish is making a rattling noise. Frustrated, I feel like kicking the damn thing. I pull my leg back do it, but I stop at the last second when sanity returns to me. I'll end up breaking my foot.

Another noise reaches us, this time a grunt followed by a thud right outside the building. Imminent danger awakens my wolf, and I allow a partial shift. My canines are longer and sharper, my nails turning into claws. I don't want to shift completely until I know what we're dealing with. Morning light pours in suddenly when the front door bursts open, making it impossible to see the dark silhouette by the threshold.

"I knew you would get into trouble." The woman strides in Billy's direction, stopping by his cell door. She turns to me, her sleek ponytail whipping around like a snake. "Hello there, Mr. Wolfe."

"Nina Ogata. A pleasure seeing you." I let sarcasm drip from my tongue, despite the fact she's here to save our asses. What can I say —old habits die hard. She was a pain in my ass when we were younger, and grew up to be an even pricklier thorn.

"How did you get here so fast?" Billy asks.

"I heard rumors your brother had taken over the pack. I was already inside the compound when I got your SOS signal."

"How did you get in? The fences were supposed to be on, and we have sentries patrolling," I say.

"The fences weren't electrified, and the gate I came through was wide open. I knew something was off. Then I heard the screams."

"Is it Valerius? Are we under attack?" Billy asks in a frantic manner.

"Yes. I saw a group of Shadow Creek wolves chasing some of your people."

"Where the hell were our enforcers?"

Nina turns to me, her gaze serious. "I saw none."

"Fuck. We need to get out of here. Can you pick these locks or not?"

With a snort, Nina pulls out a skeleton key from between her breasts, then uses it to open Billy's cell first. She does the same to mine next. Examining the key in her hand, I realize it's not one of ours.

"Where did you get that?"

She hides the key from view once more, sticking it back between her cleavage. I don't miss how Billy follows the movement, nor when his gaze stays glued to her chest. Ah hell, the kid has a crush on the fox.

"That's a secret I'll never tell. Come on, let's get out of here before Valerius's minions find us."

I follow the fox out of the building. The first thing I spot is a teen sprawled next to the bushes. He's not an enforcer yet, only a cadet. Damn it. I can't leave him behind like that. He'd be easy prey for Valerius's ruthless wolves. Bending, I pick up the young wolf, throwing him over my shoulder.

"What are you doing?" Nina asks with wide eyes.

"What does it look like? Did you have to knock the poor kid unconscious?"

"I didn't know what he was up to. I didn't want him sounding the alarm."

She starts moving toward the woods behind the prison building, in the opposite direction we need to go.

"Where do you think you're going? We need to help the pack."

Nina glances over shoulder, leveling me with a glare. "I didn't sign up for that."

"Fine, then leave." I begin to turn around when Billy gets in between us.

"Wait. Nina, you said we were partners. We can't simply turn our backs on the pack. They'll be killed. You know that."

Partners? Oh, I can't wait to hear the details of that story. The fox's expression softens a little before she catches my eye over Billy's shoulder. "I'll help you out, but I want a favor in return."

Suspicious, I narrow my eyes. "What favor?"

"Don't know yet."

She strides past me. As one, Billy and I follow close behind, sneaking around, staying close to buildings to avoid detection. The sound of fighting becomes louder, and with it, my headache increases to the point where I begin to see white spots in my vision. For fuck's sake. Now is not the time to suffer from a migraine. I suck my lower lip in, biting it until I taste blood. The sting distracts me from the throbbing in my head and clears my thoughts.

The square in front of the alpha's manor is a war zone, but it's clear who has the upper hand. Blood has been spilled, and none is from the enemy. Valerius's army is vicious, and they're going for the kill. I need to get in there, which means I have to put the unconscious cadet somewhere safe first. Retracing my steps, I return to the window we passed on the side of the building we're using for cover. I slam my palm against the wood panel, breaking the lock on the inside. Sticking my head inside the house first to make sure there's no enemy in sight, I unceremoniously dump the kid on the floor, closing the window again.

By the time I turn around, Billy and Nina have already

joined the fray, Billy in his wolf form. Nina chose to remain on two legs, and I don't understand why until she sticks her hand in the satchel by her hip, pulling a fucking sword out of it. I don't have time to wonder how the hell she did that because I feel a tug in my chest. My bond to Red has flared, which means she's here.

My head knows I should shift and help in the fight, but my body moves of its own accord, turning in her direction, the alpha's manor. I'm already sprinting toward it when the front door bursts open. My heart stops beating for a second before it jumps up my throat.

"Red," I whisper, not believing my eyes. I don't know if I want to cry or laugh.

She stares at my face wide-eyed for a split second before her gaze diverts to a point behind me. "Tristan! Watch out."

Pain explodes in my shoulder where the teeth of a Shadow Creek wolf sink into my flesh. I fall with the force of the beast's jump, locking my jaw tight as it keeps tearing at me. The sound of bone crushing comes first before the mutt's weight disappears. Bracing my forearms on the ground, I lift my torso, catching Red holding an old baseball bat. She's not looking at me, but at the fight not too far from us.

With a grunt, I slowly bring my body to an upright position. My shirt is torn, and blood is pouring freely from the wound.

"Shit, brother. He got you good," Sam says from next to me, right before he takes off at a run, shifting midair during a jump. Show-off.

I recognize Dante's white fur in the middle of the fight, thrashing his opponent like a rag doll. Not too far from him, a great brown bear fights three wolves at the same time, but he's holding his own.

No enemy is coming our way for now, allowing Red to take her eyes from the fight for a moment. Our gazes connect. Before I realize I'm going to do it, I'm pulling her into my arms, ignoring the searing pain in my shoulder. Forgetting the battle, I capture her beautiful face between my hands and kiss the hell out of her. I must look like a starved person with the way I take possession of her sweet mouth. There's no doubt we belong together. I don't care about anything else other than the woman in my arms.

She's the one who pulls back first, only to rest her forehead against mine. "Tristan, I was so worried about you."

"You're one to talk. I was going out of my mind thinking about you in the hands of that deranged monster."

She drops her gaze to my mangled shoulders, her green eyes turning darker. "You need help."

"Is Zaya still here with my mother?"

"No. We searched the manor and the clinic. There's no one there."

I curse, not knowing if Seth took Mom or if she managed to escape.

The sound of a loud explosion makes us jump back as the ground begins to shake. A large blue glow in the center of the square is beginning to fade already, allowing us to see Nina at the edge of it.

"What the—"

She turns to Billy, then yells at him to stop. But the young wolf doesn't pay any attention, heading straight for a specific wolf, his brother Seth. Grunting, I take a step forward, already feeling the tremors of the shift.

"Tristan, you can't possibly join the fight. You're hurt." Red touches my arm.

"Seth is responsible for all this. I can't let Billy face off against his brother. That's my fight."

"Where's Lyria?" Red narrows her eyes, gazing into the distance.

I follow her line of sight, not spotting the former beta anywhere. "She must have taken off already, back to her new master."

Red turns to me, surprised. "So you know Lyria and Seth were behind my kidnapping?"

Rage takes over my body, and I do nothing to tamper it.

"They'll pay for it."

"Lyria is mine," Red hisses, and the fire in her eyes makes me want to kiss her again. My cock is rock hard and begging for action. It's the most inappropriate time to have a hard-on, but lust and fury go hand in hand.

Red will berate me for it later, but I allow the shift to happen. It takes longer than normal, with double the pain. But once I hit the ground on four paws, the bloodlust overrides the discomfort. Seth and Billy are already engaged in a fight. On the other side of the quad, I see Nina swinging her sword left and right, trying to get to Billy. She must know Billy is no match for his older brother. The fact she's determined to help him makes me dislike her a little less.

In the mayhem, I see a path straight to them, but Lyria finally appears out of nowhere, blocking me.

"Lyria, get the fuck out of my way."

"What for, Tristan? So you can save your little buddy, the only wolf in this pack who still believes in you?"

"You're despicable. You betrayed your pack and for what?"

"Do you think I wanted to make a deal with Valerius? But you had to go and get mated with that fucking blonde bitch. So in a way, this is all your fault."

She leaps on me, but she's intercepted by a grey-and-white wolf—Red. I freeze for a moment, the natural instinct to protect my mate taking over my brain.

"Tristan, go. I got this," Red shouts in my head.

Forcing myself not to look back, I sprint toward Seth and Billy. Seth grabs Billy by the shoulder, throwing him against a nearby tree. The poor kid doesn't get up. Nina lets out an enraged battle cry, lifting her sword high above her head. Seth sees her, then bolts toward the tree line.

Fuck. I can't let him escape. I begin to give chase, but then I remember what happened to Mom the last time I ditched the battlefield in order to go after one wolf. Stopping in my tracks, I scan behind me, realizing we're still greatly outnumbered. It kills me to let Seth run away, but I can't go after him and sacrifice everyone else.

The smell of blood fills my nose, but even without it, I can see the carnage Valerius's wolves are leaving behind. I've lost count of how many are down on our side, but there's no sign of slowing the enemy down. They keep coming at us even when they're badly hurt. What kind of power is that?

"Why won't these motherfuckers die?" Sam asks.

"They must have the demonic chip in their heads," Dante replies.

"So Valerius is working with Martin?" I ask without slowing down. We can't afford it.

"Yes," they both answer at the same time.

"Fucking fantastic." I leap on top of a wolf who was about to deliver a killing blow on none other than Charlie, the idiot who believed Seth's lies and who was all too happy to off Mom and me.

The wolf falls on his side with a whine, but gets up a second later. Before he can attack me, a gunshot cuts through the battle noise and his head explodes. I swing around, not knowing what to expect. Relief washes over me when I see Sheriff Arantes and her officers swarm the perimeter, guns pointed at the enemy. If Valerius's wolves had any preservation instinct, they would flee. But they're mad in their savagery. In consequence, they're turned into Swiss cheese when bullets rain on them. The fight is over in the next minute, the smell of blood and gunpowder almost making me gag.

Immediately, I search for Red, relieved to sense the bond link as strong as ever. I leap over corpses and shove my own wolves out of the way so I can get to her. She's standing alone, breathing hard. There's blood on her muzzle, but it's not hers. No sign of Lyria anywhere.

Locking her gaze with mine, she says, *"She escaped. I had her, Tristan, but when the sheriff arrived, I got distracted and let her slip from under me."*

Red's tone, even in my head, is remorseful. I rub my face against hers, but what I really want is to hold her close and never let go. *"Don't feel bad about it. You'll have your chance again, sooner than you think."*

"Red, are you okay?" Dante asks as he runs toward us with Sam close behind him.

"Yes, I'm fine. I'm just pissed I let Lyria escape."

"We should shift back so we can talk to the sheriff," Dante says.

As a group, we return to our human forms, and so do all the remaining members of our pack. Sheriff Arantes walks between the corpses of friends and foe alike with care before she reaches us.

"How did this happen?"

"Valerius sent some of his soldiers to obliterate us while you were too busy following Mayor Montgomery's orders," I snap.

She ignores my jab, focusing on Dante instead. "How did they get in?"

"Seth—he's working with the enemy," Dante replies.

"And Lyria, let's not forget about that bitch," Red says, glowering.

"Oh my God," someone says from behind Sheriff Arantes. The woman turns, revealing her daughter Kenya not too far behind.

Red's friend is staring at us wide eyed with her hands covering her mouth.

"Kenya, what in the world are you doing here?" her mother asks.

"I came to make sure Red was okay since I haven't heard from her in days. What happened here and why is everyone naked?"

CHAPTER 39

RED

Kenya hasn't spoken a word since her mother explained supernatural creatures exist and the Wolfe brothers—and I—are wolf shifters. After she crashed the party—or better put, the massacre site—we all went to the alpha's manor, including the few enforcers who survived. Those who were sent to the clinic to wait for help to arrive since Dr. Mervina had been taken out of the premises by Zaya once the nurse realized she wasn't safe in the compound.

Not able to take Kenya's silence any longer, nor her staring at me like she's never seen me before, I speak.

"Say something, Kenya. Please."

"I can't believe all this happened to you and you didn't tell me."

She's sitting across from me at the great dining room table, but it feels like there's a chasm between us. I drop my gaze to my folded hands, ashamed.

"I wasn't supposed to say anything, especially since you weren't aware about the supernatural community in Crimson Hollow."

Kenya lets out a humorous laugh. "It all makes sense now. God, I was such a fool." She turns to her mother, accusation glaring in her eyes. "Why did you keep the truth from me? You didn't think I could handle it?"

Guilt flashes in Sheriff Arantes's stare, but she doesn't break eye contact with her daughter like I did. "Your father and I decided it was best if you were kept in the dark for your own safety."

"That's bullshit. I could have walked into a vampire's nest without even knowing!"

"There aren't any vampires in Crimson Hollow," Tristan says in a matter-of-fact tone, earning a glare from Kenya and strangely shifty eyes from Sam.

"It was just an example." Holding her head in her hands, she continues. "This is turning out to be one of the suckiest days of my life. First, Martin cancels our date, and—"

"You can't date him," I almost shout.

Kenya whips her face to mine, her eyes narrowed to slits. "You can't tell me what to do. You're no longer my best friend."

I wince, feeling the pain of Kenya's retort deep in my heart. "You don't mean that."

"Yes, I do. You should have told me you were turned into a wolf. That's what best friends do. I wouldn't have turned my back on you."

"Oh, for fuck's sake. Enough with this childish bullshit." Sam throws his hands in the air. "You lied to me, blah, blah, blah," he says in a girly voice. "You can't date Martin because he's a sadistic motherfucker who's been working with Valerius. Most likely, he wanted to date you to have leverage over Red."

The stricken expression on Kenya's face makes me wish Sam wasn't so callous. I turn to him, letting him know with my hard stare that he went too far.

"What? She's been going on and on about how she can handle the truth. Now that she has it, it's clear her mother was right to keep it from her."

Kenya stands up abruptly, announcing in a tight voice that she's leaving. Her mother stands as well, following after her daughter. I want to do the same, but Dante's hand on my forearm stops me.

"She needs time to digest everything. She'll come around."

My shoulders sag as I sit deflated on my chair. All the terrible things that have happened to us weigh heavily on me. Nadine enters the room, coming out of her hiding spot. I asked her to stay in the manor and guard the chips while we fought Valerius's soldiers, something she did without reluctance. I don't know if the reason was that she didn't want to fight the wolves she grew up with, or if she was afraid the box containing the chips would vanish.

Xander's gaze immediately switches to her. His animosity toward Nadine is still alive and kicking, which makes absolutely no sense to me. Does he still believe she will betray us?

"How did you know we needed assistance?" Tristan asks Santiago, the sheriff's deputy. Dante told me earlier the deputy is a druid—one who is a few centuries old and very powerful. The surprises keep coming.

"Zaya brought your mother to my son when she realized Seth had taken over the pack. After that, they stormed the city hall together with Riku Ogata and Baldwin to demand assistance from the mayor."

"And she just simply agreed?" Tristan scoffs.

Santiago smirks, making his jovial face even younger. "I went over her head, straight to the top boss of the Midnight Lily Council."

"I don't understand. I've always assumed she was the head," Dante says.

"Oh no. Her mother is, but she rarely leaves her mansion these days. With her mother on our side, Georgina had no choice but to lift the ban on assisting the supes."

"How is our mother, Santiago?" Tristan asks.

"She's okay. A little banged up, but nothing life threatening."

"We need to regroup as soon as possible," I say. "This was only the first wave of attack we can expect from Valerius. I don't know how many wolves he has under his control, but it's definitely higher than what's left of our pack."

All three brothers fix me with stares that are a mix of awe and pride. Heat creeps up my face. I don't know why they're regarding me that way. I didn't say anything they didn't already know.

Dante breaks eye contact first, shifting his attention to the others present. "And we still have Martin and his men to contend with."

"Now that Seth and Lyria are gone, the compound is still the safest place for our wolves," Tristan adds, and everyone seems to agree.

Nina enters the room in that moment with Billy by her side. The young wolf seems fine besides the bruise on his left cheek.

"You need to call every enforcer you have left back to the compound. The woods outside are not safe," she declares.

Tristan growls, and Dante watches the brunette through slitted eyes. I don't know who she is, but only Sam is not reacting negatively to her presence and statement.

"Nina is right. We need the numbers, and patrolling the perimeter of the compound is useless. We know Valerius will come back sooner or later," Billy adds, defending his companion. It fills me with pride. I knew he wasn't a doormat.

He's finally decided to step away from the submissive role of the omega. I'll never accept that the pack needs someone to be the punching bag. It's archaic and barbaric in my opinion. Maybe that's something I can change if we survive what's to come.

Then the idea hits me like a cannonball. I don't know why I didn't think about it sooner. "We should take the fight to Valerius. Catch him by surprise."

"It's too dangerous. He'll have the advantage of knowing his territory well," Tristan counters.

"Nadine can help us with that. It's better than waiting for him to come at us again with all his might. He's probably counting on that, actually."

Tristan opens his mouth again, but Sam cuts him off. "I'm with Red. Let's take the fight to that bastard's lands."

Clearly frustrated, Tristan stares at a point on the wall, rubbing his chin as he does so. It's a gesture so familiar that it causes a sudden ache in my chest. I touch his leg, trying to reassure him that all will be well. Then I see a vision of a man running toward me in the forest. His hair is dark blond, and he wears clothes that don't belong to this time. Is it a memory from my previous life? And why would touching Tristan now trigger it? I remember then what the great wolf apparition told me—that I'd find the answers I seek if I went back to the place where it all started. What if I can unlock the knowledge to win against Valerius as well?

"Before we head to Shadow Creek, there's a place we need to go first." I turn to Dante. "We need that diary you found."

CHAPTER 40

RED

I have to brace myself, encase my heart into a barrier made out of steel, in order to come face to face with my grandmother. To speed things up, she agreed to meet us at the place Natalia Petroviski—the presumed Mother of Wolves and my former self—used to meet up with her lover Robert E. Saint, one of the names on the list the imp Zeke Rogers left for Tristan.

Silver Falls is a piece of woodland farther south, on the border of Ravenwood, a neighboring town. The forest is dense, but there's no sense of danger here, which I can't say the same anymore about the woods in Crimson Hollow. But how long until Valerius's presence spreads here? We need to stop him before his power takes over the entire area.

It's easy to guess why this particular spot is called Silver Falls. Any light that manages to break through the canopy gives the crystalline waterfall in front of us a silvery sheen. But I don't have the right state of mind to appreciate the scenery. My grandmother is waiting for us at the edge of the clearing, looking healthier than ever. In fact, she seems ten years younger, which makes the resentment festering in my chest increase. Sam told me what he had learned about her deception. She lied about being sick all these years, something I'll never be able to forgive her for. Even when Dante pointed out that if it wasn't for her lie, I wouldn't have met them, the hurt didn't lessen.

We dropped off Nadine and the chips at Brian's before coming here. Something still needs to be done to destroy them. If it's the conjuring of the Eternal Fire, then the druid has to call on the witches needed for that. I don't want to have anything to do with them. Walking between Dante, Tristan, and Sam, I attempt to control my nerves. Nevertheless, my spine goes taut when I lock gazes with Grandma. I stop in my tracks, leaving a good distance between us.

"Red, it's good to see you're unharmed."

I snort. "Like you ever truly cared about my well-being." If she had, she wouldn't have sent me into those woods to be attacked by a rogue wolf.

Face tightening, she takes a step forward. "I hope one day you'll understand my reasons."

"Repeating that phrase every time we meet won't make me change my mind. Is that the diary?" I point at the tome in her hand.

"Yes."

When I don't make a move to retrieve it from her outstretched hand, Tristan does the honors. The moment he touches the old tome, he changes, becoming the man I saw in my vision. What the hell? I let out a gasp and the illusion vanishes, which doesn't make my accelerated heartbeat return to normal.

"What's the matter?" Sam touches my arm, concern lacing his words.

"Did you guys see that?" I continue to gape at Tristan without blinking my eyes.

"See what?" His eyes search around us as if he's expecting an ambush at any minute. He has no idea he's the reason I'm freaking out.

"There's magic in the diary. Tristan must have triggered it," Grandma says.

I'm still frozen on the spot, not knowing what I should do next. Now that I'm so close to learning the truth, I'm terrified.

"You have to. It's the only way," the familiar woman's voice

speaks to me, sounding so distant I can barely hear it.

"I thought you were gone."

"There's some kind of disturbance blocking me."

The chip. It must be the chip. In my haste to come here, I forgot all about it. I still need to find a way to remove the damn thing from my head.

"You have enough power in you to destroy it."

"What? How?"

The voice goes silent. Typical. Why can't I get a straight answer from any of the mysterious entities helping me? The annoying buzz coming from the chip becomes louder. Martin must still be trying to control me through it. Using all my mental strength, I push the noise to a dark corner of my mind while solidifying the barrier between my conscience and the disruptive chip.

"Red?" Dante is suddenly in front of me, his eyes riveted on my face.

"What?" I ask with a start.

"You spaced out for a moment." He touches my cheek with the tips of his fingers, and I want to lean into that caress, but if I do, I might chicken out and not face the music. We came here for a reason, to find out the truth about how I'm linked to the Mother of Wolves.

"It's nothing." I brush past him, moving toward Tristan and the mysterious diary.

As I get closer to the object, I sense its power increase, which makes me even more jittery. I'm beginning to understand why Tristan is so against witches and spells. Magic sucks.

He offers me the diary, and a huge lump gets lodged in my throat as I stare at it. Then, lifting my eyes to Tristan's face, I take a deep breath before grabbing the tome. My intention was to peer inside; I didn't expect magic to flare up from it. My scream gets swallowed up by the sound of howling winds. Tristan reaches for me, holding my arms as we're enveloped by a vortex of light. We're caught by the spinning air. As it increases speed, his grip on me begins to slip. Then he's yanked away from me, disappearing from sight.

"Tristan!"

The light surrounding me brightens before it vanishes altogether. Still reeling from the experience, I find myself sitting on a rock by the Silver Falls lagoon. The forest is quiet besides the sound of the waterfall. I'm all alone; everyone is gone. Where did they go? I stand up, ready to go search for them, when the swishing sound of fabric catches my attention. Glancing down, I see an ankle-length brown skirt, caked with mud at the edges, covering my legs. I was wearing sweatpants before. Panicking, I inspect the rest of my ensemble. I'm now wearing a tight bodice, and a thick wool cape is fastened around my neck. That's not the only disturbing detail. Instead of my blonde hair, dark brown locks tumble down my front. *Shit. Shit. Shit.* I run to the water, dropping to my knees to peer at my reflection. A stranger is staring back at me. I let out a yelp, falling back on my ass.

"Natalia!" A man's voice shouts the name, scaring me even more.

I scoot back on the dirt, but then my panic dissipates when my heart recognizes him somehow, soaring in elation. The blond man from my vision is bearing down on me, jumping over rocks and ignoring when his clothes from a different era get smeared by mud. He's a stranger. Yet, I know his face, but not from my vision. It's like an old memory I had forgotten until now. How can that be?

Unable to move, I can only gawk as he runs to me. He slows as he gets nearer, then he drops to his knees in front of me so we can be at the same level. His eyes search my face in a frantic manner, as if he's looking for any signs I'm hurt. Taken over by a sudden impulse, I throw my arms around his neck, hugging him tight.

"Robert," I say, not understanding how I know his name.

His entire body tenses before he eases off, grabbing my hands between his. "You wanted to see me, so here I am."

His voice is cold, detached, and it feels like a dagger in my chest. I drop my gaze to his left hand, seeing a gold wedding band there. He's married, a fact that makes my pain increase tenfold. My vision begins to darken at the edges right before I lose the feeling of my body. My line of sight also changes. I'm no longer staring at Robert's face; I'm hovering above a scene where a dark beauty stands before him instead. There's a thread of faint blue light linking my ethereal form to hers. Holy shit. I think that's Natalia Petroviski, the Mother of Wolves.

She drops her arms to the sides, her face now mirroring the cold mask that's on Robert's. "You need to convince the city council to stop with their witch hunting and focus on the real problem."

Robert stands, taking a few steps back, but angrily scowls at Natalia. "You should be grateful. While they're busy hunting witches, they aren't hunting you and your wolves."

It's impossible not to notice the venom in his tone. What an asshat.

"You forget I'm a witch, too." Natalia gets back on her feet, her eyes flashing a hint of ember. "Those self-righteous fools are torturing and killing *my* people."

"There's been signs of dark magic all around town. You can't blame them for their actions. If the witches aren't the cause, who is then?"

Natalia lifts her chin in defiance. "A demon."

Robert doesn't speak for several beats as he digests the news. I'm also on pins and needles.

"I beg your pardon?" he finally says.

"A demon named Harkon is behind all the killings. He says he won't stop until he has what he wants."

"Which is what?"

"Me."

The blood drains from Robert's face, and I bet if I had a body right now, the same thing would have happened to me. My mind is reeling, thinking about my close encounter with that demon in Valerius's lands. If I'm the reincarnation of

Natalia and there'd been a demon obsessed with her in the past, could it be possible they weren't able to get rid of him, and he's coming after me now?

Robert breaks the distance between Natalia and himself, holding her forearms tight. "Then we need to get you out of here."

"I can't leave!" She steps out of his hold.

"Because of your damned pack?"

"Yes and no. Don't you understand? Running away won't stop him. He'll just come after me."

Robert captures her face between his hands, moving closer. "I'll come with you; I'll protect you. We'll go someplace he will never find us."

With a shudder, Natalia closes her eyes. "Robert, I can't leave. You can't, either. You have responsibilities. You have a wife!"

Exactly, dude. She isn't a homewrecker—or should it really be we aren't?

"I never stopped loving you." Ignoring her outburst, he kisses her swiftly, hard, and I'm sucked back into her body. *Oh Lord? Why? I don't want to feel this.* The only problem is my body and heart don't give a fuck about my morals. I put up zero fight, surrendering to the kiss instead. When we break apart, I'm breathless and horny, yet the surprises keep on coming. I don't find Robert gazing at me... Instead, it's Tristan.

"What the—"

Blinding light envelops me again, forcing me to close my eyes. I'm spinning so fast I'm getting dizzy. Only when I sense the force pressing against my body is dissipating do I open my eyes again. It takes me a moment to regain my bearings. Everything is hazy. Slowly, I recover the sensation of my body. With it comes the awareness I'm in someone's arms. As I blink fast to clear my vision, Tristan's face finally comes into focus.

"Did you see that?" I whisper.

"Yes," he answers tightly.

"What the hell happened? One moment, you were both standing there, then poof, you vanished." Sam gestures wildly with his arms while Tristan helps me back on my feet.

I can't find the words to answer Sam, too overwhelmed trying to process what I learned. Was Tristan Robert E. Saint in a former life? Would that account for the animosity he felt against me when we met?

"The diary worked as a portal to memories of the past. I've seen it happen before," Grandma interrupts the *Hundred Questions* game I was playing in my head.

"So, are you saying Red and Tristan were transported to the past?" Sam swings around, studying Grandma almost disbelievingly.

"Something like that."

"And what did you learn?" Dante takes a step closer.

Tristan turns to his brother. "Valerius is not our biggest problem. The demon he's working with is."

Blinking, I face Tristan. "So you believe the demon who was obsessed with Natalia back in the nineteenth century is the same one who is here now?"

"I suspect as much. You do as well, don't you?"

Biting my lower lip, I break eye contact with him. "It's one theory."

"Why else would Zeke Rogers leave that clue for me? What purpose did that trip down memory lane serve other than making us aware a demon was after the Mother of Wolves?"

Tristan sounds almost angry. We learned other things equally important about ourselves, our link. Why is he brushing it aside?

"I don't want to jump head-first on this demon theory, but I think it's worth investigating. If a demon plagued Crimson Hollow in the past, then it must have been registered somewhere."

"Santiago is older than dirt. Wouldn't he know?" Sam asks.

Grandma shakes her head. "He didn't move to Crimson

Hollow until the 1920s."

"Maybe the diary has the answer," I say, then I realize I don't have it anymore. I search frantically on the ground. "Oh my God. Where is it? I had in my hand before Tristan and I were transported to the past."

"Don't fret, child. I'm afraid that diary had only one purpose—to give you and Tristan knowledge. Now that the magic is completed, the diary is no more."

"Oh, that sucks. All that trouble for nothing. We should have gotten all of them." Sam shoves his hand through his hair in a frustrated gesture.

"We need to find out what happened back then. How did they stop that demon?" I say.

Grandma takes a deep breath before she searches my eyes. "There's one book that contains every single account of supernatural occurrences in Crimson Hollow since its founding. The Midnight Lily Grimoire."

"Isn't a grimoire a book of spells?" Dante asks.

"Precisely. Since the Midnight Lily Coven was founded, one member in each generation was selected to record spells, as well as other interesting paranormal incidents. If there was a battle between a demon and shifters in Crimson Hollow, it's written in that grimoire."

"So basically, we're screwed. No way will Mayor Montgomery give us access to that book," Sam says.

"Georgina has no say in the matter. She's not the grimoire's keeper."

"Then who is?" I ask.

"Her mother."

CHAPTER 41

RED

I'm bone tired when we return to the compound. The events from the past few days have finally caught up with me. I can't stop yawning, a fact everyone notices. When I step out of the car, Dante touches my lower back and whispers in my ear.

"Go rest. You look like you're on the verge of falling asleep where you stand."

"I can't rest. There's so much to be done. We need to get the grimoire, figure out a way to stop Valerius and his demon, destroy the chips I stole, remove the one in my head, get—"

Dante covers my lips with his index finger, silencing me. "Shh, we can get things in motion while you sleep for a couple of hours."

I narrow my eyes at him. "You and Sam didn't get any sleep, either."

"We also weren't in captivity for the last few days."

"Besides, you know if we get into bed with you, there won't be any sleeping." Sam chuckles nearby. His comment makes me blush as I remember our previous night.

I glance at Tristan, who has been quiet the entire way here. He hasn't been the same since we came back from our trip to the past, and I want to know why.

"I'll rest in a bit." Skirting around Dante, I head in Tristan's direction.

With his arms crossed in front of his chest, he turns to me. I'm surprised to see the scowl on his face.

"What's the matter?" I ask.

"Nothing. You should listen to Dante and get some rest."

I touch his face, hating to see the tension etched there. "I won't go until you talk to me."

"I have nothing to say." Surprising me, Tristan swings around, entering the alpha's manor in a huff.

"What crawled up his butt?" Sam asks.

"I don't know, but I'm going to find out."

Resolved, I follow Tristan inside, not seeing him anywhere. It doesn't matter, though, since the bond linking us tells me exactly where he went—up to his room. Taking the stairs two steps at a time, I reach the landing in time to hear a door slam down the hallway. Pissed at Tristan's childish behavior, I stride to his room with angry steps, not bothering to knock before I push the door open. Tristan is staring out his window, and he continues do so even when I bang the door closed again.

"All right. Enough with this BS. You'd better tell me what's going on or I'll kick your ass."

He snorts before glancing at me. "Are you back to issuing challenges?"

"Are you back at being an ass? I thought we were over that."

The annoyance in his eyes fades away to be replaced by guilt. "I loved you more than anything in the world, yet I abandoned you."

"What are you talking about?" I ease toward him, afraid if I move faster, he'll leave again.

With a sigh, he faces the window once more. "I was stuck in Robert's mind. I could feel how he felt about you, how torn he was when he left you to marry another. He still did it, though, chose duty over you." Tristan drops his chin, bracing his hands against the windowsill. "If I'm him, am I fated to make the same mistake again?"

Pinching his chin between my thumb and forefinger, I make

him look at me. "You're not him. You never abandoned me, and you won't."

"How can be you so sure of that? I fucked up, Red. I let the pack down. Thanks to me, my mother got hurt. And it's all because I was weak, just like Robert was."

Tristan's eyes are filled with tears. To see him so upset and doubtful like that breaks my heart. When the first drops roll down his cheeks, I wipe them off with my fingers.

"You were drugged, Tristan. You can't blame yourself for that."

"I was drugged because I was a fool, because I was too wrapped up in my self-pity. I didn't see Seth's betrayal until it was too late, despite Dante's several warnings. All my life I've heard others say I was the one destined to be the next alpha, but they were all wrong. I'm the weakest link, the runt of the litter."

"Shut up." I raise on my tiptoes to kiss his lips. "You're not weak, nor a runt. You're a leader, Tristan. You can't give up on the pack."

"The pack will be fine without me."

"I need you."

"No, you don't. You're strong, Red. You're our queen."

Capturing his face between my hands, I force him to keep staring into my eyes. "And you are my love."

Tristan's breathing hitches while his eyes widen a fraction.

"I love you, mating bond or not. You're in my heart, and there's nothing you can say or do that will change that."

Grabbing a fistful of my hair, Tristan brings my face to his, kissing me with the ardor of a man on the verge of losing everything. I pour all my love into that kiss, wanting to make sure he knows I meant every word I said. With impatient fingers, I reach for his T-shirt, ripping it down the middle with my bare hands. Grunting, Tristan lifts me up without breaking the kiss. In half a heartbeat, we're on his bed and he's kissing down my neck while his hands are under my shirt.

Fabric rips, then cool air caresses my feverish skin. The cold feeling only lasts a moment before Tristan's tongue draws a hot path down my belly until he's between my legs, kissing and sucking my clit. Arching my back, I curl my hands around the bedspread, my body electrified. I'm so close to the edge I can almost taste the bliss already when Tristan abandons my sex to flip me over. I let out a yelp, then turn my face, looking over my shoulder. My clit is throbbing like never before. Finding Tristan completely naked behind me, pumping his erection up and down, is almost enough to make me come.

Watching me through a lustful haze, he releases his cock, then grabs my hips, lifting them. Anticipation gives me shivers as I brace my forearms against the mattress. Tristan enters me with a powerful thrust, eliciting a sharp moan from my lips. Digging his fingers into my skin, he takes me hard, pumping fast enough to make me see stars even before I climax. He then runs his fingers through my hair, grabbing a handful to pull my body upward. His warm mouth finds my neck. When he runs his tongue over the sensitive spot below my ear, I fall off the edge.

He calls my name right before his warm seeds fills me up, but he doesn't slow, which only gives me another orgasm. At this point, I don't even know where I am anymore. All I can feel is Tristan, how my love for him will never cease, never diminish. I'll always love him, the same way I will always love Dante and Sam. I never thought loving more than one person equally was possible, but my heart is not an ordinary one.

Tristan eventually slows until he collapses to the side, bringing me with him to nestle my body beside his. Our breathing is erratic, but in sync. Resting my head against his chest, I close my eyes, happy despite all the challenges we still have to face. I'm finally reunited with my mates. Together, we can face anything.

CHAPTER 42

TRISTAN

She slept, and I watched like a creep. I still can't believe she's in my arms. She said she loved me, something I hadn't expected. The mating bond is the strongest link among wolves, but it doesn't necessarily mean love. But she does, despite my flaws, despite my horrible treatment of her in the beginning.

Even knowing I did her wrong when she became a wolf, I still can't do things right. I never said I loved her, too, something that became obvious to me when I tried to bring her back from Valerius's lands. I don't even know when it happened. The feeling came so suddenly that when I realized it, I had already fallen.

It almost feels like a dream to have her back safe and sound. My heart should be full, but there's a wretched feeling in my chest instead, like a bad omen. I'd like to say I believe in Red's confidence in me, but she doesn't know the dark thoughts that have plagued my mind since the day she was taken, how all the decisions I've made in the last forty-eight hours were the wrong ones. My instincts have betrayed me again and again.

Finding out I was Robert E. Saint in my former life, a man who left his true love behind so he could abide to the rules of society, added salt to the wound. Now it festers. What if I'm doomed to repeat the same mistakes as before?

Going back and forth, I keep thinking about what I did and didn't do to the point it brings back that awful headache. I should try to rest as well, but these dark thoughts won't let me be.

No one comes to disturb us for the next couple of hours, and I don't move an inch during that time. Eventually, Red becomes restless, starting to shake her head from side to side while murmuring words I can't discern. I touch her shoulder, shaking her lightly.

"Red, sweetheart, wake up."

She blinks her eyes open, her gaze not focusing on anything. Turning her face to me, she asks, "Tristan? Is that really you? I'm not dreaming?"

I crack a smile, then kiss her lips softly. "No, I'm real." And so is the huge erection pressing against her hip. Our earlier lovemaking hadn't even begun to satiate my hunger for her.

She melts against me, sighing while she presses her face against my chest. "I had a nightmare that I was back in Shadow Creek and Valerius's demon was chasing me."

I hug Red tighter, kissing the top of her head. "I'll never let anything happen to you for as long as I live. I'll face an army of killer wolves and demons to protect you. I can't lose you again."

"You never lost me, Tristan. Not even when I renounced our bond. You know I was only trying to get Valerius to trust me, right?"

"Yeah, I know."

What I can't tell Red is I wasn't referring to losing her in the present time. I brought back with me some of Robert's guilt. More than ever, I want to learn what the witches' grimoire says. Had Robert redeemed himself in the end? Was he able to save Natalia from the demon?

A soft knock comes on the door, followed by Dante's voice. "May I come in?"

"Yeah." I sit up on the bed, covering my boner with the sheets. Not that Dante can't sense I'm aroused, because

I'm sure he could smell the bond scent from the entry hall downstairs.

Red follows my movement, also using the sheet to cover her naked torso. Dante smiles at her action, which makes her pout.

"What? I need time," she says.

"Time for what?" Sam barges in, holding a half-eaten donut in his hand. He glances at us in bed, then a huge grin appears on his stupid face.

"All right. Are we having a four-way today?"

Red gasps. "No, we are not."

Dante hits Sam upside his head. "Can't you stop thinking about sex for one minute?"

Rubbing the sore spot, he sidesteps away from Dante. "I was joking. God, when did you become so uptight, brother?"

Red saunters off the bed, still wrapped in the sheet, and veers toward Sam to steal the donut from his hand.

"Hey!" he complains when she stuffs the whole thing in her mouth.

After she swallows the treat, she gives Sam a haughty glance. "Payback for making me blush."

His arms immediately go around her waist, bringing her flush against his body. "But you love when I make you blush—among other things I do to you."

The scent of the mating bond becomes unbearable. If we don't stop this banter, we might have a four-way after all. Clearing my throat, I turn to Dante.

"Any news?'

It takes a few seconds for Dante to pull his gaze away from Sam and Red to focus on me. "Yes, Mrs. Redford is here, but she won't say anything until Red is present."

Red tenses visibly, frowning as she moves away from Sam's embrace.

"I know you don't want to hear this, but even if you never forgive your grandmother, you'll have to learn to work with her."

Dante and I gape at Sam because for once, he's serious. Red lets out a heavy sigh, glancing at the floor. "I know. It's just too soon, and the wound is still fresh."

"It will get better. Time heals everything," Sam continues, playing the wise man. Fucking surreal.

Red lifts her face, smirking at him. "Did you hit your head or something?"

Curling his lips, Sam rubs his nape. "Well, Dante did hit me on the head."

"I need a shower. I'll be down in ten minutes," Red announces. Sam opens his mouth, but she cuts him off. "And no, I don't want any company."

His smile wanes, face downcast. Dante grabs his arm, dragging him out of the room. "Come on. Let's wait for Red downstairs. Are you coming, Tristan?"

I throw him a glare. "This is my room in case you've forgotten."

"Ouch, message received," Red replies. "I'll go to my room."

"I'm not kicking you out." I get out of bed, and Red's eyes drop to my crotch. My cock that had been standing at half-mast springs back to life. Luckily, Dante and Sam are already out of the room. "I'll leave to give you privacy."

Our gazes lock, heat and lust flowing freely between us. Desire surges in my veins, and only pure willpower keeps me rooted to the spot.

"You know, maybe I could use some company," Red says in the huskiest of voices, and I'm a goner. Reaching her in two wide strides, I pick her up and head for the bathroom. I don't think we'll be down in ten minutes.

CHAPTER 43

RED

The moment I enter Antony Wolfe's former office with Tristan by my side, I know Sam and Dante are aware Tristan and I had another round of delicious, make-up-for-what-we-lost sex. Watching me through heated eyes, Sam shakes his head. In his gaze, I read the message loud and clear. He'll ask for compensation later. My toes curl inside my shoes in anticipation. I wonder if I'll always be this turned on when I'm around my mates.

I rein in my supercharged libido, steeling myself as I do so. But all it takes is one look at my grandmother to get my mind out of the gutter. It's only the five of us in the room and when the door closes, I feel an odd humming above my skin.

"I cast a protective spell in this room. No one will be able to eavesdrop," she says.

"I'm here so let's get this over with. What news do you have?" I cross my arms.

"Demetria Montgomery has agreed to let us look into the grimoire."

"That's great news," Dante begins to say.

"With a condition." Grandma raises her hand.

"Of course there had to be one," Tristan grumbles next to me, exuding frustration and anger from his frame. It's crazy how I can sense his mood now as if it's a tangible thing.

"What is the condition?" I turn my attention back to Grandma.

"She didn't give me details. But only you and I are allowed to come to the Montgomery mansion, no one else."

"That's bullshit. I won't let Red go to that house of horrors alone. Mayor Montgomery is not to be trusted, and I'm extending my opinion to her mother as well." Tristan takes a step in front of me, using himself as a human shield.

"Demetria is not like her daughter."

"Then why did you leave the coven if she was so great?" Sam raises an arrogant eyebrow.

"We did not agree on certain traditions, so I left. She won't betray us."

"You sound certain. What makes you believe that? Years have passed since you had any relationship with the woman." Dante is the one staring hard at my grandmother now, but true to herself, she doesn't seem intimidated, which is a feat in itself. Not everyone can withstand the glares of three pissed-off alphas. *Wait. Alphas? Why did I think that?*

"Because I have leverage," she replies.

"What kind of leverage?" Tristan's voice sounds dangerously low.

"Let's just say I know a secret Demetria doesn't want aired out."

Sam curses under his breath, then turns to Tristan. "You were right all along about witches. They're all conniving bit—er, people."

I hit Sam's chest with the back of my hand. "Don't be a turd."

"It's true. I haven't met one yet who wasn't hiding something."

I bite my tongue. Now is not the time to remind Sam that I have witch blood, and I was also a full-fledged one in my previous life.

"Okay, can we go now?" I say, knowing we're on borrowed time. Who knows when Valerius will decide to strike again.

"Yes, she's waiting for us."

I swing around, finding all three brothers blocking the exit. "What do you think you're doing?"

"We can't go inside the Montgomery's mansion, but Demetria never said we couldn't wait in the car." Sam smiles in a cheeky way.

Rolling my eyes, I push them out of my way, carving a path for me and Grandma. "Fine. You can all come."

"Like she had any say in the matter," Sam whispers to his brothers.

"I can hear you," I try to snap, but my reply has no bite. I can't blame them for acting so protectively of me. To be honest, I feel better knowing they'll be there. I don't trust the Montgomery matriarch, either.

⁂

Sam wasn't joking when he called the Montgomery mansion a house of horrors. The dark brick building with its lancet windows and turreted towers looks like it came straight out of a horror movie indeed. A wrought-iron gate with the family emblem festooned on it keeps strangers from entering the property unannounced. It swings open when Dante's car approaches, but no magic is involved. I spy two security cameras mounted on each side of the gate. A Renaissance-style fountain depicting an angel battling a demon is in front of the house. It looks completely out of place, as if it were an afterthought or the person who decided on it wanted to piss off the house's architect.

A young man is standing in front of the door, and something tells me he's not the family's butler. He could be a bodyguard—he's definitely dressed like he's ready for battle with his dark pants and black muscle shirt underneath his leather jacket—but why would the Montgomery family need bodyguards here in Crimson Hollow? Before this whole madness with

Valerius started, it seemed there were no dangers lurking in dark corners.

"Who is that guy?" I ask.

Grandma makes a distressed sound in the back of her throat, but doesn't answer right away.

"He looks like he came straight off the set of the *Underworld* movie. What's with the leather jacket in the summer?" Sam replies from next to me, which earns a snort from both Dante and Tristan. "What?"

"Pot, meet kettle," Tristan replies.

"Ha-ha. I ride a motorcycle; I need to wear leather for protection."

Dante parks the car right in front of the steps leading to the heavy wooden front door. The bodyguard, or whatever he is, approaches the vehicle, staring hard at the front.

"Let's go before Montgomery's minion makes a stink about you fellows." Grandma opens the door, getting out in the next second.

I was sitting sandwiched between her and Sam in the back, so I make a move to scoot on the seat, but Sam wraps his fingers around my wrist, stopping me.

"What is it?" I ask.

He cups my cheek, then leans in to kiss me. It's a peck on the lips, brief but loaded with meaning. Easing off, he stares into my eyes. "Please, please be careful."

"I will."

I face the front of the car, finding both Dante and Tristan staring at me. "Seriously, guys. I'll be careful. Don't worry."

I get out of the car before they decide to take off with me still inside. The man in black glances at me briefly before turning his attention to my grandmother.

"Mrs. Montgomery has asked me to take you to her. Your companions must leave at once."

"They're our ride. Why can't they wait in the car?" I ask, already suspicious this is a trap.

"These are my orders."

"They're staying," Grandma replies, her tone leaving no room for argument.

The bodyguard maintains his stony expression. It's then I notice his eyes are lackluster, devoid of life. It's like he doesn't give a fuck about anything.

After a moment, he tells us to follow him, not inside the house, but around the building.

"Where are we going?" I whisper to Grandma.

"We shall see soon enough."

I want to ask her about the bodyguard, see if she also noticed the lack of motivation in him. I don't know why his demeanor caught my attention or bothers me so much. I've met other people in my life who also appeared demotivated and joyless, and I never spared them a second thought. What's different about this guy?

He takes us to the back of the house where a beautiful garden in full bloom greets us. I open my mouth to ask how it's possible to have flowers in the high of the summer when I sense the burst of magic. Of course. There must be some spell in place here. I should have guessed.

Following the silent man through the garden, we reach a glasshouse bigger than Grandma's home. From outside, I can see all kinds of flowers and other plants. The door swings open on its own, and the bodyguard steps aside to let us through.

"Mrs. Montgomery is inside."

Grandma goes first, not bothering to address the man. I follow her, but glance at him to say thank you. I catch a twitch of his eyebrow, the most reaction I've seen from him until now. He doesn't make eye contact with me, though, nor does he reply. Okay, fine. It seems good manners are not in his job duties.

Pushing the slight annoyance aside, I cross the threshold into a botanical maven. The scent of several different flowers hits me at once, almost making me dizzy with the sensorial overload. I can't find Grandma for a second, then I hear her voice farther down the narrow space between all the pots and plants. Following the sound, I find her near an elderly woman with white hair who is busy trimming some plants. She stops her work, putting the sheers down, then she turns to us.

"So this is the famous Amelia Redford. I'm so glad to finally meet you." The lady smiles, emphasizing the wrinkles on her face.

"Hello, thanks for agreeing to see us," I reply.

Mrs. Montgomery shifts her attention to Grandma. "Wendy can be quite persuasive."

"You do realize we're on borrowed time here, don't you, Demetria? Or do you no longer care about the fate of this town?"

The woman's lips become a thin line. "Don't you dare question my loyalty to Crimson Hollow. I've made more sacrifices to keep this town out of the darkness than you know."

Things are getting intense here. It's obvious there's still some bad blood between my grandmother and Mrs. Montgomery. But I can't allow things to escalate any further and risk not seeing the grimoire.

"You said we could have access to the grimoire under one condition. What is it?" I ask.

The ire in Mrs. Montgomery's eyes seems to lessen a fraction. She squares her shoulders. Then, with a swishing movement of her hand, the glasshouse with all its flowers and plants disappears to be replaced by dark stony walls, and no sunlight. Torches mounted on the walls are the only source of illumination. The air is stale, and it smells of mildew. This is a dungeon.

With a gasp, I ask, "Where are we?"

"In the bowels of the Montgomery Manor. This is a secret chamber only I have access to."

I turn to Grandma, only to realize she's not there. Fuck. This is a trap.

"What happened to my grandmother?" I ask, my voice rising shrilly.

"In the glasshouse. She has forfeited her right to the grimoire when she walked out of the coven."

"But I'm not in the coven. Why are you letting me look at it?"

"Because I need a favor in return."

With another swish of her hand, a book stand appears between us. On top of it, there's a thick, leather-bound book. Powerful magic surges from the inane object, calling to something deep inside of me.

"You feel it, don't you? The call of all the witches before you."

"Is that what it is?" I say, my mouth getting dry.

"Yes. Only those with the midnight power in their veins can sense it."

"But I'm not a witch."

"Oh, my poor uninformed darling. Wendy did you a disservice not telling you about your legacy. Of course you're a witch. Now, if you want your answers, go look for them." She points at the thick tome.

With hesitant steps, I approach the bookstand, but the only thing I can hear is the sound of my heart pounding in my chest. "I don't know where to start. Is the information recorded in chronological order?"

"Put your hands on the grimoire and ask it what you want to know."

I do as she says, feeling the crackling of power as my hand hovers over the book cover. The moment I touch it, a current of electricity runs through my body, invading every cell in my being. My wolf howls as it grapples with the power taking over. I can feel the chip inside my head again, stronger than ever, trying to take control of my mind. I lose the feeling of my body, but at the same time, I hear a woman screaming. It's Natalia's voice. My head feels like it's being split in two. If I had a body, I'd be doubling over in pain by now. The frequency from the chip intensifies. When I think I can't take it anymore, it vanishes as the chips disintegrates.

Reeling from the experience, I try to catch my breath, only to be assaulted by random images, all flashing in front of my eyes at incredible speeds. It's like I'm watching a movie in fast-forward. Finally, the reel slows, and I can discern the scenes. There's Natalia in human form surrounded by a pack of wolves. They're fighting a great demon, at least ten-foot tall, with scaly skin darker than coal cracked in several spots to reveal molten lava underneath. I smell his foul stench of sulfur as if I were there myself, and I immediately know it's the same demon working with Valerius. The demon is hit by several balls of blue fire, but it does nothing to slow it down. Then Robert appears in the scene, holding a great sword that glows with power. He strikes the demon, piercing his stomach and enraging it more. The demon swats Robert with the back his forearm, sending the man flying across the clearing. Natalia screams and runs toward him, but the demon reaches her first, grabbing her by the waist with his mighty fist.

"You're mine," he says.

"Never." She struggles in his hold.

Then, a dark circle appears behind him, a portal to the demon's hellish dimension. I'm aware if Natalia lets the demon take her through it, she'll be doomed forever. She pulls a small dagger from her dress. It has an ember stone encrusted on the handle. She thrusts the dagger with all her strength into the demon's neck, and blinding light pours from where the blade struck. The demon screams in agony, but he keeps squeezing her. Natalia pours out every ounce of power she has, feeding the magical dagger. The demon begins to disintegrate and finally drops a passed-out Natalia to the ground. He explodes in a burst of light, leaving behind charred ground. The dagger falls next to Natalia's prone body, burned completely. The stone is black, spent, and Natalia isn't breathing.

A great force yanks me back, shoving me against the dungeon's stony wall. Sprawled on the cold ground, it takes me a couple of seconds to get my bearings. Mrs. Montgomery appears in my line of vision with an expectant expression.

"What the hell did you do to me?" I ask, my voice shaken.

"I helped you. You're welcome."

"That was an incredibly hellish trip down memory lane. I thought my head was going to explode." I touch my nape on a whim, noticing I can no longer sense the chip pulsing inside my brain.

"The grimoire can work as a conduit, an enhancer of power. Did you get the information you needed?"

Racking my brain, I try to organize the memories of my weird trip in a coherent fashion. I saw the great battle between Natalia and the demon. "I think so. Natalia had a weapon, some kind of dagger with an ember stone in it. I think that's what killed the demon in the end."

"She must have used one of the sacred weapons."

"What's that?"

"When the angels still deemed humanity worth their while, they gifted seven stones of power to the humans they chose as the worthiest. But as usual, humans sought to use the stones for personal gain instead of for fighting evil. Legend says that with time, some of the stones got lost and others were used in weaponry. Since the stones were blessed by angels, they can be used to fight demons, but at a great cost to the person wielding the weapon."

I know the cost. Life. Natalia died on the battlefield. I'm certain of it.

My right palm becomes warmer. When I glance down, I see light coming from within it. I'm also holding something. Unfurling my fingers, I find a blue stone there. The light fades, but inside, it seems the stone is alive. Trapped energy pulses as if it were a heart. It's the most beautiful thing I've ever seen.

"You brought back one of the stones," Mrs. Montgomery says in awe.

"How?"

"It must have been hidden inside the grimoire."

My heart skips a beat as I stare at the stone. "Can I use it to fight Valerius's demon?"

"One stone alone won't kill it. And you need to forge it into a weapon."

Mrs. Montgomery winces, then clutches at her chest. I jump to my feet to assist the elderly lady. "Are you all right?"

"I've used too much of my magic for one day. I'm no longer in my prime."

"Do you still have enough juice left to get us out of here?" I glance at the oppressive stone walls of the chamber, terrified of being trapped here.

"Yes. But first, you need to hold up your end of our deal."

Of course. Here comes the payment. I should have asked what the price was before I touched the grimoire. I hope she doesn't demand my firstborn child.

"What do you want?"

"A promise that you will look after my granddaughter when I'm gone. She's going to need strong allies to fulfill her destiny."

"I don't think I've met your granddaughter before."

"I have two. Casey is in high school, but it's Erin who will need your help."

Bearing in mind Erin is Mayor Montgomery's spawn, I have to ask my next question. "Is she nice?"

"What kind of question is that?"

"Considering your daughter's track record, I need to know if I'm promising to help someone as vile as she is."

"Erin is nothing like her mother."

"Okay, fine. I promise. Can we go now?"

"Not so fast, my dear. Words are meaningless. We need an unbreakable vow."

Out of nowhere, Mrs. Montgomery produces a small athame. She presses the sharp blade against the softness of her palm, drawing blood, then motions for my hand. I want to tell her how unsanitary and dangerous that is, but I don't think she cares about contamination. She cuts my hand as well, and then we shake hands. I expect to see light burst from our handshake, but the only indication that a spell has been cast is a tingly sensation that curls up my arm.

Letting go, she declares, "It's done."

CHAPTER 44

RED

We return to the greenhouse, Grandma is nowhere to be found, but the sound of wolves growling outside has me running for the door. Dante, Sam, and Tristan have shifted and are now cornering Mrs. Montgomery's bodyguard. The guy is sprawled on the floor with part of his jacket sleeve ripped at the seam. A long sword lay not too far from him.

"What happened?" I ask.

All three of them swing their snouts my way. A second later, Dante is brushing outside my mental shield.

"Why did you attack that guy?" I ask as soon as I drop the barrier.

"We couldn't sense the bond any longer, so we stormed in and found this puppet guarding the greenhouse. We thought something happened to you."

"I'm fine, as you can see."

"You feel different."

"Different how?" I clutch the stone in my hand harder.

"I can't explain."

"Why are you bleeding?"

I hide the hand with the cut behind my back, not that it will do any good. He already smelled my blood.

"I'll explain later. Now, can you shift back so we can go?"

Dante turns to Sam and Tristan. Together, they return to

their human forms. Mrs. Montgomery's guard finally deems it safe to stand from his prone position, eyeing my mates with distaste. At least now I know he's capable of showing emotion.

"That's why I didn't want your mates here. Wolves are so volatile," Mrs. Montgomery says, watching them with a scowl.

"Maybe you shouldn't have hidden my granddaughter's signature, Demetria." Grandma returns the glower.

"It was a necessary precaution. I've risked too much already bringing Amelia to the grimoire."

"I'm sure the benefits outweighed the risks. What kind of bargain did you strike with her? I can sense the blood vow between you two from where I stand."

"Nothing she can't handle."

"Blood vow? That doesn't sound good." Sam pulls me to his side while he positions his body in front of me.

Irritated at the two elderly ladies, I step away from Sam's human shield. "Hello. I'm standing right here." I wave my hand between the two stubborn women. "It's fine, Grandma. I didn't promise anything terrible."

"If Demetria is involved, you can't be certain of your statement."

"I thought we were leaving," Sam interrupts, and I'm glad for it.

"Yup, we are." As I start to leave, Mrs. Montgomery touches my arm, so I stop. "What is it?"

"If you want to turn that sacred stone into a weapon, Donal might be able to help you."

"Donal?"

"Oh, I forgot he goes by a stupid nickname now. What is it again?"

"Do you mean Santiago?" Dante asks.

Mrs. Montgomery snaps her fingers. "That's it. Santiago. I don't know why in heaven's name he would pick such a silly name, but alas, trying to understand that man is as pointless as trying to get him to reveal where he found the fountain of youth."

"Wait a second." Sam raises his hand. "A fountain of youth exists, and Santiago knows where it is?"

"Who cares about Santiago and his fountain of youth?" Tristan chimes in, then focuses on me. "Did the grimoire say how we—I mean, Natalia and Robert—defeated the demon?"

"Yes." I don't elaborate, because I'm not sure what to do with the knowledge I gained. If I tell my mates Natalia died in the battle against the demon, they'll never let me face him. But I might be the only one who can destroy that foul creature.

"What are you holding there, Red?" Sam drops his gaze to my fist.

I open my palm, revealing the blue stone that now lies dormant. No more pulsing energy inside, but the power hasn't deserted it.

Mrs. Montgomery's bodyguard gasps loudly, earning a curious glance from Grandma. He schools his features back into neutral quickly, but Wendy Redford isn't fooled. She keeps studying him for a while longer.

"I retrieved this from the grimoire. Now I need Santiago's help to turn it into a weapon."

"Is that how we're going to kill the demon?"

I hesitate. If I say yes, I'll be lying. Natalia died when she used the power of one stone. Yet Mrs. Montgomery seems to think I need at least two.

"I don't know yet," I say finally.

"You'll fail if you try to kill an archdemon with only one stone," the bodyguard speaks up, surprising everyone.

"He can talk," Sam says.

"Of course I can talk. And you owe me a new leather jacket, by the way." He glances at Mrs. Montgomery. "Forgive me, ma'am, but I couldn't hold my tongue any longer."

"It's fine, Freddie. I already warned Amelia that one stone wouldn't be enough."

"Wait. Why do you think the demon working with Valerius

is an archdemon?" I ask.

"Because if he were only an ordinary demon, druid magic would be powerful enough to deal with him."

Tristan curses loudly, and I share his sentiment. Of course the malefic being had to be something of great power if he'd survived that battle from centuries ago and came back for me. I wish I knew why the demon wanted Natalia.

"Where can I find another stone? I thought they were lost." I direct my question to Mrs. Montgomery.

"Albert Saint holds one. At least he did a few years back." Freddie bends over to pick up his fallen sword from the ground. I can't help my gasp of surprise when the weapon disappears in the next second. And here I was thinking this dude was human.

"How do you know that, Freddie?" Mrs. Montgomery asks.

He smirks, "I can't reveal my sources."

The old witch rolls her eyes, shaking her head. She actually has affection for her minion. Interesting.

I run a hand through my hair, frustrated we seem to be missing so many pieces of the puzzle still.

"Maybe we need to split up. I'll head to Brian and ask if he can help us with the blue stone, and one of you go after Albert."

"No. We're not splitting up, not with Valerius on the loose." Tristan's gaze turns hard. Before I have the chance to protest, Dante sends me a message mind to mind.

"He's right. We'd better stick together. I'll call Albert from the car."

"Okay."

"Since we're here, is there any chance your witches can help with the situation? I mean, we have to deal with an archdemon, a crazy alpha and his deranged wolves, plus hunters," Sam says casually, as if reciting a grocery list.

Mrs. Montgomery lets out a sigh, and it's obvious her answer won't be favorable. "I wish I could help you, but Georgina is the one making the decisions for the coven now.

I'm too old to be involved with the daily tasks. She doesn't want to get involved."

Not having had the pleasure of meeting the odious woman personally, I can't say for certain, but I'm betting I should probably stay away from her. I can't answer for what I might do. Maybe punch her in the face. Never mind that I just swore to protect her daughter. Frigging fantastic.

Since we have the information we came for, we depart the Montgomery premises. I fervently wish I never have to set foot in this place again. The visit to that dungeon has me in jitters still, but the idea is wishful thinking on my part. I'll be back—if I survive the confrontation with the archdemon, anyway. It's bizarre how I don't even consider Valerius a threat now, which is obviously a mistake on my part. Demon or no demon, he's extremely dangerous. Until we can free the wolves he has under his control, he shouldn't be brushed aside.

During the ride, Dante tries to reach Albert Saint but only gets his voice mail. He calls Brian next, but is unable to reach the druid as well. Not being able to contact two people shouldn't be reason for concern, but nevertheless, a shiver of apprehension drips down my spine, raising the small hairs on the back of my neck.

Stuck in a car for a least another ten minutes until we get to Brian's place allows me time to think about Kenya. She has all the right in the world to be mad at me. I have to speak to her, grovel until she forgives me. I may be some powerful witch-wolf hybrid supernatural, but I still need my best friend. Since I don't have my cell phone with me, I ask to borrow Dante's. I dial Kenya's number, knowing it by heart. The phone rings and rings, before her prerecorded voice tells me to leave a message. I end the call, hoping she hadn't somehow known it was me calling and purposefully ignored it.

"Are you fretting over Kenya?" Grandma asks.

"Yes. I have to explain to her why I didn't tell about my new...situation."

"You had your reasons for keeping the truth from her."

My spine becomes stiff as I catch the double meaning of Grandma's reply. "I still haven't fully processed all the changes. Eventually, I would have found a way to tell her the truth. I wouldn't deceive her forever."

"That's what you want to believe, but with time, you'll see that the truth can do more harm to people than omission."

I snort. "Yeah, right. Is that the lie you tell yourself to assuage your guilt?"

Grandma doesn't reply this time, leaving me seething. I want to yell at her, demand an apology. That's what's hurting me the most, the fact she's not remorseful about her deceit.

Sam covers my hand with his, squeezing tightly. Facing him, I catch his blue eyes watching me with understanding and even some shared rancor as well. Grandma is on his shit list, too. Oddly, that makes me feel a little better. He leans in to kiss my cheek, moving to place his lips against my ear. In a whisper, he says something I haven't heard from any of my mates yet.

"I love you."

Goose bumps break out on my forearms as warmth wraps around my heart. I close my eyes for a brief moment, overwhelmed by the swell of emotions overflowing my chest. When I open them again, they're filled with tears.

Touching his face, I kiss his lips briefly before murmuring, "I love you, too, Sam."

He lets out a shaky breath that fans over my skin. "Shit, I never said those words to anyone else before."

His admission makes me giddy. It's a selfish emotion since I can't claim the same. The first person I ever said those words out loud to was Alex, my ex. But what Sam doesn't know can't hurt him. Grandma's earlier comment flashes in my mind, dampening my mood a little. There's no point in mentioning Alex to any of my mates since he's no longer part of my life. Keeping the details of my previous relationships to myself doesn't compare to her lies.

"How does it feel?" I ask.

"Fucking amazing."

"Oh, gee, could you turn down the lovey-dovey declarations a notch?" Tristan grumbles from the front seat.

"Don't be a hater, Tristan," Sam replies, amused.

I, on the other hand, don't have it in me to find humor in Tristan's comment. He never said he loved me back when I poured my heart out to him. I'd been so happy to be with him again, I'd pushed that detail aside until now.

"Are you still sensing the chip?" Dante asks.

"Actually, the chip has been destroyed."

"Come again?" Tristan swivels on his seat, frowning.

"I don't know how it happened. When I touched the grimoire, some great power coursed through me, and it obliterated the chip."

"Just like that?" Sam peers curiously at me.

Grimacing, I remember how painful the ordeal was. "Well, I thought my head was going to explode for a moment, but as you can see, it's still intact."

Tristan keeps staring hard at me for a moment, despite my attempt at a joke. I don't understand where his attitude is coming from. It's almost like he's not happy I got rid of the chip.

The ride turns a little rough when Dante turns on to a dirt road. The vehicle shakes from side to side, jostling my bones. When I peer out the window, I can't see the sky anymore as the great ancient trees are blocking the view.

A little further ahead, the thick forest gives away to reveal a dark, two-story house that reminds me of a witch house straight out of a fairytale. Several cars are parked in front of the construction, which gets my complete attention.

"Whoa, it seems Brian is having a party and he forgot to tell us about it," Sam says.

Before we get out of the car, the druid steps out of the front door, his face solemn and preoccupied. I'm not the only who notices his demeanor.

"Oh, shit. I don't like the look on Brian's face." Tristan pushes the door open, the first one out of the car.

We all exit the vehicle. When my feet land on the ground, the sacred stone in my hand becomes warmer. Brian stops abruptly not too far from me, while his gaze zeroes in on my fisted hand.

"You have one of the sacred stones," he says.

"Yes. I was hop—"

"Shit," he interrupts me. "I can't let you come in holding that. I sense it's in its pure form, which means it's not linked to you yet."

"Why does that matter?" Dante asks.

"It matters because right now, anyone can harness its power for good or evil."

"Who would want to take the stone from Red?" Sam wraps his arm around my shoulder, pulling me closer to him in a protective gesture.

"Your mother told me everything, even about how your father was betrayed by someone from his inner circle. There are three alphas inside, and we don't know who is the traitor."

"Fuck." Tristan runs a hand through his hair. "What can Red do to link to the stone?"

I hold the stone tighter, as if that's going to make me link with it somehow. Yeah, like it would be that easy.

"She needs to embrace her witch powers," Grandma answers, earning glares from all three of my mates.

"I don't have any witch powers," I contest stubbornly.

"You know that's a false statement. Your gift was dormant before. It happens sometimes. Becoming a shifter must have ignited your powers."

"We're running out of time. If you want to connect to that stone, we have to do it now before someone else picks up on the stone's powers."

Resigned, I take a deep breath. "After I link to the stone, will you be able to turn it into a weapon?"

"I can, but it will take time."

"How much time?" Sam asks.

"It's hard to say, but I'm afraid it won't be before you have to face Valerius again."

CHAPTER 45

SAMUEL

"Okay, so what do we do now?"

"I have to go back in or my absence will be noticed. You three should come with me." Brian looks pointedly at my brothers and me.

"Hell no. I'm not leaving Red alone." I hold her tighter.

"It's best if you're not around when Red attempts to connect with the stone," Mrs. Redford says, immediately pissing me off. I don't even try to conceal my snarl.

Red steps away from my embrace, then looks at the house. "I'll be okay." She turns to me. "Don't worry, Sam."

"We just got you back." I step into her personal space again, capturing her face with my hands.

"The entire property is protected by wards. No enemy will break through," Brian says.

Ignoring the druid, I kiss Red hard, sensing the same protective vibe coming from my brothers. Not wanting to be a selfish cad and monopolize Red, I step away, giving Tristan and Dante a chance to do what they must.

Dante kisses Red as well, then hugs her tight and whispers something in her ear. When he steps away, Red turns to Tristan. He simply stares without uttering a word. Seconds pass without either of them moving, turning the atmosphere heavy with tension. He's been acting like an asshole since we left the Montgomery mansion, and I swear to God if he doesn't get his act straight, I'm going to kick his ass.

He finally moves, stopping in front of Red. Touching a strand of her hair, he doesn't make eye contact with her when he speaks, his words so low they're almost a whisper.

"I do love you. More than you know."

A gale of relief whooshes out of my lungs. For a second, I was afraid he was going to say something mean to her. Red's expression softens as she parts her lips to reply, but Tristan turns around and heads for Brian's house without a backward glance. Fuck. Here I was thinking he was over his jerk ways.

I'm glowering at his retreating back when I feel Dante's presence at the edge of my conscience.

"What?" I ask.

"Don't bite Tristan's head off yet. I sensed great turmoil within him. Whatever it is he learned when he and Red visited their past memories disturbed him profoundly."

Grumbling, I reply, "Fine. As long as he doesn't say or do anything stupid, I'll give him a wide berth."

Red turns to her grandmother. "What should I do?"

"Come with me. The further away we are from the energies of the other supernaturals, the better. You need to connect with the powers of the four elements without disruptions."

I watch Shady Grandma, barely containing my glower. "You'd better not be leading Red to another trap, witch. If anything happens to her, you'll have to deal with me."

Mrs. Redford rolls her eyes. "I'm quivering in fear."

Taking a step in her direction, I snarl viciously. Dante holds my arm, pulling me back. "Settle down, Sam."

"Jesus Christ, Sam. Are you trying to jump Grandma to defend Red? That's an odd twist to Little Red Riding Hood." Nina stands casually on the front porch of the house, her smart mouth having no problem reaching us. Billy and Nina's brother Leo flank either side of her.

"Usually the wolf is trying to eat Little Red, not save her." Billy turns to Nina in a conspiring manner, and I have to do a double take. What the hell happened to him? That's not an omega talking.

To my surprise, the fox laughs at the kid's comment before slyly saying, "Well, I suppose he did eat the girl."

Red makes a disgruntled sound in the back of her throat. When I turn to her, I find her cheeks tinged pink.

"Are you coming in or not? Tristan is already in a piss-poor mood, no surprise there, and I'm afraid he'll punch someone in the next minute or so if you don't come rein him in."

Dante and I lock gazes. Without a word, we head for the house. Something is definitely wrong with our brother if he can't be civil for a minute without our intervention. This feels like déjà vu, but I shake the feeling aside. Tristan is not Dad. He can't be.

The moment we enter Brian's living room, all eyes turn to us. I immediately spot Mom sitting on the couch, sandwiched between Zaya and Carol, Brian's wife. The bruises on her face are already fading, but she still has her leg bandaged. She gives Dante and me a small smile, before her gaze shifts to the three alphas standing together on her left.

I recognize two of them. Francois Boucher, a dark man with long dreadlocks and the best-dressed shifter I've ever met is from the Montreal pack. He's standing next to his counterpart, the alpha of the Vancouver pack, Blake Prescott, a short ginger with freckles on his face who looks like he's fifteen, not thirty. Blake just became the alpha of his pack recently, last year to be precise, when his father died in a car crash. Dad and his father were tight. Understandably, Dad maintained a close relationship with the son as well. The third man is the most intriguing one, and I can only assume he's Simon Riddle, the London pack's alpha.

Simon breaks away from the group, striding in our direction. He shakes hands with Dante first, then me, before offering his condolences. Tristan is at the opposite end of the room, observing the interaction with visible distrust. Would it kill him to pretend we don't suspect these alphas?

The British alpha is the only one who took the trouble to address Dante and me. The other two remained where they were, just watching. I don't like this. Why are they keeping their distance? Unless they have something to hide. All this time, we've only been hunting for one traitor, but what if there are more?

Jared comes up to me, clapping my shoulder. "Everything all right?"

"Not even close." I search the room, noticing someone I didn't expect to see here. Riku Ogata, Nina and Leo's father.

"What is he doing here?" I ask.

"I convinced him to step out of his hiding cave," Leo replies next to me, shoving his hands into his pockets.

"You did?"

Leo shrugs. "He can't expect to stay on the fringe forever. Eventually, every supernatural being must take a stand."

"Why are you surprised?" Nina chimes in. "Dad will do anything for Leo. It has always been this way."

"That's not true, Nina," Leo counters.

Brian strides to the middle of the room, deliberately making eye contact with every single supe there before he addresses us.

"I don't believe we're expecting anyone else, so we can start the meeting."

"Wait a second. Aren't we missing the girl responsible for this mess?" Blake says, earning angry snarls from my brothers and me.

"Red is not responsible for anything," Dante replies through clenched teeth. "Valerius has been plotting to take over Crimson Hollow before she ever entered the picture. She was just an excuse."

"Do we know how many wolves Valerius has in his army? And how about the human hunters?" Simon steps in, veering the conversation to a less volatile topic.

"We do not have an exact count of the wolves Valerius has under his control, but it's safe to say his numbers are at least double what we have," Tristan answers.

"I brought ten of my best enforcers with me." Simon turns to Francois and Blake, expecting them to speak next.

"I'm afraid I can't match Simon's numbers," Blake says. "My pack is small, and I can't afford to lose any wolves to a war that's not mine."

"So why the hell did you come here, then?" Tristan growls.

"To learn firsthand how royally your pack fucked up."

Ah, shit. I sense it before it happens; Tristan readies to jump Blake here in the middle of Brian's living room. I can't blame him for wanting to. I'm almost there, too.

Xander holds Tristan back, and there's no escaping from the bear's strong hold.

Mom stands up, then takes a few steps in Blake's direction, her eyes flashing with anger. "If you came here to create discord, I'd suggest you leave now."

Francois touches Blake's shoulder, pushing him back, before he offers an apologetic glance at my mother.

"Blake is concerned about how Valerius was able to gain so much advantage without anyone being the wiser."

"We have our illustrious mayor to thank for that," I say, unable to hold my tongue any longer. "Until a few days ago, she was siding with Valerius. She has since changed her tune now that the shit has hit the fan."

"Do you have proof Georgina was conniving with Valerius?" Riku asks.

"Not concrete evidence, but we all know that bitch has a vendetta against our pack," Tristan replies.

"Forget the mayor. Right now, she's the least of our worries. We know Valerius has several wolves in his army, and an unknown number of humans with guns that can kill us. Plus, he also has an archdemon at his disposal," Dante says.

Francois and Blake seem to blanch at the mention of the archdemon, and I wonder if their reaction is genuine or fake. Right now, those two clowns are on my list of suspects. I trust neither. Simon rubs his chin as he digests the information, a slightly uneasy expression briefly crossing his features.

"We need to act now. We can't just sit around and wait for Valerius to bring all his might here to Crimson Hollow. His war will not only affect the supernatural community, but also all inhabitants," I add, tired of this inaction.

"You're asking us to bring the fight to his territory? A place he has the advantage? That's insane," Rick counters.

"Not if we catch him by surprise," Nina intervenes, earning a glare of disdain from her father. She doesn't seem to notice or maybe she has an excellent poker face. "I suggest we blow up the building where his lab of horrors is."

Nina's comment catches me by surprise. How does she know about the lab? Maybe she acquired more intel since the last time we spoke.

"I'm all for blowing shit up," Jared's brother says.

Francois scoffs, crossing his arms. "How do you suggest we blow up a building? With druid magic?"

Nina shrugs. "If not with magic, we can always go the traditional route, TNT."

Blake lets out a humorless laugh. "And where are you going to get your hands on that, little fox?"

Billy growls low in his throat, the sound surprisingly vicious as he takes a menacing step toward the alpha. "You'd better watch your tongue, buddy."

The Canadian alpha looks Billy up and down, as if he is an insignificant insect. "And who the fuck are you?"

"He's one of our best enforcers, and very much capable of going against a brand-new alpha," Tristan replies, his eyes crackling with fury.

Faster than I can blink, Nina crosses the distance between her and Blake, shoving him against the wall and jerking him up by his neck. "What are you truly doing here?"

The alpha begins to shift, but Nina slams something into his neck, stopping the shift and somehow rendering the alpha paralyzed. No one breathes.

"Let go of me, bitch."

Nina flicks her wrist, and the alpha begins to convulse. What the fuck? Francois finally snaps out of his paralyses, making a motion to help his friend. But Dante and I block his way. Nina wouldn't attack someone without reason.

"Answer me!" she says.

"Fuck you," Blake replies.

Nina zaps him again, not stopping until his eyes roll back into his sockets. She steps away, letting him drop to the floor like a bag of trash.

"Nina Ogata. What in the world did you do?" her father asks, gaping at her.

Ignoring everyone, the fox crouches next to Blake and begins to search his clothes. A moment later, she pulls a folded manila envelope from his jacket pocket.

"What's that?" I ask.

She glances inside. With a victorious smirk, she throws the envelope to me. After opening it and figuring out what's inside, I have to count to ten in my head so I don't fucking kill that son of bitch while he's passed out.

"Motherfucker," I say, handing the envelope to Dante. "Chips. Blake had chips with him."

"Shit," Dante hisses.

"Can someone explain what the hell just happened here?" Francois glances at me, then at his fallen comrade.

"Valerius is using chips to control his wolves," Mom says. "Anthony had such an implant that eventually made him turn against his pack. That's why my sons fought him."

Francois seems distraught as he stares at Mom without blinking. "Do you think Blake was responsible for Anthony's chip?"

"We suspected someone betrayed him during the Vancouver trip. We just didn't know who. Now we do."

I turn to Nina, the question burning in my mind. "How did you know it was Blake?"

She pulls a ring from his finger before she stands up. "I saw him playing with this, and I immediately recognized it for it was. A magical object forged by fae that has the ability to disrupt wards."

I want to ask how she'd known what it was from where she stood, but the question gets lodged in my throat when all members of the Kane family let out a simultaneous loud gasp.

"What is it?" Tristan asks.

"The wards have been breached," Brian replies, his eyes wide in disbelief.

I lock gazes with my brothers, and we all have the same thought. Red.

CHAPTER 46

RED

I follow Grandma deeper into the woods surrounding Brian Kane's property, keenly aware that the farther we get from the house, the warmer the stone in my hand becomes. My heart is beating staccato; my tongue is dry. I have no idea what to expect. I've barely gotten used to the idea that I'm a wolf shifter; now I must embrace some hidden witch powers, too?

We must have walked a couple of minutes before Grandma stops by a creek. Lifting her chin, she takes a deep breath, then exhales loudly with a contented sigh.

Turning around, she smiles. "Ready?"

"No." I cross my arms in front of my chest, pouting.

"There's nothing to be afraid of. A witch's initiation is painless, natural."

"I'm not afraid. I'm just not sure I want to awaken my powers."

"Are you worried about Tristan's feelings?"

Her question gives me pause, and I frown. "Why do you say that?"

"He's never made any secret he doesn't like witchcraft."

"He's my mate, not my keeper. I can make my own decisions." I lift my chin stubbornly.

"That's good to hear. Now, place the stone on the ground in front of you. Then close your eyes, open up your channels, and let the energy from nature run through you."

"That's sound like a bunch of mumbo jumbo to me." I drop the stone to the ground. When I straighten my back, I find Grandma glaring.

"You've experienced the power you had in a previous life. You know what you're capable of, so I can only assume you're being sassy because you're angry with me."

"I'm not angry. I'm furious. But I'm not here to hear you say—for the thousandth time, I might add—that you did what had to be done."

"Very well. I won't speak a word about that again, and since my presence is getting you frazzled, I'll leave you alone."

"What? That's it? You're just going to bail?"

"I already told you what to do. You don't need me."

Good to her word, she walks away, leaving me completely alone in the forest. A shiver runs down my spine, making me rub my arms up and down. I have no reason to be afraid of being alone. Brian said the property is protected by wards. It takes a few minutes for the anxiety to leave my body, though. When I finally feel ready to connect with nature, I close my eyes, attempting to empty my mind of everything else. It's almost impossible to accomplish that considering everything I've been through.

Damn it. This is not working. I'm tempted to call upon the great wolf apparition for help, but if the property is protected, I'm not sure the guardians would be able to come. Besides, I instinctively realize I must do this on my own.

Instead of attempting to force all my thoughts out of my head, I pay attention to the noises in my surroundings. The first distinct sound is of the creek rushing by. Then I pick up the sound of birds, chirping as they fly above. I take a deep breath, inhaling the sweet smell of earth and green leaves. A soft breeze brushes over my skin. With that comes a new awareness. A soft humming around me, almost like a crackling energy shield. My legs and arms turn a little numb for a second, before heat spreads through them. Inside, my wolf's essence makes its presence known, but it's not trying to break free. It seems to be greeting this new power that's flowing freely through my veins and my mind. A rush of energy converges to my core suddenly, mixing with the wolf there. It brightens the world around me, despite the fact that my eyes are still closed. It expands until it's all I can feel, an indescribable feeling that makes me whole.

Finally, the surge of power ebbs away, not leaving me completely. It's now contained next to my wolf's energy, ready to be called upon when I need it. Blinking my eyes open, I stare at the forest. Everything is still the same, but somehow different. Remembering the sacred stone, I glance down, relieved it's still there. When I bend to pick it up, it flares with a bright light. Little tendrils of electricity escape from inside, wrapping around my hand. It's painless, but when the stone returns to its dormant state, it has a different color. It's now green. Does that mean it's linked to me?

My spine goes rigid when I sense a disturbance in the air. Turning around, I search for the source.

"Grandma?"

I hear a grunt, but it's not coming from her. It's a man's voice. The smell of blood reaches my nose, making my entire body tense. I don't know if I should run, shift, or wait where I stand.

A familiar shape breaks through the shrubbery. I haven't thought about him since my new life as wolf turned upside down, but Peter is here, badly hurt, and clutching at his middle. Without hesitation, I run to him.

"Pete. Oh my God. What happened to you?"

He falls on his knees before I can reach him, his face scrunched in pain. His hand is bloody.

"Red, please help me." He lifts one arm in a supplicant manner.

Dropping to my knees as well, I catch Peter in my arms. "How did you get here? Who did this to you?"

Voices call out my name in the distance. Dante, Sam, and

Tristan are coming for me, but it's Grandma who finds me first.

"Red, step away from Peter," she commands.

"What?"

Peter clutches me tighter, his expression morphed into one of regret. "I'm sorry, Red. He made me do it. I'm so, so sorry."

His words don't make any sense until a strong gush of wind envelops us, and I feel the tendrils of a powerful spell at work.

"Pete, what have you done?" My words are swallowed by the wind tunnel that has formed behind me.

With nothing to hold on to, I'm sucked right into it. The last thing I see is my mates running for me. Only, they're too late.

CRISTAN

"No!" I scream as I watch the love of my life disappear inside a dark wind tunnel.

The portal begins to close, and we're too far from it to make it before it vanishes. Red's grandmother reaches it first, sticking her hand inside the dark void. Somehow, she manages to not get sucked in while also keeping the passage open.

"Hurry. I don't how much longer I can hold on."

Dante, being the fastest, reaches the portal first, jumping right into the tunnel, followed by Sam and me. The moment I pass through, the opening begins to shut, but before it closes completely, I catch a glimpse of Mrs. Redford's face, drained, as if holding the portal open for us cost her a great deal of magic. She vanishes from my sight, and my body is sucked back while pressure squeezes me from all angles. Grinding my teeth, I flay my arms around, trying to find something to hold on to. There's nothing around me but air. The trip doesn't last long, maybe a few seconds, before I'm thrown out. I land with a loud thud on the rough ground, rolling a couple of times before I manage to stop the motion.

Bracing my hand on the ground, I raise my head and search my surroundings. There's a loud buzz in my ears, and I feel dizzy as fuck. A grunt nearby catches my attention. Turning toward the noise, I find Sam not too far from me, slowly getting to his feet.

"Jesus fucking Christ, what the hell was that trip?"

I sit up, the dizziness slowly receding, then I search for Red and Dante, finding no sign of either.

"Where are they?" I ask, making sure to keep my voice low.

Sam pivots on his spot, searching, before turning to me. "I don't know about Dante, but Red is not far. I can feel the bond's tug. Can't you?"

I search for the link that binds me to Red, but I sense nothing. "No. Maybe the trip through the portal messed me up."

Deep down, I know that isn't the case. I get to my feet, trying to ignore the real reason why I can't sense Red. Pain flares up in my temple, so sharp it makes me dizzy again. Sam holds my arm, keeping me steady.

"Whoa. Are you okay, bro?"

"I'm fine." I step away from his support.

Howling out in the distance, followed by a great sense of wrongness, makes my entire body tense. Sam and I lock gazes for a split second before we sprint toward the noise, shifting as we run. We should be more careful as the portal brought us to Shadow Creek, but the sense of urgency is overriding caution. We're spotted as soon as we break out of the tree line, heading straight into the square at the center of Valerius's territory.

Snarls are aimed our way coming from several wolves. It will only take a few seconds until they descend on us. But my sight is glued to the front of the burned-down gazebo ahead, where Red is on the ground, her body covering a white wolf. Dante.

CHAPTER 47
RED

One moment I'm holding my former coworker Peter in my arms. The next, he vanishes and I'm sucked into a dark vortex. A few seconds later, the world becomes bright again, and then I land on the ground hard, banging my head in the process. The impact makes me confused for one moment, until I feel his malign presence nearby.

"Welcome back, sweet Amelia," Valerius says, his voice dripping with venom.

I roll over to get to my feet, but there's a loud growl behind me, then a white blur collides with Valerius, sending him careening to the ground.

Dante somehow managed to follow me through the portal, and he has Valerius by his throat now. A loud gunshot sounds, and Dante falls off Valerius with a whine.

"Dante!" I jump to my feet, throwing my body over his prone form to protect him from getting shot again.

I don't know where the bullet hit him, but his warm blood pours freely from the wound, seeping through my clothes. I can't see shit through the tears clouding my vision.

"Dante, talk to me," I send the thought out.

"I'm okay, Red."

I sense Sam and Tristan approach, but it's the furious snarl behind me that has me looking over my shoulder. Valerius has risen back to his feet, and he's now clutching his bloodied neck. His irises are completely red while he stares at us with murder in his gaze.

"You're both dead," he spits.

My nails become sharp talons as my newfound powers mingle with the wolf. Standing on shaking legs, not due to fear but rage, I say, "No. You are."

Valerius's wolves become aware of my mates' presences, some breaking away from the circle to meet them at the fringe of the forest. I don't dare take my eyes off Valerius. This is my chance to end this monster.

Tendrils of power surge from my fingers, licking my skin as they run up my arms. Valerius's eyes drop to my now-glowing hands, rounding in surprise.

"So that's why he wanted you."

I don't need to ask to know Valerius is referring to the archdemon, who's presence I have not picked up on yet.

My hands become warmer as a sphere of energy begins to form between them. I don't know how I'm doing this. I just awakened my witch powers, so it's possible I retained old memories from Natalia, my former self. I'm ready to strike Valerius when he begins to laugh like a maniac.

"What's so funny?" I snarl.

"Go ahead. Smite me with your power, and your best friend dies."

He steps to the side, revealing behind him Kenya. She's bound and gagged on her knees while Seth holds a gun against her temple. That motherfucker. Fury makes my power crackle as I become torn between ending Valerius or Seth. I don't think I can hit both at the same time before Seth pulls the trigger.

"Not so tough now, are you?"

I sense a familiar pair of eyes watching me, then I recognize Rochelle's wolf just a little behind Seth. My heart sinks to see her among Valerius's army, until I feel a brush against my conscience.

Opening up my channel, I ask, *"Rochelle?"*
"I don't have much time."
"You can fight the chip's compulsion."
"Not for much longer. Please, remember your promise."
I lose the connection, but watching her body language, I know exactly what she's planning to do. Everything happens in a blur. Breaking into a run, she leaps on Seth, biting the arm with the gun. Kenya falls to the side, getting out of shooting range. The gun fires at the same time I instinctually draw on my newly acquired witch powers and launch an energy missile in Valerius's direction. He leaps out of the way, and the strike aimed at him knocks out some of his wolves.

Sensing movement behind me, I turn to find Dante getting onto his paws, blood covering his pelt.

"What are you doing?"
"I'm okay, Red. The bullet only grazed my shoulder."
I don't have time to argue with him as Valerius gives the order to attack. Dante leaps onto the first wolf bound our way, and I search for their alpha, spotting him heading in the opposite direction of the fight. I can't go after him when my mates need me. We're sorely outnumbered.

I make a beeline to Kenya instead, who is slowly crawling away from Seth. The backstabber is still busy trying to break free from Rochelle. How long until her chip takes over again? I feel the power surge once more as my fingers tingle. It's not as strong as the first time, but it should be enough to deal with Seth. Only, I don't have the chance to throw anything at him before a wolf leaps on me, biting my arm and bringing me down in the process. Motherfucker. It's Lyria. I bring up my free hand, shoving against her muzzle, but she won't budge.

I need to shift.

Kenya appears above us, blocking the sun. With her hands still bound in front of her, she lifts her arms, bringing them down hard on top of Lyria's head. The bitch lets go of my forearm finally, rolling off me and away from my friend's range. I see the rock Kenya is holding then.

The blow wasn't enough to deter that traitor, though. I won't be able to shift in time to defend myself, so I do the first thing I can think of. I grab the rock from Kenya's hands, waiting for Lyria to make her move. With lips peeled back, she comes at me again, hatred shining in her eyes. I don't move until the last second. Using the little bit of magic I have left in me, I swing my arm, hitting Lyria on the side of her head with a blow so powerful it cracks her skull open. No way in hell would I have been able to hit her that hard without my new witch gifts.

"Is she dead?" Kenya asks next to me, free of the silver tape that was covering her mouth before.

"I sure hope so. Are you okay?"

"Fuck no. Are you?" She drops her gaze to my bloody forearm.

"I'll heal." Springing to my feet, I pull her up with me. "Let's get you to safety."

I search the perimeter, realizing that, mercifully, only a handful of wolves have gone after my mates. The rest are standing still either in their wolf or human forms. Maybe we've overestimated the size of Valerius's army. But then, I hear shouts in the distance followed by several wolves howling. I can't be certain, but it sounds like hundreds of wolves answered the call for battle. They're coming from the direction of where the lab is. I should have known Martin would make an appearance. We have no chance.

Then, out of nowhere, I sense a change in the air, then a powerful gale rushes through the square. A dark blemish appears in the blue sky, becoming larger and larger until I recognize it for what it is—another portal. Fuck me. What's coming for us now?

I brace for the worst, maybe it's Harkon, the archdemon, making his grand entrance. Nothing could have prepared me for the person who actually leaps out of the portal, landing on the ground with soft feet and the grace of a cat.

My ex Alex.

CHAPTER 48

RED

The imp Zeke Rogers jumps from the portal after Alex, landing next to him with less grace. Then two more dark-clad people follow suit, a young woman with jet-black hair, and another familiar face, Alex's best friend in high school, Maximus Kane. Alex, Maximus, and the woman all carry in their hands a black dagger with strange designs on the blade which glows a faint blue light.

My breathing catches as Alex and I lock gazes. He still has the same dark hair, looking like it needs a cut, and the same intense dark stare. The similarities to the guy I used to date end there. There's a scar now on his right cheek, and he's also gained a few pounds in muscles. He breaks our staring contest first, turning his attention to the enemy who is approaching.

I was so ensnared by this impromptu reunion that I missed the arrival of more allies. The portal has vanished, but Billy, Xander, Brian, plus other supernaturals I haven't met yet, have come through to assist. No sign of my grandmother or Nadine. I hope both of them are far away from here.

Using my claws, I cut through the tape binding Kenya's wrists. "Run, get out of here."

"No. I can help."

"Kenya, I love you, but you're not a fighter. You don't even know how to use a gun."

Zeke runs to us. "I'll take her out of here."

I'm glad he volunteered, but I can't let him leave before he answers one burning question of mine. "What's Alex doing here?"

The imp stares at me as if my question surprises him. "You dated the guy for years, and you don't know?"

I bristle at once, but my time for questions is up. The bond is calling me to my mates' side. I don't know what that means, but I must go to them at once. I spare one final glance at my best friend, then stare hard into Zeke's eyes.

"Take care of her."

Before he can reply, I break into a run, pulling one of Sam's favorite stunts and shifting midair.

When I land on my four paws, the link between Sam and Dante becomes stronger, but I can barely feel Tristan's. Knowing that it doesn't bode well, I sprint in his direction while shouting his name telepathically. He doesn't answer.

Damn it, Tristan. You can't leave me now.

Enemies get in my way, humans and wolves alike. I dodge bullets and sharp teeth, unwilling to slow down to deal with any of them. I finally catch sight of Tristan's white form ahead, closer to the edge of the forest. He's facing three wolves at the same time, and he's losing. I jump on the back of the wolf closest to me, sinking my teeth so deep into his flesh that I find bone. The wolf lets out a yelp, but it won't stop fighting me. Despite my knowledge these wolves have no free will, my need to save Tristan trumps my conscience. I bite the wolf again, finding a major artery this time. Dropping him to the ground to bleed to death, I turn to the other two wolves attacking Tristan. There will be a time for remorse, but it's not now.

Tristan's white coat is covered in blood already, and seeing his injuries make my ire double. I deal with the second wolf as fast as I can, but not fast enough to prevent Tristan from receiving a clawed blow to his jaw from his opponent. His legs fold under him, and he stops moving.

"Tristan!"

Cold tendrils of air sneak up behind me, curling around the base of my spine and raising the hairs on my back. My heart stops beating for a second, before it lurches in my chest savagely. The archdemon is here. Damn it. I bet Valerius left the battlefield to summon the beast. I should have killed him when I had the chance.

"Red, you can't stay here. You don't have the stones," Dante says in my head.

Ignoring his words, I run to Tristan. His paw is covering his nose, but when I approach, I see that his eyes are wide open.

"Tristan, talk to me."

"Red... I... oh my God. The pain."

"What's wrong? Please tell me."

"I... you need to run...I can't." His ember eyes change then, losing their warmth. With a sinking feeling, I know what happened.

"No. You can fight it. Don't let it control you."

"What happened?" Sam asks, stopping next to me.

A savage snarl comes from Tristan as he gets back on his paws. His eyes are soulless, just like Rochelle's when she succumbed to the chip's control.

Before I can stop him, Tristan launches himself at Sam, catching his brother by surprise. Sam falls with Tristan on top. He would have been killed if Dante didn't hammer into Tristan, pushing him off Sam. This is the worst case of déjà vu. Once again, I must witness my mates fight against their own blood. I have to put a stop to it before one of them gets seriously injured or killed. Maybe if I shift back, I can hit Tristan with a spell.

The archdemon's presence is becoming stronger, but I can't flee. Making the decision, I begin to reverse the shift. I'm barely back into my two-legged version when I feel the cold touch of a gun barrel at the back of my head.

"Don't make any sudden movements or you're done," Seth sneers from behind me.

"I've always known you had no honor, but for a wolf to fight with weapons is beyond despicable."

He grabs my arm, shifting his nails into talons to dig into my skin. "You know nothing about the ways of wolves, bitch. Don't presume for a second—"

"Leave her alone, Seth." I recognize Billy's voice, and I don't know if I should rejoice or curse.

With a clicking sound of his tongue, Seth spins me around, keeping me as his human shield. "Ah, sweet brother. Tell me, have you fallen for this witch's spell as well?"

"Red has nothing to do with your grievances. Let her go." Billy's tone is harsh, his posture rigid and ready for a fight.

Taking advantage that Seth is distracted, I focus on my new powers. But either I've used all my juices or the first time I conjured a power ball was a fluke, for nothing happens now. I guess I'll have to do things the old-fashioned way. Bringing forth my memories of the nineties' classic movie *Speed*, starring Keanu Reeves, where he shoots his partner in the leg to save the guy from a hostage situation, I become boneless, as if I were passing out. It's not the same thing as being shot in the leg, but it does the trick. Not expecting the sudden shift, Seth loses his hold on me, but he still has his gun, so I grab him by his waistband as I fall, making him lose his balance. I didn't calculate him landing on top of me, though.

A black leather boot comes out of nowhere, colliding with Seth's jaw. His head whips back as blood splashes from his mouth. But it's not Billy I find staring down on me, but the odious Martin. *Out of the fire into the frying pan. Son of a bitch.* I change my attention from his face, looking between his legs in Billy's direction, but he's busy now fighting another wolf.

"Come quickly, we don't have much time." Martin offers me his hand.

What?

When I don't move right away, Martin lifts me from the ground, holding my arms a little too tight. With a jerky movement, I free myself from his hold.

"Don't touch me."

A wolf whine catches my attention, followed by a sharp pain in my chest. With my heart stuck in my throat, I turn around. Valerius is back, holding Dante by his neck. Dark veins mark the alpha's face and arms, whereas his irises are glowing red. Dante is unmoving. Behind him, I see the great shape of something dark and vile. It stands over eight feet tall easily, but it doesn't have a clear form. It doesn't matter. I know it's the archdemon from my vision. Harkon.

Fear like I'd never known crushes my chest, not because I'm worried about my fate. I'm terrified what the archdemon is going to do to my mates.

"Let him go." I take a step forward only to be yanked back by Martin.

Seth slowly staggers to his feet, wiping the blood from his chin. He throws a murderous glace in Martin's direction, before limping toward his new master, Valerius.

Tristan, who has Sam pinned down with his jaw locked tight around his throat, looks in my direction. I try one more time to breach through his conscience. At first, I only encounter static, then I force my way in, hearing the command that's pulsing in his brain loud and clear. He has to kill his brothers. Fighting the burn in my eyes, I use every ounce of mental strength I have, plunging through the dissonance caused by the chip. I bounce against the barrier and back into my own head. Tristan's eyes remain soulless.

"Tristan," I whisper, my heart breaking. I can't believe this is the end. A fat tear rolls down my cheek.

"He's gone, Amelia. There's nothing you can do to help him," Martin says.

"That's right. Say goodbye to your precious little wolves." Valerius squeezes Dante's neck tighter, digging his talons in his skin, drawing blood.

"No!" I elbow Martin's stomach, turning around when his hold on my arm slackens to scratch the side of his face.

He staggers backward before glancing at me with red-tinged eyes. A great brown bear comes charging from behind, roaring as he comes. Martin pivots, but he's not fast enough to avoid the blow of a massive bear claw to his head. He's sent flying, and then I don't care anymore about his fate. I turn around, ready to shift again when Tristan lets go of Sam, falling to the ground himself with a whine of pain.

Valerius is in halt-pivot motion, still clutching Dante by the neck, when Sam leaps on him, the momentum sending the three of them careening on the ground. Dante falls close to the archdemon's shadow while Sam and Valerius roll around on the ground, snarling and biting at each other.

Harkon laughs before reaching for Dante's prone form. I break into a run, yelling something unintelligible, a battle cry. I don't reach Dante before the archdemon grabs him by his tail.

"Say goodbye to your pet," he says in his garbled demonic voice.

Another dark portal appears to his side. With a flick of his hand, Harkon sends Dante flying through it. The portal disappears. Blinded by rage and despair, I charge the archdemon, knowing full well I'm heading for certain death, or worse, eternal damnation as his captive. I'm intercepted by someone who body slams me to the ground. Strong arms wrap around my shoulders as I fight against the hold.

"You can't fight the archdemon directly, Red," Alex says, holding me close.

"Set me free, Alex."

"Harkon doesn't have a tangible form in this plane yet. He's using Valerius to tether himself here for the time being until he's strong enough. If you want to stop him, you must kill the vessel."

"I have to kill Valerius."

"Yes."

Alex eases off me, standing up and pulling me with him. Valerius has shifted into half human, half wolf form. He resembles a werewolf in that deformed state.

"Stay out of the way," Alex orders before he runs toward the fight, magical dagger in hand.

No fucking way I'm staying out of this. I make a move to follow him, when a howl from Tristan makes me stop in my tracks. Seth is standing in front of him, gun aimed at Tristan's head. I'll never be able to stop him before he pulls the trigger. But Billy gets there in his wolf form, pushing Seth to the side. A shot is fired, but it misses Tristan.

I shift my attention back to the fight between Valerius, Sam, and now Alex. Damn it. I'm torn, not knowing who I should go to. Harkon begins to move again, toward the trio. He doesn't want to lose his vessel.

Fuck. I need something to stop him. I think about the great wolf apparition. Now would be a great time for my guardians to show up. I focus on them, calling out, only there's no surge of power from the ground, no intrinsic awareness of their approach. Something here must be blocking them.

I try once more to tap into my witch's power, but I get nothing, not even a flicker of electricity between my fingers.

Sam lets out a wail of pain when Valerius pierces his eye with his claw. Alex is on the ground, staggering to his feet, sans his dagger. I spot it between me and Valerius, partly hidden by the overgrown grass. It's now or never. I sprint toward it, bending over to pick up the weapon without slowing down. Valerius tosses Sam aside as if he were a piece of rotten meat, then turns his attention to Alex, who is braced to face the alpha relying only on his fists. I don't know what the hell Alex is, but he must have a death wish.

When I'm near enough, I leap, pulling my dagger-wielding hand over my head to pierce Valerius's exposed neck through the back. The dagger's blade pierces the monster as if it were cutting soft butter, getting buried deep to the hilt. The whole weapon turns bright blue, and as Valerius turns in slow motion, the light spreads through his dark veins, consuming the darkness in him. Now with my ass on the ground, I scoot back, getting closer to where Sam has fallen.

An enraged scream fills the square, and I'm not sure if it's coming from Valerius or Harkon. Valerius's skin begins to crack as he staggers in my direction, arm raised to reach me. The light from within him turns brighter before he explodes in a shower of dark matter, the smell too pungent to be simply ashes.

There's no time to rejoice that the vile alpha, the monster who hurt so many people, is gone. With my heart in my throat, I veer my attention back to where Harkon stood, and then my entire world comes crushing down on me and I die inside. I would scream, but there's no time.

Grabbing Tristan, he disappears.

CHAPTER 49

RED

I stare without blinking at the spot the demon disappeared from with Tristan. My chest is tight, a contradiction to the hollowness I now feel there. Focusing on the invisible thread that links me to Tristan and Dante, I can't sense anything. The bond has vanished. They're truly gone.

Dropping to my knees, I choke on an angry sob that bubbles up my throat. I forget that there's still a battle going on, that at any moment I could be attacked by the enemy. Instead, I crawl to where Sam fell, finding him attempting to stand while covering his bloody eye with one hand.

"Sam," I say, staggering to my feet.

He turns in my direction, then manages to stand as well. I break into a run, stopping only when I collide with him, almost sending us both down to the ground. He takes a step back to steady us, wrapping his arm around my shoulder to hold me tight.

"Are you okay?" we both ask at the same time.

"I'm not hurt," I answer. "Your eye. We need to get you medical attention."

"I'm not going anywhere until these fucking wolves are dealt with."

It's then I realize I can't hear the angry snarls of wolves engaged in battle. Glancing around, I see that Valerius's soldiers have stopped attacking. But there's not complete silence. Not too far from us, Xander, in his great bear form, has his paw over Martin's chest, about to crush it.

"Go ahead. Do it," the hunter says in a chilling voice.

"No!" Alex yells before he and his companions break into a run toward Xander and Martin.

Xander looks over his massive shoulder. Sensing a threat coming his way, he stands on his hind legs. He lets out a roar so savage, it makes me tremble. Alex and his friends don't seem one bit intimidated by the bear shifter. Damn it. Alex does have a death wish.

I break away from Sam's side, running after the idiots and waving my hand like a madwoman, trying to catch Xander's attention.

"Stop! They're with us."

A black blur collides with Alex, pushing him to the ground. His companions forget charging Xander to assist Alex, who is being dragged by the back of his shirt by a great black cat.

"Is that a black panther?" I ask.

"No. It's a jaguar. Fuck. I thought they were all gone," Sam replies in awe.

Instinctively, I know things are about to get messy, when a gunshot sounds in the air, freezing all parties. Santiago is standing near the charred gazebo, looking pissed beyond reason. He turns to Xander, pointing a finger at the alpha.

"You, shift back now."

When the bear doesn't obey, Santiago sends a purple-colored energy sphere toward Xander, hitting him square in the shoulder. With a grunt, Xander drops onto his four paws and shifts back. On his hands and knees, he lifts his face to throw a murderous glare in Santiago's direction.

"How dare you force me to shift?" His voice sounds more like a growl.

"You were lost in your bloodlust. I'm not going to apologize for it." Santiago switches his attention to the black jaguar who still has Alex's shirt between its teeth. "Don't make me force you, too, lass."

The jaguar lets out a low snarl before turning in my direction. A sense of familiarity hits me when our gazes lock. I know that shifter, but that's impossible. It can't be her. The jaguar releases Alex before bolting, faster than lighting, out of the square. She disappears around the corner before anyone can stop her.

"We have to go after her," I say.

Santiago is still staring in the direction she disappeared before he shakes his head. "She'll come back."

The odious Martin begins to laugh, spewing blood from his mouth as he does so. Xander is on him faster than I can blink, holding the hunter's neck in a vise hold.

"I don't need to be in my bear form to end you."

Santiago points his gun at the back of Xander's head. "Step away from him."

"Why are you so hell-bent on protecting that scumbag?" Sam asks. "He's a fucking monster."

Xander moves away from Martin slowly, his hands now up. Only when the alpha is far enough from Martin does Santiago drop his gun.

The hunter props his elbows on the ground, looking like he was indeed almost mauled to death. Three angry gashes cut the right side of his face, turning him into a stuff of nightmares. Now he has the looks to match his character.

Alex, to my surprise, drops next to the man. "Jesus fucking Christ, you're a mess, brother."

Brother?

Cold dread drips down my spine, while the heaviness in my chest becomes almost unbearable. Alex and Martin can't be in collusion, can they?

"I fucked up, mate. I fucked up so royally," Martin replies, speaking with a British accent now.

"Can somebody explain what the hell is going on here?" Sam asks.

Alex turns to us, glaring at Sam first before connecting

his gaze with mine. "Martin was an undercover agent. He infiltrated the Ravens, knowing the hunters were involved with underworld scum."

He touches the raven tattoo on Martin's neck, and it disappears. Martin closes his eyes for a brief moment, shuddering before he focuses beyond Alex, on the black-haired girl who is standing stiffly next to Maximus.

"I see that you passed the trials, sis. Congrats."

"You look like hell," the young woman replies. So, she's Martin's sister. I can see the resemblance.

Alex opens his mouth to say something else, but I've had enough, so I cut him off. "What are you doing here, Alex?"

His face becomes as hard as stone as he unfurls from his crouch. "I'm part of an elite task force called The Dark Blades. I'm a druid, Red."

"Alex?" Sam turns to me. "Is that your ex?"

Ah, shit. How does Sam know about Alex? I guess it doesn't matter how he does, only that now I have to keep Sam as far away from Alex as possible because the jealousy I see shining in his eyes means trouble, the deadly kind.

CHAPTER 50

RED

It's been a day since the terrible fight in Shadow Creek. After I killed Valerius, his controlled wolves stopped fighting and then it was over. Rochelle and the other wolves with implants were put in quarantine until Dr. Mervina could figure out how to remove the chip without causing more damage to them. Because their controlling devices were tainted with demonic energy, the procedure wouldn't be simple.

We're back in the compound since Valerius had so easily been able to break through Brian's wards. I'm in shock, refusing to believe that both Dante and Tristan are gone. I still can't sense my bond to them, but I couldn't when I was Valerius's captive, either. I have to believe they are alive.

I'm locked in Sam's room, refusing to talk to anyone while I veil his sleep. Zaya was able to patch him up, but he did end up losing his left eye. When we returned here, Brian filled me in on what happened after I disappeared through the portal. Peter had been ambushed by Martin's hunters, stabbed in the guts, and then sent to the compound carrying some kind of magical device that not only broke Brian's protective wards, but also opened up the portal to Shadow Creek. He was rushed to the hospital, but mercifully, was in stable condition. Brian assured me he won't remember a thing about what happened. He's human after all. I'm not sure how I feel about this whole scrubbing the memories of regular folks to protect the supernatural community. It leaves the inhabitants unprepared to deal with threats from evil creatures, such as Valerius and Harkon.

Thinking about that fucking archdemon makes me more enraged than afraid. Brian has not had the chance to forge my weapon using the sacred stone, nor have we heard from Albert Saint regarding his stone. So for now, I have no means to defeat Harkon.

A soft knock on the door makes me tense up. I've asked to be left alone. Dr. Mervina pushes the door open a sliver, sticking her head in.

"How is he doing?" she asks.

"Still out."

She enters, then closes the door behind her. I open my mouth to say I don't want any company, but she raises her hand and says, "You can't hide here forever."

"I'm not hiding."

Dr. Mervina pinches her lips into a scowl. "I've left you alone for a day, sensing you needed time to recover. But the time for a pity party is over. There's much to be done."

Rage simmers low in my gut. Crossing my arms, I glare at the alpha. "I'm not throwing a pity party. I needed time to think."

Dr. Mervina nods, lacing her hands together. "Very well. Anything you would like to share with me?"

"I can't sense the bond to Tristan and Dante anymore, but I refuse to believe they're dead. I couldn't sense any of them when I was in Shadow Creek, so it's possible some great power is blocking my link to Tristan and Dante now, right?"

"They aren't dead."

A wave of relief washes over me, but still, I have to ask. "How do you know?"

"You wouldn't be able to sense the bond to my sons if they weren't in this plane."

"I don't understand."

"I'm their mother. I know they're alive. The thread is weak, which is why I don't believe they're in the same dimension as we are."

Running my hand through my hair, I yank at a strand. "How are we going to discover in which dimension they are?"

"There's where Zeke Rogers and the Dark Blades come in. The imp took off as soon as he suspected you were the reincarnation of the Mother of Wolves. He went after the Blades."

Bitterness pools in my mouth when I think about Alex. A person doesn't suddenly become a druid; they're born a druid, which means he lied to me during our entire relationship. It's hard to believe another person close to me was deceitful, but just because it happened again doesn't make the bitter pill less difficult to swallow.

"Alex is my ex," I say, and I don't even know why.

"I know. I heard he's one of the best Dark Blades fighters."

I snort. Of course he is. He was always good at everything he tried. I never once stopped to consider that maybe his excellency in every single sport he attempted wasn't natural, or how he never seemed inclined to stick to any in particular.

"You're angry."

"That's an understatement."

"I get your frustration, but you'll need Alex's help to find Dante and Tristan. I hope you can move past the rancor you're feeling right now."

Dr. Mervina is right. I have to push Alex's deceit aside. But talking about him won't help me, though, so I decide to change the subject.

"My new witch powers are flaky. I could only tap into them once during the battle."

"You need time to harness them. It was already a great feat that you were able to use your powers at all."

Sam makes a small sound while he sleeps, drawing my attention to him. I touch the side of his face, glad I have him with me still.

"Did you hear anything from Kenya?" I ask, only knowing that Zeke took Kenya to her mother, Sheriff Arantes, yesterday.

"She's fine. No harm was done to the girl during her brief captivity."

I release a breath of relief. "And her memories? Are they getting scrubbed, too?"

"No. Kenya is a special case."

"Because her mother is the sheriff," I say a little stiffly.

"Among other things."

I watch Dr. Mervina closely now. Her reply makes me suspect she's hiding something. Maybe sensing my suspicious thoughts, she changes the subject.

"Your grandmother is also fine."

"Why wouldn't she be fine?" I ask.

The fact she didn't come to see me wasn't strange considering everything she has done in the past. I figured she was busy doing more important things.

"Keeping that portal open long enough for my sons to come after you took too much from her. She's with her sisters from the rogue coven, recharging her batteries per se."

Dr. Mervina doesn't elaborate, but I get the gist that wherever Grandma is, she's not to be disturbed. I'm relieved for more reasons than one. I'm not ready to talk to her yet, especially when I have to deal with another ghost from my past.

"Alex is here. He wants to talk with you."

There goes my plan to ignore my ex for as long as I could. But if he can help me find Dante and Tristan, then the sooner I speak to him, the better.

Taking a deep breath to calm my nerves, I say, "Could you please send him to Tristan's office? I'll be there in a minute."

"Of course." Dr. Mervina comes closer, then lays a hand on my shoulder, squeezing it softly. "It'll be okay, honey. We'll get Dante and Tristan back."

Her words make me choke up. The lump in my throat gets bigger. Breathing becomes hard. I bite the inside of my cheek to get my emotions in check. I can't crumble now.

Dr. Mervina walks out of the room, and when she clicks the door shut once more, I turn to Sam. His eyebrows furrow together as he become a little restless. Taking a seat on the edge of the bed, I curl my fingers around his hand. He squeezes it a little, before he opens his eye, glancing in my direction.

"Red? Are you okay?"

"Yes. How are you feeling?"

"Like hell." With his free hand, he touches the bandage covering his left side. "Did I lose it?

"Yes. I'm sorry."

Dropping his hand from the bandage, he cracks a lopsided smile. "Don't be. I've always wanted to be a pirate. You can call me One-eyed Sam now, like One-eyed Willie from *The Goonies*."

A snort bubbles up my throat. "You're absolutely crazy." I lean down, kissing his lips softly, needing the contact more than ever.

He places his hand on my arm, flaring the spark that exists between us. I pull away, not wanting to start anything right now. Sam needs to recover.

His good humor vanishes from his face. "Do we know anything about Dante and Tristan yet?"

"Your mother believes they're in a different dimension."

Sam grimaces. "My chest feels heavy. There's a dull pain there. We need to find them, Red."

"We will. Even if I have to go to hell to get them, I'll bring them back."

"And I'll be right there with you." Sam laces his fingers with mine, while the promise of retribution shines clearly in his one blue eye.

TO BE CONTINUED

ABOUT THE AUTHOR

USA Today Bestselling author M. H. Soars always knew creative arts were her calling but not in a million years did she think she would become an author. With a background in fashion design she thought she would follow that path. But one day, out of the blue, she had an idea for a book. One page turned into ten pages, ten pages turned into a hundred, and before she knew, her first novel, The Prophecy of Arcadia, was born.

M. H. Soars resides in The Netherlands with her husband and daughter. She is currently working on the *Love Me, I'm Famous* series, and the *Crimson Hollow World* novels. She also writes SciFi and Fantasy under the pen name Michelle Hercules.

Join M. H. Soars VIP group on Facebook:
https://www.facebook.com/groups/mhsoars/

Connect with M. H. Soars:
Website: www.mhsoars.com
Email: books@mhsoars.com
Facebook: https://www.facebook.com/mhsoars
Twitter: @mhsoars

ALSO BY M. H. SOARS:

LOVE ME, I'M FAMOUS SERIES:

WONDERWALL

SUGAR, WE'RE GOING DOWN

WRECK OF THE DAY

DEVILS DON'T FLY

LOVE ME LIKE YOU DO

CATCH YOU

ALL THE RIGHT MOVES